The Entries of the Black Sails

The Entries of
the Black Sails

Rafael P. DeFreitas, Jr.

I would like to dedicate this book to my mother,

Dr. Olivia J. Mack

You have been my biggest cheerleader through-out my entire life. You told me many times that you prayed for me to have certain gifts and it seems that they manifested the day I was born. Thank you, for all the encouragement and dedica-tion you gave me from my youth to now.

You have instilled in me love, courage, faith, and so much more. For that, I'm profoundly grateful and indebted to you.

I dedicate this book to you because you never gave up on me, even when I gave up on myself. Thank you, mother, for always believing in me when no one else did. Thank you, for loving me when no one else could. I love you and I thank you for everything.

Love always - *Your only son,*

Rafael P. DeFreitas, Jr.

Contents

The story of *The Entries of the Black Sails* is totally unique and one of a kind. From the story itself to the way it was developed. The title was originally *Black Sails*. I researched the name to make sure it wasn't being used and that is when I discovered it was in fact being used by a television show. So, I ended up changing the title for legal purposes and because it could be confusing for the people that would search for it.

The storyline came to me like a forgotten memory as I began to write. I didn't know how the story was going to end initially, not until I was deep into the last chapters. To this day, I stand by my word that I made up my characters' name on my own and without influence. However, being that I had issues with the naming of the book, I decided to research the character names that came to mind.

Once I researched the names to make sure none of them had been used before, I found that the meaning of some of the names fit with the story. It was weird and felt as though I was being told the story by an unseen force. For example, *Matuka* is one of the character's names. I had never heard the name or word before. I made it up! But when I searched to see if anyone used something similar it was a real word that had a meaning that tied to water and fishing, which correlates with the character and the characters' insignia of the flying fish. I found out that *Matuka* was a lure for fly fishing. I picked that name before I learned of the connection to Matuka's name or the symbol of the flying fish I was going to use! Coincidental word play!

Once I saw those coincidences, I searched nearly everything, and I found strange coincidences like before. I ended up running into a wall once I realized I didn't know too much about sailing or the appropriate terms to use while writing this book. So, after many months of research, I was able to build my story and describe it how I felt I needed to.

After three long years of writing this book, while I was writing the sixth chapter, the computer program I was working on deleted some of the book. Upset, scared, and heartbroken, I reached out to a computer service. This company ended up hacking my computer, giving me a virus, and locking me out of my computer. They were supposed to help me restore the document and ended up nearly destroying my computer in the process.

With my hope dying, my drive and motivation fading, I found another computer service a month later. This computer technician worked on my failing hard drive for a week. During this process I cried, yelled, cursed, and literally gave up on life. Then, I fasted and prayed.

A week later, I was notified that the only thing the computer tech was able to find or save from my computer was my book manuscript!! He restored the version before the program deleted it!! Hallelujah!! Soon after he retrieved the book, the computer completely crashed and failed. It was just in time!!!

It took about two months after that for me to finish the book. It's funny but I thought I learned this lesson in life all ready. But I had to relearn not to procrastinate and to get things done while it's fresh and when you're being urged to. This book is special for so many reasons. I hope you enjoy it as you dive into my imagination!

-Rafael P. DeFreitas, Jr.

Entry 1

REBIRTH

His eyes struggled to open as he coughed on the black smoke that consumed the sky with falling ash. While lying on his back, he felt the warm blood flowing underneath his body from the person by his feet. As he tried to use his hands to sit up, they slipped in blood and he fell back. The boy then looked up to the sky before he turned his head to the right and coughed up blood. The fires were blazing around him, reflecting on the darkened navy-blue water and sky with a tint of red orange.

Ships were being devoured by the fires from the battles and fatal attacks prior to his awakening. The graveyard of ships only seemed to show the hate and the pride of man.

After resting a few seconds, he sat up and looked to his feet and noticed a dead body.

"An enemy!" he said as he snapped his right foot back.

In doing so, the lad was met with vicious pains that pulsated up and down his right leg.

"Serves you right jerk!!" the boy said as he stood to his feet as he trembled from the excruciating and jagged pain.

Drenched in his enemy's blood and his own, he looked around to notice no one was moving on his ship and that there were a couple of fires kindled. He took a deep breath, gathered all the strength he had and tried to walk around to check on his fellow shipmates. The air aboard the main deck was still like that of a ghost town; the waves were beating against the sides of the boat and a gloom rested over the deck.

The fires burning the ship seemed to delay; the enormous vessel was sinking slowly. Two steps in and a chain of explosions went off from the ammunition on the burning ships nearby; causing him to fall on his wounded leg.

"Ah! Crap this hurts!" the young lad said as he looked at his leg.

Exhausted from dehydration, he began to carry a sweat from the ferocious flames and yearned for one drop of fresh water. His eyes were filled with sweat, which caused them to burn, so he wiped his face with his battle beaten shirt. Doing so left black ash covering the top of his face; almost engraved in his flesh like a tattoo. Once again, he tried to stand, in more pain than before, the fires were dancing in his eyes; he dropped his head back with his chin up and screamed.

For the boy realized that for the first time in his life, he was alone. With all his might, the boy ran a couple feet away, dropped to his knees and grabbed a heavy lifeless body. Their clothes soiled in blood, mocha skin covered with wounds, buried sins throughout their locks, the young boy wailed at the top of his lungs. While he held him rocking back and forth; as blood dripped onto the deck from them both, he screamed.

"Father! Father! Wake up! Please wake up, Father! Father!!!" the boy yelled until he was hoarse.

The boy scanned his body for injuries to find the wound that claimed the man's life.

"His right leg," the boy cried before he dropped his head.

The only sound he could hear then was the waves and fire burning the ships lost in combat, reality sat in, so he became enraged.

"Someone will pay!!!" he declared.

Barely breathing, the black smoke no longer fazed him; he stared at the destruction thriving in the distance. Captivated by its omens, he drifted into the whirlpool of revenge. After an hour passed by, the heartbroken lad was still holding onto the man's cold, lifeless corpse. Abruptly, a small explosion from his ship pushed him forward and made him drop the man's upper body on the deck.

"Okay, I can't stay here, the ship is sinking, and I need to think of something fast. Father, what would you do?" the lad cried as he looked down at the fallen Captain.

After he wiped his bloody tears, the young boy looked up towards the ocean and saw another ship in the midst of the smoke.

"Where the heck did that come from?!" he asked himself in fear.

The way the image seemed to move, he wondered if it was a mirage or if it was death himself. The ship was very dark in appearance; almost like it was layered in thick, black smoke and the sails were dark as the ocean at night. The fires reflected off the fine, silver bulwarks of the ship with blinding beauty. The ship had two masts, the first one was small and on the front deck of the ship. The second one was very steep in the middle of the ship and held the crow's nest. The back of the ship held the helm and it appeared to be spinning. His mind was plagued with all sorts of thoughts that produced more fear.

"I've never seen a ship that looked like that before. Is there anyone alive on it? Can I defend myself right now? Can my leg withstand? Do I have the strength to hold a weapon? Where's the guild's coat of arms or their crest? Why is the helm spinning, but the ship isn't moving?" he asked himself.

So, before giving it another thought, he looked for his Captain's spyglass. A look of despair greeted his face as he saw the broken glass from the aged green and gold antique. He then thought of all the other places where one could be.

"Poor Hehteh, he always hated weapons, they'll pay whoever did this to you," the boy said before he looked away from the crow's nest.

The boy started to wonder if Hehteh had a spyglass in his crow's nest and quickly looked back up.

"That's too far up for my leg and arms right now," the lad said softly.

After the boy looked from the crow's nest, he continued to look around to see if he could find a spyglass.

"Just my luck, figures," the lad said as he

looked down to see what appeared to be a black spyglass; broken on the ground near the mast Hehteh was stationed on.

After he clenched his fist from anger, he looked at his crew to see who else would have one; sadly, he realized no one else did, so he looked back to his Captain. When he felt his eyes watering, his lips shaking and teeth grinding, he took his Captain's sun-dried, black leather hat off his head to put it on. Trying to avoid overheating more than he already was, he controlled the tears and began to breathe slower to lower his heart rate.

"Okay, I got to pull it together!" the young lad said before he simultaneously slapped both sides of his face with his hands.

The boy felt a bit entitled, so he took the man's compass, spyglass, ring, and journal, then stored them in his multi-compartment quiver, that was lying next to them both on the deck. The glow from the necklace that rested on his bloody and hairy chest, introduced confidence to the young boy's soul. He strangely couldn't remember the story behind it, but he knew it was a great one.

"I refuse to let this sink into the bottom of the ocean too, he cherished this," he thought to himself.

So, he took it off the cold body of his beloved and wore it proudly. The boy cried blood and mustered strength in agony as he wrapped his leg with his Captain's bandanna. Heat beaten, injured, weak, bloody, and hardened by grief, the boy took the man under his wings to set him in his Captain's seat.

He slowly looked over his ship and saw his shipmates were all dead, shot, and decapitated. Some were stabbed with swords still in their bodies and there were a few dead enemies as well. He raised his right fist in that moment of silence then put it over his heart. His head was crowned with his beloved's black hat; that seeped honor, as his locks dripped sweat and blood. The black ash was smeared upon his face as though it has always been like a birthmark. His eyes were like the flames before him as blood crept down his cheeks and over the black ash.

The lad's chest was blessed with courage from the necklace of a hero, while a badly torn and burnt shirt caped his body. His arms and torso were wounded like he had battled with jaguars; the cuts sent forth their screams. His brown pants were ripped and dirty; his blood knew no bounds. His right leg was shot and severely wounded, the strength of his Captain's bandanna bound it like the great rivers of the north center, keeping him from overflowing. His feet were tired and extremely heavy; his boots wore the weights of his father's fathers' transgressions. After he slowly made it to the seat and put the man in it, the boy looked at him and cried. Suddenly, another explosion on his ship caused him to fall and hit his head.

"No good! I have to go now!" the young boy said as he quickly got up and tried to run to starboard side to jump.

Armed with his bow and quiver loaded, the boy looked out to the ocean.

"Okay, let's do this!" the boy said as he balled his right fist.

Ready for battle and skeptical of the unknown, he knew it wouldn't be an easy feat. The lad looked back one last time towards his Captain and dived into the water to make his way to the other boat. Immediately, the lad regretted that decision because the temperature and salt from the ocean felt like a thousand daggers cutting into his wounds.

"What was I thinking?! If I couldn't climb up to the crow's nest, how am I gonna manage to make it up that thing? That's if they don't pick me off like a sitting duck before I can even get close enough to try," the young lad said after the water began to intensify his pain.

The water was freezing, there were dead bodies everywhere, half-mutilated and torched to the bone. Everywhere he looked, he saw men, women and children, innocent casualties of a meaningless war. The sight made him sick, so he put his head down and continued to swim through the carnage and debris.

Stroke after stroke, the further he got away from the familiar, he could feel the dead stares from the innocent. He felt as though he was the one to blame for their deaths, so, tears of blood ran down his cheeks once more. With only forward as an option, he continued to push through the agony.

"How much further?" the lad asked aloud as he continued to swim.

After he shortened the distance, he looked up in complete exhaustion.

"Almost there," he whispered with relief.

The flames from the nearby boats seemed to repel against the mysterious ship. Without warning, a sudden change of weather happened immediately after he got closer to the vessel. The young boy and two ships were now wrapped in a cocoon of thick smoke and lightning, which caused him to feel trapped.

"Where the heck did all that come from? This doesn't look good; I have to hurry," the boy said as he looked around while he swam forward.

After he finally made it to the ship, he reached out to touch the black, wooden, and metal surface, then was immediately met with a vision. He saw himself as a baby, crying on a seat of a small boat that was broken in half and a woman that he felt was his mother. The lady was in the water crying, while she held onto a part of the boat that was above water. Her left arm was extended towards and over him; with something in her hand.

His tears wanted to flow, but the strange warmth of the ship comforted his broken heart and spirit through his hand. Shaken by the incident, he hesitated to climb up, although he knew that he couldn't stay in the water for much longer. The young lad knew his energy was nearly depleted and it was a vortex surrounding him.

"I didn't see anyone from afar and I don't hear any voices above on deck, that's strange," the boy said as he looked up.

The lad tarried awhile in the water to scout starboard side and tried to see if he could hear anyone aboard.

"Okay, it's cold! I… I have to get out of here!" he shrieked as the water grew colder by the second.

The lad then saw a long, white rope hanging over the ship's bulwarks, that appeared to be safe for climbing.

"I swear I didn't see that there before, am I losing it?" the boy asked with a confused look as he swam over to the white rope.

After he got to the rope, he looked up to see if he could see where it was attached.

"Freaky, I know this wasn't here, is someone up there?" the boy asked himself as he swam backwards to get a better look.

The exhausted lad then decided enough was enough and he had to board.

"Okay, here I come! Ready or not!" the boy said as he tugged on the rope to make sure it was secure.

With all his might, the boy began to climb up the white rope to a place of unfamiliarity. Grasp after grasp, he could see the finish line growing nearer and nearer.

"There we go," the boy thought to himself as he reached the silver bulwarks.

The boy then peeked over the top to see if anyone was aboard deck.

"Huh? No one?" the lad asked as he looked around.

To his surprise, it looked vacant and eerie. As he carefully boarded the ship on starboard side; quiet as a mouse, he noticed that there wasn't a soul on the main deck of the vessel. Not a burned, mutilated, dead body or blood anywhere in sight.

"Strange, it's quiet, too quiet," he whispered to himself.

The boy stood still aboard the silent deck and waited patiently to be ambushed.

"Any second now," the young boy sarcastically said as he waited for an attack on his life.

Moments passed and no one came to harm him, so he relaxed a bit.

"Okay, nothing happened. So, which way should I go? To the left, or right?" the young boy thought to himself.

While he looked back and forth; over the ship, the atmosphere aboard deck became more eerie to him.

"So weird. I should hurry, but which way first? Well, the stern is to the left, which must lead to the Captain's quarters and below deck. And the forecastle, where the crew sleeps, is to the right and I'm dead center," he stated while he looked up to the crow's nest.

After picking the forecastle, he slowly set out to comb the new environment, from top to bottom. As he grew closer to the forecastle, he noticed the beautiful workmanship of the black door; trimmed with fine silver, that led in-to the daunting quarters. Gently, the boy grabbed the warm, silver doorknob with his left hand, slightly crouched down and opened slow-ly, ready for a fight. As the door opened, it creaked so loud, he had no choice but to burst in and be ready for whatever was next. He charged through the door and yelled at the top of his lungs; prepared for battle. However, the air was still, and the room was soundless.

"I can't see anything, and no one appears to be here," he said as he walked into the pitch-black room.

He searched for a candle and lantern at the entry, but instead he stumbled down a small set of stairs.

"Oh crap!" he shouted before he hit the ground hard.

The lad then sat in silence for a second to gather himself.

"That's gonna leave a mark," he jokingly laughed.

In pain, he laid and felt the soft carpet under his drained body; he let out a deep sigh.

"How is this room still so dark with the door open? It's like the outside light is stopping at the threshold of the door; like the room itself is producing the darkness," he said to himself as he looked from the door back inside the strange room.

As he laid there on the floor of the cabin, he looked up at the ceiling and noticed something breathtaking. The ceiling had small glowing lights that looked like a map of the stars from the night's sky. The lad quickly sat up and stared captivated by the unbelievable display.

"What the heck? Am I dead or something? Did I hit my head too hard?" the boy asked as he tried to make sense of what he saw.

Suddenly, some of the lights began to grow brighter until it looked like a map to somewhere specific.

"Whoa, now that's freaking cool! What is that?" he asked himself, as he glared at what appeared to be an island forming; in the star-like constellations on the ceiling.

Without him noticing, more of the room began omitting its own light, which made it easier for him to see.

"No way!" the boy said as his eyes lit up from excitement and curiosity.

The young boy couldn't figure out if it was the star-like lights on the ceiling, the furniture within the room or something completely different and it was driving him nuts.

"Is the rest of the ship like this?! How bizarre, I can see the table and bed now," he said slowly as he stood and scanned the room.

The boy quickly realized how beautifully the brown wooden walls glowed.

"I never saw walls like this before! They're seeping light! It's causing the wood to glow its natural color," the boy shouted as he looked closer at the wood within the room.

Going down from the steps to the left, on the south wall, was a wardrobe that was wide open and had only a few clothes in it.

"That's a huge closet, not many clothes though, I wonder why," the lad said softly.

The young lad then walked over to the wardrobe to have a look inside.

"Huh? They're glowing too? How is this

possible? I really bumped my head too hard on that fall. That's weird, either this guys a dwarf, or he has a child. Cause no way can an adult fit these," the lad stated as he glanced in the wardrobe.

To his right, on the west wall, in the south corner, was the enclosed head and bathing area with the door wide open.

"Okay, now that's new, these people must be loaded," he said as he stared in the bathing room; that started to softly shine.

In the middle on the west wall, was a huge, flat-earth map and below it sat a long, skinny, golden-brown table. In the northwest corner of the room, were arrows, swords, guns, and all sorts of tools of warfare in a barrel.

"And whoever they are, they love their weapons," the boy said as he glanced at the sparkling and glowing arsenal.

After he walked over to the corner to get a closer look at the small, illuminated armory, he turned around and froze.

"How?! I could have sworn I fell right there!" the boy said with a look of confusion on his face as he began to walk.

Dead center was a beautiful, gold-trimmed; extremely detailed, hand-carved, stained oak desk. Below it was a red-leathered, golden, and detailed, wooden chair; that also radiated its own light.

Beneath the abnormal desk, set the most complex designed carpet, the lad had ever seen.

"Whoa, now this is glowing too! But how? This is like something for royalty or something otherworldly. I'm almost afraid to step on it. Ah crap! I'm getting blood all over it! Crap! No doubt about it, this is definitely the Captain's quarters and I just messed up big time! But I could have sworn this would have been the crew's quarters," the boy said with a nervous tremble as he looked down at the blood, then back up around the room.

The boy noticed that the north wall was not as lit as the others and had no visible distinctions. Going down the stairs, to the right, on the south wall, was a gold-trimmed, in-wall bookshelf. To the right of that was a bed, which headboard sat on the south wall and the foot towards the north wall. The bed glowed and was made of strong cedar wood that he seemed to smell from afar. The huge sheet was illuminated; it was red with gray and navy-blue patches on it. It seemed to be hand knit and quite frankly; pretty cozy to the boy as it glowed softly in his light-brown eyes.

"Not gonna lie, a nap would be nice, but there's no way I'm going to sleep in here," the young boy said.

As he stood in the middle of the Captain's quarters, he looked around, saw that the room was tidy and looked abandoned.

"That smell, I know it! But where from?" he asked as he closed his eyes and sniffed the air.

The room had a distinct smell that the lad could not figure out, but it smelled and felt familiar in there to him.

"I wonder if the rest of the ship is like this," the boy said as he looked to the room's door.

After he turned around to head back towards the steps to leave the room, the door slammed from the wind blowing outside aboard the main deck.

"Not cool," he said out of shock as he stepped back.

Out of nowhere, a retractable, wooden panel rolled up on the north wall; exposing a large glass porthole, which stretched along most of the wall.

"What the heck was that?" he yelled as he turned around.

The lad could not believe his eyes; he could see out the bow of the ship. He stared there for a minute to look at the rubble and fires as the storm brewed outside in the distance.

"I can't believe my eyes, where are the crew and Captain? Who made this ship?" he asked himself as he shook his head in disbelief.

After he gazed for a bit, the boy climbed

the steps, opened the door, and slowly exited the Captain's quarters. After he exited the cabin, the young lad slowly walked forward and turned around to look at the deck above the Captain's quarters. He glanced quickly and didn't see anyone above on the deck, so he turned back around to proceed forward. Slowly, the brave and bruised boy crept across the warm and silent deck.

"This is beginning to freak me out a little. There's no one up here, I thought I was kind of loud and would have alerted someone, especially with that clumsy, fluke of a fall. However, it seems I have no choice but to continue on. I'll just have to see if someone is here or not when I get below," the boy said softly as he inched forward.

The sky was screaming, and its rage was black, the smoke had surrounded, while lightning danced above. The boy knew he needed passage on the ship to survive but he didn't know if it was an enemy's ship. He knew it meant death was near if it was a foe's vessel because the ocean was calling for him to pay his debts for the lost lives.

"*I refuse to die here! I must avenge my father and crew! No adult is going to stand in my way!*" the boy thought to himself as he kept moving forward.

The boy continued to look side to side,

up, down, back, and forth, being as quiet as he could as he crept across the deck. As the boy continued, he started to admire the ship's beauty and mysterious origins.

"I've never seen a ship built like this in any shape, form or fashion before. No one is here and it's in this condition? Not to not mention, it popped up out of nowhere and so far, there is no visible damage like it was on my ship, it's freaking creepy! Yet, I feel a comfort from afar; tugging at me, pulling me in closer. Echoes from another time it seems," the lad thought to himself as he slowly crept across the main deck as the blood from his wound trailed him.

The accents seemed to sparkle and radiate more as he looked at the silver masts, trims, and bulwarks.

"Wow, I wonder how much all of this had to cost in order to make. It's almost like the Captain's room," he whispered as he got to the stern of the ship, where another beautifully hand-carved door stood.

There were two sets of stairs, one on starboard side and one on port side. Both staircases led up to the steering deck above the magnificent door.

Same as before, the lad gently grabbed the warm, silver doorknob, with his left hand and slightly crouched down. Anxious as can be, he then opened it slowly, ready for a fight.

"Huh? That's different," the boy thought aloud as he walked down the small set of stairs.

He then came to an in-wall prison cell fifteen feet away, the walls of the ship were black, and it also appeared to be made of wood. The smell on the second deck was tasteful with the scents of herbs and meat. After making himself hungry from constantly sniffing the air, the lad looked and noticed how the silver prison bars stood out from the black walls.

"The bars are glowing too? I was skeptical; I was thinking it was the Captain's quarters only. But somehow, I knew it wasn't over with the surprises because above deck on the outside is unreal," the boy said softly as he looked into the holding cell.

On each side of the cell, was a dimly lit, kerosene lamp that was beautifully designed as well. Inside of the cell, the walls were golden-brown and glowed enough to see the contents thereof.

"Even the jail cell looks clean and never before used. The bed looks pretty comfortable and it looks pretty warm too," the boy acknowledged as he stared at the gray sheets on the bed.

He then turned around and noticed hallways on both sides of the stairs.

"This should be fun. I must be careful, there may still be people on here," the boy whispered as he contemplated which hall to go down first.

Room by room, he checked thoroughly, each one unique with its own quirk and style.

"Interesting, this place is foreign to me; yet I feel like I'm home, but that's impossible. Snap out of it! I have to be on alert! There could still be someone around any corner," the boy said as he closed a room door.

The further the lad explored, he began to feel uneasy and lonely; he missed souls he never knew although he felt as though he had. After he checked all the rooms on each side, he gradually walked towards the bow of the ship.

"Okay, I have to keep moving, I just pray someone doesn't find my blood trail all over their clean ship before I find them," the lad said as he walked to an opened entrance of another room.

To his amazement, there was a huge galley and saloon in the middle, that connected both hallways. They were clean, fully loaded and prepped for use.

"No one here either, strange, I smelt food earlier. But there's nothing prepared," the boy said as he looked around the galley.

After he left the galley, the boy headed towards the bow of the ship once more.

"Now that's something you definitely don't see every day!" the boy said as he walked into another large room.

On the other side of the kitchen's north wall, were two, huge rooms for the head and bathing area. It appeared that the east side was for males and the west side was for the females.

"I faintly remember homes that didn't have bathhouses like this. This is crazy! I'm beginning to think there's no one on this level of the ship too," the boy said.

The boy then crept to the other side to check the other bathing room.

"Yep, this deck is definitely empty and there's only one place to go now. Below," the lad said as he walked to the hallway and stared towards the bow of the ship.

Behind the north wall of the bathing rooms, were a set of stairs at the bow of the ship that led down into the gun deck. The brave boy quietly delved deeper into the belly of the mysterious ship; reaching the gun deck that was as silent as he. The boy could see the entire deck from the stairs, and it was empty from all souls but his. Everywhere as far as his eyes could see were heaps and piles of different weapons that were partially disassembled. Some he saw before and some he had never; that even looked otherworldly.

"No freaking way! What are those?!" he shouted as he grabbed his face and tried to hurry down the stairs.

The lad was rushed with excitement and energy from seeing all the unique weapons.

"This ship is absolutely incredible! It looks like it has never had anyone on it, but it's fully stocked and has style. From the crew's rooms to the Captain's quarters, to the galley, quality of material used to build it, this ship is legendary! It doesn't add up! And now there's just weapons laying around on here?! Is this a trap? No, if it was, I would have been done away with by now," he said as he walked around the huge gun deck while his blood trailed behind him.

The young lad continued to look around the deck in search of at least one soul.

"A lot of these weapons are disassembled. It'll take a couple of naturals and maybe even a genius to figure this one out. But none of this makes sense! There are places I haven't been yet on here; I have to assume that there could still be people on here. However, this ship…" he uttered as he looked at the three separate sets of downward stairs that led into different chambers below the deck he saw from the main stairs.

There was one staircase on the left, one on the right, and one in the middle towards the stern. Each with their own regal door; inviting him with imagination and promise, so, he continued. After half an hour of scouting the vessel, the young lad made his way back up to the main deck.

"This is undeniably the finest, the coolest, the freakiest, most expensive, cryptic vessel, I ever set foot on! If I hadn't been here, there's no way I'd believe such a story of such a creation. But how is there no one here to claim it?! Luckily, there's food and fresh water too! That's unbelievably rare to have. I completely forgot to look to grab some before leaving my ship. This is kind of weird; what's strange is that I feel comfortable, but I know something is off at the same time," the young lad said.

The young boy then looked around more and began to doubt himself and his capabilities.

"Can I even handle this thing? I mean, I remember enough to survive but can I manage this thing all by myself? Sure I can, father taught me well, but... No, I couldn't, it's lonely here. I could easily be overthrown if someone decided to attack. I can't do this alone and I don't know a thing about medicine to keep this wound from getting infected.

Now that I think of it, I don't even remember father teaching me anything, that's weird. How come I can't recall the times he taught me, but I meticulously know the stuff I know? Whatever, I'll get back to that. Look at this place; it's so great I could curse! I can get my revenge on whoever did that to my father and crew, but I need help," he said softly.

The boy then walked to starboard side, where he saw a basin of flammable oil.

"There's no sign of a struggle, and there's no blood but my own," the lad said before he shrugged his shoulders and laughed.

After shaking off the nervousness, he looked up to see his ship in the distance still above water.

"How is that even possible? It should have been sunk, unreal, it's like time is confused here," he said as he reached behind his back and dug inside his quiver for a couple of arrows.

His mood changed from chipper, back to a mourning state, for he knew his ship was sinking and he had to take a brave new journey into the unknown. With his arrows nearly ready for flight, he recited his guild's song as he slowly dipped the arrowheads in oil. A parade of tears leaped from his eyes as he released the three thunderous-like strikes. All three took off at the same time from his bow; they sparked from release and fell like fire from heaven.

Aimed for the exposed ammo, gunpowder, explosives, and flammable oil basins next to the fires, the once magnificent ship went up in flames. As it slowly began to sink, the tears of a lonely child did not fall onto deaf ears. To witness his beloved, his home, his crew, and memories get erased from existence, left him gasping for oxygen.

All of a sudden, the wind seemed to hear his request for a fresh taste; a miracle happened. A strong gust of wind came through from the east, which carried the smoke from his burning ship to in front of him. The spirits of the Captain and crew appeared in the smoke that camped in the graveyard of battalions that day. The sky grew darker; exposing flares of lightning and then the ship he was on began to vibrate. He dropped down to his knees in more pain than before he started his journey. Completely drained from the entire ordeal, his eyes watered, and his mouth dropped. The fresh air had come and gone; his lungs were clear once again. By this time, some of the fires dwindled that were in the vortex but not the ones beyond it. The mood was heavy as the sun seemed to cease its light and time appeared as if it froze.

The waters raged more as fog arrived to meet desperation. Even the creatures of the ocean came up to see the prophecy and farewell from the might of Schivala. Outlined with striking silver, their eyes were like a thunderous-white; the Captain began to speak.

"My dear boy..." his spirit said, before being quickly interrupted.

"Father!! Father!! I'm sorry!! I'm sorry I

was weak and couldn't help you all, it's my fault you're all dead! Forgive me!! Father!! Father!! I'm so sorry!! I'm so, so sorry," the lad cried.

"It is not your fault. So, don't beat yourself up if you are already weakened. You are indeed strong, and you must know it. You must know although the distance between us has grown and the notion of time has changed, we will never part for we are one. It is not your fault. You have been given a very special opportunity, a second chance; fate has called. It's up to you Matuka to carry on, to be the salt of the earth and thy brother's keeper. Be kind to others, run from no fight, you have the strength to overcome any opposition. You will be one of the strongest warriors amongst the continents and even known to man. The waters of the rain, the rivers, lakes, ponds, swamps, bayous, canals, puddles, the oceans, and seas will be your footstool.

The animals will hear your cry and aid you always and forever. For you are their alpha, their friend and protector, but only after you declare it so! The thunder only stands still for you and the Creator; it dances at your fingertips. Fire from your soul burns deeply, so make sure to let it out once in a while. The fog will be your shield everywhere you go; your mystery will even captivate the blind because this vessel has no limits. This is your ship and you are its Captain! It will be linked to you and your crew, a gift from the ocean, you can say. So, learn to make friends! Learn to trust, forgive, and live honorably. Live everyday like it's your last. Try not to ignore people and their feelings, especially the ones who care for you and who you claim to care for. Learn to make a way that everyone around you could live peacefully and be the best version of themselves," the spirit of the Captain said.

"Father, I don't even remember anything! The battles, how they started, the injuries, nothing! And what are you talking about?! I can't do the things you said I can, I didn't even remember my name until you said it. How will I remember all of what you said?! I've already forgotten most of it!" Matuka yelled as he cried.

"You will remember what you need to when the time comes. Nothing is ever truly forgotten, just hidden," the spirit said as he looked on at the weeping boy.

"And look around; the pickings look a little slim on friends, father! Oh, let me guess, I'm supposed to get the seagulls and sharks to be my crew, huh?!" the young boy yelled and cried.

This caused the Captain and crew to chuckle in unison.

"Have the hard lessons learned not taught us anything? Haven't you learned already that the things seen are because of the things not seen? Have faith in yourself! And don't worry, you'll remember what you need to know with time. Wear that tri-cone hat proud and with some heart! You are royalty!" the spirit of the Captain proclaimed.

With the mighty shout from the Captain, a thunderstorm appeared over Matuka and the ship he was on.

"Matuka, remember the words of truth, keep them in your heart always. Don't forget your natural skills and find the ones you lost long ago before time coming. It's urgent you locate your crew, they need you Matuka," said the Captain's ghost.

"Everyone does!" yelled the crew immediately after.

As the thunder and swirling of the cocoon of smoke increased, the strong winds lifted Matuka off the deck. That is when a small shower of rain hugged the vortex of smoke and thunder with precision.

"Father!!! You guys!!! Don't leave me!!! Please take me with you!!!" he pleaded.

"Matuka, the mighty, you have the strength," the spirit said softly as they all vanished.

"Father!!!" Matuka yelled and cried.

For it was too late, the spirits of the Captain and crew were gone. All the sea creatures descended back from whence they came; in a new contract with Matuka as soon as he declared it so. The vortex immediately dispersed and Matuka dropped to his feet, in stagnant pain still; he sat and cried. He had nearly forgotten all of what his beloved said and couldn't believe what he just saw. Immediately after, the young boy became dizzy and vomited all over the deck.

"Father," the young boy said softly with his head down.

Without warning, another huge gust of wind blew away; nearly all the smoke and fires from the deadly battles that surrounded him. The waves washed his bile off the pitch-black deck, along with his pride. In his vision were shipwrecks, rubble and bodies floating as far as the eye can see. The young lad's heart began to race as he looked out to sea.

"What is this feeling? Why is my heart racing? It's not fear necessarily; could it be anticipation? Or is it that I'm about to pass out?" he asked himself.

It was a little past noon and the sky was still dark from the smoke that was beyond the dissipated vortex. Matuka then stared towards his ship's helm, trying to remember the words of his beloved.

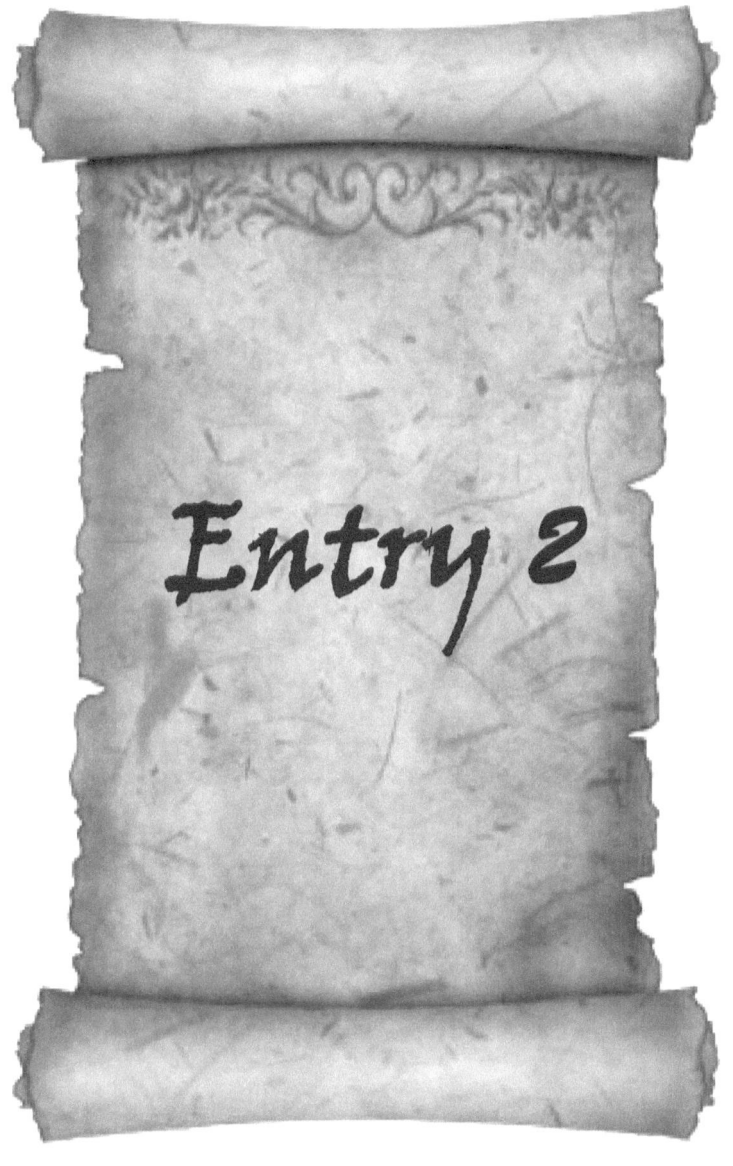

Entry 2

THE CRY OF THE FORGOTTEN

He realized that it was his first time ever being a Captain of his very own ship. So, he brightened up a little and tried to walk proudly over to his destiny. Step after step, Matuka looked around his deck at the beautiful black paint. He admired the carvings and workmanship of the metal details. He glanced at his black sails, how they seemed to cover like the night sky. He was reminded of the Captain and crew's last words, so, he couldn't help but to feel comforted. Even though he was engulfed in the beauty of the majestic ship, Matuka saw that it was quiet and that his crow's nest was empty. He felt the loneliness from the vacant galley and bedrooms he saw earlier.

By the time he made it to the helm, he was already covered in so many emotions. Matuka then stood there with his hands out ready to grab but he hesitated and paused.

"Did all that just really happen? I mean like really? Am I going crazy?" he asked aloud.

That's when sharp pains shot through his wounded leg as he watched the green, soaked bandanna, trickle blood down his leg.

"Nope, that really happened," Matuka said as he looked up.

Matuka then grabbed the helm with both hands and froze. Suddenly, an invisible wave of energy exploded from around him and went out to the sea in all directions.

"What the heck was that?!" he screamed.

Fidgety already, he tried to pull away and realized he couldn't.

"What the heck?! Why can't I let go?!" he screamed out of frustration and fear.

Simultaneously, he was met with a vision of a young girl floating within the debris. He saw that she was still alive but barely holding on and needed help immediately. Tears of blood fell from his eyes, while warmth from his soul transferred from his body, through his hands, to the ship's helm. Fog quickly seeped from the boat's exterior until the ship was completely shrouded in a blanket of invisibility. Suddenly, the ship took off like a bullet, blasting through all the wreckage.

"Unbelievable! It's so fast and where did this fog come from? It's not blowing away. Wait! Is it coming from the ship?!" he asked with a wide opened smile.

Out of nowhere, the grand vessel stopped as fast as it started. If it wasn't for his hands being supernaturally glued to the helm and feet to the ground, he would have been propelled off the ship into the water. The fog quickly disappeared and Matuka could see better than before.

"Déjà vu," he whispered.

He then stood to his feet and looked around at the rubble in the water.

"Wait a sec, this looks like..." he said before being interrupted.

"Hey!! Help!! Help!! Hey!! Help!!" a young girl screamed.

Not knowing his hands were free, he pulled away hard and fell to the deck. Numb to the pain because of hearing her voice, he quickly got up and ran over to the side of his ship, as fast as he could. The blood squirting from his wounds and numb tendons tearing, were not going to stop him. As Matuka held the side of his ship, he looked over in disbelief.

"That's the same girl from my vision! What's going on here?!" he shouted as he looked on at her.

A sense of concern and joyfulness engulfed him because he knew she was in danger, but at the same token, he was no longer alone.

"Let's assess the damage, she's floating on a piece of wood and she looks pretty beaten, how can I get to her or get her to me?" he thought aloud as he leaned over the bulwarks.

As quick as he could blink, a dark shadow covered Matuka like a blanket over a newborn. Matuka slowly looked up and saw a figure jumping as though it came from the crow's nest. Eyes stretched wide; he could only wonder how long the entity had been on the ship.

With an impression-making landing, the tall, dark lad stood in front of Matuka, unveiled his hooded cape and smiled. The first thing he noticed was the lad's dark, navy-blue cape-like cloak, that hung around his neck and shoulders. A soft purple shirt underneath that seemed to be made from fine material. He wore pale forest green pants and there was white bandage tape wrapped around his legs, ankles, and feet. They were stained with fresh blood and covered with the falling ash.

He had a gray bandanna wrapped around

the left side of his face, while it seemed to have a slit cut into it, so his left ear could be exposed. The right side of his face was exposed, which revealed his snow-white eyebrow. His exposed eye was dark-brown and intimidating. He had beige, wooden earrings that stretched his earlobes. His persona and confidence spoke all throughout his hair loud and clear. His hair was short and black on the sides. There was some black hair on the top of his head as well. However, the middle portion of his hair was much longer and snow white.

"Who the heck are you?! How long have you been here?! When did you get on here?! And what the heck is up with your hair?!" Matuka demanded to know.

"*That necklace, where have I seen it before?*" the young lad thought as he crossed his arms and closed his eye.

"Hey! Don't you dare ignore me!" Matuka shouted with his fist balled up towards the stranger.

The tall lad stood there silent before the young Captain; all the while as he pondered on Matuka's necklace.

"I saw you speeding past, so I caught a ride," the lad stiffly replied with a smirk as he opened his right eye and threw his palms up in the air.

"Oh! You caught a ride?! Do you think

I'm some stupid idiot?! That's impossible! And if so, this is my ship and I'm the Captain! You think you can just jump on someone's ship and stowaway?!" Matuka asked enraged and in fear, although he knew he had just done the same thing in a way.

The mysterious lad looked on with a smirk as Matuka tried to make sense of his presence.

"How long was he up there? I didn't see him when I looked before. Was he hiding all along? Was this his ship? Is he one of the crew? No, wait!" he thought to himself as a memory began to surface.

The words from his Captain began to softly ring in his ears.

"Father said that this was my ship and that it was a gift from the ocean. So, who is he? How and when did he get on here? I'm sure father would have told me if someone was aboard. So, what? He's some kind of creeper peeper? Just who in the heck does he think he is? He could have killed me if he wanted," Matuka thought to himself.

The lad continued to stand there with a sneaky smirk upon his face, which ignited Matuka's fire even more.

"You think this is funny or a game?! You've invaded my haven and purposely hid yourself! Now what is your name?!" Matuka screamed while he reached in his quiver for an arrow.

"I can think of other things that are way more important," the lad sarcastically responded.

"Oh yeah? Like what?!" Matuka asked as he tried to grab an arrow.

"Her," the lad replied before he pointed to the girl in the water.

A look of embarrassment haunted Matuka's face, once he realized he forgot the young lass, who was in desperate need of help. By this time, she was no longer moving and had gone silent for a few seconds.

"How about we save her first and then we can discuss this later?" the young, tall lad asked as he stepped closer.

"Right," Matuka replied before he quickly turned around to check on the young girl.

"Well, what's the plan Captain?" the lad asked sarcastically before he closed his eye.

"Okay," Matuka whispered as he prepared himself to issue his first command as a Captain.

"Well, being I'm shot and can barely walk and she's about sixty-feet away, it'll be in our best interest if you jump in and swim her back to the ship. However, there is a lot of debris, waste, and bodies in the water, so getting to her won't be a walk through the meadow.

Also, the water is too cold; you do not want to be in there for too long. When you retrieve her and make it back, get close enough and I'll let down the net and pull you both in. By then, I'll have some warm towels for you both," Matuka replied as he observed the situation.

"How do you plan on doing that with your arms in that condition?" the tall lad asked with an attitude.

"Don't worry about me, just save her!" Matuka said as he lifted his right arm and balled his fist.

With a small gust of wind, what followed was a huge splash in the water, the lad jumped in with no hesitation.

"Wow, unreal! He's freaking fast! Maybe he wasn't lying," Matuka said, shaken from disbelief.

Stroke after stroke, the lad gained speed and shortened the distance between the young girl that seemed to have passed out on the piece of debris.

"Crap, I hope I'm not too late," the young lad said after he released water from his mouth and as he ferociously swam to her.

The mysterious lad proved he had a strong gut as he passed all the casualties. The distance grew even smaller than before and he didn't slow down until he reached her.

"Finally," the lad said as he swam up in

front of her.

The water was cold; filled with countless casualties and time was running short.

"She must have passed out when she saw the ship. She's beautiful," he said as he reached in to lift her arm to carry her.

The young girl was unconscious, over-heated and badly bruised, so the lad knew he had to hurry her back to the ship. Without hesitation for his mission from the Captain, he strapped her around his back and began to swim. In the distance, the lad saw Matuka preparing for their return with warm blankets, so he picked up his speed.

"Well at least she isn't heavy," the lad thought aloud as he began to swim faster.

All of a sudden, the lad and young lass were snatched backwards because their clothes had gotten hooked onto some of the debris.

"Crap! This isn't looking good," the lad said as he tried to keep them from going under.

Looking on from the ship, Matuka noticed the boy got caught up in the debris and dove in the water without second guessing. With a wounded leg and holding onto a net grabbed from the ship, Matuka struggled to make it to them.

"Ah!! Come on! What's the point of being Captain if you can't save them when they're in need?!" Matuka yelled to himself.

Breath after breath and thrust after thrust, he found himself exceeding his limits. Matuka felt his ligaments tearing as the sweat, blood, and saltwater in his eyes burned without ceasing. His mouth was dry from the ocean's spray and he was well past dehydration. He was extremely fatigued but didn't give up. His arms and legs were on fire on the inside, but they were freezing on the outside. Even though he realized that he was risking his own life for strangers, he continued because he would have rather died there than be alone. A cry of desperation soon leaped from his mouth for strength to carry on.

"Father, help me!" Matuka yelled as he raised the net entwined around his right hand and before he regained some of his strength back.

The pain no longer mattered to him and he wasn't going to give up. With his bow snugged tightly around his quiver, he pushed on. The lad seen it all and found Matuka intriguing yet stupid while he watched him struggle to get to them.

"What is he thinking? Is he trying to kill himself? Why didn't he get rid of the weight off his back? What a moron," the lad thought aloud as he cut the fabric that had them ensnared on the broken mast head.

As soon as Matuka made it to them, he

handed the mysterious lad some of the net.

"Just had to play hero huh?" the lad asked.

Matuka picked up his half-submerged head out of the water and smiled.

"No, I thought you wouldn't make it alone, so I jumped in, how is she? How are you?" Matuka asked with an exhausted laugh.

"She's out cold but she's alive," the lad replied.

"And you?" Matuka questioned with a serious face.

"I'm okay, just got snagged on a piece of metal, would have been better if you weren't here slowing me down," the boy replied stoically.

"Good, I'm glad you're both okay," Matuka said with a smile before he slowly fainted.

"What the hell?!" the lad asked.

The mysterious lad immediately grabbed for Matuka's shirt with his left hand as he held the young girl's arms with his right hand, over his chest. When they all began to sink, the net that Matuka was holding started glowing white.

"What the?!" the lad asked before water entered his mouth.

The net simultaneously wrapped around all of them and began to retract, which brought their heads all above the water-line.

"No way they're gonna believe this," the lad said before he passed out as the net continued to retract.

A couple of hours had gone by and the first one to come to; was the young girl.

"Where am I?" the young lass asked as she sat up and tried to look around.

After the throbbing headache subsided and her vision cleared up, she noticed Matuka and the lad still unconscious on the ship's beautiful black deck.

"Did they save me? Who are they? Where is their guild's coat of arms?" she asked as she stood up.

Skeptical of the young lads, the young lass didn't hesitate to pull out her dagger she had hidden in her left pant leg pocket. The young girl noticed that there were towels on the deck, but they were soaked with water and blood from the boys. She then made her way over to the two boys; hovered over them, saw they had injuries and that they were soaking wet.

"The younger one has been shot and sliced up pretty bad. He needs attention as soon as possible. But first let me disarm him of that loaded quiver and bow. How did he get it to stay secure? Oh okay, clever," she said as she took off the bow and quiver from the unconscious young Captain, before she placed it next to him.

She then looked back to the ocean and stared for a second or two, as she tried to remember what happened prior to awakening on a strange ship.

"What happened? What day is it? Heck, what year is it?" the young girl asked as she looked at the destruction around the ship.

She soon realized she couldn't remember anything, and it scared her. After she gave up on trying to remember the events prior to, she looked back to the other lad that was lying unconscious on the black deck.

"This other guy, he looks a little older, he has blood all over him, but it's not his. He must be a brute or a warrior, looks kind of mean too," she said as she examined his body and the situation.

"The youngest has a Captain's hat on but no way he could be the Captain. Maybe this is his father's ship. But in all honesty, he does look the part. And he's kind of cute too. Okay girl, snap out of it! I got to search for supplies.

"Huh?" the girl suddenly asked as she glanced at Matuka's necklace.

The golden necklace drew the young lass into a deep thought as she gazed upon it.

"That's weird, it looks so familiar, focus girl! Okay, I see he has wet linen here, I need more," she said before she snapped her fingers as though she had an idea while she put up her dagger.

The young girl looked towards the bow of the ship at the forecastle's door, then towards the stern of the ship.

"I hope this is the way," she said as she ran towards the rear of the ship.

While she was running, she looked down and saw Matuka's trail of blood leading her to the majestic, hand-carved door.

"Yeah this is definitely the way," she said as she burst through the door.

The girl stood frozen as she admired the ship's design and beauty.

"Whoa, it has a man's touch but it's fancy and sleek as well," the young lass said because she couldn't believe how clean and astonishing the vessel was.

The girl continued to look around and became more captivated by the second.

"Such fine detail, who made this ship? Look at the cell! It's spotless besides the trail of blood. A little too clean for a good for nothing!" she said before she rolled her eyes while her left hand rested on her hip.

She then walked down the steps and was immediately drawn to her right, down the hallway on the left side of the ship. There were two doors to choose from on her left and down the hall on the right; there were two openings into other rooms.

"I'm going to guess and say those two are more cabins or maybe the galley," she said as she looked down the hallway.

Suddenly, the young girl screamed because she began to vibrate and levitate off the ground.

"What's going on?!" she screamed and cried.

After she was magnetically pulled to the first door on the left, it flew open and she fell inside. The door slammed shut and the room was pitch-black, leaving her with no vision.

"Hey! Help! Help! Help me, please help!" she screamed repeatedly as she banged on the door as loud as she could.

However, the young lads above on the main deck were still out cold. After minutes passed and she gave up, she sat still in the darkness. The young lass then braced herself for the unknown and inevitable. That's when little by little, until it was bright enough to see, the room began to glow the purest, most beautiful shades of green, she had ever seen. An immediate sense of safety and warmth filled her spirit. The energy was familiar, so she felt calm and relaxed as though she belonged. Her mouth fell open as she viewed the objects in the room, radiating their own light.

"Oh my God, look at this room! Are you

kidding me?!" the young lass said as she looked around the room.

As the lights grew brighter so did the beautiful and tasty fragrances.

"This is amazing! And it's beautiful! And the theme is green! And it's huge!" she screamed with excitement as she covered her face.

The young lass continued to scan the peculiar room with more excitement growing from within.

"Green is my favorite color! How is this even happening?! What is this ship? Is the floor made of grass?! It is and it's real! There are flowers, fruits and herbs growing in here from the floor?! How is this possible?! It smells so good!" she said as she looked around, stunned from the magical and colorful display.

She then spotted a huge, jade, in-wall bookshelf to her right by the door. It had recipe books on medicine, labeled jars with familiar and strange vegetation, that also emitted light. One jar had beach sand, while another had volcanic ash. There were a few items that had labels she could pronounce, but most of them she couldn't.

The walls were covered in radiant vines that were producing rare flowers. However, the rare flowers were only growing on a portion of the glowing, golden-brown walls.

"Wow!" the young girl shouted as she inched pass the delicious glowing fruits that lit up the room with tasty scents.

As she looked to her left, there was a huge comfy looking bed that ran along the south wall. The support was surrounded by lavender and was made from the finest tree stumps that she had ever laid eyes on.

"Wow, the wood is sparkling and glowing golden-brown. It looks like a gold nugget held in the sun," the girl said as she found herself overwhelmed from curiosity.

The bed had an enormous green leaf that looked as though it was made of silk as it rested upon the soft glowing, white, feather-stuffed mattress. On top rested two large, sparkling green pillows that were covered with glowing, pink dust. Directly in front of her was the west side of the ship, there was a huge wardrobe with doors opened already, that revealed all sorts of gorgeous women clothing and accessories. Without thinking twice, she ran to the wardrobe and started pulling things out.

"Oh yes girl, this is so you!" she laughed as she stretched out the long sleeve blouse to see if it would fit her by comparing arm lengths.

She twirled and laughed before she looked to the right to notice there was a beautiful brown, glowing table that ran along the entire north wall. On top, the floating table was fully stocked with medical supplies that gave off a light-green aura as well. Above the table was a huge mirror where she was able to see herself. After she saw her reflection, she felt ashamed, forgetting why she came in the first place. The girl dropped the clothes and ran to the table to examine closer, from elixirs to surgical tools, she had all she needed to help her rescuers.

"This is perfect and more than enough! Yeah, this should be all I'll need to get them fixed up," the young lass said as she leaned over the illuminated table.

The young girl grabbed what she needed, turned around and the door opened for her.

"Why thank you," she said as she curtsied.

The young girl bolted out the door down the hallway and then the door closed gently. As she was running, the door to the main deck opened before she turned left from the hallway. Once she made another left up the stairs; out onto the deck, the door closed behind her as well. As she dashed to the unconscious boys, she looked towards Matuka and then towards the taller lad.

"The big guy's injuries aren't as severe as the younger one. Let me help this one first," she said as she hurried and knelt over Matuka.

The young girl slowly and gently untied the blood-stained, green bandanna from around his wounded leg. She was being as careful as she could to not awake him with more pain, so she supported his right leg with towels and pulled the soiled bandanna, from out of his ripped pant leg.

"Okay cool, doing good there sir," the girl said as she laid the bandanna right next to herself on the smooth, black deck.

The young girl kept a towel over his wound to keep it from bleeding as she grabbed for one of the tools.

"Okay, here goes," the young lass said as she leaned in.

Sweat began to drip down from her nose, so she stopped and wiped.

"Girl, you've done this a million times, why are you shaking? Wait, have I?" she asked herself as her memory escaped.

After she wiped her face from sweat, confusion, anxiety, and nervousness, she then proceeded to remove the bullet from his leg. The closer she got to Matuka the brighter her silver retractor glowed green.

"Whoa, that's new! His wounds are dis-appearing! All except his blood," she said as she marveled at the sight and inched closer to him.

Suddenly, the bullet sprung from his leg

onto the deck and Matuka screamed as he sat up. All over his body, the wounds were healed immediately after the bullet was removed. All that remained was his blood and she could not believe her sight.

"Ahh! What the hell was that?! My leg, my leg!" he yelled with his eyes closed.

"Really?" the girl asked with a sarcastic chuckle and smile.

When he opened his eyes and turned his head to the left, he nearly fainted again. Simply because she was the beautiful young girl from the vision, and she was extremely close to his body. From top to bottom he admired his healing angel; his eyes were as big as an owl's while he stared at her. Her golden-brown hair, styled in an all-natural, curly afro, bounced with life, and smelled like hazelnut. Her thick and smooth, golden-honey eyebrows sparkled as sweat dripped off her face, due to the blazing fires still around them. Her eyes nearly melted his heart as he deeply gazed in the browns, the oranges, and greens of her iris.

The young girl's face was sprinkled with freckles, which made the colors in her eyes stand out. He followed her cute button nose down to her soft and welcoming, darkened-pink lips. Her lovely, light-caramel brown skin glistened from the flames as they danced about the wreckage. Her skin also gave off a honey and vanilla aroma as she began to sweat. She had on an emerald green blouse with a brown leather bustier that hugged her bosom tightly and her thin waist. She had on dark-brown tights with brown leather boots that also hugged her curves. The young boy took a big gulp as he contemplated speaking to her, so he grabbed his green, blood-soaked bandanna and wrapped it back in the same spot on his leg.

"What is your name?" Matuka asked nervously.

The girl stood up to stretch, stuck her right hand out and smiled.

"I'm Yanielle, thank you for saving me, what is your name?" she asked with a smile.

That's when Matuka saw the uninvited boy lying unconscious on the deck.

"*Why is he unconscious? Did he pass out?*" he thought to himself.

Matuka stood up slowly and let out a sigh. He had a regretful look in his eyes because he knew he could take the full credit, but he'd be lying, and it would not be honorable. He grasped her hand, smiled proudly with his chest out as his necklace rested on it and smiled.

"I'm Matuka and this is my ship, I'm the Captain," the young boy said before he let go of her hand.

"How are you the Captain?! You are just

a kid! No offense, but this ship is too nice to be yours. The room that I was just in was absolutely magical, these tools and medicine, magical! This boat is far too complex for a preteen to handle. Sorry, I'm not buying. What's the real story?" Yanielle demanded to know.

"Wait a second! How did we all get up here?" Matuka whispered before he dropped his head, crossed his arms, and grabbed his chin as he tried to remember.

"Hellooo? So, you're just going to ignore me?" the young lass shouted as Matuka walked away.

As he pondered on how they survived, he completely ignored the young girl and her questions.

"Oh yeah?! Whatever you jerk!" she yelled before she stuck her tongue out.

Matuka continued to walk away as he tried to bring the memory back to the surface.

"Let me just help this guy out then," she said as she walked over to the lad lying lifeless.

She immediately noticed him bleeding on his left side, so she grabbed for the towels and one of her surgical tools. As the noon sky blackened from smoke and the eternal fires of the destruction showed no mercy with heat, the young girl hurried to aid the other lad. His wounds did not appear fatal at first, but time showed something different.

"How come I didn't see this earlier?!" Yanielle asked as she leaned over the boy.

Same as before, when she placed one of her tools close to him, it started to glow a deep, sparkling-green and before she could blink, the blood was gone and so were all his wounds. Consumed in the mystery of how they were all saved from the abyss, Matuka missed the light show Yanielle created.

"So why did your blood disappear instead of his? Hey, did you see that?! You jerk!" she yelled as she looked over her shoulder in Matuka's direction.

Her mouth dropped as Matuka completely ignored her. Matuka stood by the side of the vessel and gazed deeply into the water.

"What happened?" Matuka asked before he walked closer to the silver bulwarks.

"I can't believe that guy," Yanielle said before she turned around to notice that the unconscious lad was missing.

"What the heck?!" she asked with a confused look on her face.

A quick gust of wind moved about the ship towards and over Matuka. Out of nowhere, the once comatose lad dropped from the air and landed on the silver bulwarks in front of Matuka. The boy thought Matuka would be frightened and would jump back quickly, but Matuka did not move a muscle.

"He's different from before, like he has split personalities or something. This side is more serious, while the other side is more childlike," he thought to himself as he stared at Matuka.

"You jerk! I bring you back from the brink of death and you can't even say thank you? You both are big jerk holes!" she yelled as she walked over to them both.

Matuka and the older boy both smiled with a shameful grin, then dropped their heads.

"Sorry," Matuka said first, followed by a quick sorry from the tall lad.

"Ugh! Whatever!" she yelled as she stepped closer to them, which put them in a tri-angular position from each other.

"You're awfully quiet, what's bugging you?" the lad asked Matuka stiffly.

"I ask the questions here! You boarded my ship uninvited and hid! You lied about how you got aboard and still haven't told me your name. So, I ask the freaking questions here! What is your name?!" Matuka demanded with a stern, sure voice that sent chills down Yanielle and the older boy's neck.

"I already told you! Did you not just see me land here? Or what about before when I jumped down and scared you?!" the lad asked Matuka with an annoyed look on his face.

Matuka stood there unfazed as an unbending glare resided in his eyes; he needed more proof and the lad could sense it. The lad then looked up towards the sky and jumped with unbelievable speed towards the crow's nest. Matuka and Yanielle's eyes grew big once they witnessed such a sight for the first time in their lives.

"Oh my God, did you see that?!" she turned to Matuka and yelled from being astounded.

Matuka looked up with a serious face towards the boy and said, "I'm sorry, I stand corrected, you were telling the truth."

The lad looked down and cracked half of a smile and shouted, "Jubilaree!"

Yanielle looked to Matuka for his guess to what the mysterious lad said.

"Huh?!" Matuka yelled in response.

"The name is Jubilaree!" the boy yelled from the crow's nest.

"Well, my name is Yanielle! And you better get used to it, jerk!" Yanielle screamed before Jubilaree jumped down to the ground with speed and grace.

"Amazing," Matuka said with a serious look as he watched the boy's cape flow in the wind.

"So, we're gonna act like this is normal huh? Like this entire freaking ship is normal?!" Yanielle screamed and cried.

"Speaking of ship, what happened after I passed out Jubilaree?" Matuka asked as he walked over to him.

"Never got your name," Jubilaree said.

"Sorry, my name is Matuka," the young Captain said proudly as he extended his hand to greet him.

Jubilaree reached out and firmly shook Matuka's hand before he stood and thought for a second. Suddenly, Jubilaree remembered it like a dream resurfacing after a good night's slumber.

"It's strange, I remember now. Yeah, I remember you passing out and nearly going under water when I reached for you. I had her on my back and I was holding her too, then I think I went under. Yeah, I did! The next thing I remember was being pulled from underwater, bound in the net you brought with you. It was glowing and it was wrapped around all of us. It began to reel us in and that's when I passed out," Jubilaree said as he sat down on the deck with his feet crossed.

"Freaky," Yanielle said softly as she sat next to Jubilaree.

"What is this ship?" Jubilaree asked with a concerned look upon his face.

"A very special gift; our new home, if you two would like to stay," Matuka said with a gentle smile after his serious facial expression changed.

"Uh, yes! I picked my room," Yanielle immediately responded before she leaped up from the deck.

"Ah yes, I know which room you've picked by what you have here lying on the deck. That room fits you, it's unreal, it's like it was made just for you. There's a room for you too Jubilaree on the second deck. If you're going down the stairs, on the left there's a hallway which is on starboard side, the second door on the right is definitely yours. I think you belong there; it suits you. Maybe that's what he meant," Matuka said as he gripped the golden necklace with his left hand and stared off into the sky.

"What who meant?" Jubilaree asked as he looked up to Matuka from the floor.

"Is this ship enchanted or something?" Yanielle asked with a soft, yet serious voice.

"I wish I could answer all of your questions," Matuka dropped his head and said as he began to walk towards the helm.

As he started to walk, he noticed his bow and quiver lying on the deck where he was earlier. He leaned over, picked them up and put them on. After doing so, the young Captain looked towards the helm once more; ready to sail.

"Well, I think it's a pretty easy answer if

you ask me, I just want to hear you say it," Yanielle said as she got up and followed Matuka up the stairs to the steering deck.

"Yeah, this ship is pretty weird from what I noticed," Jubilaree said as he stood up.

Matuka turned around to listen to what they were saying before fully reaching the helm.

"Like for starters, the rudder looks like it's only for fashion and not use..." Jubilaree said before he was interrupted by Yanielle.

Matuka stood in silence as he looked on at them while they stood by the stairs.

"How come you didn't use any of the medical supplies that were in the room that I grabbed them from?" Yanielle asked as she walked up the stairs onto the helm deck and leaned in close to his face.

"That's easy, he doesn't know anything about medicine, am I right?" Jubilaree asked as he walked halfway up the stairs to Matuka and Yanielle with his arms crossed.

Matuka turned around, nervously walked up the small set of steps to the helm, stood in front of it, and then paused.

"The last time I grabbed this helm, the unimaginable happened, you two better hold on," Matuka said as he looked down at the detail of the workmanship on the ship's helm.

"Wait, what?!" Yanielle asked.

Jubilaree turned around and immediately jumped up into the crow's nest before Matuka could touch the helm.

"Hold on guys!" Matuka yelled as he grabbed hold to the helm and as Yanielle turned around to face the bow of the ship.

Just like before, Matuka was met with a vision of a young female in need of rescue, but this time the young lass was sitting and meditating on rubble. Once again, tears of blood fell from his eyes, while warmth from his soul transferred from his body; through his hands, to the ship's helm and his locks began to float in the air. The fog quickly seeped from the vessel's exterior until the ship was completely cloaked in a cocoon of mist, which made them invisible to the naked eye.

Suddenly, the ship took off like a bullet; blasting through all the wreckage once again, which caused the blood-soaked towels to fly off the ship. Yanielle was screaming for her life when Matuka looked over and noticed she was supernaturally glued to the deck as well. Her hair was flowing in the wind, but she was standing as still as the masts on the ship.

"Ahh!! What the heck is happening?! Why can't I move? Somebody help!" she screamed.

"Don't worry you're safe Yanielle! This is normal!" Matuka shouted as he looked to his right towards the frightened girl.

"What do you mean this is normal?!" Yanielle screamed as she looked around the ship and back to Matuka.

"He can move a little too huh?" Jubilaree asked as he watched Matuka move around enough to tell Yanielle she'd be fine.

Jubilaree then looked up as his left eye that was covered, began to glow red behind his gray bandanna.

"Ahead Captain! Port side!" Jubilaree screamed after he saw a young woman sitting on a piece of debris from a distance.

This alerted Matuka and Yanielle to be on a look out, for whatever that was next to come.

"Is that a girl? If so, then what's her deal? If it wasn't for this ship being so fast, I probably would have never spotted her as quickly. This ship is remarkable, Matuka," Jubilaree said under his breath as he looked down from the crow's nest.

"*How can he see through this fog?*" Matuka thought to himself as he tried to see through the thickness of the fog.

"You can see Jubilarec?!" Yanielle shouted in total disbelief as she struggled to look up to him.

"Not her too," Jubilaree said as he looked down and over his left shoulder at Yanielle, which was somewhat able to move as well.

"*Is his eye glowing?*" Yanielle thought as she looked up at Jubilaree with her mouth opened.

Unexpectedly, the ship began to slow and instinctively Matuka arms began to steer the helm to the left. As he continued to steer to the south, Jubilaree's left eye stopped glowing red behind his bandanna. As the ship began to completely slow down, the fog disappeared as fast as it showed up, however, the smoke remained. When the ship stopped, the crew was no longer glued to its surface and were able to move freely.

"What the heck? Did I just see that? Hey, why is Jubilaree looking like that? Huh? Matuka too?" she asked softly as she looked from Jubilaree to Matuka.

Yanielle then walked down the stairs, over to port side's bulwarks and looked into the water. Everyone stood there in silence as they watched the beautiful, foreign-looking girl meditate on a burning, wooden door. She was unfazed, her eyes were closed, and explosions were going off all around her.

"Oh, nah girl, is she crazy?" Yanielle asked as she looked over her left shoulder towards Matuka for confirmation.

Matuka walked over to the bulwarks on

port side of the helm deck in silence as he watched the young lass sit on the brown door. While blood continued to slowly drip from his eyes, the young Captain began to smile. Yanielle's mood changed to sad when she saw Matuka's eyes bleeding from the distance.

"Are you okay Matuka?" Yanielle asked after she walked up the helm deck and stood by his side.

Matuka looked to his right at Yanielle, closed his eyes and smiled.

"I'm fine, are you?" he asked before he looked her in the eyes.

"You can stop showing off now! We don't have all day!" Jubilaree yelled to the girl sitting amongst the rubble.

"Jubilaree!" Matuka yelled as he turned from Yanielle to look back up to the crow's nest.

Immediately and unexpectedly, the girl's right eye flew open and she looked up towards Jubilaree. She continued to sit while her right eye pierced his right eye.

"Such primitive behavior and arrogance are beneath me," the foreign girl said under her breath as she closed her eye.

"I heard that missy! You wanna say that to my face?!" Jubilaree yelled with his left hand pointed towards the girl and the other gripping the fine, silver bulwarks of the huge black, metal crow's nest.

"Jubilaree cool it man!" Matuka yelled as he looked towards him.

"She's probably not coming now, I know I wouldn't, not after all that," Yanielle said as she placed her right hand on her hip.

Matuka stormed by Yanielle leaving her kind of mad and jealous as she watched him walk away. Matuka quickly walked down the stairs towards the mast that the crow's nest was stationed on, to silence Jubilaree. As he looked up, he signaled a threat to Jubilaree by punching his left hand and running his finger across his throat in a cutting fashion.

"Pst, yeah, whatever," Jubilaree said before he closed his eye, tooted his nose up and crossed his arms.

Yanielle rolled her eyes, turned her head, and crossed her arms. As Matuka began to walk towards port side, Yanielle couldn't bear the sight, so she closed her eyes. Matuka saw that the young girl was a good distance away from the ship by the time he reached port side's bulwarks.

"Hey there! I'm sorry about that! I think he means well! Are you okay?! Do you want to board? Do you need help?!" Matuka yelled to the beautiful young girl that was sitting on the burning door.

The girl let out a deep sigh, threw her

head back with her eyes closed and then dropped her head. After she stretched, she stood up slowly and yawned.

"Wow, such balance, remarkable," Jubilaree said softly as he watched the gorgeous young lass on the door.

Suddenly, she looked up towards Jubilaree and smiled as she moved the hair from in front of her face, to behind her left ear.

"Did she hear me?" Jubilaree asked himself as a soft shiver overtook his body.

Immediately after, the girl on the door winked at Jubilaree, Yanielle noticed and then laughed. Jubilaree began to blush and turned around immediately so no one would see, however, the young foreign girl did anyway.

"Are you blushing Jubilaree?" Yanielle slowly teased and danced as she looked up to him.

"Shut up!" he yelled with his back turned to everyone; being he was deeply embarrassed.

Swiftly, the young girl ran atop the remains of dead men, women, children, and debris. Everyone was astonished at her tenacity and speed, so they patiently watched as the girl made her final leap.

"What the?!" Yanielle asked as the girl jumped past her face.

With ease, the beautiful lass nailed an impression-making landing onto the ship, in between Matuka and the mast Jubilaree was on. Suddenly after, the gust of wind that followed her also carried her tantalizing perfume to all the others' noses. The boys were captivated by the young girl's fragrance and beauty. Yanielle grew even more jealous when she noticed the boys, so she crossed her arms, frowned, and sucked her teeth.

She had long and straight, shiny-black hair. Her eyes were slanted, and she had a creamy, tan colored complexion. Her blouse was a deep and dark burgundy red, that almost looked like fresh, rich blood. The young lass' eyebrows were long and smooth also. Her lips were thick, and her ears were pierced. She wore red and yellow feathered earrings with a brown leather bustier. Her tights were a dark-brown and her boots were brown. They were made of a strong, unknown material and you could tell they were good for kicking. Jubilaree quickly turned around to avoid being seen looking at her but it was already too late.

"She's so gorgeous, I never saw anyone who looked like her," Matuka thought to himself as he walked towards her.

The young brave Captain then wiped his hands from sweat and approached the young lass.

"Hi, I'm Matuka and this is my ship, I'm the Captain," he said before Jubilaree turned around and peaked over the edge of the crow's nest.

"*It took you long enough, I heard you coming a mile away,*" the young girl thought to herself as she walked over to Matuka.

"You may be even faster than Jubilaree up there," Matuka said with a smile as he turned to look at Jubilaree while he reached for her hand to shake.

"Oh, I am," the girl said with a smile as she bowed and before she shook Matuka's hand.

When Matuka and the girl both laughed, Jubilaree sucked his teeth and quickly turned his head again.

"Welcome aboard," Matuka said as he let go of her hand.

"Hi, I'm Kotoyami, thank you for coming for me, I knew you were," she said with a serious face and deep stare.

Matuka stood paralyzed because what Kotoyami said caught him off guard and he didn't know how to react.

"*She must feel it too,*" Matuka thought to himself as he smiled.

Meanwhile, Yanielle was watching and began to get highly annoyed by how the two were laughing and talking like they always knew one another.

"*Who does she think she is? All foreign*

and beautiful and graceful and strong and amazing," Yanielle thought to herself before she let out a deep sigh.

Matuka and Kotoyami continued to laugh while Jubilaree grew annoyed as well.

"*No way I can compete with her, ugh! He's mine! No! Wait! He's not! Did I just say that?! I don't even really know him! But he seems so familiar somehow. What are these feelings?! Ugh! Snap out of it, girl! What's going on?!*" she shouted within her mind.

Yanielle then dropped her head, hunched over as though she was tired and gave up on the battle that was going on in her mind. Before too much time could pass, Yanielle lifted her head, smiled, and went over to meet the new passenger.

"Hi, I'm Yanielle, nice to meet you," she said as she admired the girl's beauty.

"Hello, I'm Kotoyami, the pleasure is mine," she said with a smile as she bowed to Yanielle then reached for her hand.

The two shook hands, hugged, complemented one another, and laughed. That's when Kotoyami looked up to Jubilaree and noticed he was staring at her. As soon as he saw her looking, he started to blush and then he quickly turned his head again.

"Hey lover boy! Aren't you gonna come down to say hi?!" Yanielle shouted towards the crow's nest.

"Yeah, come on down Jubilaree! Introduce yourself!" Matuka shouted as he and Yanielle looked up.

"I'd rather not," Jubilaree whispered with his arms crossed.

"Girl don't worry about it, these two can be jerks!" Yanielle screamed as she looked towards Jubilaree.

Out of nowhere, Kotoyami ran five feet up the mast, leaped all the way to the crow's nest and landed inside with Jubilaree.

"You're good, who cares?" Jubilaree asked with his eye closed.

"Obviously, you do," she said with a chuckle.

Jubilaree opened his eye and turned around; only to see her smiling at him, which made him blush even more.

"Hey! What are you doing?" he asked as she inched in closer on him.

"I'm Kotoyami, nice to meet you," she said when she bowed to him then reached for his hand.

With a nervous blush and sweat building, he quickly reached for her hand, shook it, and let it go.

"I'm Jubilaree, nice to meet you, show off, now leave," he said as he turned his back to her.

"See you later, sucker!" she said before she kicked him in the back of the right knee, which made his legs buckle.

"You little!!" Jubilaree said furiously as he turned around.

By then, she had done a backflip out of the crow's nest and blew a kiss at him before she landed onto the black, wooden deck.

"Amazing," Jubilaree said softly as Kotoyami and he locked eyes.

"*Outstanding,*" Matuka thought to himself while he watched Kotoyami look up to Jubilaree.

"Ew girl, I know you don't like no dusty tail Jubilaree," Yanielle said as she walked over to Kotoyami and rested her hand on her back.

"Mind your own damn business!" Jubilaree shouted bashfully.

"Hey, up yours jerk! Anyway, you gotta teach me those moves, girlfriend," Yanielle said to Kotoyami after she yelled at Jubilaree.

"I think we all could learn a few moves from you, Kotoyami," Matuka said as he walked over to the two, young lasses.

"Sure, no problem, anyone who wants to learn, I will teach," she said as she laughed and looked up to Jubilaree.

Jubilaree turned his head once again and closed his eye as he started to blush.

"Okay, let's get you out of here before I

get sick," Yanielle said as she gestured for them to head below.

"Yes, take her below deck; the room next to yours will fit her just fine. Make yourself comfortable Kotoyami, stay as long as you want," Matuka said while he turned around to look back at the ocean.

"Thank you, Matuka," Kotoyami said as Yanielle grabbed her hand.

The girls giggled and laughed until they were out of sight of the boys.

After Matuka turned around and faced the bow of the ship, he noticed soon after, without all the distractions earlier, just how huge the war was. One would argue it covered the entire ocean that day.

"How upsetting, so many lives lost," Matuka whispered as a lonely tear rolled down his check.

He stood silent as he stared at the havoc thriving outside his vessel. The wreckage also caught the attention of Jubilaree as he stood facing in the same direction.

"There's more out there," Matuka said calmly; knowing that Jubilaree could hear him.

"I figured you'd eventually say something like that," Jubilaree said with his arms folded.

"I can feel them," Matuka said with a deep stern gaze in his eyes.

"So, are we the pity guild now?" Jubilaree asked with a chuckle.

Matuka cringed when he heard Jubilaree, so he turned around and looked up.

"How could you say that? When our separate guilds caused all of this! Look around Jubilaree! Those are babies! Mothers! Fathers! Children! And some are even our age! We owe it to anyone that's alive out there to save them! Friend or foe!" Matuka yelled as blood from his eyes fell to the deck.

The wind was blowing and Matuka's locks were flowing in his face. Jubilaree knew he was serious from his stare and demeanor, so he dropped his act.

"Fine," Jubilaree said as he looked away with his nose in the air.

"Huh?" Matuka asked from being shocked that it would be that easy.

Jubilaree looked over the edge of the crow's nest, then jumped down to the deck and began to walk over to Matuka.

"I said fine, you don't have to be a crybaby over it, Captain," Jubilaree said with a smirk.

Matuka's look of confusion turned to a smile before he dropped his shoulders and head out of relief, from being mentally exhausted.

"Okay cool," Matuka said slowly as he stood back up.

"Where to now? Oh, brave one," Jubilaree asked sarcastically as he put his left hand on Matuka's tri-cone hat to push it down on his head correctly.

"A bed, for a quick nap, I need to rest," Matuka laughed as he stretched his arms out above his head.

"That wasn't the answer I was expecting to hear," Jubilaree replied.

"Well wouldn't you agree it's been a crazy start of a day? I don't know about you but I had a pretty rough morning so far and now it's a couple of hours past noon; the day hasn't even kicked our butts yet," Matuka said as he placed his right hand on Jubilaree's left shoulder.

"So what? Am I supposed to play babysitter and watch the ship?" Jubilaree asked with an attitude.

"You're the one who likes the crow's nest; pretty odd place to be if you're not willing to be the eyes. But, like I said before, there's a room for you down below, if you do not want to oversee the ship. Besides, something tells me it doesn't need anyone to watch over it," Matuka said as he looked around the vessel.

"What does that supposed to mean? And how do you know these rooms supposedly fit us?" Jubilaree asked with a raised right eyebrow.

"I have a feeling we will all find out soon

enough," Matuka said softly and very quickly.

"What was that?" Jubilaree quickly asked.

"I'm the Captain, why shouldn't I know where people belong on my ship?" Matuka asked with a smile.

"Yeah, okay, whatever," Jubilaree replied.

"But anyway, after you go through the door and down the stairs, make a left onto the right side of the ship's hallway; your room is the second door on the right. On the left side, the first opening is the galley and saloon, further down at the second open wing is the head slash baths. Behind that wall, on the front end of the ship, is a door that leads below to the gun deck," Matuka said as he pointed towards the door underneath the helm deck.

"Speaking of below deck, what are those two loud mouths up to?" Jubilaree asked.

"Not sure but you can find out, I'm gone for now," Matuka said as he turned around and threw his right hand back to wave goodbye.

After Matuka entered his Captain's quarters and closed the door, the main deck was quiet once more. That's when Jubilaree turned around and stared at the door that led below deck. Meanwhile, the girls were below deck, leaving Yanielle's room.

"See girl I told you, it's beautiful but

freaky too!" Yanielle said as she and Kotoyami stepped out into the hallway.

"I've never seen anything like this before and my people are very advanced. Wait! How do I know that? My memory has been hazy since I woke up. Can you tell me what happened to cause this war? I don't even remember the name of my guild or country," Kotoyami said with a concerned look in her eyes.

"That is weird, speaking of that, I can't remember either, I guess it's been one thing after another, so I really haven't had time to think about it until now," Yanielle said as she looked up to the black ceiling.

The two young lasses stood in the hallway and tried to force a memory to resurface; that they seemed to both had lost.

"This is insane, not even one name! My head hurts," Yanielle said before she dropped her head and closed her eyes.

"Maybe you should stop. Without the proper training in meditation, the pain could prove itself unbearable or even deadly," Kotoyami said as she looked at Yanielle.

"Well at least we can still look at your room that Matuka picked," Yanielle said as she wrapped their arms around one another to walk down the hall.

"Matuka, the young Captain, kind of cute, isn't he? You guys together?" Kotoyami asked as if she wanted to get a reaction from Yanielle.

"What?! No way! That jerk wouldn't know love if it pulled a bullet out of his leg and saved his life!" she shouted dramatically as she blushed and frowned.

Two steps in and suddenly, Kotoyami laughed because she began to vibrate and levitate off the ground, which pulled the two girls apart.

"What's going on Yanielle? Have I finally reached the ultimate ascension? Has my mediation finally paid off?" Kotoyami asked as she floated four feet off the ground.

"I'm not exactly sure but something similar happened to me!" Yanielle shouted frantically as she looked on with concern.

All of a sudden, Kotoyami was quickly and magnetically pulled ten feet away to the second door on the left. After it flew open, the young lass was dropped inside. Yanielle tried to run to her but she tripped and fell to the floor. The door slammed shut and the room was completely black, which left Kotoyami with no vision. Unfazed by the ordeal but a little stunned from the fall, Kotoyami rose to her feet in the dark room. At that time, Yanielle was banging on the room door but Kotoyami could not hear her on the other side.

While she stood in the dark meditating

on the silence, the room began to glow the purest, most beautiful shades of red, which caused her eyes to open. Little by little, until it was bright enough to see, the room sparkled with different red auras. A sense of safety and warmth filled her spirit as she gazed around the room. She quickly started to feel calm and relaxed as though she belonged. The smell of cinnamon and apples filled her nose which caused her mouth to fall open. When she viewed the objects in the room radiating their own light, she couldn't help but to be amazed and drawn into its beauty.

"Whoa, this is amazing! This room is glowing too! It's not just Yanielle's… but how? And its' red!" Kotoyami said with a smile.

As her hands covered her mouth, tears began to form in her eyes.

"What is this light? Where is it coming from? I don't see any candles, so how? It's so strange. However, red is my favorite color! How did he know? How is this even possible? How did this ship come to be? Is the floor made of grass too? It is and it's real! It's glowing green as well! How are there fruits and vegetables growing in here from the floor? How are they glowing? It smells delicious! Wait! Are those weapons and kitchen ware on the walls? Is that cheese and meat over there? How is this food still good? This almost feels like a trap and strategically planned," the young girl said as she looked around at the condition of the room.

As she looked to her right, there was a huge comfy-looking bed that ran along the north wall. The support was made from the finest steel she ever laid eyes on.

"It's spotless," she said as she looked back at her reflection.

The bed had an enormous, red leaf that looked as though it was made of silk, resting upon the soft, glowing-white, feather-stuffed mattress. On top rested two large, sparkling-red pillows with glowing red orange dust that covered them. Directly in front of her was the west side of the ship and there was a huge wardrobe with doors that were already opened. The open wardrobe revealed all sorts of clothing and accessories, just like in Yanielle's room. Without thinking twice, she ran to the wardrobe and started pulling things out just like Yanielle did before.

"These shall do," Kotoyami laughed as she stretched out the long sleeve blouse to see if it would fit her by comparing arm lengths.

She smiled and twirled, then looked to her left to notice there were two beautiful, silver, and black tables that ran along the entire south wall. The top of the floating table was fully stocked with cooking ware. It also had weapons and training gear that gave off a light red orange aura as well. All the while, Yanielle was sitting on the floor by the door with her head down. Suddenly, the door opened and Kotoyami came out of the room smiling.

"Oh my God, are you okay?! You couldn't hear me banging on the door?!" Yanielle stood up and asked as she grabbed Kotoyami by the arms.

"I'm fine and no I couldn't, but I have a lot of questions for our so-called Captain," Kotoyami said with a serious face.

"Well good luck with that one, I've been trying since I got here," Yanielle replied.

"Well what more can you answer?" Kotoyami questioned.

"Well I told you everything I knew when we were in my room when you asked then. Speaking of rooms, let me see it girl!" Yanielle said with a huge smile.

"See what?" Kotoyami asked.

"Your room, your room!" Yanielle shouted with a laugh.

"Oh, yes, sure, go ahead," Kotoyami said as she gestured for Yanielle to enter.

"Oh, my, God, this is made for a princess! It's beautiful, girl! Look at your rags!" Yanielle screamed as she ran to the wardrobe.

The girls laughed as Jubilaree walked down the stairs to go to his very own room; he too wanted to get some well-deserved rest that he was lacking.

"That's different, a cell here of all places? I guess it makes sense in a way but still strange to see. That's their hall I'm guessing by the noise," he said as he peaked around the corner to his right from the stairs.

After looking down the girl's side of the ship, he turned around, walked across the stairs, and continued to the left, down his side of the ship.

"He said the second door, right? Well, I want to see the first room damn it!" Jubilaree said while being highly aggravated as he walked up to the first door.

As Jubilaree reached for the doorknob, electricity met his hand quickly and caused him to swear quite a bit.

"What the hell?! What's up with this place?! Did he freaking rig the doorknob? Why I oughta!!" Jubilaree shouted as he began to turn around, to head back up to the main deck, to awake and confront Matuka.

Abruptly, the second door flew open down the hall and Jubilaree was pulled to the floor.

"What the hell?!" Jubilaree screamed as he hit the floor.

The lad started to get pulled by his ankles, by some unseen force, into the dark and mysterious room. Before the door could close all the way, the lad let out an unnoticed cry.

"No! No! Wait! No! Ahh!" Jubilaree screamed as he was completely drugged into the room.

The lad had no hope for escape and the door slammed shut as if it was never opened. The halls were silent, and the girls heard nothing at all, even with Kotoyami's door being open. After lying on the floor in the dark room for a few seconds, the room began to glow the deepest, purest shades of blue.

"Whoa. It's glowing in here, how bizarre," Jubilaree said softly as he hesitantly stood up from the ground and glanced around the cabin.

As he looked to his left; with the door behind him, there was a long table that sat on the north wall. It was glowing silver and it was accompanied by a long, glowing, navy-blue cloth that covered it ever so gently. Above the table, in the middle of the wall, rested a flat-earth map that had a small, red glow on it in a random place. On top of the table was a huge, silver, empty bird's cage that was glowing quite brightly.

"Well see, that's where you're wrong buddy, I don't have no stinking bird of any sort," Jubilaree said with an annoyed grin as he balled his fist and closed his eye.

After he looked up again, he noticed next

to it was a silver and brown-leathered gauntlet for holding sharp-clawed animals that also emitted its own light.

"Just who in the heck do he think I am?" Jubilaree asked aloud.

Also, on the table was a silver and royal-blue spyglass that had a sparkling-steel compass lying next to it. The walls were black with blue, sparkling glitter-like lights all over it, as well as the ceiling. Directly in front of him was a wardrobe that also radiated navy-blue hues. As Jubilaree looked to his right, he saw the biggest; most comfortable looking hammock that stretched along the entire south wall. The support ropes were white, and they too had a light embedded from within. The fabric atop was gray and gently illuminated its surface.

Laid neatly over the fabric were three huge, blue, soft pillows that emanated their own light. Lastly, what really caught his eye was an enormous, dark-purple blanket with a light, forest-greenish threading, which was also radiating light. As he looked away from the hammock, he then noticed the floor and saw that a huge floor pillow was glowing visible in the middle of the room. He then looked up to see that there was a series of aged white nets hanging from the ceiling that made another hammock to sleep or relax on. However, these ropes' lights were dimmer than the ones that were floor level.

"That's strange, I didn't see that up there before or that on the floor," Jubilaree said as he walked near the glowing, tan floor pillow to examine the ropes on the ceiling.

The floor was a black polished wood with glowing hues of blue seeping from the cracks and crevices. The room was cozy, he couldn't resist the feeling of safety and warmth as he stood captivated by the view. After he looked away from the ropes and the rest of the glowing objects, he looked down by his feet.

"It seems comfortable," he said as he leaned over to touch the floor pillow.

As he started to touch the seating area, he looked up and noticed that the wardrobe had his style of clothing inside.

"Well I be…" Jubilaree mumbled.

He then stood up and looked into the illuminated wardrobe.

"That's why he said that, these look just like my cape and my style of clothes. How is it my size?!" he said after he walked to the wardrobe and pulled out the hooded cloak.

Jubilaree then took his cape off and dropped it to the floor to the right of himself. He then threw the black fancy cape over his head and lowered it over his body.

"He really is something else," Jubilaree said with an annoyed smile as he looked at the fancy cape.

After looking over the room a bit more with peace and familiarity beginning to build in his heart, the young lad decided to take a nap on the well-suited hammock. Three hours had passed, and all the ship's inhabitants were sound asleep in their own rooms, resting for the next voyage that was yet to come.

Entry 3

THE GLOW OF THE DARKEST NIGHT

Above deck in the Captain's quarters, Matuka was tossing and turning in his new comfy bed from having an intense dream.

"I will!! We will!!" he screamed.

As he jumped from his sleep and looked around at his quiet, cozy suite, the darkness was gentle on his eyes and the air in the room was still.

"Huh? What was I just dreaming?" he asked himself as he sat and tried to recover the fading images.

The young Captain crossed his arms and grabbed his chin as he tried to remember his dream.

"Shoot! I can't remember! What's up with my memory lately?" Matuka asked himself before standing to stretch.

He let out a deep sigh and yawned while he walked to the middle of his room, next to his desk.

"Now how did it close? Wasn't it open last time? I guess I was too tired earlier to notice when I came in or am I just losing it? How did it open before? That's right, the wind slammed the door shut and the wall rolled up, but… is there a lever or something?" Matuka questioned.

He then scanned the walls and looked around the room for a lever.

"Nothing there, where could it be?" he asked as he started to walk backwards towards the stairs.

As Matuka walked backwards, his left heel slowly pressed down on the hidden lever, which caused a soft creaking sound. Then suddenly, the wall rolled up and revealed the vessel's window.

"And there you have it!" Matuka said.

As he stared out the porthole; amazed as if it was his first time, he saw the view and his heart began to race.

"I must have stepped back on this as I was leaving," Matuka said as he looked down to the floor at the overlook-able lever.

Matuka looked up and stared out of the giant porthole; captivated by the beautiful sunset peeking through the dark clouded sky, his heart began to race even faster.

"I know you're out there; I can still feel the rest of you. It's only a matter of time before we're all together, just stay strong and survive. I just hope that you all can look to me as your Captain, no, like a friend, a brother," he thought to himself as he gazed upon the fires and setting sun.

With a deep sigh released, Matuka looked back to the lever and stepped on it. He then proceeded up the stairs and out the door as the brown wooden wall once again, concealed its secret.

"I'm surprised to see you up," Jubilaree said from the crow's nest as Matuka opened the door and stepped onto the main deck.

"Likewise," Matuka said as he walked towards the helm deck.

As Matuka got halfway and near Jubilaree's post, he looked around his vessel and began to smile. Joy filled his spirit after he admired all the fine details he did not notice before. He noticed how the silver dipped in and out of the black, polished wood. Not to not mention, how the silver looked as though it vibrated with a glow. Matuka realized the dark clouds made it feel cozy and warm; like sitting next to a fireplace to rest your boots.

"Where are the girls?" Matuka looked up to the crow's nest and asked.

"Beats me, probably still sleeping, which is fine by me," Jubilaree said with his eye closed and arms crossed under his dark cape.

"Yeah okay, you can fool them but not me," Matuka said before he laughed and smiled at Jubilaree.

"What was that?! I'll come down there!" Jubilaree yelled as he blushed from embarrassment.

"I wonder if I should move the ship or not?" Matuka questioned himself aloud as he looked towards the helm deck.

Without warning, Jubilaree jumped down to the main deck and landed next to Matuka. At the same time, both girls walked through the door onto the main deck.

"Well, everyone is here now," Jubilaree said with his eye closed and arms crossed as usual.

"Not everyone," Matuka said as he looked to his right towards the ocean.

Jubilaree's eye opened and he looked down to his right at Matuka.

"What are y'all over here mumbling about?" Yanielle said as Kotoyami and her walked up to the boys.

"I was deciding whether or not to move the ship…" Matuka said before quickly being interrupted.

"Wait a darn second! The last time you did that I nearly had a heart attack! Absolutely not!" Yanielle screamed as she waved her arms around in the air; like a small child throwing a tantrum.

"Aww, is the baby scared?" Jubilaree teased as he leaned in and smiled towards Yanielle.

"Hey up yours, jerk face! Don't you got a pole to climb or something?" Yanielle replied with her arms crossed.

"You two cut it out, we have a long journey ahead," Matuka said as he put his right hand on Yanielle's left shoulder and his left hand on Jubilaree's right shoulder.

All the while, the anxious Kotoyami, was waiting for her time to speak.

"Long journey? Oh no honey, as soon as we see dry land, I'm ditching and going home," Yanielle said before she paused and stared off into space.

"Home," Jubilaree said softly as he

looked down to the black, polished deck.

A moment of silence captured the mouths of everyone and left them searching inwardly for answers.

"I can't remember my home; why can't I remember my home Matuka?" Yanielle asked aloud in a panic.

"It is indeed strange, all I can remember is waking up from the war; lying on that door," Kotoyami thought to herself while she reached for Yanielle's hand to comfort and calm her.

"I've too noticed I have some lost or missing memories," Matuka chimed in.

"What guild are you from? Where's your insignia? And what country are you from?" Kotoyami asked Matuka with a serious look in her eyes.

Her eyes were focused on him and her hair was blowing in the wind, in front of her face. Yanielle and Jubilaree looked to Matuka as they silently hoped he'd remember something because they could not. Matuka was caught off guard by Kotoyami's questions, so he took his hands off Jubilaree and Yanielle's shoulders then closed his eyes.

"What guild do you belong too?! Where's your branding?" Matuka asked Kotoyami while Jubilaree and Yanielle searched for theirs.

Kotoyami stared at the top of her right

hand and stood silently because her branding had vanished.

"Impossible, how could that be? When did it vanish? I didn't even notice. Wait, did I see it at all since I woke up?" Kotoyami asked herself while she checked her other hand.

"You don't remember, do you?" Matuka asked Kotoyami as he pointed at her with his right hand.

Kotoyami stood speechless with her head down, ashamed and tormented from amnesia.

"And what about you two? Any memories you'd like to share with us?" Matuka asked as he looked to Jubilaree and Yanielle.

They both looked away and started to whistle as they rocked side to side.

"I thought so. So, none of us can remember our past. The question is how did you remember where to look for your insignia? Or better yet, how do we remember some things but not all?" Matuka asked as he crossed his arms.

Matuka then walked past Yanielle and Kotoyami to head to the left staircase that led up to the helm deck. Everyone was facing Matuka by the time he reached the helm and slowly reached for its warm, black-polished, wooden handles. The silver trimming and detailed engravings shined in his eyes as he let the lights take him on a mental journey.

Engulfed in the ship's beauty, Matuka paused to gather himself. The waves were beating against the side of the ship and the sound of the wind seemed to draw everyone into a deep thought; for nature was speaking. Yanielle then walked up to the helm deck to softly encourage Matuka because she felt his anxiety.

"Are you okay?" she asked as she put her left hand on his right shoulder.

Matuka then looked to his right towards Yanielle and smiled.

"Yes, I'm okay," Matuka said.

"Good. Then I'm going to need you to respond to people when they ask you something, you jerk!" Yanielle screamed.

Everyone except Yanielle started to laugh, which caused her to blush and pout. The sun had set and there was a glow in the distance. It grew brighter and brighter as the night's sky began to take control. The red orange glow seemed to increase as a huge mushroom cloud formed above it.

"Do you guys see that?" Yanielle asked which caused Jubilaree, Kotoyami and Matuka to turn to look to the west.

"Whoa," Jubilaree said as his right eye stretched open.

"What could cause that?" Yanielle asked as she looked to Matuka for comfort and a peace of mind.

"I've only seen it once before, I can't remember where, but I do remember it," Kotoyami said as she began to walk towards the bow of the ship.

Jubilaree and Yanielle quickly turned their heads to look at Kotoyami, while Matuka stared at the sky.

"So, you've seen this before?" Jubilaree asked Kotoyami.

"What causes it?" Yanielle asked Kotoyami immediately after.

Matuka then looked to Kotoyami as he grew interested in her response. Kotoyami stood there silent for a second with a serious face before she dropped her head from uncertainty.

"So how does this work?" Kotoyami asked Matuka as she looked back over her left shoulder before she fixed her hair behind her left ear.

"Huh?" Matuka asked as he focused in on her question from daydreaming about her answer.

"How does it work? Moving the ship? Do I just stand?" Kotoyami asked as she turned around to face Matuka.

"Oh, yes, sorry. Yes, just stand and the ship will do the rest," Matuka said with a smile as he closed his eyes.

"So, when are you going to explain this

ship?" Kotoyami asked Matuka.

"Good luck," Jubilaree and Yanielle said in unison.

Kotoyami then let out a deep sigh and turned around to walk towards the bow of the ship. As Kotoyami walked up the right sides' stairs; that led up to the deck above the Captain's quarters, Jubilaree looked up to his right at the crow's nest and jumped, which caused a strong gust of wind to follow. After Kotoyami reached the deck, she proceeded to the bowsprit, where she stood at the tip.

"Girl, what are you doing?!" Yanielle asked Kotoyami out of concern.

"It's okay," Matuka said as he turned to his right and looked at Yanielle.

"It's okay?! Are you crazy?! She can fall and hurt herself!" Yanielle screamed in response.

"From seeing what she and the ship can do earlier, I feel she's in her rightful spot. Until she says otherwise, I think we should let her be," Matuka said.

Yanielle then looked back and forth between Matuka and Kotoyami with concern.

"Okay," Yanielle said after she let out a deep sigh and looked back towards Kotoyami.

"Hold on if you like," Matuka said to Yanielle as he quickly grabbed the helm.

Simultaneously, Matuka was met with a

vision of two boys at the root of the glow in the darkness when he grabbed the helm. Then just like before, the fog crept from the ship and made it invisible to the naked eye.

"Huh?" Yanielle asked.

Before she knew it, she was immediately bombarded by a huge force of wind to the face.

"Ahh!!!" Yanielle screamed as the ship sped off through the wreckage.

"*So, fog comes out from somewhere and hides the ship, interesting,*" Kotoyami thought to herself as she stood at the edge of the ship's bowsprit, while the wind ferociously blew in her hair.

"*So as long as we are on the ship's surface, it'll hold us at these speeds. Good, even if not, I can tell she has more skills then she's letting on,*" Matuka thought as he stared at Kotoyami from afar.

"You jerk! You don't give a warning and immediately act afterwards! Are you trying to kill me?!" Yanielle shouted to Matuka.

"Sorry," Matuka said softly.

A couple of minutes passed, the glow was growing bigger and bigger as the distance had finally closed in.

"*This is taking longer than usual; it must be pretty far. I didn't think the war was this vast,*" Matuka thought to himself as the ship carried them at speeds not witnessed before.

"Straight ahead Captain," Jubilaree said as he pointed towards the fires.

"Huh? How come he can see but I can't? Maybe it's the height?" Matuka asked softly as the dancing image became clear to him, while he stood and held the helm.

"How can she breathe with all of that fog and wind up there?" Yanielle asked Matuka as she looked forward at Kotoyami.

"*The question is how can we all breathe at this speed?*" Kotoyami thought to herself from hearing Yanielle from afar.

Matuka started to remember how the ship stopped the last two times, so he grew concerned about what would happen to Kotoyami.

"Kotoyami! Brace yourself!" Matuka screamed as loud as he could, so she could hear him through the sound of the high-speed winds.

"Okay, you don't have to yell," Kotoyami said as she turned around and began to walk from the edge of the bowsprit onto the deck.

"What the hell?!" Matuka shrieked.

"How?!" Yanielle asked in total disbelief because of what she saw.

"How absurd! I can barely lift my arms and she's walking?! Dammit! How?!" Jubilaree shouted out of frustration as he leaned over then grabbed the edge of the crow's nest.

As Jubilaree watched Kotoyami walk onto the deck above the Captain's chambers, jealousy grew within his heart.

"*She's amazing! Just who is this girl?*" Matuka thought as he stared at Kotoyami.

"You're strong Jubilaree!" Kotoyami said as she looked up to the crow's nest.

"Huh?" Jubilaree questioned softly while he looked confusedly at Kotoyami as she continued to walk steadily.

"You are physically strong, just in the instance of seeing me walk, you broke through limits. But you lack the mental strength," Kotoyami said as she walked down the left staircase onto the main deck.

"What kind of a compliment was that?!" Jubilaree yelled down from the crow's nest.

"It wasn't," Kotoyami quickly replied with a wink.

Jubilaree leaned up, closed his eye, and crossed his arms as usual. Out of nowhere, the ship stopped as fast as it started without warning. When Kotoyami made it to port side's bulwarks, the fog had completely vanished from sight. Everyone could not believe their eyes as the flames bounced around; two figures emerged from them.

"Are you serious?" Kotoyami asked in disgust as she looked into the ocean.

"What girl?' Yanielle asked as she walked over and stood next to Kotoyami.

"These idiots," Jubilaree said as he slapped his forehead with his left palm, threw his head back to the dark sky and closed his eye.

"Unbelievable," Yanielle said as she looked to the water.

"Finally," Matuka said as he smiled and looked past the flames.

In the water, amongst the rubble were two lost lads. One of them was in the same age group as the rest of the lads and lasses, while the other one was a little younger. The two were getting drunk while they ran around on top of debris; shooting guns at each other and throwing explosives. The two boys were so intoxicated they were shooting just to shoot, which caused a random bullet to fly towards the ship.

"Look out!!" Jubilaree screamed.

Unexpectedly, an unseen barrier deflected the stray bullet, which caused it to ricochet back and hit the youngest one in the left arm.

"Are you morons crazy?! What's your problem?!" Yanielle screamed towards the boys after being scared from the flying rounds.

"I think I'm hit," the young boy said to the older boy.

"Nice," the older one replied as he ran over to the younger one, before they sat down side-by-side, on a piece of debris.

The boys were floating about one hundred feet away from the ship, which caused Matuka to walk over to port side to get a closer look. As he stood at the silver bulwarks on the helm deck, he noticed the boys started moving again.

"Another sip little bro?" the oldest boy said.

"Drip, drip, sip, sip!" the youngest lad replied before they laughed hysterically, while they took turns sipping from the bottle.

"I know you not letting them on this ship," Yanielle said as she turned to her left to look at Matuka.

"Oh, but I am," Matuka quickly replied as he walked down the left staircase from the helm deck, to the middle of the ship by the bulwarks.

"They'll destroy it! Look at them!" Yanielle shouted to Matuka as she hoped he'd understand her distress.

By the time Matuka walked up to Yanielle, he was smiling with tears of blood flowing from his eyes.

"Oh," Yanielle said softly from realizing his eyes were bleeding again.

"Let's have a look," Matuka said as he grabbed Yanielle by the waist and brought her to his side, causing her to blush.

"These two are ridiculous, who gave

these two guns?" Jubilaree asked from the crow's nest as everyone looked on.

"Everyone look; do you know what I see? I see two lost, young, and scared boys, with no one around but each other. Afraid of what's to come, with death surrounding them and promising to take their lives. That wine was their breaking point, their farewell because they lost hope. I'm sure they were shooting because they would have rather had died that way, than of starvation.

From the looks of it they're obviously brothers. So, that is what I see when I look at them. My only thing is that you look at them; like you would look at yourself if you were in the water again, and if I had never showed up. We don't even know how long they've been out here, they could not be mentally there right now," Matuka said as he held Yanielle while a tear rolled down her left cheek.

Yanielle then covered his right hand that was on her waist, with her right hand.

"More the reason we shouldn't just allow anyone one on here, they could try to shoot us all and take the ship for themselves," Kotoyami said as she walked over to Matuka and Yanielle before they quickly let go of one another.

"I agree, we should figure these two out before we do anything," Jubilaree said before he jumped down from the crow's nest.

"Dang, you don't get tired of doing that?" Yanielle asked with an annoyed face.

"How could I when I know you love it so much?" Jubilaree asked as he leaned in and smiled mischievously.

Before Yanielle could reply with her outburst, Matuka screamed to the boys.

"Hey! You two! Hey!" Matuka yelled.

"You hear these clowns big bro?" the youngest boy slurred before he lifted his heavy head.

"Yeah, it's about time," the eldest boy slurred as he stood to stretch.

"So, no one is going to ask about that weird invisible shield thing that lit up over the ship when the bullet came our way?" Jubilaree asked softly as he looked towards the girls.

All three huddled up in a triangle behind the focused Matuka.

"I'll be the first to say, I'm glad for the shield because from the looks of it, it was heading right towards me," Yanielle whispered in the huddle.

"This ship seems to have no bounds and I don't think we even scratched the surface yet," Kotoyami said soft and quickly.

"So, which one of you ladies would like the honor of asking sir Captain over there?" Jubilaree whispered sarcastically.

"Why can't you? And don't think I

didn't see your eye up there in the crow's nest earlier before we found Kotoyami!" Yanielle immediately snapped back.

"What is she talking about Jubilaree?" Kotoyami asked with an annoyed smirk.

The two girls looked to Jubilaree while they all were huddled together behind the young Captain. Suddenly, Matuka quickly extended his right arm and held out his hand to the boys in the water. Blood danced down Matuka's cheeks from his eyes before the breeze of the ocean gave passage to his scarlet tears.

"You see that big bro or am I squiffy?" the youngest brother said as he fell and burped.

"Yeah, I see it, déjà vu," the eldest brother said with his eyes wide open and a look of horror upon his face.

"It's our dream, we're saved," the little brother said softly before he passed out.

"Crap!" the eldest yelled as he grabbed his younger brother before he could fall in the water.

"They look like they need me, I'm going!" Matuka frantically said as he prepared to climb the fine, silver bulwarks; after throwing his hat to the black deck.

"Wait!" Yanielle screamed from the huddle, which caused Matuka to lose his footing, hit his head on the bulwarks and fall in the water anyway.

"Great job," Jubilaree sarcastically said before he broke the huddle, walked to port side, and looked overboard.

"That's my cue," the eldest said as he threw his younger brother over his shoulder.

The elder brother held his younger brother's legs with his right hand and their wine in the other. With nothing else to do, he chugged the last of the bottle, threw it down on the mahogany chest floating next to him and took off running towards the ship.

"He's fast, maybe even faster than you, Jubilaree," Kotoyami said as Yanielle and her walked towards Jubilaree.

"Aren't you going in to get him?! I think he hit his head!" Yanielle shouted to Jubilaree.

"Why don't you have a look for yourself," Jubilaree said as he crossed his arms under his flowing cape and closed his eye.

Yanielle quickly ran and pushed her way in between Jubilaree and Kotoyami to look overboard into the water. Yanielle's face lit up when she saw that Matuka was still alive and floating in the water as she walked to the left of Jubilaree. In a blink of an eye, the eldest brother of the two lads grabbed Matuka with his left hand and leaped up onto the bulwarks. A sudden gust of wind caused the three above deck to jump back from being startled as the lad landed on the bulwarks.

"Did you lose this guy?" the eldest brother asked with a smile before going unconscious; nearly falling into the ocean with Matuka and his younger brother.

"Hey!" Jubilaree yelled as he grabbed the eldest brother.

Kotoyami grabbed for Matuka and Yanielle grabbed for the younger boy before they could fall as well.

"Just in time," Kotoyami said as Yanielle sighed from relief with her head down and hands up, holding the boy.

"Alright, let's pull them in!" Jubilaree said as he looked to his left and right at the girls.

After they got all three of the boys onto the ship's deck, Yanielle immediately noticed the young Captain's head wound and ran towards the door that led below deck. Before Jubilaree and Kotoyami could say a word, she was down the stairs and out of sight.

"What is up with you people and passing out?" Jubilaree asked after he picked up Matuka's hat, walked over to him and put it on his chest.

"I didn't take you for the sentimental type," Kotoyami said with a smile before she chuckled and ran her finger through her hair while she looked at Jubilaree.

Frozen from embarrassment, he turned around to hide his blushing with a slight frown. Then, out of nowhere, he jumped up with a tornado-like gust of wind around him, to the crow's nest.

"Aw did I say something?" Kotoyami teased softly as she looked to the hidden Jubilaree.

At that very moment, Yanielle burst through the door with the same tool she had before when she magically healed Matuka and Jubilaree.

"I'm here!" Yanielle shouted as she bolted up the stairs onto the main deck with tears in her eyes.

Yanielle then shot past Kotoyami, towards the unconscious boys on the deck.

"Hmp," Kotoyami mumbled as she watched the extremely energized Yanielle.

"I'm here," Yanielle said as she ran and slid next to the unconscious Matuka.

After removing Matuka's hat from his chest and placing it on the deck, she preceded to exam him. Yanielle quickly grabbed her retractor when she saw the puddle of blood increasing beneath Matuka's head.

"Crap…" Yanielle whispered before being interrupted by the sudden change of color and brightness from the retractor.

In a flash, Matuka's wound was healed

but his blood didn't disappear again.

"Weird," Yanielle said as she looked from Matuka to the youngest brother.

Yanielle's eyes grew big as she looked on at the young lad, for his damage was great too.

"Here I come, here I am," she reiterated to the youngest boy as she got up, ran over and knelt next to him.

"She has much potential, she lit up when it was time to serve, hmm," Kotoyami thought to herself as she looked on at Yanielle.

With sweat in her eyes and her beautiful golden-brown hair hanging over her face, she looked in her left hand at the silver glowing retractor. Once again, drawn into its beautiful carvings, she gazed upon it and then positioned it towards the young boy's left arm.

"Okay, let me move this first; here we go again, don't let me down," Yanielle said as she placed the retractor over his wound; after moving around his cloak to reveal his folly.

As before, the once silver-glowing tool, started to glow the prettiest shades of green.

"Closer," Yanielle thought to herself as she motioned closer to the wound while a teardrop rolled down her right cheek.

By this time, Jubilaree had fully stood up in the crow's nest to watch, while Kotoyami had walked closer to see as well. Abruptly, the eldest brother sat up from his slumber; like he was brought back to life with unseen lightning.

"Hey, what are you doing to my brother?!" the eldest brother yelled as he squeezed his right fist towards Yanielle.

At the same time, the bullet shot from his younger brother's arm onto the warm, black deck, which caused the eldest to pass out again. Jubilaree sucked his teeth and turned his head as the breeze flowed through his hair.

"*He seems to have a strong will to live,*" Kotoyami thought while she stared at the unconscious elder brother, lying on the deck.

Yanielle then waved her hand from right to left over the youngest and all his wounds were mended.

"Impossible, she has the power of life?" Jubilaree thought aloud as he stood in the crow's nest over them.

"Let's see, you next, crazy," Yanielle said as she looked to the eldest brother and leaned over him.

With one wave from right to left over his body, the boy was no longer bloody and bruised. Immediately after all their wounds were healed, the once glowing-green tool returned to its soft, silver glow and she stood up to look at all three of them.

"*See, how come everyone else's blood healed instead of Matuka's?*" Yanielle thought as she stood up over the boys and scratched her head, before she placed her retractor in her right, pant leg pocket.

"Yanielle, so these are the tools you spoke of when we were in my room?" Kotoyami asked as she walked completely over to Yanielle.

"Yeah," Yanielle said as her face went from serious to a smile when she looked at Kotoyami.

"It's one thing to hear about it, but to see it, that's something else," Kotoyami said as she walked over to the unconscious Matuka.

Yanielle started to blush and frown when she saw how Kotoyami squatted down over him to stare at him.

"Amazing," Kotoyami said as she gazed at Matuka's necklace.

"What? Did she just call him amazing?" Yanielle thought to herself as she stared at them both.

"Aw, is the poor baby jealous?" Jubilaree teased Yanielle from above.

"Hey! How about you just shut up, you big dummy!" Yanielle screamed as she turned to look up at the smiling Jubilaree.

Without hesitation, she stormed over and kicked Matuka's left leg as she proceeded to the door that led below deck.

"Shame on you," Kotoyami said as she

stood and looked up towards Jubilaree.

"Wait!" Jubilaree shouted as he looked down on Yanielle.

"Let me guess," Yanielle said as she stopped walking.

Suddenly, Jubilaree jumped down from the crow's nest and faced Kotoyami as Yanielle stood with her back to his left.

"How did I know he was gonna jump down?" Yanielle asked as she rolled her eyes and turned around to look at Jubilaree.

"We can't leave these two up here," Jubilaree said as he looked towards Yanielle.

"We? I was leaving, they're okay, they got y'all two," Yanielle said as she started to turn around and head towards the regal door.

"Okay, I'm sorry," Jubilaree said softly as he threw his head back and slapped his forehead with his right palm.

"What was that?" Yanielle quickly responded with an attitude as she turned around.

"Sorry or whatever!" Jubilaree yelled before he turned his head to the right, away from her sight.

Both girls started to laugh as Yanielle and Kotoyami closed the gap on Jubilaree.

"Jerk," Yanielle said as she punched Jubilaree on his left arm with her right fist.

By the time all three of them were standing in a triangular position from another, they all looked up. The night's sky was the darkest recorded in history and the glow was seen for miles upon miles. The ocean was filled with waste from destroyed ships and had an endless supply of blood from its guests. The aftermath of the brothers' pain caught the eyes of many that day. With the incapacitated Captain and two new strangers aboard, the conscious trio stared to the sea with uncertainty in their hearts.

"You guys want to hear something weird?" Yanielle asked Jubilaree and Koto-yami.

Both Jubilaree and Kotoyami looked towards Yanielle as they waited for her response.

"We've moved from cold to warm waters and I haven't seen any sharks. Let's be honest, it's like bodies everywhere. Why don't we see any of them feeding? I didn't think it could be possible for this much death at once," Yanielle said softly as she shook her head from side to side.

Jubilaree turned his head and closed his eye, while Kotoyami turned around in a circle; to look into the water from different views of the ship.

"Strange, so how does the steering work?" Kotoyami asked as she looked to the right past Yanielle at the helm deck.

Jubilaree immediately turned to Koto-yami and unfolded his arms as Yanielle crossed her arms.

"I'm unsure, all I ever seen him do is grab the helm and we take off," Yanielle said as she looked to Jubilaree for confirmation.

"I haven't seen a working boom or rudder and a few more things, now that I think about it," Jubilaree said as he began to survey the ship for inconsistencies.

"Let's find out," Kotoyami said as she looked to Yanielle and Jubilaree.

"I don't think that's a good idea," Yanielle said as she unfolded her arms and put her right hand on her hip.

"Don't you want to go home?" Kotoyami asked Yanielle as she turned to face the helm deck.

"Yeah but, we don't even remember home, yet alone how to control this thing. It's obviously not a normal ship; do you even see an anchor to lift?" Yanielle replied out of frustration and fear.

"All we can do is try," Kotoyami said as she started to walk towards the staircase that led up to the helm.

"Wait," Jubilaree said as he dropped his head and walked over to Kotoyami.

"Not you too," Kotoyami said as she fully turned around to face the tall and intimidating, young warrior.

"I don't feel right, the weather is changing," Jubilaree said as he looked up.

"Huh?" Kotoyami and Yanielle asked in unison as they both looked up to the sky.

At that very moment, a strong wind from the west came and completely silenced the fires. The oceans began to consume the lost souls in the graveyard of battalions and their faces began to sink into the abyss.

"What's happening?! They're all sinking at once?!" Yanielle screamed while her eyes grew big.

"Sharks?" Jubilaree sarcastically asked.

"I'm going to act like I didn't hear that," Yanielle said as she continued to look to the water.

Once the wind purged the sky from the once glooming appearance of death and mayhem, it left only a clear night's sky; lit up with trillions of stars.

"I'm going, don't try to stop me," Kotoyami said as she looked back to Yanielle and Jubilaree with a serious look, as the wind blew in her eyes.

"Yeah, let her go," the youngest brother said who was thought to still be unconscious.

"This should be good," the eldest brother said as they stood, stretched, and yawned.

"Not you two idiots again," Yanielle said as the conscious trio looked at the boys.

"Hey, wasn't I hit big bro?" the youngest

lad whispered to his brother as he searched his arm for the bullet wound.

"Yeah, you're right, you were, and we had scrapes and cuts all over us, blood too. Now it's gone," the eldest brother said softly as he searched over his body for injuries.

"Hey where's that other guy, the one we had a dream about?" the youngest boy asked his big brother as he dusted his cloak.

"There, I noticed him when I first woke up, I had the dream again. He was standing with blood in his eyes and fire was coming from his hand. He had an aura around him; you could almost see a visual of what peace and safety was, it was crazy," the eldest brother whispered to his little brother.

"I had the same dream again too bro, who is he? Why do we keep having the same shared dream? Isn't that supposed to be impossible? And why do I feel okay here with these weirdos?" the youngest boy asked as he looked up to his older brother.

"What are you two mumbling over there?" Yanielle asked with an attitude as she glared at the brothers.

"Wait a sec! I remember, I woke up and you were doing something to my little brother!" the eldest brother said as he faced Yanielle.

"Doing what big brother? She can do whatever she likes to me anytime, anyplace," the younger brother said as he blew kisses and winked at Yanielle.

"Ew! And by the way, you jerk! I saved his life and possibly yours too!" Yanielle screamed at the eldest brother.

"My earth angel," the youngest brother said as he started to drool and blush.

"Control your dog," Jubilaree said to the eldest brother as he turned his back to them, to face the stern and helm deck.

"Excuse me?" the eldest brother questioned as he began to walk towards Jubilaree.

"Yeah! Excuse me?" the youngest brother asked as they both walked side-by-side, until they were behind Jubilaree.

"You don't want these problems," Jubilaree said and laughed as he looked over his right shoulder.

"Quiet! I have had it with you all!" Kotoyami shouted, which silenced everyone.

"Wow! Now that's what you call a woman," the eldest brother said as he looked on at Kotoyami; which caused Jubilaree to get jealous.

The annoyed and ready to leave Kotoyami, walked up port side's black, alligator skin-like staircase that led to the helm. All but Matuka was awake to watch the young, foreign girl take a big leap of faith. Immediately after, rain clouds started to gather over the ship and thunder began to stir.

"This doesn't look good," Yanielle said as she covered her face with her left forearm from the wind and rain building.

"Koto," Jubilaree whispered with his eye closed.

"Yes?" Kotoyami whispered in response to hearing the distant Jubilaree.

"Be careful," Jubilaree replied as he opened his eye and looked to her.

By this time, Kotoyami had reached the black and silver engraved helm with anxiety seeping from her pores.

"Bang, bang!!!" the youngest brother shouted before he laughed hysterically.

"Drunkards," Jubilaree mumbled from being annoyed.

"I heard that!" the eldest brother shouted as he stared at the dark, deep-blue cape on Jubilaree's back.

"We just getting started," the youngest boy said as he pulled out another small bottle of wine.

"Oh, hell no! They gots to go!" Yanielle demanded as she walked over to the brothers.

"Come on bro, let's go find a better seat," the eldest brother said as they walked away and sat down on the deck next to the comatose Matuka.

"Hey, get away from him!" Yanielle

screamed at the brothers as they shared their wine.

Without warning, the rain began to fall heavier, and flashes of lightning could be seen across the earth. Still unfazed by the warnings of nature, Kotoyami reached for the helm. Without warning, a huge lightning bolt struck the helm and caused Kotoyami to be jolted backwards, against the bulwarks.

"Bang, bang!" the youngest boy yelled as his eldest brother spit out wine from laughing.

"You guys are jerks! She could be dead!" Yanielle screamed and cried as she ran up the stairs to Kotoyami.

At the same time, Jubilaree leaped from the middle of the ship to the back of the helm deck, where Kotoyami furiously sat.

"Did you see that bro?" the youngest brother asked as he took a sip and passed the bottle.

"Yeah, I saw it," the older brother said as he took a sip and passed the bottle back to his little brother.

"And here I thought you were dead," Jubilaree said as he shook his head and turned around from seeing Kotoyami angry.

"Girl are you okay?!" Yanielle asked with tears in her eyes as she made it up to where Jubilaree and Kotoyami were.

The blackened and frizzy haired Kotoyami; let out black smoke from her mouth as she coughed and stood.

"She can stand?" the youngest brother asked as he sat up shocked and wiped his mouth from spilling his wine.

"Seems like we ran into quite the bunch, huh little bro?" the eldest lad asked as he looked to his younger brother.

Angry from what seemed to be a fluke or coincidence, Kotoyami got up, yelled, and ran to the helm to grab it again. She was so upset, that she nearly slipped on the wet surface before she grabbed hold to it. As soon as she touched the helm, she was struck again by another bolt, this time nearly throwing her backwards overboard.

"Hey! What the hell is your problem?! You got a death wish?!" Jubilaree yelled as he grabbed Kotoyami before she almost fell.

"Girl are you crazy?! What are you thinking?!" Yanielle screamed from being upset with tears in her eyes after she slapped Kotoyami.

"That's it, maybe I need his hat!" Kotoyami quickly leaped from the helm deck in front of the eldest brother; next to Matuka, which caused a gust of wind to push back Yanielle.

"Oh no she didn't," Yanielle said as she watched Kotoyami vanish and reappear on the main deck.

"Okay, I think I'm in love and twice as much, cause I'm seeing double of you baby," the oldest brother slurred, before he burped and blushed.

"Shameful," Kotoyami said as she watched the eldest brother rock back and forth, trying to keep his balance, while sitting.

"Yes, shameful we haven't met before," the eldest brother replied quickly with a smile. '

"You should be ashamed of yourself, leading a child to strong drink," Kotoyami said as she leaned over to grab Matuka's hat.

"I make my own decisions little lady," the younger brother said after he burped loudly before Kotoyami retrieved Matuka's hat.

Kotoyami then turned around and leaped back onto the helm deck, where the concerned Yanielle and Jubilaree were waiting.

"You're crazy if you think I'm going to let you touch this helm again," Yanielle said as she extended her arms out to signal no passage.

"Yeah, I think the ship, weather and even God is trying to tell you something," Jubilaree said as he walked forward to Kotoyami from the helm, down a couple of steps onto the helm deck.

"Get out of my way; this is your last warning!" Kotoyami yelled to Jubilaree and Yanielle before the thunder roared in the background.

Yanielle dropped her soaked head and moved out of the way, while Jubilaree stood still.

"I knew you would stay," Kotoyami said as she quickly tied her hair up in a knot to prepare for battle.

Jubilaree stood still and looked forward as though he was looking through Kotoyami. As the wind and rain danced, the thunder spoke. Kotoyami then crouched down in her fighting stance as she stared at Jubilaree and admired his bravery.

"Please move," Kotoyami whispered as the rain dripped down her forehead to her nose and onto the deck.

Jubilaree hesitantly moved out of the way from the raging Kotoyami; for being torn by his emotions. He did want to know if any of them could move the ship but did not want her to die in the process. Jubilaree then walked down port side's set of stairs onto the main deck, where Matuka and the brothers were, to distance himself from the mayhem.

"Feel like sharing?" Jubilaree asked the brothers as he extended his hand to shake the eldest brother's.

The eldest brother passed the bottle to his younger brother and stood. He then grabbed Jubilaree's hand to shake which caused the youngest to stand as well.

"Jubilaree," Jubilaree said stoically as he observed the brothers in detail.

The eldest brother was the same height as him; their skin complexion wasn't far off as well. He had long, thick, blonde locks that were tied up in a ponytail. His eyes were brown and gently resting from the strong wine. He wore golden-brown shorts and both his legs were completely wrapped in bandages up to his thighs. His ankles and feet were covered in the white cloth, but his toes and heels were exposed. Almost all his upper body was wrapped with the exception of his right and left arm. His shoulders and right pectoral muscle were exposed as well. Although his neck and face were uncovered as well; the rain seemed to cover them with unyielding force.

"The name's Dayhoon and this here pistol; is my little brother, Umbati," the eldest brother said to him.

Umbati then stretched out his right hand to shake Jubilaree's before he passed the bottle to him with his left hand.

"Bang, bang!!!" Umbati screamed at the top of his lungs as Jubilaree reached for the young lad's hand.

Instantaneously after the outburst, a loud crackle and light lit up the sky. The temperature rose and Kotoyami flew towards the back of the helm deck once more. Jubilaree couldn't help but to flinch after he heard Kotoyami's impact, so he immediately grabbed Umbati's hand to shake and took the bottle to drink from it.

"Ahh, that's good," Jubilaree said softly as he held his head to the sky with his exposed eye closed.

While the rain fell down on his face, he waited silently for Kotoyami to react irrationally.

"So, what's with the bandanna? Did something happen to your eye?" Umbati slurred as he asked Jubilaree.

Dayhoon looked down to Umbati, then back up to Jubilaree before he noticed the restraint in words. Jubilaree lowered his head with his eye closed and took another larger shot, which caused Umbati to get annoyed.

"Hey, don't kill it!" Umbati slurred as he jumped face high to Jubilaree and snatched the bottle.

In that moment Jubilaree's eye opened and he could see the young boy's blonde, huge, curly afro, dripping wet from the rain. His large, golden-tan cloak shined from little pieces of glass caught within its fibers when the lightning flashed. Beneath that, he wore a dark-red shirt and light-brown pants, which were torn at the hem. His feet were wrapped but his heel and toes were exposed. The younger brother also resembled his elder brother so much that he looked like a younger version of him. As Umbati landed, he took a swig of the bottle and threw it to his older brother Dayhoon.

"You never answered my question," Umbati said as he looked up to Jubilaree; with his finger pointed towards him.

Dayhoon took a sip of the bottle and sat down in the rain next to Matuka, followed by Umbati; then Jubilaree.

"That necklace," the brothers said softly in unison before they looked at each other.

"Am I the only one who has noticed that it's raining only over the ship?" Jubilaree asked as he looked towards the brothers.

"Huh?" Umbati asked as he looked around as he rocked side to side.

Dayhoon also looked around at the night's sky. All he could see was the sky filled with flashes of lightning, a huge cloud above them and cold rain falling.

"Nice try Jack! You're not slick, you curved my question," Umbati slurred before he saw the soaked and beautiful Yanielle walking over to them with her head down in defeat.

"Jack? It's Jubilaree," Jubilaree said as he snatched the bottle from Dayhoon and took a sip.

"Hey!" Dayhoon immediately yelled.

"My love! You're back!" Umbati

screeched with a smile as Yanielle walked up behind Jubilaree.

"Not now, I need a drink," Yanielle said as she stood with her arms crossed and head down in the rain.

"Have a seat," Jubilaree said as he gestured for her to sit next to him on his right.

Yanielle hesitantly sat down with the boys until she saw that she could sit to the right of Matuka and watch over him while he was unconscious. As Yanielle sat down, Umbati tried to take the bottle from Jubilaree to give it to Yanielle but Jubilaree wouldn't let it go.

"Hey! Hands off," Umbati screamed as the two yanked for it. Suddenly, the bottle flew out of their hands onto the black, wet deck and broke instantly.

"Nooo!" screamed the four in unison as the wine flowed from the deck to the silver scuppers.

Yanielle dropped her head into her hands and cried as the boys looked to each other.

"Don't worry my love! Your savior is here!" Umbati said with a boastful smile as he stood up and reached behind his back, underneath his cloak, once more.

"Impossible!" Jubilaree said as his eye grew large.

"Where?!" Dayhoon asked as he looked at his brother.

"I don't want to know," Jubilaree quickly said.

Everyone looked confused as they stared towards the young lad when they noticed he had yet another, even larger bottle of wine than before. Umbati then smiled as he held the bottle extended outward to Yanielle, with his right hand.

"How?" Yanielle asked with a smile as she grabbed the dark-green bottle of red wine from Umbati while he gloated.

Yanielle took an enormous shot from the bottle and only left a little more than half behind.

"Dang girl," all the boys said in unison as they stared at Yanielle.

"What? You thought I was an amateur?" Yanielle asked before she wiped her mouth and burped loudly.

"Now that's my kind of lady," Umbati said as Yanielle passed him the bottle of wine.

"That seemed planned, like he intentionally broke it," Jubilaree said as he looked to Dayhoon for confirmation.

"Totally," Dayhoon quickly replied as he looked at Jubilaree then back to his little brother and Yanielle.

As Umbati took a sip of the bottle, Yanielle crossed her legs, leaned back with her arms extended out behind her to hold herself up, then threw her head back up to the sky as the rain fell through her afro.

"So, what happened?" Jubilaree questioned slowly and softly as he looked to Yanielle.

The rain seemed to fall even louder as she sat quietly to try and gather her thoughts. Yanielle lowered her head and sat upright, when Umbati looked towards her.

"Are you okay my love?" Umbati asked Yanielle as he passed the bottle to Dayhoon.

After she opened her eyes, Yanielle looked towards the helm deck and took a deep breath.

"How can I be? Look for yourself, she's pacing and contemplating on doing it again, I can't watch her kill herself," Yanielle said after she looked over her shoulder at Kotoyami.

She then turned her head to the left to look down on Matuka and noticed how drenched he was. The boys immediately looked to the helm deck and noticed that Kotoyami was walking over to them.

"This should be good," Umbati sarcastically joked as he looked to Dayhoon.

Everyone stood up together as Kotoyami swiftly made it over to where they all were.

"Out of my way! It's the necklace!" Kotoyami screamed as she pushed past Yanielle and Jubilaree.

"Hey!" Jubilaree shouted.

Jubilaree then grabbed Kotoyami's right arm while she was trying to get to Matuka.

"What's your problem?! It's not that serious!" Jubilaree yelled to Kotoyami as he held her by the arm.

"It's his necklace! It's the key! Then we all can go home," Kotoyami said with a smile of a lunatic.

"I think the bolts fried her brain," Umbati said as he looked up to his right at Kotoyami.

"I'm surprised she's not dead," Dayhoon replied to his younger brother.

"The only thing you're gonna be successful at, is going home to your maker! You will die Kotoyami!" Jubilaree yelled to Kotoyami before she pulled away from his grasp.

"Let me go! I don't have to take this!" Kotoyami shouted as she walked away from Jubilaree until she was standing over Matuka.

Suddenly, the huge, dark cloud lowered, and the bolts grew larger than before; with immense heat protruding them. The exposing light caused Jubilaree, Yanielle, Dayhoon and Umbati to quickly step back.

"This is very bad," Jubilaree said as he looked to the sky.

As the bolts grew in heat, the others stepped further away from Matuka and Kotoyami.

"Uh guys, this doesn't look good," Day-hoon said as he looked to Jubilaree for confirmation.

"Bang, bang!!!" Umbati screamed, which made Yanielle look towards Jubilaree then back to Matuka.

"Stop! You may kill him in the process!" Yanielle screamed as she looked at Kotoyami.

"Then bring us back to life, earth angel!" Kotoyami sarcastically screamed to Yanielle as she prepared to lean and reach for the necklace.

That's when the cloud grew and the weather became extremely violent above the ship.

"What's going on?!" Dayhoon yelled as he covered his face from the wind and rain with his forearms, while he held the bottle of wine.

"She must be pissing someone off up there!" Umbati tried to yell over the sound of the rain and wind.

As Kotoyami leaned in more and more, everyone noticed how the bolts from the cloud began to come together to form one big ball of lightning.

"Jubilaree!" Yanielle shouted as she looked to Jubilaree for help.

"*This is not gonna end well,*" Jubilaree thought to himself as he looked up to the cloud above the ship.

As the bolts prepared for launch, far from the ship was a young boy being chased by a shark and he was headed straight for the crew.

"Interesting, you can't say you see that every day," the lad said as he skated on the water with what appeared to be some sort of mechanical type of shoes on his feet.

Once the shark began to close in on him, the lad tried even harder to escape and make it to the ghostly vessel. The quicker and quicker he skated, the brighter the shoes lit up with a light-blue colored light that came from the sides of them. Back on the ship, Kotoyami was ready to try her luck for the final time; for she swore she had figured out why the ship would not move.

"Here goes something!" Kotoyami screamed as she reached all the way in to grab the golden, mysterious necklace.

Instantly, the enormous ball of electricity shot down one huge bolt. However, this time instead of hitting Kotoyami, the bolt struck Matuka's necklace, which caused Matuka to stand to his feet and grab Kotoyami by the throat. Everyone could not believe their eyes that Matuka was still unconscious and standing.

As he stood still, he was surrounded with a layer of electrical charged energy. Everyone was speechless and couldn't find the words to express their fear as their hearts raced much faster, at deadly speeds. When Matuka's eyes opened, all they could see was the electricity making them glow white as the energy tried to escape his body.

"Let me go!" Kotoyami tried to scream as they both began to rise until her feet were dangling off the ground.

"Uh, someone should do something," Umbati said as he looked around at everyone else.

"Someone should definitely do something! He's killing her!" Dayhoon yelled.

"I never seen him like this before, I don't know what to do, it's like he's still unconscious," Yanielle cried out in fear as the rain and wind picked up even more forcefully.

"Hey, hey!" a voice screamed from the ocean, which caused everyone to look to the water.

"Huh?" everyone asked in harmony as they tried to make out what appeared to be a boy in the ocean, running on the water.

"Huh? Interesting," the lad in the water said as he fixed his glasses while he looked at the cloud above the magnificent ship.

The young lad skipped over the water and through the rubble as fast as he could in order to escape his demise.

"Not today buddy!" the lad said as he ran above the water; through the rain after the large and ancient shark's mouth passed over his entire body, with a shadow of death.

After the boy escaped and put more distance in between him and the shark, he started to smile.

"I must be three sheets to the wind," Umbati said as he wiped the rain from his eyes.

"No, you're definitely not tripping bro, I see it too," Dayhoon said as he placed his hand on his little brother's wet afro.

"Impossible," Yanielle said as she looked on at the boy in the water.

"There's something chasing him, wait, it's a shark! How come I didn't see it before?! Its huge!" Jubilaree shouted as he ran to the side of the ship and grabbed the silver bulwarks, which made everyone else run over as well.

"Hope he doesn't bring that thing over here!" Yanielle screamed from fear as she witnessed the boy run from the shark.

"Yeah," Jubilaree and the brothers said in unison with a fearful look on their faces.

"Hey, don't forget about me," Kotoyami tried to yell as she hung in the air, while being stared down by the white, glowing eyes of Matuka.

Everyone then turned around back to face Matuka and Kotoyami. Being they were afraid for her life, one by one, they walked closer to where Matuka was holding her hostage. Suddenly, there was a loud bang on port side that caused the ship to jerk. Simultaneously, Matuka stopped glowing and dropped to the floor with Kotoyami on top of him. The rain and storm immediately disappeared as well, which left a clear night's sky; accompanied with trillions of stars.

"How?" Dayhoon asked as he looked around at the sky.

"What the?! What the hell was that?!" Jubilaree yelled as he ran over to the side of the ship where they saw the lad in the water.

Without warning, the young lad quickly crawled up the side of the ship, which caused Jubilaree to jump back. As the young boy crawled over the bulwarks, he fell onto the deck in front of Jubilaree, where he laid and tried to catch his breath. At that very moment, Matuka began to wake from his slumber and noticed Kotoyami on top of him.

"What happened? Did I miss something?" Matuka asked softly as he looked at the unconscious Kotoyami.

"*She must have passed out from the strain,*" Jubilaree thought to himself as he stared at the lifeless Kotoyami, lying atop Matuka.

That's when Dayhoon and Umbati walked to the young Captain and Kotoyami.

They each grabbed an arm of Kotoyami's and lifted her off Matuka; onto the deck next to him.

"Thanks," Matuka said slowly as he sat up and grabbed the back of his head with his right hand.

"No prob, I'm Dayhoon and this is my little brother Umbati, we've been waiting on you," Dayhoon said as he extended his hand for Matuka to grab and use to stand up.

"Glad to have you back," Jubilaree said as Matuka stood up.

"What happened?" Matuka questioned as he tried to catch his balance.

"What do you remember?" Jubilaree asked Matuka as he walked over to him, Dayhoon and Umbati.

"The last thing I remember was seeing them in the water drinking, and I think, no, I saw the youngest get hurt and I prepared to jump in," Matuka said as he scanned the two brothers for injuries.

"What's he looking for?" Umbati asked Dayhoon as Matuka walked around them in a circle.

"She healed us, if that's what you're wondering," Dayhoon said as he pointed towards Yanielle.

Yanielle then blushed, turned her head, and began to twiddle her thumbs after Matuka looked to her with a smile.

"Aren't you going to tell him about our dream big bro?" Umbati whispered to his older brother.

Dayhoon ignored Umbati and gestured for him to stop, which caused Jubilaree to get suspicious of the two of them.

"And what happened with Kotoyami?" Matuka asked as he pointed to her on the deck while she laid unconscious.

"Long story," Yanielle dropped her head and said as she walked over to Matuka and the rest of them.

"I have time," Matuka said as he looked at Yanielle.

"Well where do I start?" Yanielle asked as she looked to the rest of the crew.

"How about I tell you," Jubilaree interjected as he unfolded his arms and walked closer to Matuka.

A few minutes passed and Jubilaree finished briefing Matuka on what happened on his ship; from the time he went unconscious.

"Interesting," the lad that was being chased by the shark chimed in; after he peeked from behind Yanielle, while he sat on the deck.

"What the?!" the crew yelled in unison as they turned to see where the voice came from.

They were immediately reminded of the

boy's presence as he stood to his feet and kicked off the metal shoes; he had around his normal shoes.

"You left him out of the story Jubilaree," Matuka said as he looked on at the boy before he noticed his glowing and broken, mechanical shoes.

"I guess he was so worried about poor Kotoyami, he couldn't remember anything else," Yanielle said with a sly grin and with her arms crossed.

"You got a death wish too?" Jubilaree quickly asked Yanielle before he closed his eye and crossed his arms.

As Matuka looked to the lad, he saw the boy had brown locks and light-brown skin. He wore big, thick glasses and was skinny. He had a dark, turquoise green satchel on his left shoulder that was thrown over his head and hanging on the right side of his body. He wasn't wearing a shirt and he wore dark-beige pants that were torn at the knees. His normal shoes were a dark-tan color and looked different from any pair of shoes they've ever seen before.

"Hi, I'm Tahma, thanks for allowing me on, you guys are life savers, you must be the Captain," the lad said as he walked up to Matuka to shake his hand.

"How did he know? He gathered all that from our conversation?" Yanielle asked the others as the boy stood in front of Matuka.

"What happened?" Kotoyami asked as she sat up from the wet, black deck.

Everyone was shocked to see that Kotoyami was awake and trying to move.

"You shouldn't move Koto," Jubilaree said with his head bowed and eye closed as Yanielle rushed to her side.

"Koto? So, we have sweet names now?" Matuka jokingly asked while he looked towards the blushing Jubilaree.

"Hey knock it off!" Jubilaree shouted as he turned around from everyone.

"Kotoyami, I heard you've been very busy in my absence," Matuka said as he walked over to her and extended his hand for her to use to stand up.

"Sorry," Kotoyami said as she dropped her head from being embarrassed.

"Well, at least you're not dead," Matuka laughed and smiled.

"Speaking of such, I'm Tahma, an eager alchemist and inventor and I'd like to study you," Tahma said as he went in to shake Kotoyami's hand.

"Kotoyami, nice to meet you too?" Kotoyami replied as she hesitantly shook his hand.

"Weren't you being chased by a shark?" Umbati asked.

"Yeah, how did you escape that?" Dayhoon asked as he looked to Tahma.

"Yeah and what are those?" Umbati slurred and jokingly asked as he pointed at Tahma's shoes.

"I'm glad you asked, I invented them, the metal casing you seen me wearing around them; not only helps me float on water but skate on water as well. I was unable to outrun the shark but..." Tahma said as he looked back to port side and began to walk over to the bulwarks he climbed over.

"Well?" Yanielle questioned as everyone looked to the lad.

"The shark, it stopped, like it was afraid or like something made it turn around when we got closer to the ship," Tahma said as he looked to the ocean for the shark.

"Bizarre," Jubilaree said before he turned around, folded his arms, and closed his eye.

"So, what's next?" Dayhoon asked Matuka as he stood there with the bottle in his hand.

Matuka then took the bottle from Dayhoon and walked over to Tahma, then took a big sip.

"Whew, that's strong!" Matuka said as he coughed on the strong red wine and passed it to Tahma.

"I don't drink but something is telling me to do this, interesting," Tahma said as he hesitantly reached for the bottle.

After Tahma took a sip of the wine, the ship began to vibrate.

"What's going on?" everyone except Matuka yelled in unison, as they looked around for an answer.

Just as quickly as the ship started to vibrate it stopped and the crew was speechless as to what happened.

"Am I the only one who just felt that?" Umbati asked.

"The vibrating?" Yanielle asked as she turned to Umbati.

"Of course not, I just got a strange feeling," Umbati stated to the crew.

"I think I know the feeling," Dayhoon replied.

"Yeah," everyone except Matuka agreed.

"What are y'all talking about?" Matuka questioned everyone as he looked around.

"Like a weight of responsibility," Jubilaree replied.

Suddenly, a gust of wind picked up Matuka's hat from the floor of the helm deck and carried it right in front of his feet. At that moment, Matuka felt the same feeling as well and leaned over to pick up his hat.

"You've done it, you've found us all, now it's time to lead the way, Captain," Kotoyami whispered in Matuka's ear as she took his hat from him and placed it on his head.

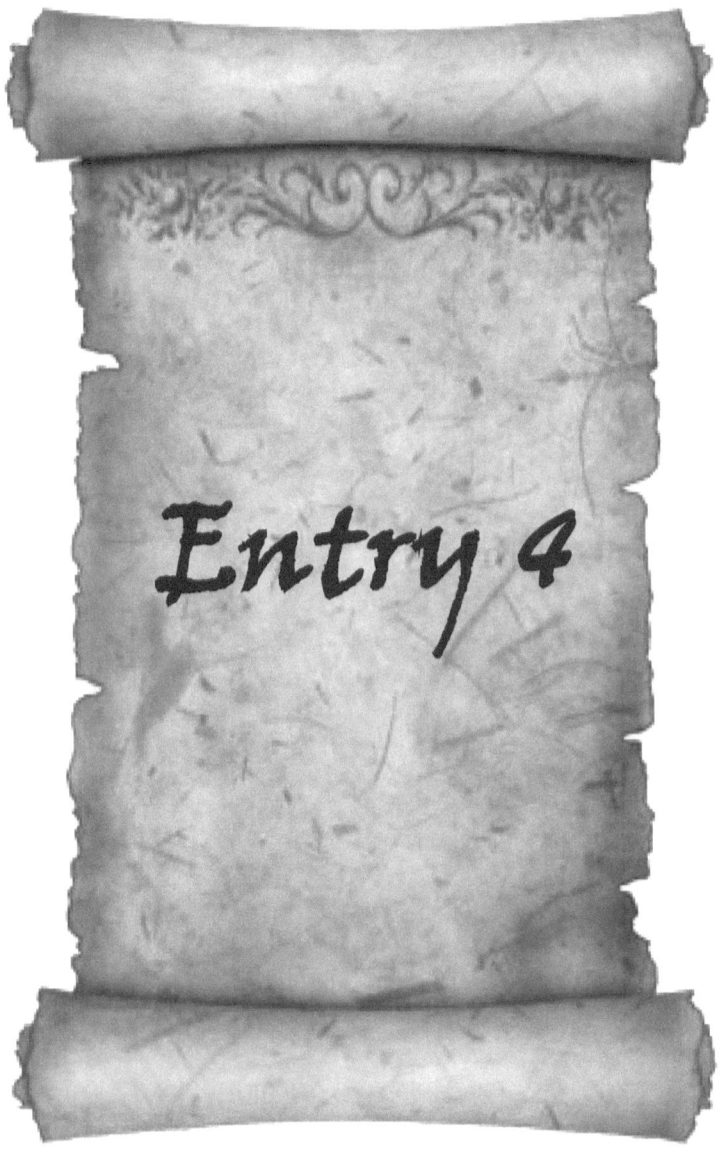

Entry 4

BIRTH PANGS

"So, what's next?" Umbati asked as he staggered his way in front of Matuka from being intoxicated.

Matuka looked towards his helm deck and abruptly was met with a familiar pain. A familiar sound that growled as loud as the singing whales of the deep; rang in their ears.

"I know that sound, okay, let's go girl," Yanielle said as she gestured for Kotoyami to follow her.

"Huh?" Kotoyami asked as she looked

towards Yanielle a little confused.

"I'm sure we all could use a bite, let's go check out the galley. We know that we both have food growing in our rooms, but we haven't checked out where we will prepare it," Yanielle said with a smile as she grabbed Kotoyami's hand.

"Food sounds pretty good right now," Dayhoon said as he looked to Umbati while he grabbed for the bottle of wine.

"Food growing in your rooms? Interesting," Tahma said as he fixed his glasses with his right hand.

"Yeah, what's that about?" Jubilaree asked.

"In due time guys," Matuka said with a smile.

"Yeah, I'm starving big bro," Umbati said as he looked back to Dayhoon.

"Come on, let's go girl," Yanielle said anxiously with a smile as she pulled Kotoyami off to head down below deck.

"Okay fine," Kotoyami said before the two girls laughed and headed through the door.

After Matuka looked away from the girls, he looked to the brothers, Tahma and Jubilaree, and then smiled.

"Some kind of day, huh guys?" Matuka asked the boys with an exhausted smile.

"Yeah, some day," Jubilaree said as he

uncrossed his arms, slouched, and leaned forward out of exhaustion.

Without warning, Tahma moved in awfully close to Matuka to view his necklace. It made Matuka a little uncomfortable to notice how close Tahma got without being detected, so he stepped back.

"Interesting," Tahma said as he fixed his glasses on his face with his right hand.

"What's that?" Matuka asked as he stepped backwards to gain even more breathing room.

"It looked like he was about to give you a kiss," Umbati said before he laughed and took a sip of the bottle; after he grabbed it from Dayhoon.

Suddenly, before Umbati could move the bottle from his lips, Tahma was already close to his face, staring with his gleaming glasses.

"Hey man, you ever heard of personal space?" Umbati asked with an annoyed voice as he passed the bottle back to Dayhoon.

"Interesting," Tahma said as he fixed his glasses.

"Clearly not," Dayhoon said as he looked down at Tahma.

Without warning Tahma stood up, turned towards Dayhoon, and leaned in close to look at his bandages over his body.

"The bandages on my feet and knees

used to be bloody, I can make them like that again, if you want," Dayhoon slurred as he raised his left knee.

"Some kind of day," Jubilaree said as he began to walk away from the group of boys.

"Hey! Where are you going?' Matuka asked as he watched Jubilaree slowly walk towards the door that led below the main deck.

"Going to bed," Jubilaree replied stiffly as he looked back to Matuka.

"What about supper?" Matuka asked as he stepped forward to Jubilaree before he completely vanished.

"Hey, whatever he doesn't want I'll take," Umbati said with a chuckle as he walked over to Dayhoon.

"You know where to find me," Jubilaree said as he threw his left hand in the air and waved goodbye; before he went through the door.

"Interesting, a place of rest would be nice to have and a good meal too," Tahma said as he turned around to face Matuka.

"You guys are more than welcome to stay; I have a room for you all. You can stay as long as you like. I have the perfect rooms for you guys. Follow me," Matuka said as he waved for the lads to follow him as he walked forward towards the stern.

One behind another, they followed

Matuka across the deck to the door that was under the helm deck. With Matuka leading, Tahma next in line, then Umbati and Dayhoon; the new visitors were in for a shock of their lifetime. The boys looked around at the ship and admired its beauty all the way until they reached the regal door.

"Interesting," Tahma said as he fixed his glasses with his right hand and walked over to the door to look at the detailing.

"Who is he? How did this all come to be? This ship is unlike anything I've seen so far. You'd think he'd be worried about adults coming and taking this from us, but, for some reason, he's not. I don't remember much but he reminds me of home and that dream; that dream was unreal," Dayhoon thought to himself as he gazed upon Matuka; who had grabbed the doorknob and opened the door.

"You're sure about this big bro?" Umbati asked as he turned around and looked up at his older brother.

Dayhoon smirked, leaned down to his brother, closed his eyes, and placed his right hand on Umbati's head. That's when Matuka proceeded through the door and out of sight into the darkness.

"Interesting, it's so dark," Tahma said after he fixed his glasses with his right hand and walked through the door, out of sight.

"I'll follow you to death brother," Umbati said as he looked up to his brother.

"No need for that Umbati, let's go," Dayhoon said with a smile as he walked his little brother forward into the darkness.

"No way," Tahma stuttered as they walked through the black and silver engraved door to be joined with the others again.

"Is this real alligator skin?" Umbati asked as he looked at the broad stairs and then the black, wooden floor of the second deck.

Matuka turned around with his eyes closed, put his left hand behind his head and smiled while he stood in front of the glistening prison cell.

"You didn't notice them on the other stairs outside above deck?" Dayhoon asked Umbati as Tahma walked down the large, half-circle staircase next to Matuka.

"Well there was a lot going on and everyone is acting like this crap is ordinary!" Umbati shouted to his older brother as he looked around at the pitch-black walls of the ship's interior.

"Are you guys ready?" Matuka smiled as he waved for Dayhoon and Umbati to come.

Meanwhile, the girls were leaving their rooms from gathering their supplies to head over to the galley and prepare supper.

"Hey girl, what did you bring?" Yanielle

asked Kotoyami while she held a huge, wooden bowl full of vegetables and herbs.

"I see you came prepared," Kotoyami chuckled as she uncovered her basket of cooking ware, cheeses, and meat.

"Oh yes girlfriend, let's go get this started," Yanielle said then laughed before Kotoyami noticed the boys at the end of the hallway, peaking around at them.

"Okay?" Kotoyami said slowly with a raised eyebrow as she looked past Yanielle.

"Huh? What happened?" Yanielle asked as she turned to look.

"Quick, quick!" Umbati whispered as he pushed the other boys around the corner so they couldn't be seen gawking.

"Unreal," Yanielle said before they both dropped their heads, while they held onto their food carriers.

"Let's go see what they want," Kotoyami said as she lifted her head.

"Uh, let us not. They're just perverts being creeps!" Yanielle said as she turned around to look to see if they were looking again.

"Quick, quick!" Dayhoon whispered as he pushed the other boys around the corner so they couldn't be seen staring again.

"You're right let's go say hello," Yanielle said as a vein extruded from her forehead while she balled her right fist and frowned.

The girls put down their baskets and began to walk down the hallway. As they passed the candles that lit up the black wooden walls, Matuka was seemingly pushed out from around the corner.

"Uh, hey girls," Matuka said as he closed his eyes, smiled, and put his left hand behind his head.

"Oh, so just cause you're Captain; you think you can be a creep?" Yanielle walked up and shouted.

"Yanielle, let's give him a chance to answer," Kotoyami said after she noticed Tahma, Dayhoon and Umbati peek around the corner again.

Kotoyami and Yanielle then looked to Matuka for an explanation for the staring.

"Well, I was wondering if it'll be cool if you two waited a sec for these guys to get into their rooms; before you started cooking. Something tells me that they will have something to bring as well," Matuka said after he opened his eyes and walked closer to them.

"Really? I was doing this for you," Yanielle stated with an annoyed attitude and with her hands on her hips.

"Hey, this will give you two enough time to check out the saloon, I'll be fine," Matuka quickly responded as he grabbed both of her hands.

"Hey!" Yanielle shrieked before she started to blush.

That's when Umbati came around the corner with a frown and an evil look in his eyes; followed by Dayhoon and Tahma.

"Hey! That's my girl, so hands off!" Umbati slurred as he tried to look cool when he walked over to Matuka, Yanielle and Koto-yami.

"Ew, first of all, I'm no one's girl! Second, Matuka, I don't want to cook for these perverted little morons, and I don't think I should have to. Matter of fact; I'm not and you can't do nothing about it buddy!" Yanielle said as she snatched her hands from Matuka and tried to walk away.

Matuka quickly grabbed Yanielle's left hand as she tried to push past Kotoyami.

"Hey, I know you don't, but it'll be nice if you did, and I think we all could benefit from what's to come. What do you say?" Matuka asked with a smile.

Yanielle turned around to see him smiling and it melted her heart, so she started to blush again.

"Okay, fine but me and Kotoyami get to prepare everything," Yanielle quickly stated before she snatched her hand back from Matuka.

"That's fine," Matuka said before he waved and as Yanielle took Kotoyami by the hand to lead her back to their food carriers.

"Unreal, what jerks!" Yanielle said as she looked to Kotoyami for confirmation and agreement.

"I wonder if he can tell you like him," Kotoyami said with a chuckle.

"Hey! I don't like him like that!" Yanielle screamed back before she started to blush more.

Meanwhile, Matuka sneezed at that very moment as he watched Kotoyami and Yanielle cross the threshold of the galley before they disappeared out of sight.

"This isn't over," Umbati said to Matuka before he turned around and headed back the way they came.

"Okaaay, anyway, Tahma, right? Follow me," Matuka said as he walked past all the boys around the corner.

After Matuka passed the jail cell, he headed down the hallway on the opposite side of the ship.

"Matuka, this ship's detail is astonishing. I haven't seen anything like this, only in my imagination," Tahma said as they all followed behind Matuka.

"Oh, just wait," Matuka said as he turned around and laughed.

As Matuka and Tahma got close to the first door on the right, it swung open loud and hard, which caused all the boys to jump.

"Huh?" Matuka asked softly while he looked at the opened door.

Suddenly, Tahma began to vibrate and lift off the ground.

"Interesting, the magnetic field here is interacting with my body on a subatomic level," Tahma said as he fixed his glasses with his right hand.

"No way!" Umbati shouted while he looked on at Tahma as he floated in front of him.

"How is this possible?" Dayhoon questioned Matuka.

"I'm unsure, this is my first time seeing this, but if I had to guess, I would say this is the room's way of choosing its occupant," Matuka slowly replied.

In an instant, Tahma was pulled into the room and the door closed.

"Not cool," Umbati said as he grabbed his older brother's hand.

"The room chose? This is insane! Come on bro, we're out of here," Dayhoon said as he grabbed Umbati's hand.

"Bro where will we go?" Umbati asked Dayhoon.

"Far from here," Dayhoon quickly replied as he walked Umbati back down the hall the way they came.

"Hey! Wait!" Matuka yelled to the brothers.

Suddenly, the last door on the right flew open hard just like before, which caused Matuka and the brothers to turn around.

"What the hell?!" Dayhoon shouted as he was snatched from the ground into the air.

"Bro I'm scared!" Umbati yelped while he reached for his brother's hand after he was lifted off the ground as well.

Without warning, the boys were quickly pulled down the hall, past Matuka and into the room where they were dropped.

"Hey! That hurt!" Umbati screamed.

"Let's go Umbati!" Dayhoon yelled as he tried to stand.

Without warning, the door quickly slammed shut the moment Dayhoon and Umbati tried to run out.

"What's with all the noise?" Yanielle asked as she and Kotoyami stuck their heads out from the galley's right-side entrance.

"Something strange," Matuka said as he looked to both Tahma and the brothers' door.

"Come, have a seat Captain," Kotoyami said before waving him over.

Matuka took one last look at the two doors and paused.

"I wonder why they didn't come out or try to. I'm surprised I didn't hear any banging.

Are the rooms soundproof? But how? It's a ship not a fortress," Matuka thought to himself while he looked back and forth between the doors.

The silence was beginning to pick at his brain so much that he was tempted to check on them.

"And why didn't Jubilaree come out, he must have heard all of the commotion, didn't he?" Matuka thought to himself while he stood in front of Jubilaree's room door.

"Hey, you're just gonna ignore our invite? You jerk!" Yanielle questioned before she chucked a huge onion at Matuka's head.

"Ouch!" Matuka screamed down the hallway, which caused Yanielle to pull her head back in the galley and hide.

"Are you blushing?" Kotoyami asked Yanielle, who was twirling her thumbs.

"No way!" Yanielle said and blushed as she looked at Kotoyami.

"Well he's coming, and he doesn't look too happy," Kotoyami quickly replied.

"What the heck was that for?!" Matuka yelled after he walked up on the girls from the hallway.

Meanwhile, Tahma was still sitting with his eyes closed by the room's door. Although his eyes were closed, he could begin to see light piercing the darkness of his eye lids.

"Interesting," Tahma said after he felt the ground and realized it was grass.

As Tahma sat in the dark, he tried to feel how deep the grass and dirt went into the floor with his fingers.

"Interesting, the roots of the grass and soil go pretty deep," Tahma said after he opened his heavy eyes from the drawn-out contemplation.

As Tahma stood to his feet, the room became even brighter.

"Wow, amazing!" Tahma said as he leaped off the ground.

As he looked to his right, which was the south wall, a long and wide bed took up most of the wall. The support was made from fine silver and had engraved designs that also were glowing. Tahma then noticed that the mattress was also emitting its own light. It was white, thick and it appeared as soft as a feather. He looked and saw how huge the cover was that gently laid across it.

The cover was light blue, it had silver, glitter-like dust throughout its fibers and it too was also radiating light. He then noticed that his pillow was letting off immense light, so he walked slowly over to it to have a closer look. By the time he reached the bed and had leaned over it, his glasses were lit up from the pillow's light show. The pillow was silver and had light-blue, glitter-like dust within its fibers, which was the exact opposite from the huge cover on the bed.

"Interesting," Tahma said as he fixed his glasses with his right hand.

Suddenly, out from the corner of his left eye, he saw something else that began to glow brighter.

"Huh?" Tahma asked as he looked to his left in the southeast corner of the room.

In front of the bed was a corner desk that ran along the south wall and the east wall. It was made from fine silver, same as the bed support; it was engraved and looked expensive. There was also a small, silver stool in front of the desk that gave off an aura as well. The desk was also emitting its own light, when he noticed two more tables in the middle of the east wall, side-by-side.

They were skinny and long, they were sticking out from the wall and had equipment on them. The one closest to him was the smaller of the two; it was made from the finest wood he had ever seen. The wood was glowing golden-brown and was engraved with perfection. On top of it were all sorts of beakers, notebooks, tools, and each gave off their own light as well.

"*I can't believe my eyes, Matuka, what kind of ship is this?*" Tahma thought to himself as he surveyed the room.

Tahma then stood in awe from the mysteries that were before him for a moment.

"How is it glowing in here, it's not what I think it is, no way, it couldn't be," Tahma said.

He then walked to the other table, which was about four feet away from the other one, to get a better look.

"Interesting, I wonder," Tahma said softly while he scratched his head.

Tahma then walked towards the other table and then looked to the corner of the north east wall. It was pitch-black still, so he decided to walk around to the other side of the longer table. The young genius began to wonder if the area would light up from sensing his movement as he got closer. After he got to the other side of the longer table, he immediately noticed that it was made of a metal he hadn't seen before.

"Interesting," Tahma said as he fixed his glasses with his right hand.

On top of the table were sugarcanes that were cut in halves, and sitting inside of three enormous, metal food bowls.

"What type of metal is this?" Tahma asked as he looked at the glowing table and its contents.

That's when the room's wall began to emanate its own light. The walls of the room were wood and glowed a golden-brown color, while the cracks were seeping hues of aqua blue. Tahma then looked up to the ceiling and nearly fell backwards on the floor from being astonished.

"What the?!" Tahma yelled as he was poked by something on his rear.

After turning around to see what it was, the dark corner began to glow and Tahma could then see what it was that poked him.

"Sugarcanes?" Tahma asked as the small sugarcane field in the corner of the room began to glow a deep shade of green.

Tahma immediately looked back up to the ceiling once he knew what it was that stabbed his rear.

"Interesting! It's beautiful! It looks like the stars in the sky," Tahma said as he watched the aqua blue lights shine on his ceiling.

After somewhat stargazing for a few minutes, Tahma looked to the north wall and noticed a wardrobe in the northwest corner of the room that was nearly empty.

"Interesting," Tahma said as he fixed his glasses with his right hand while he walked over to the wardrobe.

By the time Tahma got to the wardrobe, he could see that the walls were made from the same wood as the room walls and they too were also glowing. The inside of the wardrobe had the same blue glitter-like dust sparkling throughout its surface that the pillow had.

"Matuka, Captain of the ship with the black sails, just who are you?" Tahma asked aloud as he looked around the room in total disbelief.

Tahma then noticed an exceptionally large, dark-walnut colored storage cabinet that reached from the floor to the ceiling of the room. It too was emitting light like all the other furniture in the room and appeared to be awfully expensive.

"Interesting, I didn't see that before," Tahma said as he fixed his glasses with his right hand while he walked over to the large, dark cabinet.

Meanwhile, Matuka, Yanielle and Kotoyami were still in the galley waiting for everyone to come out of their rooms.

"So, what are we going to do from here on out?" Kotoyami asked Matuka with a serious stare while she sat across from him.

Matuka then put his elbows on top of the table and rested his face in his hands.

"Why you even ask girl?" Yanielle asked Kotoyami as she turned around and sat on top of the table at its edge.

With Kotoyami to her right, Matuka to her left and the entry to the galley in front of her, she dropped her head back to the ceiling, then let out a deep sigh. At that time, Dayhoon and Umbati finally worked up the courage to open their eyes in the dark room where they were magnetically dragged in.

"Whoa, unreal," Dayhoon said as the room became brighter and brighter.

"Am I tripping or is the floor made of grass?" Umbati asked as he stood up and looked around the room.

"You're definitely not bro, unless we both are," Dayhoon quickly replied as he stood next to his younger brother before he placed his right hand on his head.

"But how?!" Umbati demanded to know while he looked up to his older brother.

"I'm unsure brother, that's a question for Matuka," Dayhoon replied as he looked around the room.

The first thing Dayhoon noticed was that there were two desks in the room, one on the right side of the door and the other on the left. Both desks sat on the west walls and both were producing their own light. The desk to the left of the door was made of tigerwood and it was glistening with splendor. It had two large, polished tungsten bowls that were gleaming and kind of hard to look at for long. As Dayhoon looked back to the other desk on the right side of the door, he noticed it was made from stainless-steel. Just like the other desk, it was glowing and had contents on top of it.

"Is that weapon cleaning and upkeep supplies over there Umbati?" Dayhoon asked his younger brother as he gestured for him to have a closer look.

Umbati then walked over to the table on the right that was three feet away and immediately paused.

"What's the matter bro?" Dayhoon asked Umbati, who had become incredibly quiet.

By the time Umbati was ready to reply to his older brother, something caught both of their eyes.

"Whoa!" the brothers said in unison as they stared to the right side of the room.

"That's so freaking cool! Have you ever seen anything like it, big brother?!" Umbati yelled from excitement before he looked to Dayhoon for a response.

"Not even close man, not even close," Dayhoon said as they both walked up to the majestic beds.

There were two large, floating beds protruding from the walls unlike anything they had ever seen. The bottom bed was enormous, the support was made from stainless-steel and it too had its own glow. The bed was connected to the east and south walls as well as the one above. The mattress was white, thick, soft and glowing. It radiated the purest color of white and was draped in multiple covers. The first cover was tan; the second was orange and the last was dark-green. All three of the covers were emanating light and seemed to be made from fine quality material.

The bed above it was a little smaller in width and was raised about five feet from the bottom bed. This bed's support was made from stainless-steel as well and glowed also. The wall had three sets of steps sticking out from them that lead up to the second bed from the floor. The steps were made from tungsten as well and seemed to glow brighter as Umbati walked closer to them.

"Now that's something you don't see every day," Dayhoon said softly as his younger brother grew closer to the steps that were protruding from the wall.

"I call the top!" Umbati yelled as he ran up the three steps and jumped onto the bed.

The white, soft glowing mattress that was covered with a sparkling large tan blanket, seemed to hug him back as he fell into its sweet, comforting hold. Suddenly, Umbati sat up immediately and dropped his mouth from shock.

"What's wrong bro?" Dayhoon asked with a concerned look in his eyes.

Umbati was frozen and all he could do was point to the ceiling, which made Dayhoon look up quickly.

"What the hell?!" Dayhoon asked aloud before he fell back to the floor.

The brothers noticed that the ceiling was black but glowing with orange and silver, glitter-like lights that mimicked the stars in the night sky.

"How?" Dayhoon questioned aloud as he looked up at the magnificent sight.

Without hesitation, Umbati jumped from the top bed onto the bottom one, then to the floor, to help his older brother, stand back up.

"You okay bro?" Umbati asked as he extended his hand to his older brother.

"Yeah, I was just caught off guard," Dayhoon replied as he stood up.

"What do you think it is?" Umbati asked Dayhoon as they both stood and looked up at the ceiling of the room.

"I have the slightest clue bro," Dayhoon said as he looked down to Umbati with a serious facial expression.

Out the corner of Umbati's right eye, he could see the northeast corner beginning to brighten.

"What is that?!" Umbati screamed as he looked in the northeast corner of the room.

"Is that what I think it is?" Dayhoon asked Umbati.

"No freaking way!" Umbati yelled as they both walked over to the northeast corner of the room.

There were two large squares: one inside of the other. The outer square was dirt and had a bean garden growing from it, while the inner square had a small wheat field inside of it.

"How is this even possible?" Umbati asked his older brother while he knelt to get a closer look.

By this time, the room was fully lit and glowing from all the furniture and ceiling, the brothers could see everything in detail. Just like the other rooms, the floor was made of green, lush grass that glowed and sparkled as if it were wet from dew. Unlike the other rooms, it had two different auras; orange and silver that merged like a symphony.

"Is it real?" Dayhoon questioned Umbati as he knelt next to him.

Umbati then grabbed a bean from the glowing plant, wiped the dirt from it and placed it in his mouth. After chewing and swallowing the bean, Umbati jumped to his feet with a huge smile upon his face.

"What's the matter bro?" Dayhoon asked the overly joyed and yet quiet, Umbati.

"That was the best bean I ever tasted bro! It tasted like it was already seasoned," Umbati explained as he leaned over, grabbed another and passed it to his brother.

Dayhoon quickly realized why his

younger brother was excited to eat a mere bean.

"Whoa, unreal, you weren't exaggerating, this is good!" Dayhoon quickly said as he devoured the bean.

After Dayhoon stood to his feet, Umbati noticed that there was a large wardrobe in the northwest corner of the wall that stretched to the center of the north wall.

"Hey, look at that bro!" Umbati said as he pointed to the wardrobe that was fully opened.

"Huh?" Dayhoon replied as he turned around to look at what his younger brother had seen.

"Nice, it has our sizes and styles," Umbati said with a huge smile as he grabbed a dark-brown cloak from the wardrobe.

"Matuka, you are something else man," Dayhoon said softly while he looked into the wardrobe.

Everything in the room had its own glow and aura, which made an awesome light show for the brothers who were captivated by its beauty. The walls were pitch-black but were seeping out tiny orange, glitter-like lights that appeared to pulsate like the stars. The brothers couldn't stop themselves from looking around at their new domain with joy; for they knew right then that the room was made specifically for them. Meanwhile Matuka, Yanielle, and

Kotoyami had begun to grow impatient because of their growling stomachs.

"How long do we have to wait before we can eat?" Kotoyami asked with an aggravated tone of voice.

"Yeah, cause I'm getting tired of waiting myself," Yanielle said as she looked towards her right at Matuka.

"I'm unsure but I can go check," Matuka said as he got up from under the picnic-style table, while his hands rested on the table's surface.

"Well in the meantime; I'm going to get started," Kotoyami replied as she stood as well.

"Okay, that's fine," Matuka said as he walked away and exited the galley.

As Matuka began to walk down the east hallway, he admired the beauty of his ship; the black, polished walls and smooth black deck was comforting to him. As Matuka got in front of the brothers' room and was prepared to knock, the door opened on its own.

"Okay, that's weird," Matuka said as he looked at the opened door.

Matuka then stuck his head in the room and realized that the brothers were fast asleep.

"That wine and running around must have got the best of them," Matuka said with a smile as he looked at the sleeping brothers.

Matuka then closed their door and headed down the hall towards Jubilaree's room.

"I wonder if Jubilaree is awake," Matuka said as he walked in front of Jubilaree's door.

Suddenly, like before, the room's door opened and Matuka could see Jubilaree asleep on his hammock to the right of the room.

"You too huh? Trying to stop Kotoyami must have taken a lot on him mentally, he must really like her," Matuka said softly while he stared at Jubilaree.

Jubilaree's back was turned and his face was towards the wall, so Matuka could not see that his eye had opened. Not knowing that by the door opening he had awakened Jubilaree, Matuka closed the door and continued down the hall towards Tahma's room. As Matuka got in front of Tahma's door, he had expected for it to open on its own but was shocked to see Tahma standing in the doorway.

"You're awake? That's great! The girls are preparing a meal for everyone; we'd love it if you joined us," Matuka said as he stood at the opening of the room.

"Interesting, I would but I have so much research to do in here. This ship is impossible on so many levels. So, I'm going to have to take a rain check, because the things I'm finding are things that would be in a fairytale," Tahma said with a smile.

"Are you sure? You'll have plenty of

time to do research, besides a nice hot meal will give your brain the energy it needs to focus," Matuka quickly replied to Tahma with a smile.

Tahma then scratched his head and paused to think about what Matuka said.

"Interesting. No, I have to do this now, thank you Matuka, but you've given me a mission indirectly by placing me in a room of wonder such as this," Tahma said as he reached for Matuka's hand to shake.

"Okay, if you are sure then there's nothing more I can say about it. Just don't stay up all night, make sure you get some rest eventually," Matuka said as he shook Tahma's hand.

"Will do Captain," Tahma replied with a salute after he let go of Matuka's right hand.

"Goodnight Tahma," Matuka said as he began to walk away.

"Goodnight," Tahma said as he closed his room's door.

As Matuka began to walk back towards the galley, he realized he was missing something important and dear to him, so he began to grow nervous.

"How could I be so stupid?" Matuka asked as he turned around and ran back down the hallway.

After Matuka began to run, he accidentally kicked the red onion that Yanielle threw at him into Jubilaree's door.

"What the heck was that?" Matuka asked as he looked backwards and noticed it was the onion from earlier.

Matuka then continued until he got down the hall and around the corner. Once he did, Matuka then ran up the stairs and out to the main deck to look for what he lost.

"Where the heck is it?" Matuka asked as he profusely looked for what he lost earlier.

Out of the corner of his left eye, Matuka saw what he was looking for lying on the black, polished deck.

"There it is!" Matuka yelled.

The young lad couldn't hold his excitement as he ran over to port side, where his lonely treasure rested.

"That was too close for comfort, I should be more careful, I didn't even notice it came off. It must have happened when the lightning struck my necklace," Matuka said while he picked up his bandanna and tied it back around his leg.

After that, Matuka headed to his Captain's quarters to change and get more comfortable for the meal that was coming his way. Meanwhile, Yanielle and Kotoyami were still in the galley preparing the meal to come.

"I wonder what's taking so long," Kotoyami said to Yanielle as they stood over the red-cedar table where they were prepping the food.

The galley was extremely clean; the floors and walls were made from golden-oakwood that made the entire room smell pleasant. Coming from the east hallway facing inward, you could see out the other exit that led to the west hallway. Dead center was a huge picnic-style table that was made from red-cedar as well; that had enough space for everyone on the vessel to sit. To the right was the north wall, against it was a red-cedar table that contained three large, wooden barrels; filled with salt and fresh fish. In between the table and counter was a short, brown bin filled with sand; that was used for lighting the fires to cook the food.

In the northeast corner was another table that ran along half of the east wall. Over half of the east wall was taken up by a large cabinet that housed plates, silverware, and mugs. On the southwest wall, stood a tall storage closet with many shelves. To the left of the feeding table was the entry into the saloon; that had a bigger opening than the doorways leading into the galley.

The saloon was made from the same material and contained multiple collapsible chairs; that was arranged in a circle in the middle of the room. The collapsible chairs were made of metal and painted black. The seat cushions were black suede and nicely designed. On the east and west walls, sat large, long seats that took up most of the walls.

On the south wall was a wide bar that ran along the entire wall, which was fully stocked with wine and rum. The bar had seven black stools lined up under it, the legs were made from red-cedar and the seats were made of black leather. Both rooms were well-lit with kerosene lamps that made the rooms appear warm and comfy. Yanielle walked to the entry of the saloon and stood there amazed at its cleanliness.

"This ship is too much," Yanielle said as she leaned up against the doorway with her arms crossed before she shook her head.

"What do you mean?" Kotoyami asked as she reached for a fish out of one of the barrels beneath the counter where she was working.

"I never seen anything like this, it's like it has human touches but at the same time otherworldly," Yanielle said as she looked into the room.

"Elaborate Yanielle," Kotoyami said as she turned around to look at Yanielle.

"It's like, I know it was made by human hands but I kinda feel like maybe not all of it was. The design of this place is unreal, it has practical things in it that make you believe it's a normal ship but then there are things missing and things added that shouldn't be. Perfect example, fresh water, food already cooked, the speed of this vessel, the rooms, this place is loaded!" Yanielle explained as she turned around to face Kotoyami.

"I understand what you mean," Kotoyami said as she held a small tuna fish in her left hand.

"And I pray that Matuka finds or has a way to lock up that rum and wine from those two drunks down the hall," Yanielle said as she pointed over her right shoulder towards the room filled with alcohol.

"Indeed," Kotoyami replied then laughed before she turned around to continue prepping the food.

"Is that gonna be ready in time without being too salty?" Yanielle asked Kotoyami as she walked to her right side.

"I don't think so; it usually takes hours to soak in water to remove the excess salt. We should have done this the moment we got on the ship. We did the easy part by chopping up the vegetables, herbs, and cheese. The meat in my room was strangely already cooked so all we have to do is heat it up. However, it's not going to be enough for everyone. This meat would only be able to feed two, there is more fish but it's all too salty," Kotoyami explained to Yanielle as she looked down at the counter at all of the food.

"Where the heck is Matuka and those jerks?! He said they'd have something to add to the meal!" Yanielle shouted as she looked towards the east entry of the galley.

"Maybe you should go check on him," Kotoyami said while she looked to her right at Yanielle.

"Yeah, maybe I should," Yanielle said as she stormed off towards the east hallway.

By the time Yanielle reached the brothers door, she was infuriated because of her empty stomach. She then knocked very loudly on the boys' door; demanding that they open it.

"Hey! I know you're in there! Come out!" Yanielle screamed at the top of her lungs while she banged on the bedroom door.

After a couple of minutes of nonstop banging, she gave up and went to the next door.

"This is ridiculous!" Yanielle shouted as she arrived at Jubilaree's room door.

She then proceeded to knock on Jubilaree's door but to no avail, for he too did not answer her call.

"I hope you all starve!" Yanielle shouted as she walked away from Jubilaree's room onward to Tahma's.

The young lass was growing more angrier by the second as a loud growl hummed in her stomach.

"The nerve of these guys! Where the heck is Matuka? Is he in one of their rooms?" Yanielle asked as she walked up to Tahma's bedroom door.

Yanielle then paused to control her breathing and frustration as she rubbed her vacant stomach.

"Hey! Open up! We're tired of waiting!" Yanielle screamed to the door as she knocked continuously.

Without warning, Tahma opened the door quickly and came out of the room.

"You ever heard of personal space, weirdo?" Yanielle asked after Tahma walked up to her and leaned in awfully close to her face.

"Interesting," Tahma said as he fixed his glasses with his right hand.

"Back up!" Yanielle said as she pushed Tahma away, which caused him to stumble back into his room.

"Hey, that hurt," Tahma said in a soft voice as he caught his balance.

"Well you shouldn't get so close! Anyway, have you seen Matuka? He said all of you had something to add to the meal. Where is he? And what's up with no one answering their doors?" Yanielle asked with an attitude.

"Interesting, I have no idea, I didn't even hear you knocking, I was coming out to go ask Matuka a question and there you were. But I told him I was skipping supper and he left afterwards," Tahma said as he scratched his head with his left hand.

Yanielle then remembered that Kotoyami said she couldn't hear any knocking as well, so she calmed down a little.

"So, you don't know where he went?" Yanielle asked the young genius as he stood in the door.

"Sorry, but no. But hey, here, this is for the meal," Tahma quickly replied as he handed her a stalk of sugarcane.

"Great! Thanks for nothing," Yanielle said before she threw the stalk down the hallway towards the galley.

As she walked away stomping and pouting, Tahma decided not to follow her to Matuka, so he closed his bedroom door to continue his research. As Yanielle turned the corner to head up the stairs to go to the main deck, Jubilaree came out of his room. The tired lad then looked down only to notice the red-onion and sugarcane in front of his door.

"Huh?" Jubilaree asked as he looked at the sugarcane and onion.

After he saw the food that was laying by his door, Jubilaree looked back and forth down the hallway. Jubilaree quickly decided to keep the food, so he picked it up and then closed his door. Meanwhile, the enraged Yanielle had reached the Captain's quarters.

"When I get my hands on you," Yanielle mumbled as she started to knock on the door.

Suddenly, the Captain's quarter's door opened on its own and Matuka wasn't at the door.

"What the?!" Yanielle shrieked from being surprised.

Yanielle then decided to peek her head inside to see if Matuka was in the room.

"It's really dark in here," Yanielle said as she stuck her head in the door.

After she fully stepped in his cabin, the room and all its contents began to glow.

"Whoa, now this is what you call a room," Yanielle said softly as she scanned the room for Matuka.

To Yanielle's surprise, she saw Matuka lying in bed asleep with all his clothes on.

"Really?" Yanielle asked as her rage turned into sympathy.

Yanielle then walked over to the sleeping Matuka and took off his left boot.

"You could have told me you were more tired than hungry; you know?" Yanielle asked as she reached for the other boot to take off.

After Yanielle took off his boots, she walked over to the head of the bed and removed his tri-cone hat.

"You are something else Matuka," Yanielle said with a smile while she stared at the young, unconscious, Captain.

Yanielle then grabbed Matuka's blanket that was red with gray and navy-blue patches on it; that seemed to have been kicked to the foot of the bed, to cover him.

"There you go Captain," Yanielle said while she blushed.

After she covered Matuka with his blanket, Yanielle turned around and proceeded out of the Captain's quarters. Before she left the room, Yanielle took one more look at Matuka and smiled.

"Goodnight, my King," Yanielle said before leaving his room.

When she left his room and closed the door, she leaned up against it with her back, then threw her head to the sky.

"Whoa," Yanielle said after a shooting star shot across the night's sky.

She then took a moment to stare at the trillions of stars in the sky. As she admired the beauty of the Creator, she became overwhelmed with peace and joy.

"This can't be life though," Yanielle said as she took a deep sigh and dropped her head.

Yanielle then decided to head back to the galley because she realized how late it had become and she was still very hungry. By the time Yanielle made it back to the galley, Kotoyami was gone and so was the food she was preparing.

"Are you kidding me?!" Yanielle shouted from frustration as she looked around the empty galley and saloon.

She saw that the fish was still sitting in one of the stainless-steel bowls that was filled with fresh water, along with her vegetables and herbs lying on the table. The hungry and upset Yanielle let out a ferocious scream before she left the galley. She swore quite a bit as she walked down the west hallway to Kotoyami's room door.

"Kotoyami! Open up!" Yanielle shouted as she knocked at Kotoyami's door.

After a couple of minutes went by, Kotoyami opened the door in her sleeping apparel.

"Yanielle? What are you doing here?" Kotoyami asked Yanielle as they both stood in the doorway.

"What do you mean? You couldn't hear me knocking?" Yanielle asked.

"No, not at first, I was asleep, you can't tell?" Kotoyami questioned.

"Well what happened? You didn't wait for me? Why?" Yanielle asked with a frown.

"Look, I was tired and hungry. I got nauseous waiting for you because you took too long to return," Kotoyami quickly replied with a stoic face.

"But you knew what I was going to go do. You didn't even save me any," Yanielle replied with an attitude.

"Listen, if you weren't so busy trying to please Matuka and the others, you could have eaten just like I did," Kotoyami immediately snapped back.

"Oh really?" Yanielle said with a shocked look on her face.

"Yes, you're so in love with the Captain, you put your own needs aside for him. Not me, I come first, and I will always make sure I'm okay before anyone else," Kotoyami said as she looked Yanielle in the eyes with a piercing stare.

"Excuse me for not being selfish!" Yanielle said before she stormed off down the hall to her own room.

"Whatever," Kotoyami said as Yanielle slammed her door after she entered her room.

Kotoyami then closed her door and headed back to bed, while Yanielle let out her frustrations in her own room.

"The nerve! I can't believe her! None of them! They're all jerks!" Yanielle said as she stood in the middle of her room crying.

After a couple of minutes, Yanielle wiped her tears and grabbed a handful of green grapes from a vine growing in her room from the floor. As soon as Yanielle finished eating her grapes, she plopped down on her bed and fell asleep from being mentally exhausted. It was two hours past midnight, and everyone was sound asleep from the busy day that they all experienced.

The ocean was calm, the air was cold, the sky was clear and accompanied with trillions of stars. The moon reflected off the ocean waves and the black vessel shrouded itself with its own fog. The next day brought about a new wind; for war was brewing and was about to rear its ugly head once more. Matuka was lying in bed when his retractable north wall slid upward and exposed the sunrise, peeking into the bow of the ship. Hues of aqua-blue, yellow, pink, and orange shined in the room from the sky and beautiful ocean. A most magnificent display of light danced around the young Captain's room which caused him to awake with a deep yawn.

"Good morning," Matuka said after he deeply yawned and before he got out of bed.

After Matuka stood to his feet and faced the west wall, he leaned back to stretch with his arms spread open.

"That was some of the best sleep I think I ever had. Okay Matuka! What are we doing today?" Matuka asked aloud while he looked around his quarters.

After admiring his room, Matuka looked

to the northwest corner of the room at his closed-off bathing room and decided to get cleaned up.

"I don't think I ever took a bath in a place as nice as this before. It's completely private and only has room for one," Matuka said as he walked over to the doorway of the small bathing room.

After getting undressed, Matuka sat in the large wooden tub of warm water as he contemplated the plans he had for the day.

"Maybe I should show them around today, yeah, that'd be cool. I'll take Jubilaree and Kotoyami to the training deck. Then Tahma, Dayhoon and Umbati to the gun deck so they could have a look at those weapons. Then for Yanielle, I'll take her to the stowage deck where all the live and prepped food is," Matuka said as he rested in the warm water with his arms up on the edge of the tub, and his head leaned back to the ceiling.

Meanwhile, it was the hour past daybreak and Yanielle was in the kitchen cooking her breakfast and still upset from the night prior. She was at the north wall's prepping counter cleaning the fish that had soaked overnight in the stainless-steel bowl.

"I can't believe them! Such jerks! They're lucky that I had an unbelievably good night's rest!" Yanielle shouted as she threw the fish down on the counter to her right.

At that very moment, Jubilaree walked in the galley from the east hallway and peered in at Yanielle. She did not notice Jubilaree staring at her, so she continued by picking up the fish she had thrown and started to descale it. Suddenly, Yanielle's eyes began to water, her nose began to twitch, and she started to cough.

"What in the hell is that?!" Yanielle screamed as she covered her nose and turned around.

She immediately saw that Jubilaree was facing and sitting behind her on top of the picnic-style table.

"What's your problem brat?" Jubilaree asked softly with his arms crossed as he looked up with his right eye.

"Is that you? Man! You stank as hell! You ever heard of a bath?" Yanielle asked as she covered her face with her right forearm while she looked to him.

In that moment, Matuka, Tahma, Dayhoon and Umbati all walked into the galley from the east entrance.

"Oh my! You guys do know that there are two bathing rooms on the other side of this north wall, right? The one on the west hallway is the girls, and the one on the east hallway is the guys. Don't worry, they are completely blocked off from another. So, feel free to bathe now," Matuka stuttered after he walked in and covered his nose.

"Interesting," Tahma said as he fixed his glasses with his right hand and then covered his nose.

"Whoa that's raunchy, what's that smell?" Dayhoon asked and chuckled as he looked down towards Umbati.

"Man, y'all stank as hell in here!" Umbati laughed as he covered his nose with his left hand.

Immediately after that, Kotoyami walked in the galley from the west hallway and instantly paused before she went all the way in.

"Shameful, you all should be ashamed," Kotoyami said before she quickly walked up to where Yanielle was.

She then took a piece of fish out of the left, wooden barrel underneath the red-cedar table and walked back towards the west entry.

"Well good morning to you too," Jubilaree said with his arms crossed, eye closed and head down.

"Excuse me? I know you not getting slick out the mouth," Yanielle quickly replied to Kotoyami before she could exit.

"Did I miss something?" Matuka asked Yanielle and Kotoyami as he looked at them both.

"I'll be in my room," Kotoyami replied

before she quickly exited the galley.

"Oh my God!" Umbati screamed as he grabbed Dayhoon's left hand with his right hand.

"What bro?" Dayhoon asked as he turned to his left and looked down to his younger brother.

"Look!" Umbati said as he pointed into the saloon from noticing all the wine and rum.

"No way!" Dayhoon shouted as he and Umbati's eyes lit up from excitement.

"Oh, hell no! I don't think so, Matuka stop them!" Yanielle shouted as Dayhoon and Umbati scrambled into the saloon.

The brothers were in the saloon at the bar; grabbing bottles before the rest of the crew could blink their eyes.

"Matuka, may I have a look at this gun deck you spoke so highly of?" Tahma asked as he turned to his right and looked at Matuka.

"Well, uh," Matuka stuttered as he looked back and forth from the brothers to Tahma.

"Are you just gonna ignore me?" Yanielle screamed from the red-cedar table.

Suddenly, a parade of knives flew into the middle of the galley's floor, which caused everyone to stop what they were doing to focus on what had happened. Dayhoon and Umbati walked out from the saloon; each with a bottle of their own in hand, they looked to the west entrance of the galley.

"If I wasn't mistaken, I'd think you were aiming at me and missed," Jubilaree said with a serious voice as he looked to his left towards Kotoyami.

"All of you are like babies! Just shut up!" Kotoyami screamed with her eyes closed and arms down by her side.

"Now's our chance!" Tahma said as he quickly snatched Matuka's shirt collar and drug him out of the galley, down the hallway, towards the bow of the ship.

"Tahma, you little weasel! And who the heck are you accusing of acting like babies?! Let's get it right girlfriend, you're the one who was salty about everyone not showing up last night for supper! That's why you took everything you made to your room and ate it all for yourself! Just admit it, your feelings were hurt Kotoyami!" Yanielle screamed as she looked to her right towards the angry and heavily panting Kotoyami.

Kotoyami's eyes began to glow and she began to walk quickly towards Yanielle. That's when Jubilaree leaped in front of Kotoyami before she could reach Yanielle.

"Oh! You want some of this?! Well come on!" Yanielle screamed with her fist balled towards Kotoyami.

"This is too much, I'm headed back to the saloon," Umbati said as he looked on at Jubilaree, Kotoyami and Yanielle, who were arguing.

"Sounds good to me brother," Dayhoon said as he looked down at Umbati.

The two brothers walked away from the mayhem back into the saloon where they sat at the bar.

"Let me go onion breath!" Kotoyami kicked and screamed while Jubilaree held her off the ground in a bear hug.

"I don't think so! Not if you don't calm down!" Jubilaree shouted back at Kotoyami while she tried to wiggle and hold her breath from smelling him.

After Jubilaree calmed down Kotoyami, she snatched away from him and exited the galley once more from the west entry.

"That was close," Jubilaree said after he let out a deep sigh with his head down.

"I'd be mad too if your stank-self tried to hold me down too!" Yanielle said as she looked towards Jubilaree.

"You know what?! Next time I'll let her just kick your butt!" Jubilaree shouted before he stormed out of the galley into the east hallway.

Meanwhile, when Matuka and Tahma finally reached the gun deck, Tahma nearly had a heart attack from what he saw.

"Interesting! Is that a? No way! Are those?! What the heck Matuka?!!" Tahma screamed as he leaped with excitement.

Tahma then ran down the stairs and around the huge gun deck that was filled with all sorts of mechanical treasures.

"I told you so, all you need now is the brothers, Dayhoon and Umbati," Matuka said with a smile as he watched Tahma run around the deck in circles.

Tahma couldn't help himself as he looked at the heaps of weapons and mechanical parts.

"Unbelievable!!" Tahma said as he purposely ignored Matuka's response.

"Did you hear me Tahma?" Matuka questioned as he walked up to the thrilled young genius.

"Yes, I did, I'd rather take my chances with trying to teach a fish to help me," Tahma quickly replied as he picked up a couple of large, dusty scrolls he saw on the floor to his right; next to a large heap of weapons.

"Don't be like that Tahma, I'm sure they will be of good service, I'm sure you feel it too," Matuka said as he gently placed his left hand on Tahma's right shoulder.

"Interesting, okay, sure, I'll give it a try, Captain," Tahma said as he fixed the scrolls in his hand.

Unexpectedly, Yanielle burst through the door, walked down the black, alligator-skinned stairs onto the gun deck, as the brothers cursed and stumbled behind her.

"Interesting," Tahma said as he fixed his glasses with his right hand.

"I can't and will not deal with these two anymore, Matuka!" Yanielle screamed as she pushed Tahma out of the way with her body so she could stand in front of the young Captain.

"Hey! That hurt!" Tahma said as he looked up at Yanielle from the ground; before he tried to gather the scrolls again.

"Hey, hey, calm down. What's the problem Yanielle?" Matuka asked as he looked into her beautiful eyes.

"These two are morons!" Yanielle screamed.

"Why thank you," Dayhoon replied sarcastically as Umbati belched very loudly.

"You see?!" Yanielle screamed towards Matuka as she pointed to her right at the brothers.

"Honestly, I don't, Yanielle, why do you let them get to you?" Matuka asked as he looked to his left at the brothers.

That's when Umbati passed gas obnoxiously loud, which made Dayhoon and him laugh.

"Score!" Umbati yelled with a laugh.

"Freaking sick bro," Dayhoon laughed as they gave each other a high-five.

"You're blind if you don't see that! They're freaking gross, they drink like adults, they curse every other word, and they're perverts!" Yanielle shouted as she grabbed Matuka by the shoulders.

"Come with me," Matuka said as he grabbed Yanielle's waist with his left arm and made her walk with him.

When Matuka and Yanielle rushed past Tahma, they nearly knocked him back down to the floor again.

"Hey! You're just going to leave me here with these two?" Tahma screamed as he turned around to look at the brothers, then back to Matuka and Yanielle.

"You'll be fine Tahma! I believe in you," Matuka said as he looked over his left shoulder.

"It's not me who I have a problem believing in Matuka," Tahma said softly as he slowly turned around to face the brothers.

Further down on the gun deck towards the stern of the ship, Matuka and Yanielle were out of vision from the others.

"Where are you taking me Matuka? I mean Captain," Yanielle asked Matuka as she pulled away from his side.

"Do you see those three sets of stairs leading down Yanielle?" Matuka questioned as he looked towards her.

"Yeah, and so what?" Yanielle asked while she looked on at the steps.

"The one to the left leads down into the food stowage, the one in the middle leads to the training deck, and the other leads down into a room of miscellaneous supplies. I'm currently taking you to the food stowage so you can have peace of mind around things you enjoy," Matuka said with a smile as he grabbed Yanielle's hands once more, which caused her to blush.

"*How does he know what I enjoy? Jerk!*" Yanielle thought to herself as she smiled and frowned repeatedly.

Meanwhile, Tahma was growing more impatient as the brothers interrupted his studies with noise and commotion.

"What are you doing four eyes?" Umbati slurred as he stood on the crowded table and leaned over the quiet Tahma.

Tahma only had a small place to put up his arms and the scrolls so he wasn't moving.

"Bang! Bang!" Umbati screamed before Tahma jumped and fell backwards.

"Hey what's your malfunction?" Tahma said as he looked up at the intoxicated Umbati.

While Umbati was interrupting Tahma's studies, Dayhoon was drinking and wasting rum on the scrolls Tahma had found.

"No wait! Look at what you're doing!

You'll ruin it!" Tahma screamed as he watched rum pour from Dayhoon's mouth and brown, round-based bottle, onto the fragile scrolls.

"Oops!" Dayhoon laughed as he and Umbati played with broken weapons atop the large table.

"That's it! I have had it! You two are impossible! I hope you choke on a pile of bullets!" Tahma yelled as he grabbed the scrolls, stood up and stormed away from the table.

Up the stairs and out the door, Tahma angrily stomped until he had made it to the main deck.

"Ah, finally, some fresh air," Tahma said after he pushed through the door beneath the helm deck.

Tahma then proceeded onto the all black, polished deck. With the scrolls under his left arm, the young lad looked from right to left at the ship.

"Interesting, it's remarkable," Tahma said as he headed to the left towards port side.

After Tahma got to the bulwarks, he laid down his scrolls next to the scuppers on the deck and rested his arms on the silver bulwarks. With his head down, Tahma let out a deep yawn and sigh.

"The curious space invader has had too much of people for today? It's two hours before noon, the day hasn't even started yet," Jubilaree said before he jumped down to the main deck behind Tahma.

"Interesting, that doesn't hurt? One would think it would be hard on the knees," Tahma said after he completely turned around to see Jubilaree; standing with his arms crossed and eye closed.

"No," Jubilaree said as he walked over to the bulwarks and looked to the sea.

"Interesting," Tahma said as he crept closely to Jubilaree to have a closer look at his face.

"You got two seconds," Jubilaree threatened Tahma after he closed his right eye.

"Interesting, I wonder," Tahma said as he reached for the bandanna that was wrapped around Jubilaree's head that covered his left eye.

In an instant, Jubilaree grabbed Tahma's right hand and bent back his wrist until he nearly broke it.

"Ouch! Hey! That hurts! Stop it!!" Tahma screamed at the top of his lungs.

"Just what in the hell do you think you're doing?!" Jubilaree yelled as he pushed Tahma to the black deck.

"I was just trying to see what happened to your eye," Tahma said as he grabbed his right wrist and sat on the deck.

Tahma was in too much pain, so all he

could do was look up to the angry Jubilaree.

"Mind your damn business! My eyes are of none of your concerns!" Jubilaree shouted at Tahma before he stormed off and went back below deck.

Suddenly, a gust of wind came and pushed the scrolls down the silver-outlined scuppers into the ocean.

"No!" Tahma screamed loudly as he watched the scrolls sink into the ocean.

At that time, Jubilaree was walking to his room when he noticed the drunken brothers standing in front of their door.

"Hey, look big bro, it's onion breath," Umbati laughed before he burped and gave his brother a high-five.

"You're two to talk, you can't even hold your rum but want to drink like you can. You smell from here! And at least I can keep a conversation and function while smitten by the drink," Jubilaree quickly replied in a stoic manner.

"How about we head up to the main deck and I'll show you how well I can handle you and this rum," Dayhoon said as he took a sip from the large rum bottle.

"You keep it up and you'll have to show me bastard," Jubilaree said before he walked into his room and slammed the door.

"Chicken," Umbati quickly said after Jubilaree closed his door.

"Hmp," Dayhoon muffled as he opened their room door and walked in.

Meanwhile, at that time, Matuka left the stowage deck where he took Yanielle and had stepped onto the empty gun deck.

"Where are the guys? I thought it could be absolutely nothing that could pull them away from this place; strange," Matuka said as he looked around the gun deck.

Meanwhile, Kotoyami was leaving her room to go take a bath. As Kotoyami walked down the west hallway with just her towel wrapped around her body, she looked at the walls and floor of the ship in detail. After Kotoyami got closer, she hoped no one was in the galley, so she quickly ran past its entry and continued. About twenty-five feet from the galley's entrance was another door on the right that led into the girls bathing room. When Kotoyami got to the entry of the head and bathing area, the first thing she noticed from looking inside was that it appeared to be completely made of dark-oakwood.

"Wow, this is incredible, the seats of ease are normally in the front of the ship near the bowsprit. I knew it was strange when I didn't see any. However, these are separated from one another with their own wall," Kotoyami said as she peeked into the huge bathhouse.

At that time, Matuka had left the gun deck and finally reached the second deck. As Matuka walked down the east hallway towards the bow of the ship, he passed the galley and peeped inside.

"No one is here; I wonder what everyone else is up to. I should probably prepare supper early; we don't need a repeat of last night," Matuka said as he fully stepped into the galley.

While Matuka stood at the counter on the north wall of the galley, he noticed that there was food still out on top of it that needed to be cooked immediately.

"Wow, this stuff has been out since last night, it needs to be cooked or else it will go bad," Matuka said as he picked up the same fish from last night and earlier.

After an hour passed Kotoyami was finally leaving the bathing room.

"That was the best bath I think I ever had," Kotoyami chuckled as she wrapped her dark-red towel around her body.

After leaving the bathing room, Kotoyami continued down the hall until she reached the west entry to the galley.

"Crap! Did he see me?" Kotoyami asked herself after she nearly walked past the doorway of the galley while Matuka was inside.

With her back against the wall, she leaned over to peep around the corner into the galley's entrance.

"What's he doing?" Kotoyami questioned while she looked on at Matuka.

Matuka continued to clean and prep the food because he did not see Kotoyami watching him from the hallway. Kotoyami then decided it was time to run to her room before anybody else could see her. After Kotoyami ran past without being seen, she continued all the way to her room and closed her bedroom door.

A few hours passed and the sun had begun to set; while Matuka had finally finished cooking, everyone came out of their rooms into the galley, one after another.

"Hey guys, so the whole crew is here. Are you guys hungry? I felt bad for the way things went last night and I wanted to make it up to everyone, so I cooked," Matuka turned around and said with a smile before he opened his eyes to look at everyone.

"Yeah, it smells like you burnt something in here jack," Umbati slurred and laughed as he looked at the food platter Matuka was holding.

"Well at least he tried jerk!" Yanielle shouted from the west entry of the galley towards Umbati.

"Hey, don't talk to my brother like that you godless Jezebel," Dayhoon yelled back to Yanielle.

"Jezebel? You know what? Up yours sideways scallywag! Don't talk to me like that! It's the truth! He needs to be more grateful!" Yanielle screamed.

"Shut your mouth before I close it for you," Dayhoon quickly replied.

All the while, Umbati stood there confused and torn because he didn't know which side to take.

"Hey quit bro!" Umbati screamed to Dayhoon.

"What? I know you're not taking her side! Especially when I was defending you!" Dayhoon yelled back to Umbati.

The brothers then stared fiercely at each other while Kotoyami grew more frustrated.

"She's only standing up for Matuka because she likes him," Kotoyami said with an annoyed facial expression.

"Calm down everyone, let's have some peace and order here," Matuka calmly said to the crew as he looked back and forth to everyone.

"You got one more time to try me homegirl and we are gonna have serious problems," Yanielle said as she turned around, then stood up from the picnic table and looked at Kotoyami.

Tahma then walked over to Kotoyami, got awfully close to her face, and stared at her.

"Interesting," Tahma said as he walked up, fixed his glasses with his right hand, and glared at Kotoyami.

Without warning, Kotoyami pushed Tahma backwards until he fell into Yanielle, who was sitting down at the table. When Tahma fell into Yanielle, the hot cup of cocoa she was drinking flew all over Dayhoon.

"Damn it! Watch what the hell you're doing you idiot!" Dayhoon yelled to Yanielle.

Suddenly, Umbati pushed Dayhoon backwards, which caused him to fall into Matuka. When Dayhoon fell on Matuka, all the food he had been preparing on the counter was thrown to the floor.

"It was the chicken head virago you're so in love with that caused this!" Umbati screamed as he pointed to his older brother.

Everyone except Matuka began to yell at each other. It didn't take them long to start throwing kitchenware and food around the galley.

"That's enough! I have had it with all of you! I tried my best today to do right by you all! But this is what I get for trying?! Well guess what?! I'm done trying! You can feed yourself you ungrateful heathens! I'm going to my quarters and don't you dare even think about bothering me!" Matuka yelled before he stormed out the galley to head to his cabin.

"This is your fault!" Yanielle screamed to Kotoyami as she walked up to her with her fist balled.

"You have five seconds to get out of my face before you regret your decision of walking up to me," Kotoyami said as she cracked her knuckles.

Throughout the night, the lad and lasses argued every time they crossed paths. There was no peace below deck and the young Captain had no idea what was going on in his absence. The next day brought about disaster and mayhem for the crew; an epic battle at sea, for it brewed all night. Matuka was in a deep sleep and was having the worst nightmare imaginable.

Everywhere the young lad looked was horrid, fires were kindled; explosions were kept, and smoke came with wide open arms. There had appeared to be a great loss amongst the sea; for the young Captain saw his destiny forming at hand. The lads and lasses were on the floor of a strange vessel and they were all dead; lying in a circle formation, covered in their own blood.

"Oh no! What happened?! How?! No! No! This can't be! Why?!" Matuka cried as he looked at everyone, including himself.

Matuka then dropped to his knees in mid-air as he floated above the scene. Unexpectedly, the ocean began to bubble, and a loud voice came with the waves that splashed onto the deceased.

"Remember, remember the pact!" the mysterious and loud voice shouted to Matuka.

"Huh? The pact?" Matuka asked softly as he tried to make sense of what he just heard.

All of a sudden, the vessel disappeared and Matuka fell into the ocean as though he was on the ship to begin with.

"Help! Help!" Matuka continuously yelled while he futilely grabbed for the surface of the water.

"Remember the pact or die!" the mysterious voice yelled to Matuka.

"I don't know the pact! I can't remember the pact!" Matuka screamed and cried as he tried to stay afloat.

In an instant, Matuka awoke from his dream and looked around his room before he wiped the sweat from his forehead.

"That was intense," Matuka said softly while he looked out the bow of his ship through the large porthole.

Matuka wiped his eyes and turned to sit on the edge of the bed while he faced his bathing room.

"*That was the weirdest dream ever and it felt so real. Not cool,*" Matuka thought to himself as he stood and stretched.

That's when the room went from a beautiful array of colors to a dark gray; instantly.

"Huh? That's weird," Matuka said as he looked through the retractable wall's porthole at the sky.

The thunder was crackling, and the wind added to the strength of the waves, which caused the ship to rock.

"Whoa, I should go check on the crew," Matuka said as he began to get dressed.

After Matuka got fully dressed, he looked to his quiver that was lying on the bed and paused.

"I should empty this from the important stuff now," Matuka said as he grabbed the black-leathered quiver and walked over to the middle of the west wall; where a long, skinny, golden-brown table sat.

As Matuka stood in front of the table and emptied out the quiver, he could see the lightning flashing into the room. Matuka then carefully looked at his beloved's aged compass, spyglass, ring, and journal once it fell onto the table.

"I'll be taking that," Matuka said as he quickly picked up the gold and green emerald ring from the golden-brown, warm table's surface.

After admiring the ring, he placed it on his right middle finger, he looked towards his beloved's journal and began to get dizzy.

"That's weird, whoa, that kinda hurts," Matuka said as he grabbed his forehead with his right hand.

Matuka then caught his balance and looked to the main compartment on his quiver; where he noticed he was running low on arrows.

"That's no good, but we can fix that," Matuka said as he looked to the right at the northwest corner of the room; where guns, swords and all sorts of weapons were located.

That's when it started to rain without any remorse and the winds grew more violent.

"This weather is ridiculous," Matuka said before he let out a deep sigh.

Matuka then walked over to the northwest corner and dug around in the barrel that was filled with weapons.

"Wow, I never seen arrowheads like these before," Matuka said as he looked at the arrowheads.

After grabbing some unfamiliar arrows, Matuka filled his quiver, threw it over his head and draped it around his left arm. Matuka then walked past his beautiful desk and up the stairs to his room door. As soon as Matuka opened his door, he saw Dayhoon fly into the wall to the right of him.

"What the hell?!" Matuka asked as he

stared at the bleeding Dayhoon.

"You son of a mitch!" Dayhoon yelled to Jubilaree, who kicked him from the middle of the deck into the wall with ease.

Dayhoon then charged for Jubilaree, when Tahma went flying across the ship from the right, into the riggings and lanyards. Immediately after that, he saw Umbati running and sliding in the rain, chasing after Kotoyami.

"What the hell is going on here?!" Matuka yelled but to no avail because no one was listening, so the fighting continued.

Matuka then ran to the middle of the ship; where he screamed and tried to plea with the crew to stop. All of a sudden, Matuka began to feel uneasy and his dream resurfaced to his memory.

"Déjà vu," Matuka said as he looked around his ship in fear of the chaos that was taking place.

Yanielle was then punched into the jib by Kotoyami from the helm deck and fell, which caused Kotoyami to laugh. Shortly after that, Tahma came swinging from the riggings and lanyards and kicked Kotoyami in the face.

"That's for earlier!" Tahma screamed to Kotoyami as he jumped to the wet deck.

"You're mine! You little worm!" Kotoyami screamed as she looked down to Tahma.

"Oh no you don't!" Yanielle screamed as

she grabbed Kotoyami from behind and wrapped her arms around her waist.

"How?!" Kotoyami screamed as she quickly looked back to Yanielle.

"Never underestimate me again!" Yanielle screamed as she squeezed tighter onto Kotoyami.

Yanielle then picked up Kotoyami backwards over her head to slam Kotoyami on the ground. At that time, Tahma had run and kicked Dayhoon in the back of the left leg as Jubilaree clotheslined him from the right side onto the deck. That's when Jubilaree and Tahma were punched in the face by Umbati, which cause them to be pushed into Matuka very hard. Matuka was simultaneously flung off the ship into the ocean; where the water was cold, and the waves were as violent as they ever were. Everyone saw Matuka fall into the ocean at the same time but continued to fight without ceasing. All the while, Matuka was sinking fast in the cold dark waters.

"I'm gonna die, we're all gonna die! I failed father, I'm sorry! I was too weak!" Matuka thought to himself as he sank deeper and deeper.

The closer Matuka got to the bottom of the ship, the darker it became, and more oxygen slipped from his lungs. All of a sudden, Matuka heard a familiar voice and opened his eyes immediately.

"The pact!" the voice said loudly.

Matuka nearly drowned in that moment because he let out half of the oxygen he had left; in less than a second.

"What the hell is that?! I'm dead! I'm going to die!" Matuka thought to himself as he stared to the bottom of the ship.

For behold, at the bottom of the black vessel was the King of all octopi; the ancient and prehistoric gigantic sea tyrant of times passed. It was attached to the bottom with ease as if it was just simply holding on like a barnacle on a joyride.

"The pact!" the creature yelled telepathically at Matuka.

"What pact? Damn it!" Matuka asked as he urinated on himself from being completely terrified.

"Remember or die!" the creature yelled telepathically.

That's when Matuka was met with the memory of the day he spoke with his beloved for the last time. The vision of the Captain and crew grew clearer as the ocean grew darker.

The young Captain faintly heard the words of his beloved, "My dear boy, you are indeed strong and you must know this, though the distance between us has grown and the notion of time has changed, we will never part for we are one. It is not your fault. You have been given a very special opportunity, a second chance; fate has called. It's up to you Matuka to carry on, to be the salt of the earth and thy brother's keeper. Be kind to others, run from no fight, you have the strength to overcome any opposition. You will be one of the strongest warriors amongst nations and even known to man. The waters of the rain, the rivers, lakes, ponds, swamps, bayous, canals, puddles, the oceans, and seas will be your footstool. The sea animals will hear your cry and aid you always and forever, for you are their alpha, their friend and protector, but only after you declare it so."

Matuka was going unconscious but immediately awoke when he heard the final words.

"That's it! I remember! Thank you, father!" Matuka thought to himself as he closed his eyes.

"The pact!" the prehistoric creature yelled one final time.

"I declare it so, from this day forward that I, Matuka, will protect these oceans and seas with my life! I declare that I will forever love and respect the water's inhabitants! And that from this day we will never part!" Matuka screamed in the water with all his heart before he began to fall unconscious.

Without warning, the boat began to vibrate, and the crew paused in their fighting. Back beneath the ship, the prehistoric King octopus detached from the bottom of the ship and swam beneath Matuka. The moment the creature touched Matuka, he awoke and could breathe underwater.

"What?! I can breathe?! How?" the shocked young Captain questioned.

"As long as you touch me or any other aquatic animal, you'll be able to breathe," the gigantic octopus replied telepathically.

Matuka rested on a tentacle and could see the creature's eyes as they looked back into his own; they were bright yellow with specks of green in the iris. He could feel the creature's emotions and hear its thoughts fully. Suddenly, all sorts of sea creatures came and started swimming towards Matuka.

"*Whoa!*" Matuka thought as he witnessed all the sea creatures that came to surround him and the giant octopus.

There were some he was familiar with and ones he never thought existed. One of each kind came and swam up against him with their bodies to show their loyalty was now his. A few of the sea creatures had some of his arrows that fell out of his quiver, so they brought it back to him.

"Thanks guys, I didn't even realize I dropped any," Matuka said telepathically.

"My pleasure, sire," a killer whale replied telepathically as he swam past and dropped the arrow.

After all the sea creatures quickly introduced themselves, from fish to the turtles; to the sharks to the unknowns, the large grayish-brown and dark-purple spotted ancient beast, started to rise to the surface. Back above water, on the main deck, the fight had resumed but was about to come to an immediate halt. While the entire crew was still fighting and throwing blows, the water began to bubble erratically. Without warning, Matuka quickly emerged from the water as he stood atop the head of the King of all octopus.

"Ahh! What the hell is that?!" everyone screamed in unison as they looked up to Matuka, who was standing taller than the ship on an ancient monster.

"Interesting," Tahma said as he fixed his glasses with his right hand.

"I can't believe what I am seeing!" Jubilaree shouted.

"Unreal!" Dayhoon yelled immediately after.

"Unbelievable," Kotoyami whispered.

"Matuka what the hell?!" Yanielle screamed.

"Cool I want to try!" Umbati shouted last.

Matuka then began to walk off the beast head as though he planned to fall into the ocean.

"Hey, what's he doing?!" Jubilaree shouted.

Simultaneously, the tentacles of the King octopus began to make a stairway for Matuka to walk down to get to the crew's level. As Matuka got close, the last tentacle he stepped on carried him in front of the crew. Everyone ran near to port side where they looked on at Matuka and his beast.

"Whoa!" Jubilaree said as they all witnessed every creature; they could think of sticking their heads out of the water; surrounding the beast and Matuka.

"What are those?!" Umbati yelled as he pointed to two very strange-looking sea creatures.

"Silence! This fighting and discord has gone on long enough!" Matuka yelled as the rain picked up harder and the lightning flashed more viciously.

The crew stood still in the rain and waited for the young Captain to speak; for they were too afraid to move another step.

"I Matuka, Captain of the ship with the black sails, call you all forward to your destiny! We have been given a very special opportunity, a second chance at life and fate has called us all into her chambers. It's up to us to be our brother's keeper. Our people have destroyed so much and took so many lives. We owe it to the lives lost and the ocean to be kind to others. We will obviously never run from any fight because we have the strength to overcome any opposition.

We will be the strongest guild amongst the continents and known to man. The waters of the rain, the rivers, lakes, ponds, swamps, bayous, canals, puddles, the oceans, and seas will be our footstool, from this day forward. The animals will now hear our cries and aid us always and forever. You are their friends and protectors; we are their family. The fog will be our shield everywhere we go; this vessel has no limits. This is your ship, you are now and forever more, a member of the Hyungetta, the crew with the black sails," Matuka shouted as the wind and rain flowed harder.

"Hyungetta? What's that? What if I don't want to?" Yanielle asked as the rest of the crew looked back between Matuka and her.

Without warning, the ship began to vibrate and on all the sails appeared the silhouette of a flying fish with sharp fins, large sharp wings and three sharp fins on its back. At that moment, the same symbol appeared on the top of the crew's right hand, including Matuka's. After everyone noticed the new guild crest and emblem on their hand, the prehistoric beast placed Matuka back on the ship gently with its long thick tentacle. When Matuka was let down, he turned around and thanked the octopus for saving his life.

"Thank you, Iraja," Matuka said as he smiled and waved to the giant octopus.

All the creatures then descended back into the ocean from whence they came, and the King of the octopi connected back to the bottom of the ship in his original place.

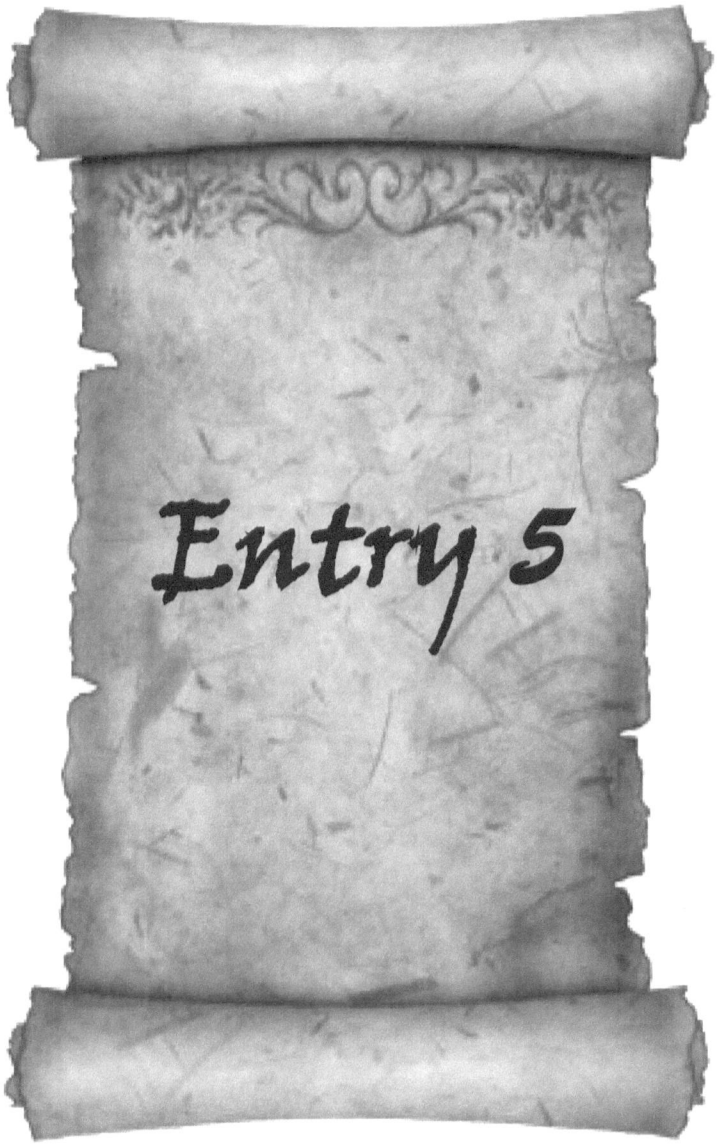

Entry 5

THE BOND

The crew stood in fear and awe as they looked upon their young, brave Captain. They all had so many questions to ask and little did they know; that it was the beginning of a bond that could never be broken. A bond that would last through all the ages and to the end of time, a crew, a guild, a family, the Hyungetta had been established.

Just as it started, the thunderous rain-storm suddenly stopped; the clouds disappeared, and the sun came out to dry their wet, wounded bodies. As Matuka walked to the crew with his head held high, they quickly encamped around him.

"So, just like that, huh?" Jubilaree asked with a smirk as he looked down at his right hand, then back to Matuka.

"What do you mean?" Matuka asked with a smile as he grabbed the back of his head with his left hand and then closed his eyes.

"I see you're back to your normal self," Jubilaree said with a smile before he closed his eye and crossed his arms.

"Interesting, it appears to be something supernatural going on here, there is more to research," Tahma said as he fixed his glasses with his right hand while he looked to Matuka.

"Definitely," Kotoyami quickly said as she and Tahma walked closer to Matuka.

"I can dig it," Dayhoon said as he shrugged his shoulders and then looked down to his left at Umbati.

"As long as he teaches me that, I'm down!" Umbati shouted with an eager smile.

"So, what the heck was that about?! Am I going crazy?! Why is everyone acting like that didn't just happen? He was on top of a freaking octopus! And it was freaking huge! And it didn't kill him! Then all those animals! There were thousands, maybe millions. They were all synchronized in their swimming! They actually acted as if they were listening to him and seemed to understand!" Yanielle shouted before everyone started to chuckle and laugh.

This caused Yanielle to grow even more frustrated and upset by not being able to fully grasp the situation.

"Why are all of you laughing?! You're going to piss me off!" Yanielle shouted as she separated from the crew to turn and face them, while she balled up her fist.

"Calm down Yanielle," Matuka said gently as he slowly walked over directly in front of her.

"What do you mean calm down?! What happened to finding our home and memories? I want to know who I am! And it's not only that, from the time this ship arrived and supernaturally saved me, it has been freaking nuts!! To when the room pulled me in, from the design of the room and medical tools, it has gotten weirder and weirder!! From the speed of the ship, to its weird capabilities to shield and protect, then the weird weather and lightning that nearly killed Kotoyami!

Then, you awakened in a subconscious state only to choke her! And then to top it off, here comes you; riding big ole gargantuan like its nothing! The rooms and the ship was too much already! You're just a kid! You could have been killed! I thought I was okay for a second being here, but I was wrong. Now you're telling me, no, all of us, we're a guild and family now?! Right after a damn fight Matuka?! That we've been given a second chance? Yeah to live, not die! And that these animals will be our friends and crap?!

Listen, I know we probably had some part in the war; even if we were just pawns but why should this responsibility be on us?! We're just freaking kids?! Don't get me wrong, this ship is amazing and magical, but I don't know if I can take all of this anymore! I just want to go home!" Yanielle screamed before she dropped to the deck, as many tears fell.

Matuka knelt, wiped her tears with his right thumb and placed his warm hand on her left cheek. Yanielle began to cry more as she could feel the love and concern through his hand. The rest of the crew walked over and surrounded the two as Matuka helped her stand to her feet.

"It's okay Yanielle I understand," Kotoyami said softly with a smile as she placed her left hand on Yanielle's right shoulder.

"Yeah, you don't have to be a baby about it," Jubilaree said with a smile as he looked down to his left and softly tapped her right cheek with his fist.

"We're in this together," Dayhoon said

with a smile as he threw up his left thumb and stood to her right.

"Yeah in the meantime, we'll be your family, we're in this together," Umbati said as he looked up to Yanielle while he stood in between her and Matuka.

"Indeed," Tahma quickly said.

"You see? We're all here willing to put the past behind us and move forward. Yes, we all have the same mission, to find our memories, but I was told that it was more to it than just that. To be honest, from me having this ship and seeing the rooms, to what I was told; to the way you guys came together and the guild crest appearing not only on the ship but our hands, I believe it's more to this after we find our memories.

Now what you all decide to do after we find what we're searching for is clearly up to you. But in the meantime, all we have is each other, there are no adults around. It seems our guilds have caused a great war that left so many casualties. I don't know about any of you, but I feel partially responsible for it all. So, I'm going to right my wrongs all the way to my memories if I have to," Matuka said as he looked at each one of them.

Yanielle then looked around at everyone and could feel the sincerity pulsating off them.

"You guys," Yanielle softly cried as she

gestured for a group hug.

Everyone then grabbed onto one another before their tears started to flow. They all stood there holding and comforting themselves through the worried pains of the unknown. That's when peace began to grow from within them all. Suddenly, Yanielle's surgical tool began to glow beautiful shades of green that encompassed the entire guild.

"Whoa," Umbati said as he looked at her right leg pocket.

"What is it doing?" Dayhoon quickly asked Yanielle before he gazed around at the green auras.

"Interesting," Tahma said as he fixed his glasses with his right hand and leaned in closer to observe her retractor.

"That's strange," Kotoyami said as she looked at her arms.

"What's that?" Jubilaree asked quickly as he glanced at Kotoyami.

"She's healing us without even holding it," Matuka immediately and softly said with a smile.

Everyone then stared to Yanielle and thanked her in unison while the vivid green lights grew more transparent. After everyone loosened their grasp to look at Matuka, he turned around to face the bow of the ship and stared up towards the heavens. It was a few hours past daybreak and the sky was as beautiful as ever. The clouds were placed ever so perfectly in the firmament that it looked like a painting; yet moving slowly from a nice breeze that accompanied light sprays of the ocean.

"Who's hungry?" Matuka said with a smile as he turned around with his eyes closed.

The crew laughed and wiped their tears as Matuka gestured for everyone to follow him below deck after he walked past them. One by one, they followed Matuka into the depths of the ship until they reached the galley in search of a meal.

"Wow!" Matuka said as he stood in the east doorway of the galley; shocked at what he seen.

"Yeah, things got a little out of hand," Dayhoon said with a smirk as he walked past Matuka and picked up a large knife off the galley's deck in front of the table.

That's when Yanielle walked through the east entry, past Matuka and dropped her head.

"But never again Captain," Dayhoon said as he looked to Matuka then to Yanielle.

Yanielle then proceeded to pick up a large handwoven bowl lying by the large picnic table closer to the west entry.

"Yes, never again," Yanielle said with a smile as she looked at Matuka and Dayhoon.

"Hey, I wanna pick up stuff too," Umbati

said as he quickly pushed past Matuka and picked up a large potato he saw lying on the floor next to the brown bin filled with sand.

Kotoyami then walked past Matuka into the galley, gathered the destroyed food near the entry and put them in a bin that was near the northeast wall's corner.

"Interesting," Tahma said as he kneeled and fixed his glasses while he stared at a large, cooked corn stalk.

As Tahma picked up the corn, Jubilaree came up to the threshold of the entry and stood next to Matuka.

"After this I'm going downstairs to have a look around," Jubilaree said before he walked into the saloon and started to clean.

"I wouldn't have it any other way," Matuka smiled and said as Jubilaree walked away.

"Hey, you think you'll be good up here? I'm going to head back to the gun deck to try and get some research and progress done down there," Tahma said as he walked over to Matuka.

"Uh, sure. I think we can handle this," Matuka said with a smile as he looked at the eager young genius.

"Great! Thanks, Matuka, I mean Captain," Tahma said as he fixed his glasses with his right hand.

"You don't mind if we tag along, do you?" Umbati asked as he walked over to Tahma and Matuka.

"Yeah, sorry for the way we acted, it wasn't cool," Dayhoon said as he walked over with his head down and arms crossed.

"Interesting, I didn't see that coming," Tahma said softly as he looked on at the brothers.

"I promise to be a big help and well behaved," Umbati said with a cute childish grin.

Tahma then stood quiet for a couple of seconds to think about it.

"Sure, why not? Only under one condition," Tahma said with his left index finger in the air.

"What's that?" the brothers asked in unison.

"Last one there has to organize the deck," Tahma shouted before he bolted out of the east entry of the galley and down the hallway.

"Oh, you're so on," Dayhoon said with a smirk as he looked up to the entry before he took off running after Tahma.

"Hey! No fair! Wait for me!" Umbati yelled before he chased after them both.

Matuka stood in the middle of the galley and smiled because he felt everything was beginning to come together. Shortly after the three boys left, Matuka walked back over to Yanielle and Kotoyami, who were still focused on cleaning. Matuka then grabbed a rag he saw lying on the main table, kneeled to the deck and began to wipe. The three were moving so fast around the room and floor that they crossed paths many times without colliding, until...

"Ouch!" Kotoyami said sarcastically.

"Oh, hey," Yanielle said as a soft blush appeared across her face.

All three of them ran into one another while hand scrubbing the deck. They then were all lying in a pile on the floor.

"Sorry," Matuka said with his eyes closed and a smile.

"Why are you apologizing? We all ran into each other," Yanielle questioned Matuka with an annoyed and blushing look on her face.

"Why are you cleaning anyway?" Kotoyami asked as she fixed her hair behind her right ear.

"Huh?" Matuka confusedly asked.

"You're the Captain, you shouldn't be cleaning anyway," Kotoyami said as she leaned back on her arms with her palms on the deck.

"Girl don't tell him that!" Yanielle said as she looked to Kotoyami with a smile.

Matuka then slowly stood up over the two girls, laughed with his eyes closed and with his head back.

"No, no, it's okay. It's my ship, so I should keep it clean and maintained, besides, it makes me feel like we're a family with order instead of a systematic dominance without love," Matuka said as his face grew more serious.

"Hey Matuka, I'm… I'm sorry okay?!" Yanielle shouted as she dropped her head and her golden afro bounced.

"Huh?" Matuka asked confusedly once more.

"For the fight! For everything; you big dummy!" Yanielle shouted while she lifted her head to reveal flowing rivers from her eyes and soul.

"Yeah, sorry for that, it was out of character for me," Kotoyami said as she looked up to Matuka.

"Somehow I doubt that," Matuka mumbled with his eyes closed and with a smile.

"What was that?" Kotoyami quickly asked as she glared at him.

"Oh nothing," Matuka said as he waved his arms gesturing no.

He then reached out his hands so both could grab hold to stand up. The two girls blushed and reached for the young Captain's hands that were silently calling for them. Meanwhile, Jubilaree had finished cleaning and was leaning against the wall, listening on the other side in the saloon.

"Listen, it's okay, really it is. I'm the one that should be sorry, I haven't been the best Captain thus far and I regret every second I can't give everyone here a peace of mind; not knowing what's really next to come. So, I should be sorry," Matuka said then smiled as he looked back and forth between the two.

"Yeah, sure," Yanielle said with a suspicious look on her face.

If it wasn't for the fight, I wouldn't have met Iraja or recovered that memory. Not to mention this guild crest appearing on my hand, no, all of ours," Matuka thought to himself as he looked down to his right hand.

Without warning, Kotoyami placed her hand on Matuka's head and leaned in close to his face, which caused Yanielle to blush and get a little jealous.

"You think too much Captain, you'll need to clear your head if you want to survive my training," Kotoyami said as she pushed down his hat over his eyes and stepped back.

"Fair," Matuka said before he lifted his hat.

Kotoyami and Matuka then began to laugh while Yanielle grew more jealous and frustrated.

"Whatever! We should get back to cleaning," Yanielle said with her eyes closed and arms crossed.

"Yeah, I suppose you're right," Kotoyami said as she glanced at the main eating table.

The three of them began to resume their cleaning when Kotoyami paused. The young lass stood quiet for a second before she walked closer towards the table with a blank stare on her face. After Kotoyami reached the large, red-cedar, picnic-style table, she picked up a small tuna and stared at it.

"Girl you okay?" Yanielle asked Kotoyami, which caused Matuka to stop cleaning as well to look.

"How about we skip lunch? You and me throw down a massive feast; that even our bellies will tell tales of for years to come," Kotoyami said as she walked up to Yanielle with the fish in her right hand.

"Oh my gosh girl! Yes! Let's do it!" Yanielle shouted with joy as they both lightly jumped off the deck in excitement.

"Look at these two, I'm glad to see them getting along, just earlier they were at each other's throats. But it's different now, this ship, Iraja, my crew, we have a purpose now, finding our memories and what caused all of this," Matuka thought to himself while he held his necklace.

Matuka smiled then looked at the joyful girls as they laughed and plotted together.

"What's all the excitement about?" Jubilaree asked stoically as he walked out the saloon into the galley as if he wasn't listening.

"Oh, hey Jubilaree," Matuka said as he turned around to his left to see Jubilaree walking towards them.

"What are you two babbling about now?" Jubilaree questioned with a smirk as he got closer and stood next to Matuka.

The boys then looked at one another; smiled and greeted each other by tapping their fist.

"None of your business, me and Yami is going to surprise you all with something spectacular," Yanielle said with her hands on her hips before she stuck out her tongue at Jubilaree.

"Yami?" Jubilaree asked.

"Yeah, you got a problem with that buddy?" Yanielle asked as she walked over with a balled fist towards Jubilaree and Matuka.

"No, but I guess that makes you Yani, huh?" Jubilaree leaned in and asked as he placed his left hand on her soft, curly afro.

"Hey!" Yanielle shouted before she blushed and knocked his hand off her head.

"Hey Cap, I'm headed below to go check out what's so interesting," Jubilaree sarcastically said as he turned around to his right and looked down at Matuka.

"Sure, but hey while you're down there, I have something you may want to see," Matuka quickly replied with a grin.

"Oh?" Jubilaree asked as he turned to face Matuka.

"Once you go below to the third deck and down the stairs. Walk all the way towards the bow, there will be three sets of downward stairs. The one to the left leads down into the food stowage, the one in the middle leads to the training deck and the other leads down into a room of miscellaneous supplies," Matuka said with a smile.

"Training deck you say?" Jubilaree asked Matuka with a smirk and with his eye closed.

"Exactly, go have a looksee," Matuka said with a smile.

"Don't mind if I do, later brats," Jubilaree said as he looked over his shoulder and waved back at the girls.

Suddenly, the small tuna Kotoyami was holding was launched at the back of Jubilaree's head. Without warning, Jubilaree caught the fish with his right hand and threw the tuna at the prepping table that sat at the north wall; without even turning around to see. As the fish landed in a stainless-steel bowl, Jubilaree was out the door and down the hall.

"That guy really pisses me off," Yanielle

said as she looked to Kotoyami.

"Yeah," Kotoyami quickly replied.

"He means well, I promise. But we should finish cleaning if we're going to use this space to cook and eat later. It's just a little bit more to straighten up," Matuka said as he walked over to the girls until they all were in a triangular position.

Just outside in the hallway, Jubilaree was standing against the wall; listening, with a smile on his face before he stood up straight and walked away to go below deck. All the while, Tahma and the brothers were diligently working together in harmony as they constructed weapons. The entire gun deck was still and calm; they were seated at a long, brown, wooden table that sat closer to starboard side. They sat atop black stools with fine, black-leathered cushions. The table was covered with all sorts of gears, belts, disassembled arsenal, and otherworldly looking parts as well as tools.

"Interesting, hey Dayhoon," Tahma said as he looked diagonally to his left across the table.

"Yeah?" Dayhoon asked as he placed a gunsight on his right index finger, closed his left eye, pretended his hand was a gun and slowly aimed around the gun deck.

"Interesting, could you pass me those?" Tahma asked as he pointed further down the table closer to where Dayhoon was sitting.

"Sure, hey, do you think you can make me a glove with a sight on the right index finger like this?" Dayhoon asked as he looked to Tahma with a smirk.

"Hey, I want one!" Umbati yelled across the table to Tahma.

"Interesting, sure, why not? But why on your glove when there's one on the weapon already?" Tahma asked with an intrigued look and glare in his glasses.

"Let's just say it's a trade secret for now, soon to be open to the public," Dayhoon said then chuckled with a shady grin.

"Interesting, so in other words you didn't master the technique you're trying to create," Tahma said as he leaned over the table towards Dayhoon and fixed his glasses.

"What?!" Dayhoon immediately snapped back.

"Ooh! Burn! One time for Tahma!" Umbati exaggeratedly cheered as he greeted Tahma with a balled fist.

"Huh?" Tahma childishly asked as he stared towards Umbati's extended left fist.

"Pound it, dap it, gimme some love brotha!" Umbati jokingly said as he slightly slurred.

"It's a greeting amongst friends, family, siblings, brothers and sisters," Dayhoon said as he crossed his arms and closed his eyes.

"Come on bro let's show him," Umbati eagerly said as he faced his brother.

"All right, sure," Dayhoon said as he faced his left towards his younger brother.

"You see Tahma all you gotta do is this, one fist starts at the top with a pound downward on the other and then..." Umbati said before being interrupted by Dayhoon.

"The other one comes back on top of the other and pounds downward as well," Dayhoon said as he demonstrated the greeting to Tahma.

"Now! Let us try Tahma," Umbati joyfully said as he extended his right fist to the young genius again.

"Interesting," Tahma said as he fixed his glasses before he dapped Umbati's hand.

"That's the way," Umbati said with a smile as he looked back to Dayhoon.

That's when Tahma extended his right fist to Dayhoon and paused.

"Interesting," Dayhoon said with a smirk before he leaned over the table and dapped Tahma's hand.

The three boys laughed and continued to work on the mysteries that laid before them. Moments passed when Jubilaree entered the third deck and paused to look at the three boys working in harmony. The boys didn't notice Jubilaree's smooth entrance, so they continued to talk.

"Interesting, I think if you put that this way Umbati, it would create more room for another deadly attachment," Tahma said as he passed back the two pistols to Umbati.

"I don't know Tahma, I was thinking about switching this around and removing this to add that," Umbati said as he showed the compartments of his firearm and then pointed down the table where Dayhoon was sitting.

"Interesting," Tahma said as he fixed his glasses to look between the weapons and parts.

"You know little bro, you should really take his advice, besides this little baby is mine for the taking," Dayhoon said as he stood up from the table, grabbed the weird mechanic, looked towards Umbati and Tahma then laughed.

"Interesting," Tahma said as he fixed his glasses.

"Hey! No fair bro! Hands off!" Umbati whined with anger and a balled fist.

"You don't need it, the kickback will be too strong for you," Dayhoon quickly replied with a creepy grin.

"What are you trying to say?" Umbati asked with a creepy smile as the room began to get dark and wind started to gather around the brothers.

All the while, Jubilaree could hear them

from afar and he began to laugh so loudly it alerted the three boys.

"What the?" Dayhoon asked as he looked up to his left towards the staircase.

"You two should put that energy to good use," Jubilaree said softly with a grin before he jumped from the staircase to in front of the table next to the others.

"You gotta show me that man," Dayhoon said before he walked towards Jubilaree.

"Hey! Jubilaree! Check this out man," Umbati eagerly said as he cut in front of his older brother.

"Hey you little, I oughta!" Dayhoon said with an ominous look on his face and balled fist towards Umbati.

That's when Umbati turned around, used his right index finger to pull down the skin below his right eye and stuck out his tongue.

"You little imp!" Dayhoon said as he started to rush towards Umbati who was directly in front of Jubilaree.

"You two quit the crap," Jubilaree quickly snapped.

Suddenly the gun deck grew still and quiet because Jubilaree seemed to have their attention.

"I have somewhere to be and I would really like to get there. Now, didn't you have something you wanted to show me squirt?" Jubilaree asked coldly with his arms crossed beneath his cape as he looked down at Umbati.

"Interesting," Tahma said as he looked on at Jubilaree and the brothers.

"What the hell's so interesting Tahma? Huh?! If I hear you say interesting one more time, I swear, I'm gonna! Ahhh!!" Dayhoon yelled as steam escaped from him.

"Interesting indeed, it seems a little button has been pressed on the small circuit board in your giant cranium," Tahma said with a slick smile and glare in his glasses before fixing them with his left hand; as he leaned over on the table.

"Okay, bring it on four eyes," Dayhoon said with a deranged grin on his face and fist balled towards Tahma as he too leaned over on the table.

"Anyway, don't worry about these two, they'll be fine. Look at what I have here, isn't it amazing?! Well?!" Umbati cheerfully and excitedly asked Jubilaree who was holding the weird, enhanced, and unconventional gun.

Jubilaree stood there speechless as he looked at the weapon, which caused Umbati to grow impatient with the delayed response.

"Hey what gives? If you don't like it hands off!" Umbati yelled as he quickly waved his arms up and down.

"Cut the crap," Jubilaree said coldly with

a piercing glare as he gave Umbati back the device.

"Okay," Umbati quickly said after he opened his eyes and dropped his arms to his side.

"It actually looks pretty cool; I just wouldn't know the first thing about these things really. Now if you wanna learn what I can do or at least try to, you know where I'll be," Jubilaree said with a grin and arms crossed before he started to walk off.

"Hey, wait a damn minute Jubilaree! You're not getting off so easy! My mind could use a break, but my body is just getting fired up!" Dayhoon yelled with a disturbed grin as he turned around and looked to his left at Jubilaree.

"Yeah me too! No offense Tahma, but I need a break too," Umbati said as he turned to his left towards Tahma and smiled with guilt.

"Interesting, no it's fine guys, I need a break from you too, I mean I need a break too," Tahma said quickly as he fumbled over his words.

"What was that four eyes?!" Dayhoon quickly snapped back as he looked back at Tahma.

"I'm leaving," Jubilaree stated loudly as he walked off towards the stern of the ship.

The two brothers dropped what they

were doing and immediately followed him to avoid being left behind. Meanwhile, Yanielle was headed down from the galley to get to the stowage deck for all the other foods needed.

"This place is really something else, huh Tahma?" Yanielle softly said as she unintentionally snuck up next to Tahma.

"Ahh!" Tahma shrieked before he cut his left hand pretty badly from being startled.

"Are you okay? I'm sorry! I didn't mean to," Yanielle said then paused as she reached in her right pant leg for her healing tool.

Yanielle quickly grabbed Tahma's hand and held it inside her own, so she could try to heal it.

"Interesting, it seems to react to you, Yanielle," Tahma said while he pushed his glasses up on his face with his right hand.

"What are you doing any way genius?" Yanielle said softly with an annoyed tone of voice and sincere look in her eyes.

"Interesting, I don't know if I should take that as you recognizing my genius or if I should take it as sarcasm," Tahma said as he looked on at the beautiful lass.

"Whatever floats your boat brainiac," Yanielle said as she looked down at her retractor that was emitting different shades of green light.

A few seconds went by and the gun deck

grew still. It was incredibly quiet and the only thing that could be heard was their breathing.

"Okay! All done!" Yanielle said with a smile as the light show dissipated and before she began to put away her retractor.

"Interesting, hey is it any way I could have a quick look at your surgical retractor?" Tahma asked Yanielle as he fixed his glasses and leaned in closer to her.

"Uh, sure, just be careful. I don't know how it works or how to fix it, so you better not break it," Yanielle said with a serious look as she passed her retractor to Tahma.

Tahma immediately sat down and put the retractor under his desk magnifier to get a closer glance.

"Interesting, I'm sorry Yanielle," Tahma said as he continued looking through the magnifier at the healing tool.

"What's interesting? And what are you sorry about?" Yanielle asked as she looked on at Tahma.

"Interesting, well, it seems to be engraved with something, looks like words, but a different language," Tahma said as he fixed his glasses before he looked up to Yanielle.

"Let me see!" Yanielle said as she quickly pushed Tahma aside out of the chair he was sitting in; to look at her tool under the magnifier.

"Interesting right?" Tahma said before he stood up from the ground and began to look around the gun deck in awe.

"Yeah, its super weird writing, but it looks familiar somehow. You never answered my other question by the way," Yanielle said as she looked to her left towards Tahma, who had walked away from the table.

Tahma stood in silence as he looked around the gun deck, which made Yanielle grow impatient enough to get up and knock on his head like a door.

"Helllooo! Earth to Tahmaaaa," Yanielle said as she gently knocked on his forehead and waited for him to reply.

"Interesting, you get easily frustrated," Tahma said to Yanielle after daydreaming about the ship.

"Oh, you're gonna find out real soon how frustrated I can get genius," Yanielle said as she put her hands on her hips and frowned.

"Interesting, I said sorry because if it wasn't for me going up to Kotoyami and being pushed into you, maybe the fight wouldn't have happened," Tahma said before he dropped his head, turned around and walked a couple of steps away.

What Tahma expressed caught Yanielle off guard and she began to feel sorry for him. As her face went from aggravated to sympathetic, her healing nature wanted to mend his broken spirit.

"Interesting," Yanielle said then chuckled before she reached and placed her right hand on his shoulder.

Tahma was shocked by her gentle hand and reply so he turned back around to see her face. Yanielle was smiling and the boy genius couldn't understand how she could be in good spirits about what he said to her.

"You shouldn't worry about that stuff anymore Tahma. If I didn't respond the way I did, maybe it wouldn't have happened. So out of us two, if anyone is to blame; it's me. Besides, look at your right hand. You have the same branding as me and the others, we're practically family now," Yanielle said as she looked up to Tahma and punched his left arm with her right fist.

"Interesting, you were the one that wanted to get off this ship the most, what happened?" Tahma questioned Yanielle with a curious face.

"I think when you all gathered around me earlier; it helped out a lot. I was at a breaking point and you guys gave me comfort I wasn't expecting to get," Yanielle said as she smiled and closed her eyes.

That's when a slow lonely tear began to roll down her left check and Tahma hurried to wipe it off before it fell to the deck.

"Hey! What's the big idea jerk?!" Yan-ielle asked after blushing and slapping Tahma's hand away.

Tahma stood there shocked and afraid to move because the once calm had turned vicious again.

"You think you can just touch someone? Trying to get fresh with me huh? I got some-thing for you buddy!" Yanielle said as she stormed off to go to the stowage deck.

As she began to walk away, Yanielle be-gan to wrestle with her inner voice and was forced to stop.

"Hey jerk!" Yanielle shouted to Tahma across the gun deck before he lifted his head from surprise.

She stood there quiet for a moment as she still struggled with her inner thoughts and voice; trying not to have a meltdown.

"Thank you!" Yanielle screamed before she ran off down the left flight of stairs to the stowage deck.

"Interesting," Tahma said with a low voice as he watched her disappear out of sight.

Meanwhile, Matuka and Kotoyami were finished cleaning the galley and they were seat-ed at the main eating table. Side-by-side, facing the north wall, the two sat in exhaustion.

"So, Captain. What happened down

there? You know, during the fight. How does all this work? You know, the gifts of the oceans. Why you? Why us? And I don't want you to think otherwise, I'm down for the cause, I just want to learn," Kotoyami said gently with a serious yet interested facial expression as she looked to her left.

Matuka then leaned back, smiled, and put his left hand behind his head.

"Well, you see, I was actually gonna explain that tonight for everyone," Matuka nervously chuckled with his eyes closed because he could feel the cold, piercing eyes of Kotoyami trying to glare into his soul.

Kotoyami suddenly broke her cold stare, crossed her arms, threw her head back and sighed. This caused Matuka to stop grinning so he looked onto Kotoyami with a concerned look in his eyes.

"I just wanted to be of service, with a few half and hazy memories; it's hard not to crave the knowledge," Kotoyami said softly as she looked up to the clean, high ceiling.

All the while, Matuka was thinking how much Kotoyami had grown with her attitude and how far it seemed she came, in a noticeably short amount of time.

"This is why I knew I'd love talking to you; I mean! I promise you will know all I know tonight," Matuka shrieked and blushed as he tried to wave off his words from embarrassment.

Kotoyami started to blush softly and nodded her head in his direction.

"Hey, Kotoyami," Matuka said as he looked at her with a serious look.

"Yes, Captain?" Kotoyami asked as she looked to her left towards Matuka.

"Tell me, what all can you do? You know, how high, how far you can jump? Your abilities," Matuka asked with a childish grin and with his eyes closed.

Kotoyami looked with a cold glare at Matuka, jumped up from the table to face him and then began to laugh with a sinister echo.

"Hahahahahahaha, oh how fate has called it!" Kotoyami laughed as a small lightning storm surrounded them.

"Uh, Kotoyami, what's going on?" Matuka shrieked as he saw a flash of small lightning.

"Destiny calls us, hahahahaha!" Kotoyami yelled and then continued laughing with both of her arms extended out.

Suddenly, the storm completely dissipated, Kotoyami walked up to Matuka and pushed his nose in with her right index finger.

"Now you have to wait until tonight to find out!" Kotoyami said with her eyes closed before she stuck out her tongue.

"Touché, well could you at least help out Jubilaree down there? You know, make sure he's not destroying the training deck because of unanswered questions from me, I'd really appreciate it if you did," Matuka questioned in a way like an order.

Immediately, he felt the cold glare of Kotoyami again but didn't see a faint blush across her face because his eyes were closed. Kotoyami then pushed off his nose with her finger, which caused his head to fly back.

"Oh, I'll go alright! And I'm on to you, you're not slick! I'll physically train him until he freaking dies!" Kotoyami shouted with a sinister laugh as she walked out of the galley into the west hallway.

"Everyone here seems to have a split personality," Matuka said with a concerned look in his eyes as he watched her exit the galley.

Matuka smiled and looked around the galley because he was amazed at how clean it was again.

"Wow this is exactly how it looked before anyone was here. However, my blood stains weren't able to come up. I wonder if it's gonna be like that with the rest because I left some all over the ship," Matuka said softly after he stood up and looked at the trails of blood around the galley and saloon.

Meanwhile, Tahma was still working below on the gun deck on a few new weapon archetypes.

"Interesting, I bet if I remove this and tweak that, I can make this go…" Tahma said as he looked up and saw Kotoyami about to walk past him.

Tahma was nervous but knew he had to speak then or forever hold his peace.

"Kotoyami!" Tahma quickly shouted as he stood up from the table.

Kotoyami stopped and turned to look at Tahma, who was sweating profusely as he leaned over the table.

"Yes, Tahma?" Kotoyami asked gently before she walked over to the table where he was.

"Interesting, I'm sorry okay?! It was wrong for me to hit a lady and I'm truly sorry!" Tahma yelled as he bowed his head extremely hard and fast which mistakenly slammed atop the crowded table.

Kotoyami stood there and observed the young genius as he bowed in her respect.

"I know that hurt, so go ahead and lift your head up," Kotoyami said with a smirk.

"Interesting, no! I will not! I'm not moving until I am forgiven!" Tahma replied with a shout.

"Oh, really? This can get really interesting Tahma, if you'd like," Kotoyami said with a glare as she looked on at Tahma.

"I'm not moving until I am forgiven," Tahma reiterated as his head rested upon gears and other sharp objects.

"Fine, stay there, we'll see," Kotoyami said as she turned to walk away.

"Interesting, I'll be here woman! You wait and see! If I have to die here!" Tahma shouted before Kotoyami paused from walking.

"We'll see Tahma, if he does, it'll show great promise for discipline in the future," Kotoyami thought to herself as she crossed her arms, walked to the stairs that led below and smirked.

Meanwhile, on the training deck, the brothers were sweating and in much pain from the training Jubilaree was enforcing.

"I can't take it anymore," Umbati struggled to say to Dayhoon.

"How much more damn it?!" Dayhoon yelled to Jubilaree while he stood in front of them.

Suddenly, the door burst open and Kotoyami was standing there with a gleam in her eyes as she scanned the room. The training deck was not as big as the gun deck but was still generous with space. The training deck was divided into five parts, four squares and one rectangle. The first square to her left, was made of black dirt.

The square to the right of it was made of beautiful seashells and beach sand. The square behind the black dirt was made of rocks and gravel. The square next to that, which was behind the seashell and beach sand patch of land, was a field of low grass. The final area was larger and behind both the rock and grass squares.

The area was made of the finest mahogany wood ever seen. The walls of the training deck appeared to be made of gneiss rock; that sparkled its magnificent colors off the black, gray, and white surface. The ceiling was also made of the same type of rock that covered the walls of the training deck. The room was giving off its own light just like the bedrooms of the ship, so it was extremely visible.

"We're saved!" Umbati screeched as sweat dripped off his face.

"I don't think she's here to help bro," Dayhoon quickly stated to his younger brother.

That's when Jubilaree jumped from the square the brothers were in, to the floor at the back of the training room. Kotoyami quickly noticed the brothers were in the handstand position, on one hand, surrounded in a pool of their sweat within the rock and gravel square. Kotoyami then quickly looked to Jubilaree while he stood on the sleek mahogany surface with his eye closed, and arms crossed.

"Here we go," Jubilaree said under his breath before dropping both his hands.

The moment Jubilaree lowered his hands, Kotoyami was already throwing a kick towards the right side of his face with her left leg.

"Nice try," Jubilaree said after he instinctively blocked Kotoyami's left foot with his right forearm.

The huge gust of wind from her leaping to Jubilaree; caused the brothers to fall forward from their handstand positions, and land on their backs.

"This is what you call training?" Kotoyami questioned with a smirk as she stood in front of the tall lad after she lowered her left leg and stood upright.

"No, my training doesn't include you missy," Jubilaree said as he closed his eye and crossed his arms.

"What possibly could you teach them besides gaining brute force?" Kotoyami asked with a smirk as she turned around to look at the brothers.

"That's more than enough and more than what you can't teach, damn it!" Jubilaree yelled and blushed in response to her comment.

Kotoyami then started to walk over to the motionless brothers, which made Jubilaree follow as well.

"What on Earth is it that you two are trying to learn from him?" Kotoyami asked as she pointed over her right shoulder; towards Jubilaree with her right thumb.

"Strength to defy the laws of nature," Dayhoon struggled to say as he and Umbati sat up.

"You see? They already get it," Jubilaree said as he walked to Kotoyami's right side.

Kotoyami immediately looked to her right at Jubilaree and glared at him.

"You're strong physically but not where it counts," Kotoyami quickly stated.

"Oh yeah? Well you're mentally strong but you are as weak as they come. Your kick needs improvement, it may have worked on someone else but not me," Jubilaree said with a sure smile on his face.

The tension began to build in the room and the brothers could see electricity flying off the two of them as they stared each other down.

"Seems like you two would make the perfect couple, a mix of strength and brains, if you two could only get along," Umbati said with a sneaky grin as he looked to Kotoyami and Jubilaree.

That's when Jubilaree, Kotoyami and Dayhoon all told Umbati to shut up in unison. Dayhoon then whacked Umbati on the head with his left hand, grabbed him and put him in a choke hold.

"Hey let me go!" Umbati yelled as he tried to escape his big brother.

"Oh, they make a good couple huh? You said that on purpose to piss me off! Didn't you? You little worm!" Dayhoon yelled to his brother as his grip grew tighter.

By then, Jubilaree and Kotoyami had their backs to one another as they frowned to keep themselves from blushing.

"I bet I could help them achieve their goal quicker than you can," Kotoyami said with her eyes closed.

"You are so on," Jubilaree said with a smile as he opened his eye and unfolded his arms.

"Wait, what?" Umbati asked out of exhaustion.

"Listen guys, little missy here says she can do a better job than me, so we are gonna see just what she has to teach," Jubilaree said before he chuckled and turned around to face Kotoyami.

That's when Kotoyami turned around and faced Jubilaree with the same intense stare as before. Dayhoon and Umbati looked at each other, dropped their heads, then sobbed because they knew what was coming; wasn't going to be much fun as well. Back above on the second deck, Matuka was preparing to grab an important ingredient for their meal.

"I need fish, this fish is too salty to have ready for tonight. Think Matuka, think," the young Captain said very softly as he paced the galley back and forth.

A few moments passed and the young Captain was met with a memory from before when he was under water with Iraja.

"That's it!" Matuka yelled before he grabbed a huge, handwoven basket and ran out the east entrance of the galley.

Matuka quickly made it down the hallway, past all the boys' rooms, around the corner, up the stairs and out onto the main deck. As the young Captain reached the middle of starboard side, the wind flowed through his locks and a wave gently sprayed water onto his face.

"Friends of the ocean, my guild is having our first real meal together for the first time as a crew. I want it to be special and a night we'll never forget. I hope I'm not asking for too much already…" Matuka said before being interrupted by Iraja.

"Just command what you want to eat to jump into the basket you are holding Master," Iraja said telepathically to the young Captain.

"Iraja? Oh, hey! I didn't know you were paying attention to my babble up here," Matuka said with a smile as he closed his eyes.

"I'm always paying attention to you and your crew, looking out for your safety above and below the water," Iraja quickly replied to Matuka.

"I didn't want to seem pushy, greedy or ungrateful. It's hard asking something or someone to lay down their life and be eaten by you. It almost feels wrong," Matuka said before he dropped his head.

"Master, there is a hierarchy in the ocean, from strength to brain capacity, to length and weight, we know which sea creatures to feed on, which to respect and which to avoid. There are some fish whose purpose was to be harvested from the beginning of time and are just merely food with no intelligence. So, you should not feel bad. It is honorable and of good heart to feel this way, but we are here to serve you, your crew, the Hyungetta," Iraja said as he made the ship vibrate.

"Wait a sec, was that you this entire time? Causing the ship to vibrate?" Matuka asked Iraja as he looked to the ocean.

"Yes and no Master, sometimes it's me and sometimes it is not," Iraja slowly replied.

"What was it the other times?" Matuka quickly asked with a look of curiosity.

"The ship itself," Iraja replied telepathically.

"How strange, hey Iraja," Matuka said as he looked back to the ocean from the black, polished deck.

"Yes, Master?" Iraja asked the young Captain.

"The next time it isn't you, could you let me know?" Matuka asked as he walked closer to the side of the ship.

"Yes Master, now, lift your basket and command your food to come, you are the king of the waters, they will listen," Iraja shouted with an encouraging tone.

Matuka slowly lifted the brown, hand-woven basket above his head and closed his eyes as blood began to creep down his cheeks.

"Food! Come to me and be a part of me forever!" Matuka yelled with a mighty shout.

The waves were beating against the ship as normal and the sound of the ocean was peaceful to the ears of its listeners. Suddenly, the water in front of starboard side began to grow uneasy as an army of endless bubbles rose to the surface of the water.

"Whoa," Matuka said as a wave began to form and tower over the ship.

Without warning, a school of flying fish poured into his basket from the wave.

"Whoa! Too much! Too much!" Matuka yelled as his knees began to buckle from the weight of the fish in the basket.

As quickly as the wave of fish came, is how quickly they stopped pouring into his basket.

"Now there is fish everywhere, what am I gonna do?" Matuka asked as he lowered the basket in front of him and looked around at all the fish, still on the deck.

"Tell them to return and they will Master," Iraja said telepathically to the young Captain.

Matuka then placed the handwoven basket down next to him on the black deck and looked to all the fish.

"Alright, here goes nothing! You may all return!" Matuka yelled to the fish that were still flopping on the deck.

That's when every single fish, including the ones in the basket flew off the ship and back to the sea.

"Huh? Hey! What was that?!" Matuka yelled as he ran to starboard side and looked over the bulwarks.

"Oh Master," Iraja chuckled telepathically.

"What happened?" Matuka questioned Iraja aloud.

"You told all of them to go back, you may have to be more specific with the less intelligent sea creatures," Iraja explained telepathically.

Matuka then dropped his head, chuckled as well, then stood upright and looked to the ocean.

"Alright! Let's try this again!" Matuka shouted with an eager smile.

Meanwhile, back down on the training deck, Kotoyami was leaving all the boys broken and drained.

"And that's how you do it Jubilaree," Kotoyami said with a smirk as she ran out the door and up the stairs to the gun deck.

Before she fully left, Kotoyami glanced back to smile at Jubilaree, Dayhoon and Umbati. They were nearly unconscious, soaked in sweat and in a lot of pain.

"She's crazy!" Jubilaree said before he went unconscious.

"She's evil!" Umbati screamed before he fainted.

"What a woman," Dayhoon said before he passed out on the field of grass.

At that moment, Yanielle was coming up the stairs from the stowage deck and Kotoyami ran into her, nearly knocking all the food on the ground.

"Oh no!" Yanielle screamed before Kotoyami quickly caught everything before it fell.

"Got it," Kotoyami said with a smile as she balanced food on her arms, legs, and head.

"Girl you scared me," Yanielle said with

a smile as she helped Kotoyami carry half of the supplies and ingredients.

"Wow, all of this was in the stowage deck?" Kotoyami asked Yanielle as they made their way to where Tahma was.

"Yes, and you won't believe what is all down there. Uh, what is he doing?" Yanielle asked Kotoyami as they walked up to Tahma.

The young genius was quiet and still had his head bowed down on the table.

"I completely forgot. You are forgiven Tahma," Kotoyami chuckled as Yanielle and her stood in front of the table.

"Oh God, thank you," Tahma said as he lifted his body and slouched down on his stool.

"Did I miss something?" Yanielle asked Kotoyami and Tahma with a raised right eyebrow.

"I'll tell you on the way, let's get this meal prepped," Kotoyami said as she gestured for them to keep moving.

"Hey, did you tell the boys what our plans for tonight are?" Yanielle quickly asked before moving another step.

"Good thinking, I nearly forgot, hey Tahma," Kotoyami said with a smile after she looked his way.

"Yes?" Tahma quickly replied as a drop of sweat rolled down his forehead.

"Tell those three babies down there that

there will be no lunch but a massive feast to-night and to bring what they can to the galley as soon as possible," Kotoyami said as she glared at Tahma with a sinister smile and with a glow in her eyes.

"Interesting, sure! No problem!" Tahma said as he saluted Kotoyami.

"Girl what you did to that poor boy?" Yanielle questioned with a look of concern while she looked back to Tahma as they walked away from the table.

"Oh, nothing yet," Kotoyami laughed, then glared back at Tahma.

Tahma immediately dropped his head and began to work again as the girls walked up the stairs and out the door. By the time the girls made it back to the galley, Matuka was already back and seated at the main eating table with the basket full of flying fish.

"I wasn't expecting this," Kotoyami said as she walked up to Matuka, who had his head down on the table.

"What in the? Did you do something to him too Yami?" Yanielle asked as she looked to Kotoyami.

"This wasn't me," Kotoyami quickly replied.

The two girls walked over to Matuka, placed their supplies and ingredients down next to the handwoven basket.

"Earth to Matuka!" Yanielle said with an elevated tone as she stood over the young Captain.

"Where did this fish come from?" Kotoyami asked softly as she looked in the basket that was in front of Matuka.

"Hellloooo, Captain?" Yanielle sarcastically asked as she poked on Matuka's right shoulder with her left index finger.

Unexpectedly, Matuka popped up from his nap and had a fish stuck to his left cheek.

"Huh? What I miss?!" Matuka shouted with a look of concern as the fish slid down his face onto the table.

The girls looked at each other, then back to Matuka and burst into laughter.

"Classic!" Yanielle laughed and snorted as she walked around the table to face him again.

"I don't think I'll ever forget this scene," Kotoyami giggled as she walked to the main prepping counter on the north wall.

Matuka then noticed why the girls were laughing and began to laugh himself as he put his left hand behind his head. Moments after the laughter stopped, Matuka and Yanielle began to help Kotoyami with the rest of the meal prepping.

"So where did you get that basket of flying fish?" Yanielle asked Matuka with a gentle, yet serious voice.

"It looks just like the empty, missing basket I had here on the counter earlier," Kotoyami chimed in with a suspicious look on her face.

"I promise I'll explain everything tonight, just know it's kind of a funny story," Matuka quickly replied with his eyes closed and a nervous grin across his face.

Matuka could feel the glares from Yanielle and Kotoyami as he stood in between them at the north wall's counter, so he backed up a bit.

"So, you can bring us food to cook but not tell us how you got it?" Yanielle asked with an annoyed grin before she turned around to face Matuka.

That's when Kotoyami stabbed the knife into the countertop and turned around with a sinister glow in her eyes.

"How about we add him to the meal? Since he doesn't want to fess up," Kotoyami said with a deranged smile as she looked to Yanielle and then back to Matuka.

"Great idea Yami," Yanielle said as she looked back to Matuka with the same deranged smile.

"Now ladies look!" Matuka said with a nervous smile as he backed up even more.

Kotoyami and Yanielle eventually

walked Matuka into the large eating table where he fell back and sat on the bench.

"Now you stay right there and help us by cutting up all the vegetables and fruits," Yanielle said as she cleared the table from the things she brought up from the stowage deck.

"And if we need you for anything else, we'll let you know," Kotoyami said sternly before she picked up the handwoven basket and carried it away to the main counter.

"Sure thing!" Matuka said with a nervous smile as he turned around to chop up the vegetables, herbs, and fruits from the girls' room.

A few hours passed and the ship was almost completely quiet. Matuka was almost finished chopping up all the ingredients that were placed before him and the girls were steadily cooking. Below deck, the three boys on the training deck were still unconscious and Tahma was still head deep in his research.

"Whew, my hands are wrecked! I don't see how y'all do it, but I have a deeper respect for you, that's for sure!" Matuka said as he stood up, stretched, and yawned after he finished his duties.

"Awe, thank you Matuka," Yanielle said after she turned around to look at him.

"Perfectly done Captain!" Kotoyami said after she reached the table and saw the good job

Matuka did.

"Well gosh! That's why your hands hurt!" Yanielle said as she looked at the table after she walked over to it.

"Yeah, I'm beat!" Matuka said as he dropped his head and shoulders.

After a few more minutes passed, Tahma, Jubilaree, Dayhoon and Umbati all walked into the galley's east entrance.

"Interesting," Tahma said as he fixed his glasses with his right hand.

"That smells sooo good," Umbati said as his mouth began to water.

"How much longer guys?" Dayhoon asked with a smirk as he stood with his hand on his belly.

Suddenly, a loud familiar sound echoed in their ears, which caused them to turn around and look at Jubilaree.

"What? You never heard a stomach growl before?" Jubilaree asked before he closed his eye, crossed his arms, and turned his back to everyone.

"Don't worry, I'll have you fed soon," Kotoyami said to Jubilaree, which made everyone except Dayhoon and him snicker.

Jubilaree began to blush while Dayhoon got a little jealous and sucked his teeth.

"Alright fellas, we are almost ready to party! I need everyone with something growing in their room to bring a small bowl of it so we can add it to the meal," Yanielle said as she looked from the food that was cooking back to the crew.

"I don't have anything growing in my room," Jubilaree replied as he turned and faced the group.

"Interesting," Tahma said as he looked to Jubilaree.

"Your room knew you didn't have a nurturing spirit," Kotoyami chuckled as she walked over to Jubilaree and punched him on the right arm.

"Knock it off!" Jubilaree yelled to his right at Kotoyami before he frowned and blushed.

Everyone began to laugh as Matuka walked over to Jubilaree to ease his mind.

"Don't feel bad Jubilaree, my room doesn't have anything growing in it either," Matuka said with a smile as he looked up to the annoyed Jubilaree.

"Well Captain, you ignore a lot of asked questions so technically you could be considered detached as well," Yanielle said with a nervous smile as she twiddled her thumbs.

"Oh really?" Matuka asked with a shocked smile and raised brow as he turned around to look at Yanielle.

"Last time I checked, the Captain and I

were the ones who risked our lives to save you, brat!" Jubilaree said with an attitude.

"And how did that work out for you?" Yanielle snapped back with an attitude.

"Ouch!" Umbati said as he looked up to his older brother to the left of him.

"Burn!" Dayhoon said as he looked down to his younger brother before they gave each other a dap.

"Well you are alive, aren't you?" Jubilaree asked with a grin before he closed his eye.

"Interesting," Tahma said before he headed out the galley's east entrance.

"Where you going Tahma?" Umbati asked as he followed.

"Well, Yanielle did ask us to bring the food that is growing in our rooms, so I'm headed to mine to collect some sugar cane, hopefully they'll find something to do with it," Tahma said as he looked down to his left at Umbati.

"Well, me and Dayhoon have beans and wheat growing in our room," Umbati said with a cunning smile; knowing it would intrigue the young genius.

"Really? Interesting, I'll meet you there," Tahma said before he bolted down the hallway to his room.

"You coming big bro?" Umbati asked as he looked to Dayhoon from the hallway.

"Sure thing bro," Dayhoon said as he

walked out the galley towards Umbati.

"Alright, back to work," Kotoyami said with a glare as she looked at everyone left in the galley.

Yanielle quickly ran to her side and continued to stir the pot over the fire while Matuka began to clean up the mess he made at the table earlier.

"If you're going to stay, you could help me with this Jubilaree," Kotoyami said with a smirk as she held up a sack of garbage filled with peelings and bones with her left hand.

"Hold on, I have more!" Matuka quickly chimed in as he ran over to Kotoyami.

Jubilaree then let out a sigh, leaned off the dish cabinet by the east entry, dropped his head and unfolded his arms.

"What do you expect me to do with that?" Jubilaree questioned as he opened his right eye and looked at Kotoyami.

"You can always eat it," Yanielle said with a smirk as she continued to look at the pot she was stirring.

"How about I..." Jubilaree said before being cut off by Matuka.

"Hey, just throw it overboard, Iraja told me he'd take it," Matuka said with a smile as he looked at everyone.

After Matuka spoke, a silence swept the galley and the air was still as a mountain.

"It's definitely gonna take some time getting used to hearing that," Yanielle said as she continued to stir and add ingredients to the stew she was brewing.

"You want me to do what?" Jubilaree asked Matuka with a nervous facial expression.

"It'll be fine," Matuka replied with a gentle smile as he walked to stand in front of Jubilaree.

"Are you chicken?" Yanielle asked with a sneaky smile as she stopped stirring to look towards Jubilaree.

Yanielle and Kotoyami began to giggle, which caused Jubilaree to blush.

"Fine! Whatever!" Jubilaree yelled before he walked past Matuka, snatched the garbage from Kotoyami's hand and walked out of the galley.

"So easy," Yanielle said as she looked to Kotoyami.

"Like a charm," Kotoyami said as Yanielle and her gave each other a high-five.

"I heard that!" Jubilaree yelled from down the hall as he continued.

"Huh?" Matuka asked with a confused look on his face.

Yanielle and Kotoyami began to laugh because they thought it was cute that their Captain was clueless at the moment. Meanwhile, the brothers were showing Tahma their room that he was so anxious to see.

"Interesting," Tahma said as he hurried to the northeast corner of their room.

"Told you it was pretty awesome," Umbati said as he looked down at his right hand's fingernails; while he leaned against the glowing table made of tigerwood on the west wall.

"It's okay," Dayhoon said as if he too wasn't impressed as he leaned in the doorway.

That's when Dayhoon noticed Jubilaree rushing past their room with an attitude.

"I wonder where he's off to," Dayhoon said as he watched Jubilaree bend the corner down the hall.

"Interesting! I think we have enough here guys! Let's go give this stuff to the ladies so they can add this stuff in time," Tahma said as he stood up and turned around to look at the brothers.

At that time, Jubilaree had made it up to the main deck and was slowly walking over to starboard side's bulwarks.

"This is insane," Jubilaree mumbled as he looked into the water.

Suddenly, one of Iraja's huge tentacles lifted out of the water and towered over the ship.

"What the hell?!" Jubilaree yelled as he looked up to the dripping wet, large grayish-brown and dark-purple spotted tentacle.

"It is okay young Master; I will not harm you," Iraja said telepathically to Jubilaree.

"*What the hell?! Where did that voice come from? It sounds like it's coming from all around? Is it him?*" Jubilaree thought to himself as he looked back and forth, then back up to the tentacle.

"It is I, Iraja. I am a servant to your Captain, to you and all the rest of the Hyungetta members. I'm here to protect you," Iraja said to Jubilaree telepathically.

"How are you speaking to me?" Jubilaree quickly asked before he tossed up the brown, handwoven trash sack.

"Thank you Master, it's called telepathy, it's communication from one mind to another," Iraja said as his large tentacle took the sack under water.

"Telepathy," Jubilaree said softly before he crossed his arms underneath his dark-blue cape and closed his eye.

"In time you'll know how to do so much more, especially with that special left eye of yours," Iraja said before he tossed back up the wet, handwoven garbage sack.

"What?!" Jubilaree shrieked as his eye flew open after he realized Iraja knew about his eye.

Meanwhile below deck, everyone except Jubilaree was down in the galley.

"This smells amazing!" Umbati said as he walked over to Yanielle, who was slicing up a loaf of bread.

"Interesting," Tahma said as he watched Kotoyami make a tea out of the sugarcane he brought to her.

"I was wondering what you were gonna do with the wheat I brought you," Dayhoon said with a satisfied smirk as he looked to Yanielle.

Yanielle smiled as she continued to drain the cleaned wheat berries so she could pour it into a pot of boiling water.

"This is a lot of food!" Matuka said with a smile as he looked around the galley.

"Yeah and the sun is setting," Jubilaree said from the east entry of the galley as he leaned against the threshold, holding the lightly-dripping garbage sack.

"Hey you! Cyclops! You're making a mess on the floor!" Yanielle said with an attitude as she looked at Jubilaree.

Jubilaree let out a deep sarcastic sigh before he walked over to the northeast corner of the galley and placed the sack back under the counter.

"Happy?" Jubilaree asked softly with an annoyed tone of voice as he turned around and looked at Yanielle.

"I'd be happy if all of you got out of here so we could finish!" Yanielle quickly snapped back as she looked to her right behind Koto-yami at Jubilaree.

"The food is nearly done, how about we all get cleaned? I mean, take a real good bath and meet back here to eat," Matuka said as he leaned over to look at the different pots filled with food.

"Interesting," Tahma said after he smelled beneath his left arm pit.

"Great idea Captain!" Yanielle said with an attitude as she looked at Jubilaree.

"Ugh, whatever," Jubilaree said as he walked to the galley's east entrance.

"Hold on a second Jubilaree, we can all go together, I haven't even shown you guys yet," Matuka said as he walked past Tahma, Dayhoon and Umbati to get to Jubilaree.

"A bath would be nice," Kotoyami said as she looked to her left at Yanielle.

"I mean, I guess we could take one, the food is basically done. We could let it sit, I guess," Yanielle said as she looked at Koto-yami.

"Fine, it's official. We'll commune back here after we get clean," Matuka said as he turned to look at everyone in the galley.

"Well what are we waiting on? Let's go! I'm starved!" Umbati said before he ran past Matuka and Jubilaree into the hallway.

The boys then exited the east entry of the

galley and the girls followed by exiting on the west. Matuka then led the band of boys into the uncharted bathing quarters to be their guide.

"Just around this corner is an oasis of re-juvenation, well at least I'd like to think," Matuka said as he turned around to look at the group of lads following him.

When the group of boys fully entered the bathing room, they could see its splendor and uniqueness. As they bent the corner to the right, they immediately saw a huge, warm, steamed filled bath, running along nearly the entire west wall. At the end of the tub, near the northwest wall was a seat of ease that had its own private door; that was open. On the north wall sat a large linen storage closet that ran along most of the wall, which held towels. In the northeast corner of the room was another seat of ease with its own private door as well. The middle of the room was open and bare.

However, the east wall held another stor-age closet full of different natural soaps and oils that engulfed the room with an aroma of tran-quility. The material of the bath house was made of dark-oakwood that smelled of pine trees. The ceilings let off a soft, white glow that almost resembled daylight and lit the room quite well.

"Interesting, the plumbing and construc-tion of this place is something I've only seen in my imagination," Tahma said as he looked into the giant tub after he walked up on it.

"And you can remember something like that?" Dayhoon asked as he walked next to Tahma and looked inside of the tub as well.

"Yes, strangely," Tahma quickly replied as he looked to his right towards Dayhoon.

"Well, I don't know about you guys but I'm starving so I'm hopping in!" Umbati said as he took off all his clothes and looked at the rest of the guys.

"Right behind ya lil bro," Dayhoon said as he got undressed.

"This will be my first-time bathing in here; I have my own bathing room in my quarters. However, it's in no form as nice as this!" Matuka said as he looked at everyone.

"Interesting, this place is highly advanced. It seems only a couple of places have kerosene lamps but everywhere else is lit with an array of auroras and filled with abundant light from within the objects themselves," Tahma said as he took off his satchel and shoes.

"You're awfully quiet Jubilaree," Matuka quickly stated as he looked to his left towards Jubilaree.

"Yeah, I haven't heard a peep from you since Yanielle got under your skin," Dayhoon said with a smirk as he looked to his left at Jubilaree.

"You have a death call?!" Jubilaree quickly snapped back before he blushed and closed his eye.

"Only if you can answer!" Dayhoon screamed before jumping into the enormous bathtub, which caused the water to splash all over Jubilaree and the others.

"Bastard!" Jubilaree screamed before he quickly snatched off all his clothes; except his bandanna, and angrily stomped over to the tub to inflict harm on Dayhoon.

"Now there guys, we are here for a relaxing bath before this amazing feast the girls and I have prepared," Matuka said while he walked over to the tub as Jubilaree jumped in to pummel Dayhoon.

"I'm pretty sure it was the girls," Umbati whispered to Tahma and Dayhoon before he jumped into the large community bathtub.

"Interesting, the plumbing on this ship is truly unrealistic," Tahma said before he stepped into the large and warm, steaming tub.

"What are you waiting on?" Jubilaree asked with a stoic tone, eye closed and with his arms crossed.

"Yeah, I'm hungry! The sooner we get done, the sooner we get fed!" Umbati said as he looked out towards Matuka, who was still standing out the tub.

"The sooner we get fed the sooner we get

drinks," Dayhoon quickly added as he relaxed in the water.

"And the sooner we can get some answers," Jubilaree said lastly as he looked up to Matuka.

"Interesting," Tahma said softly as he looked from the boys to Matuka.

Matuka then took off his hat, his shirt, his boots, then his pants and then his bandanna.

"Well that's why he's the Captain," Dayhoon said with a shocked look upon his face.

"Jealous?" Jubilaree quickly asked with a smirk as he looked to his right at Dayhoon.

"Interesting," Tahma said as he tried to wipe his steam filled glasses.

"Shut up Tahma! And how about I snatch that bandanna off your face so you can really see if I need to be jealous!" Dayhoon said as he stood up out of the water and looked at Jubilaree.

"Please, I seen bigger shrimps on a plate," Jubilaree said as he closed his eye and dropped his head with his arms crossed.

"Burn!" Umbati said as he splashed over to Jubilaree to give him a high-five.

"Why you little!" Dayhoon screamed as he grabbed and held Umbati under water.

"Someone, help!" Umbati yelled as Dayhoon jokingly tried to drown his younger brother.

Matuka, Jubilaree and Tahma began to chuckle at the brothers, which made Dayhoon start laughing as well.

"I'm glad you guys think this is funny!" Umbati said after Dayhoon let him up so he could breathe.

"Alright guys let's calm down so we can get to the main event," Matuka said as he stepped into the large and warm bathtub.

The room had grown quiet for a few moments and very peaceful to the young lads. While everyone was relaxing and cleaning themselves, Umbati jumped up with a desperate look in his eyes.

"What's biting you?" Dayhoon said as he looked to his right towards his little brother.

"I just had a severe epiphany!" Umbati said with a sneaky, glared grin as he looked at Dayhoon.

"Oh yeah?" Dayhoon asked with a raised brow.

"Matuka?" Umbati questioned as he walked over to the young Captain.

"Yes Umbati?" Matuka asked as he looked forward towards Umbati.

"Are the girls' bathrooms just like this, you know, the same floor plan, or is it different?" Umbati said as he twiddled his thumbs underwater with his head down.

"Interesting," Tahma said as he looked to

his left towards Umbati and Matuka.

"Well, it's the same floor plan but opposite, so the girls' tub is on this shared wall, why?" Matuka asked as he looked towards Umbati.

"I know where this is going," Dayhoon said as he dropped his head and fell back in the water.

"Pervert," Jubilaree said as he began to blush with a frown.

Suddenly, Umbati's nose began to bleed and he rushed out of the water, stood on the one-foot ledge, then placed his ear to the wall.

"Right now, the only thing holding us from manhood is this measly wall. Just on the other side is heaven fellas! Two gorgeous hotties, dripping wet, washing each other's back!" Umbati carried on as his mouth watered and his nose began to bleed more.

Suddenly, Dayhoon lifted his head out of the water and the other boys grew quiet from their imaginations.

"Brother! Kotoyami's over there right now with my earth angel," Umbati said as he slowly turned his neck with a creepy smile to look at Dayhoon.

"Interesting, he has a point," Tahma slowly said as he looked to his left towards Matuka.

"Oh, not you too," Jubilaree said under

his breath before he submerged under water and came back up.

"I'm pretty sure if they knew what you were doing; they'd be furious and probably try to kill you," Matuka said with a nervous smile as he looked over his left shoulder towards Umbati.

"Oh, don't think they're not talking about us right now, Captain. On a ship with total strangers and with no memories! Oh, they're talking about all of us!" Umbati said with a smile as he looked to all the guys.

"Interesting," Tahma said before he walked over to the ledge and raised out of the tub to listen as well.

"If you can't beat them, join them," Day-hoon said before he stood up, walked over to the ledge, and leaned his ear against the wall.

"Captain I'm just saying, you found and basically saved these ladies lives! I'm sure they're exchanging deep, secret words of grati-tude for you. And Kotoyami could be giving you, Jubilaree, a lot of praise from earlier in the training deck. You did out last Dayhoon and me after all," Umbati said with the same creepy, perverted smile as he looked to Jubilaree.

Unexpectedly, Matuka and Jubilaree quickly got up and rushed to the wall to listen as well with the others.

"That a boy Captain," Umbati said with a

sneaky, satisfied grin.

Meanwhile, the girls were next door in the bath as well and had just sneezed in unison.

"I have a strange feeling that we're being talked about," Kotoyami said as she turned around and looked at the shared wall.

"It's probably those little perverts! Now that you mention I have a strange feeling too," Yanielle said as she stood up and walked over to the ledge on the east wall.

Back on the other side of the wall, the group of young lads were trying their hardest to hear the words of the young females.

"All I need is one peek," Umbati yelled before he panted and drooled over himself.

At that very moment, the boys were jolted back from the wall because Kotoyami and Yanielle had both kicked the wall at the same time. All the boys except Jubilaree, fell backwards into the large tub and landed on one another. Jubilaree was able to withstand the kick more than everyone else but eventually, he too had fallen victim.

"There onto us!" Jubilaree said before he fell backwards into the water.

"Ew! This not what I had in mind when you said we'd be bonded like a family!" Umbati screamed as he tried to swim away from the group.

"This is bad," Matuka said as he quickly

got out and grabbed a towel from the east wall's cabinet.

"What are you going to say?!" Jubilaree asked with a nervous look on his face.

"I don't know but you guys wait like fifteen minutes before you get out and get dressed," Matuka said as he quickly dried off and got dressed.

"Fifteen minutes? That's forever! I'm starving," Umbati whined before he fell backwards in the tub out of frustration.

"Shut up! This all your fault!" Jubilaree said with his eye closed and arms crossed.

"You wanna go?!" Umbati asked Jubilaree after he sat up in the water.

"This is not the place small stuff," Jubilaree said before he uncrossed his arms and leaned his head back against the ledge.

"I got your small stuff!" Umbati said as he splashed water on Jubilaree.

"Guys cut it out! I have to make sure we are not all dead. Meet me in the galley in fifteen minutes!" Matuka said as he put on his boots and hat.

"Interesting," Tahma said before Matuka quickly walked out of the large bathing room.

Meanwhile in the girls bathing room, the girls were enraged and getting dressed.

"A girl can't even get a little privacy around here!" Yanielle said as she tightened her leather bustier.

"There will be bloodshed," Kotoyami said with a serious face as she continued to get dressed.

On the other side of the wall, the boys were fully dressed and afraid to leave the bathing room.

"This sucks! I'm so hungry!" Umbati whined as he fell to the floor.

"Shut up! This is your fault!" Dayhoon said as he looked to his little brother.

"My thoughts exactly," Jubilaree said before he walked to the entrance of the bathroom.

"You two are just as guilty as me! Right Tahma?" Umbati asked as he looked up to Tahma.

"Interesting, you may have a valid point. However, we were warned," Tahma said as he sat down next to Umbati and crossed his legs.

"Well, we have no choice but to see what Matuka is going to do to save our necks," Jubilaree said before he turned around and joined the group of lads again.

"Whatever it is I hope it's soon," Dayhoon said as he sat down next to Tahma.

"You can't rush this type of thing, if it goes wrong, we are all dead," Jubilaree said before he sat down next to Umbati.

At that time, Matuka was alone in the galley making all the plates and setting the table.

"Okay, there we go, as long as the girls can come straight in and eat, their minds won't be on the incident," Matuka said as he sat the last plate on the table.

The table was full of food and the room held the most fantastic aroma, that began to take hold on the entire second deck. Matuka then continued to fill the cups on the table with the warm tea Kotoyami had prepared.

"This all looks so amazing," Matuka said with a smile as he looked over the table.

Ten minutes passed and Matuka was nearly done setting the table with the silverware.

"Now all I need is the handkerchiefs and everything will be set," Matuka said as he placed the last fork on the table and looked to the southwest wall at the cabinet for the handkerchiefs.

After Matuka sat the final handkerchief unto the table, both the boys and girls walked in the galley from their side of the hallway.

"Hi everyone, I took the liberty of making all the plates and setting the table. I know you girls have worked hard in here all day and I know you guys tried your hardest not to interrupt them. So here is my token to you all, the Hyungetta, the crew with the black sails!" Matuka said with a nervous smile as he looked to the crew and prayed that the girls wouldn't start fighting the boys.

"Interesting," Tahma said softly while he fixed his glasses.

"Speaking of interrupting!" Yanielle said as she began to walk forward into the galley.

That's when Kotoyami grabbed Yanielle's left arm and signaled for her to drop the subject.

"*Well played, Matuka,*" Jubilaree thought to himself as he looked on at the girls and back to Matuka.

"Alright is everyone ready?! Take a seat! Let's eat!" Matuka said with a satisfied and relieved smile as the crew walked closer to him.

One by one, the crew began to sit down at the table that had been prepared for them by their Captain. Umbati, Dayhoon and Tahma sat on the south of the table, while Jubilaree, Kotoyami, Yanielle and Matuka sat on the north side of the table.

"Gonna say a prayer Captain?" Jubilaree asked Matuka stoically with his eye closed and arms crossed.

"Come on guys! I'm starving! It smells so good!" Umbati quickly whined.

"Quiet! We're already here, one more minute won't kill you, bro," Dayhoon said as he looked down to his right at his little brother.

"Fine!" Umbati said as he crossed his

arms.

"Everyone bow your heads and close your eyes," Matuka said softly as he closed his eyes and bowed his head.

"Don't even think about it!" Kotoyami said with her eyes closed as Umbati tried to sneak a bite.

Umbati frowned and then immediately dropped his fork, bowed his head, and closed his eyes.

"Dear God, we are gathered here under unusual circumstances. We are without memories, family, and direction. We know all things happen for a reason, so we welcome the unknown along this journey. We thank you for this meal and are asking you to bless the cooks. We are asking you to make it safe and nourishing for our bodies. And last but not least, I thank you for bringing all of us together. Keep us safe from harm and danger, Amen. Let's eat!" Matuka said with a big clap before he lifted his head.

"Finally!" Umbati screamed as he grabbed his fork and began to eat.

The crew sat quietly at the table as they stuffed their hungry mouths with the delicious food that sat before them.

"So, Yanielle, Kotoyami, do you want to tell us what exactly this amazing food is?" Matuka said as he looked to his left.

"You want to tell him?" Yanielle asked with a smile as she wiped her face.

"Sure, well, I made a tea from the fruits and herbs from Yanielle's room. I added the sugarcanes from Tahma's room for sweetness. It includes oranges, lemons, ginger, mint, and sugarcanes. The stew was made from the vegetables from my room which includes carrots, celery, onions, peppers, and potatoes.

It also had some fish thrown in there. The salt was added from the bins over there as well. The flying fish that all of you see before you, was fried over the fire. The wheat that was in Dayhoon and Umbati's room, I boiled the wheat berries and prepared it like rice. The beans were strangely already seasoned, so all I did was boil them to soften them. The fruit platter is from the fruits from Yanielle and my room. It consists of pineapples, apples, oranges, peaches, mangos, pears, and blueberries. Finally, the bread and seasonings was from below in the stowage deck," Kotoyami said before she lifted her fork to eat.

"Well this is amazing!" Umbati said with a stuffed mouth before the crew laughed and continued to eat.

"Do you like it Jubilaree?" Kotoyami asked as she looked to her left towards Jubilaree.

"Yeah, it's pretty good," Jubilaree said

as he blushed softly.

"I'm glad you like it," Kotoyami said with a smile before she continued to eat.

"Well I like it too!" Dayhoon said with a jealous tone of voice as he looked across to Kotoyami.

"Thank you Dayhoon, I'm glad you like it as well," Kotoyami said with a smile as she fixed her hair behind her right ear.

Dayhoon blushed and then smirked with an evil look in his eyes as he stared at Jubilaree.

"Interesting, I wasn't expecting such an extravagant meal. The colors are beautiful, the smell is tantalizing, and the taste is unreal," Tahma said as he looked across the table to his right at Yanielle and Kotoyami.

"Thank you Tahma, we appreciate it," Yanielle said with a smile as she continued to eat.

"We couldn't have done this without Matuka, he did the dirty work, by cutting up all the vegetables and fruits. So, we thank you for your help Captain," Kotoyami said as she leaned forward and looked to her right past Yanielle to Matuka.

"Aww, my pleasure, I was just happy to help serve," Matuka said with a smile and his eyes closed.

"Well maybe you can help me by passing that fruit platter this way," Umbati said with a stuffed mouth.

Everyone except Umbati stopped eating and began to laugh.

"Did I say something?" Umbati questioned with a serious face.

"Here you go Umbati, eat up!" Matuka said with a smile as he passed Umbati the fruit platter.

After the crew ate, they sat at the table and could barely move.

"I'm stuffed!" Umbati said with a satisfied smile as he leaned forward on the table with his arms.

"You should be, you ate nearly all the extras," Dayhoon said with a smirk and with his eyes closed.

"Well I'm glad you liked it Umbati," Yanielle said with a smile.

That's when Kotoyami stood up and began to clear off the table.

"You didn't have to do that Kotoyami," Matuka said with a smile as he stood up from the table to help clear it.

"It's fine, plus these scraps and extras are going to Iraja," Kotoyami said with a smile as she turned around and emptied some of the scraps into the garbage sack.

"Good thinking, I nearly forgot about Iraja," Matuka said with a guilty smile as he helped clear off the table.

"Interesting, I have so many questions," Tahma said as he stood and passed his plate to Matuka.

"Story time!" Umbati cheerfully yelled as he stood up on the bench he was seated on.

"Yeah, we have a lot of questions Matuka," Jubilaree said with a serious face before he passed his plate to Kotoyami.

"Yeah, so let's get these drinks going," Dayhoon said with a smile before he stood up.

"I knew that was coming. Oh well, can't beat them, join them," Yanielle said as she stood up from the table.

"Alright, well let's finish cleaning and then we can go in the saloon to talk," Matuka said as he cleared off the table.

After a couple minutes of cleaning, the crew returned the galley to its splendor.

"I'm going to take this to Iraja, don't start without me. I'll be right back," Kotoyami said before she ran out of the galley with the nearly-filled sack.

"Alright, then guys let's go in and get things situated for her return," Matuka said as he looked to the rest of the guild.

The rest of the crew went into the galley and got comfortable on the recliner chairs that were stationed in the middle of the room. At that time, Kotoyami had just made it up to the deck where one of Iraja's tentacles was already waiting.

"So, you knew I was coming?" Kotoyami asked aloud as she stared at the huge and wet tentacle.

"I did, young Mistress," Iraja quickly said telepathically.

"Here you go, I hope you enjoy," Kotoyami said as she tossed the garbage sack in the air.

"Thank you, young Mistress!" Iraja said after he grabbed the sack and took it underwater.

"Amazing," Kotoyami said before the sack was tossed back up on the ship's deck.

"Hmmm tasty," Iraja said telepathically before he made the ship vibrate.

"I guess you did like it," Kotoyami said with a smile.

"I always loved your cooking," Iraja said telepathically.

"But you only had scraps earlier, and a small taste just now, how can you say you always loved it?" Kotoyami questioned Iraja telepathically with a suspicious look on her face.

The night had grown dark and the stars were out and shining beautifully. The moon was golden and the clouds gave it its room to shine without interruption. There also was a nice breeze flowing about the deck and the waves were relaxing to the ears of its listeners.

After a few moments passed, Kotoyami and Ira-ja finished their secret conversation.

"Okay, well goodnight Iraja," Kotoyami said to Iraja aloud.

"Goodnight, young Mistress!" Iraja responded telepathically.

Kotoyami then slowly proceeded back to the saloon where everyone was waiting. By the time Kotoyami reached the saloon, everyone was in a chair and happy to see she finally made it back.

"There she is!" Yanielle said with a smile as she looked to her left towards the saloon entry.

"Hey, I have a seat for you right here next to me!" Dayhoon said with a smirk before he looked across to Jubilaree.

"Oh please," Jubilaree said sarcastically as he closed his eye and crossed his arms.

After Kotoyami got closer, she let out a deep sigh and plopped down in her chair.

"Everything good girl?" Yanielle quickly asked as she looked to her left.

"Yeah, just ready for some answers," Kotoyami said as she looked to the left towards Matuka.

The night was upon them, the ship was as still as could be and it was finally time to talk.

"Alright! Umbati, go grab a couple of

bottles," Matuka said as he looked across at him.

"Say no more Captain!" Umbati yelled with a smile before he quickly ran and grabbed two wine bottles from behind the bar.

"If you haven't noticed everyone, there is a mug on the side of your chair," Matuka said as he picked up his brown, wooden mug, that was to the right of him on the floor.

One by one, everyone picked up their mugs to be filled by Umbati.

"Alright Umbati, let's get these mugs filled," Matuka said as he gestured for Umbati to come.

Mug by Mug, Umbati poured until all their mugs were completely filled.

"A little heavy on the hand much?" Yanielle sarcastically asked as she wiped the side of her filled mug.

"Sorry," Umbati said with a childish grin.

"Interesting," Tahma said as he looked over his right shoulder at the bar.

"What's that Tahma?" Matuka asked as he looked at the curious young lad.

"Oh, it's nothing, we'll have time to discuss," Tahma replied.

Once Umbati filled everyone's mug, he went back to his chair to sit.

"Alright, now that we all are ready, I

would like to make a toast! So, everyone raise your mug. I would like to toast to meeting you guys; to still being alive and surviving this war somehow. To being the only family I have right now! I toast to our friendship, to our destiny, to our memories being found! I toast to this crew, the Hyungetta!" Matuka said as he raised his mug in the air.

"What does the Hyungetta even mean?" Yanielle asked as she looked to her right at Matuka.

"I have no idea, it just came to me," Matuka said with a smile and with his eyes closed after he faced Yanielle.

"Interesting," Tahma said as he fixed his glasses with his right hand.

"To the crew with the black sails! The Hyungetta!" Umbati yelled with a smile as he lifted his mug even higher.

"To the Hyungetta!" everyone yelled in unison.

After the crew took their first sip of the wine, the ship began to softly vibrate.

"Was that you Iraja?" Matuka asked aloud in front of everyone.

"No young Master, that was not me. However, the one a few minutes ago was me when Mistress Kotoyami fed me the delicious food you helped prepare," Iraja said telepathically to everyone this time.

"Whoa!" Umbati said as he sat up in his reclined chair.

"That's so cool," Dayhoon said before he took a sip from his mug.

"Interesting, we all heard him this time," Tahma said before he fixed his glasses and took a sip.

"It's definitely time for some answers Matuka," Jubilaree said as he took a sip with his eye closed and then looked to Matuka.

"Indeed," Kotoyami quickly chimed in as she raised her mug to Jubilaree.

"Story time!" Umbati yelled with a drunken smile as he looked to Matuka.

"This should be good," Dayhoon said as he sat up in his reclined chair and looked to-wards Matuka.

That's when Matuka sat up with a serious look on his face and took a large gulp.

"Wow, okay," Yanielle said as she took a large sip as well.

"Where should I start? Let's see. Well, it all started for me when I woke up. I awoke to a dead enemy at my foot. The very next thing I saw was my father. He was dead and lying on the deck a few feet away. I noticed he died from bleeding out of his right leg," Matuka said before he took another large sip and gestured for Umbati to come pour him another cup.

"Interesting," Tahma said as he fixed his

glasses and looked at the green bandanna that was tied around Matuka's leg.

All eyes were on Matuka; they could feel his pain and began to feel sorry for him.

"But after I grabbed him and cried for hours it seemed, I noticed this ship in the distance. It was like a feeling of relief but also a feeling of fear. After I decided to leave my own ship, I made my way over to this one. The water was ice cold and there were bodies everywhere; literally. The pain from my wounds nearly took me under a few times it seemed. The moment I reached the ship and touched it; I was met with a vision of myself as a baby. I was on a half-broken rowboat, with a woman in the water next to me; holding onto the broken boat and holding something over me," Matuka said before he took a small sip.

"Interesting," Tahma said as he took a sip out of his mug.

"Yeah, that's weird," Yanielle quickly and softly said as she looked to her left at Matuka.

"I think she was my mother. Well at least that's the feeling I got from the vision. That's when the ship seemed to mend my breaking heart, and I began to feel peace. I also knew I couldn't stay in the water for long, so I snapped out of it. After I climbed up a rope that wasn't initially there, I boarded this empty vessel.

Room by room, I checked for someone. But there was no one, absolutely no one," Matuka said as he looked at everyone.

"Yeah, you left your blood everywhere and it won't come up. And! How come your blood didn't disappear when I healed you? Everyone else's blood did," Yanielle said as she looked to her left towards Matuka.

"That's a very good question Yanielle, however I don't know the answer to that," Matuka said as he looked to his right at Yanielle.

"Get back to the story!" Umbati whined before he took another sip.

"Okay, so, I went back up to the main deck, reached for a couple of arrows, dipped them in oil and sent them flying to my ship where the exposed ammo, gunpowder, explosives, flammable oil drums and fires were kindled. I watched my home go up into flames. The only memory I had left was fading fast, and that's when the unthinkable happened. The spirit of my father and crew appeared to me from the smoke of the ship. My father said a lot. He told me I was strong and though the distance between us had grown and the notion of time had changed, that we will never part for we are one," Matuka said before he took a sip from his mug.

"Interesting," Tahma said as he finished

his nearly emptied mug.

"He then told me that it wasn't my fault and I have been given a very special opportunity, a second chance. He told me to be kind to others, run from no fight and I have the strength to overcome any opposition. He told me I will be one of the strongest warriors amongst nations and even known to man.

That the waters of the rain, the rivers, lakes, ponds, swamps, bayous, canals, puddles, the oceans, and seas will be my footstool. He reassured me the animals will hear my cry and aid me always and forever, for I was their alpha, their friend and protector, but only after I declared it so. He also told me that the thunder only stands still for me and the Creator," Matuka said as he stared down at his mug.

"Wow, I was wondering where you got all of that strange talk from after the fight," Yanielle said before she took her last gulp and then gestured for Umbati to refill it.

"Yeah, I know it is strange. He then told me that the fire from my soul burns deeply, so make sure to let it out once in a while," Matuka said as he looked around to the crew.

"Sounds like our dream big bro," Umbati said as he looked towards his brother before he got up to refill Yanielle's drink.

"Indeed, little bro," Dayhoon said as he took another sip of wine.

"He also said the fog will be my shield everywhere I'd go, and that this vessel has no limits. He said that this is my ship, that I'm the Captain and that it will be linked to me and my crew. He then said it was a gift from the ocean," Matuka said before he took another sip and dropped his head.

"How strange," Kotoyami said as she took a large sip.

"Yeah, he told me to make friends, to learn how to trust, forgive and live honorably. He told me to live everyday like it was my last and try not to ignore people and their feelings, especially the ones who care for me," Matuka said as he lifted his head.

"Well you can definitely work on that one," Yanielle said before everyone began to chuckle.

"Touché, I remember telling him I wouldn't remember what he said, it's funny, cause he said I'd remember when I needed to and nothing is truly forgotten, just hidden. I guess he was right because I haven't remembered any of this in detail until now. I even remember getting a little out of line when I told him to look around because there was no one in sight to befriend. He then told me that the things seen are because of the things not seen.

He told me to have faith in myself; to wear this tri-cone hat proud and with some heart. He said I was royalty and not to worry, that I'd remember what I need to know with time. He warned me to not forget my skills; to find the ones I lost long ago before time coming, whatever that means," Matuka said as he looked around at the crew.

"Interesting," Jubilaree said with a smirk as he looked to Tahma before he could say it.

"Hey, that's my line," Tahma said with a smile before he took a sip and looked back towards his left at Jubilaree.

"The final thing he said was that it was urgent that I located my crew, and that you all needed me, and that's when the spirits of my crew said everyone did as well. Next thing I knew, the thunder and swirling of the cocoon of smoke increased, and the strong winds lifted me up off the deck. A small shower of rain hugged the vortex of smoke and thunder, and just like that, they were gone, and I was all alone," Matuka said before he took another sip of the fine wine.

"That's insane," Yanielle said as she sat back in the chair and looked up to the ceiling of the saloon.

"Yeah," everyone else said in unison before they all took a sip.

"But the moment I touched the helm I was met with a vision of Yanielle floating in the water amongst the debris. Once I saw that, I tried my hardest to pull away but couldn't, I was glued to the helm, and the deck. Next thing I know, I was speeding off and headed to you, Yanielle," Matuka said with a smile as he looked to his right towards Yanielle.

Yanielle began to blush so she took another large gulp and finished her mug.

"Another one please!" Yanielle said with a smile as she looked to Umbati.

"Dang girl! You drink like a fish!" Umbati said with a smile as he wobbled over to Yanielle to fill her mug.

"Well that's where I come in," Jubilaree said as he sat to the edge of his chair.

"Huh?" Matuka asked confusedly as he looked to his right towards Jubilaree.

"So, my story starts with me waking up on a floating, wooden table. I awake to death and carnage with a massive pain in my left eye. I saw Captain here, coming up to my left very fast, so, with all the might I had, I jumped all the way to the crow's nest and rested until he stopped. After he stopped, I jumped down from the crow's nest and landed behind him," Jubilaree said with a smirk before he looked to Matuka.

"Yeah, thanks a lot for that, I thought I was a goner!" Matuka said with a chuckle before he took another sip and finished his mug.

Umbati then got up and refilled everyone's mugs who had finished their drinks.

"There you go," Umbati said with a smile as he refilled Tahma's cup.

"Why thank you kind sir," Tahma said with a smile as he drunkenly rocked in his reclined chair.

"Well, after that, I guess that's where I come in," Yanielle said as she took a small sip.

"Sounds about right," Matuka said with a smile as he took a small sip and looked at Yanielle.

"All I remember is waking up in the water; already fighting for my life. I was trying not to drown but my clothes were ensnared on sharp and dangerous debris. Next thing I knew, I woke up and saw you two on the deck unconscious," Yanielle said as she looked from Matuka to Jubilaree.

"Yeah, the Captain here tried to save us after I got snagged on something trying to save you. By the time he got to us, he was already going in and out of consciousness. That's when he passed out and I tried to grab for him, and I began to sink. Next thing I know is the net he was holding while he swam to us, wrapped around all three of us and began to pull us out the water," Jubilaree said before he took a sip of wine.

"That's freaky," Umbati said as he took a large gulp of wine from his mug.

"Yeah, that's super weird," Dayhoon said as he looked to Jubilaree.

"Like the rest of this ship is not?" Yanielle questioned sarcastically before she took another small sip.

"Yeah I guess you're right," Dayhoon said as he looked down to his half empty mug.

"Yep, so after I ran below deck; strangely drawn to my room, I gathered supplies and headed back up to heal Matuka and Jubilaree. The rest is history I guess," Yanielle said as she looked around to everyone.

"I guess this is where I come in," Kotoyami said as she sat on the edge of her reclined chair.

"Yep," Matuka said with a smile as he looked to his immediate left towards Kotoyami.

"Well, the only thing I can remember was waking up on that door and realizing I was all alone. I just knew I was going to die, and I began to prepare for it. I was going to meditate until I reached the great beyond. But amongst the quiet destruction, I was able to hear something or someone coming my way. I didn't know if it was a friend or foe, so I prepared with my meditation. I was preparing to kill you three if needed," Kotoyami said as she looked to Matuka, Yanielle and Jubilaree.

"Ouch!" Yanielle said before she took a sip from her mug.

"That's pretty rough," Dayhoon said as he looked to his right at Kotoyami.

"What do you expect? I'm a young girl in a world of bad men, I would have had to do something if it wasn't Matuka here that found me," Kotoyami said as she took a sip of wine.

"Agreed," Matuka quickly chimed in before he took a sip.

"Well, when you put it like that," Dayhoon said before he shrugged his shoulders and took a gulp.

"So, the rest is history, I don't remember anything from before I woke up," Kotoyami said as she sat back in her chair and took a small sip.

"Well I guess that brings the story to us huh bro?" Dayhoon questioned as he looked down to his left.

"Are you guys ready for the most epic story?!" Umbati yelled before he took a large gulp from the bottle and finished it.

"I wouldn't have it no other way," Matuka said with a smile as he looked to Umbati and Dayhoon.

The saloon grew quiet as the crew waited to hear Dayhoon and Umbati's story.

"This should be good," Yanielle said sarcastically, which made Kotoyami chuckle and spit out some of her wine.

"I'm going to act like I didn't hear that.

Anyway! So! There we were…" Umbati said before being interrupted by Dayhoon.

"Wait! Start with the dream," Dayhoon said as he stood up, opened the second bottle and proceeded to refill everyone's mug.

"I just like how you thought I wasn't going to start there," Umbati said with an attitude.

"Cut the crap and get to the story," Jubilaree said with a stoic and stern voice before he had another taste of the fine wine.

"Okay! So! It seems me and my brother had the same exact dream at the same time," Umbati said as Dayhoon sat down from pouring drinks.

"Yeah, it felt real," Dayhoon quickly chimed in as he looked to his brother.

"So, there we were, in the same dream together. We were in the water; it was night and the waves were devastating. We could barely hold on any longer when we saw Matuka standing with blood in his eyes and fire was coming from his hand. He was on this very ship and the aura around him; you, anyone could see a visual of what peace and safety was. We eventually woke up from that dream and saw that it was mid-day.

Dayhoon was the first to notice all the death around us. While I was the one who noticed all the floating bottles of rum and wine. We were floating on one large plank of wood, there were explosives on sinking ships nearby and we got bored..." Umbati said before being interrupted by Yanielle.

"See, I told you Matuka! You were giving them too much credit," Yanielle said as she tasted her drink.

"Now wait a minute little lady, I'll have you know that it wasn't so simple, right little bro?" Dayhoon said before he punched Umbati in the right arm.

"You're gonna make me tell them?" Umbati whined.

"Yep," Dayhoon quickly replied with a stern look.

"Ah whatever! Anyhow, while we were sitting there, we were asking each other what we thought the dream meant. I thought it meant death was coming, to escort us to our graves in the abyss. However, Dayhoon had more faith. I was scared okay?! So, I began to cry! I was hungry, with no memories. All we knew was that we were brothers. I got thirsty and Dayhoon tried his hardest to resist giving the rum to me.

But he didn't want me to die! So, I did drink and was given energy again. Dayhoon followed with a drink from guilt of giving it to me. We began to think, if we were going to die out there, why not go out with a blast! So, we ran atop the debris, picking up all the explosives and found guns with ammo on dead, floating bodies. We made a vow that we would die together if we had to and that's when we started shooting at the explosives," Umbati yelled and cried before he took a big gulp.

The rest of the crew felt sorry for the brothers and raised their mugs to them.

"Thanks guys," Dayhoon said as he looked around the circle.

"So, eventually, Captain shows up just like he did in the dream, minus the fire and aura. We knew it was him immediately. It was even the same boat from our dream. However, you guys weren't in sight in the dream," Umbati said after he wiped his tears and before he took another sip.

"Yeah, after Umbati here got shot, and I passed out with him and Captain in my hands, we literally fell into the same exact dream," Dayhoon said as he looked around to everyone.

"Interesting," Tahma said softly while he fixed his glasses.

"I didn't know, I'm sorry," Yanielle said as she raised her mug to the boys once again.

"Forgiven," the brothers said in unison.

Everyone got silent for a moment and stared at their mugs.

"But yeah, after that, I'm pretty sure we know who came running into the story, literally," Dayhoon said as he looked to Tahma with a smile.

"Oh, it's my turn? Interesting, where do I start? Well, let's see. I woke up mid-day as well as you two; it seems, and I noticed that I was in an area with a lot of wood, scrap metal and supplies. I looked down and picked up one piece at a time, one by one, all the pieces that were near me. Before I knew it, I had subconsciously made those shoes you all saw without even remembering how to, it was almost like instinct.

By that time, the sun was setting, I had seen the aftermath from Dayhoon and Umbati, so I decided to hurry. Later, before I could finish, I could see a storm brewing near the explosion I saw earlier in the distance. That's when I looked back at the shoes and couldn't remember how I knew how to build them. Even though I didn't remember how, I didn't care because shortly after, that's when I saw the mother of all sharks headed my way and fast!

So, I hurried and put them on and took off as fast as I could! Eventually I ran into you guys and could see the weird lightning activity over the ship. Well at first, I couldn't see the ship but one of the flashes exposed the ship. I think because of the way it struck down. If it wasn't for that, I wouldn't have seen the ship because it looked nearly invisible to the naked eye, due to the fog. But, after I saw the image of the ghostly ship, I knew it was my only chance for survival. So, I ran and ran," Tahma said before he took a large gulp.

"Yeah, all the way into the ship, literally," Umbati laughed before Dayhoon and him gave each other a high-five.

"What happened to the shark?" Matuka asked with a curious and eager smile before he took a sip from his mug.

"That's what I'd love to know," Jubilaree said as he opened his eye and turned to his right towards Tahma.

"I don't know," Tahma said softly before he relaxed back in his seat and took a sip.

"It was I," Iraja said with a loud stern voice telepathically to all the guild.

Everyone was in the middle of drinking when they heard Iraja's voice, so they all spat it out in unison from being caught off guard again.

"Whoa!" Dayhoon said as he wiped his mouth.

"No freaking way! That's so freaking cool!" Umbati said as he looked around the room for confirmation on what he heard.

"No one messes with the Hyungetta! The crew with the black sails!" Iraja shouted telepathically to everyone.

"Interesting, Iraja? If you can speak to us telepathically, isn't it possible for you to comb through our memories as well?" Tahma asked, which made everyone very curious to know his response.

"The truth is young Master; I know all about each and every single last one of you," Iraja said to the group telepathically.

"Wait! What?!" Matuka questioned aloud as he stood up.

"Yes, I know all about you and your past, but I cannot tell you or show you," Iraja said with a sad tone of voice telepathically to everyone.

"Interesting," Tahma quickly said softly before taking a large gulp of wine.

"Why not?" Matuka asked Iraja before he sat back down.

"Because it could possibly destroy all of our brains, his included," Jubilaree said as he took a sip of his mug.

"Yes, he told me the same thing earlier," Kotoyami quickly stated.

"So, you mean to tell me, you know everything about us, and you won't tell us?" Yanielle asked Iraja aloud with an aggravated tone before she had another sip from her mug.

"Not won't, he can't," Jubilaree said immediately in Iraja's defense.

"So, what now?" Kotoyami asked Matuka as she took a large sip as well as the others in that moment.

"I'm sorry young Masters and Mistresses, I can promise you this; you will remember when the time is right. I have said enough so I'll say goodnight for now young Masters and Mistresses," Iraja said before going silent.

"Goodnight Iraja," Matuka said as he walked to the bar to grab yet another bottle.

"That's number three already?" Yanielle asked before she burped and blushed.

"We didn't even get a chance to ask about anything serious," Umbati said as he stood to his feet and emptied his mug in his mouth.

"Gross," Yanielle said after Umbati burped obnoxiously.

"You're one to talk," Jubilaree said with a smirk as he looked to his left towards Yanielle.

"Look don't start with me one eye!" Yanielle snapped back at Jubilaree.

"For your information! I have two eyes damn it!" Jubilaree said before taking a massive sip.

"And goodnight you go!" Dayhoon said before he gave Umbati a high-five as they both looked to Jubilaree.

"Score!" Umbati said as he waved his empty mug around in the air.

"So Matuka, how did you get all of the fish?" Kotoyami quickly asked.

"Iraja told me to command the less intelligent creatures to serve as our dinner, so a huge wave full of fish formed and towered over the ship. After they all fell into the basket, they continued to rain onto the ship. The deck was covered and we clearly didn't need all of them..." Matuka said before being interrupted by Dayhoon.

"Maybe you should have gone twice, since Umbati here ate nearly all of it," Dayhoon said with a smirk as he looked to his younger brother.

Everyone then started to laugh, all except Umbati of course.

"Whatever! So, what happened next?" Umbati said before he looked to Matuka.

"Well, after I realized I had too much fish, I told them to return to the ocean, and that's when all of them did; instead of just the extra ones. Iraja and I then began to laugh once he told me I had to be more specific with the less intelligent sea creatures," Matuka said with a chuckle and a smile as he looked to Kotoyami.

That's when everyone except Tahma began to laugh at what Matuka said.

"Interesting," Tahma said as he took a sip of wine.

"But anyway, what all can you do Kotoyami?" Matuka asked as he walked closer to the group again.

"Uh, Captain. You don't want to know," Dayhoon quickly chimed in.

"Yeah!" Umbati said as he looked to Kotoyami.

Kotoyami then moved the hair in front of her face to behind her left ear and smiled with a gleam in her eyes.

"Okay then! How about some music?" Matuka asked as he walked around the circle of chairs to refill everyone's drink.

"Great idea!" Yanielle quickly said.

"Interesting," Tahma said as well.

"I can dig it," Dayhoon said before he took a small sip and stretched his arms.

"You ready bro?" Umbati said with a smile as he too stretched.

"What did you have in mind Captain?" Kotoyami asked as she blushed and stared at Matuka.

Suddenly, Dayhoon and Umbati began to beat the chairs with their hands and tap the floor with their feet.

"I like that!" Yanielle said as she stood up and started to dance with her mug in her hand.

"Interesting," Tahma said before he started to whistle and incorporate the melody into the sound that the brothers were creating.

That's when Kotoyami stood up and began to dance as well with her mug in her hand.

"Come Captain!" the girls said in unison as they danced to the sound of Tahma, Dayhoon and Umbati.

After Matuka took a big gulp, he nervously stood up and tried to walk over to the girls.

"You too Jubilaree, don't think you are off the hook that easy!" Yanielle said as she turned to look at Jubilaree from the middle of the circle.

"I think not," Jubilaree said with his eye closed.

Suddenly, Jubilaree was snatched up by Kotoyami and forced to dance with his mug in his hand. Everyone started to laugh except Jubilaree, which made him embarrassed, so he finished his mug and threw it to the deck.

"Alright, you want some of me? Well here goes!" Jubilaree said before he started dancing and having a good time.

"That's the way!" Dayhoon said with a smile as he continued to beat the edge of his chair and stomp.

"Ayyyyee!" Umbati cheered on as Jubilaree danced.

"Smooth," Kotoyami said to Jubilaree with a smile.

"I see you now, jerk!" Yanielle said with a smile as she danced around and looked towards Jubilaree.

"What?!" I would have never thought I'd see the day," Matuka thought to himself as he watched Jubilaree dance with everyone.

The crew continued to drink and laugh the night away until each soul had passed out. A couple of hours later, Matuka was awakened to Jubilaree sneaking out of the room, so he followed him silently. However, Matuka didn't know that the rest of the guild had awakened as well, and they also followed behind their Captain. By the time Jubilaree got to the main deck, he was in a lot of pain. He struggled to walk as he held his left eye and didn't know he had an audience. Suddenly, Jubilaree fell to his knees in the middle of the deck near the main mast. That's when Matuka immediately ran over to Jubilaree; to see what was wrong with his crew member.

"What's going on?!" Matuka asked after he dropped to his knees in front of Jubilaree.

"What the hell are you doing up here?" Jubilaree asked Matuka.

"You woke me up, so I followed, so what's the matter?" Matuka asked as he rested his right arm on Jubilaree's left shoulder.

"My left eye! It's on fire!" Jubilaree said before he snatched off his gray bandanna.

"Oh wow!" Matuka said as he looked at Jubilaree's left eye that was glowing red.

Suddenly, Matuka's necklace lifted off his chest and began to float in front of them both.

"What the hell?! What's happening?" Jubilaree asked as he looked to Matuka's necklace.

"I never saw this before," Matuka said as he watched the golden, astrolabe necklace begin to open and spin out of control.

Once the red light from Jubilaree's left eye shined down on the necklace, a white beam of light shot out of Matuka's necklace and soared up to the sky.

"Whoa," Matuka said as he looked up to the beam.

"Unreal," Jubilaree said as he looked also.

The beam then exploded at its top then fell back down towards the ocean many miles away.

"Tell me you're seeing this too!" Jubilaree said while they both followed the beam of light.

Matuka and Jubilaree could not believe their eyes under the night's sky. For there in the distance, was an entire island that looked as if it were glowing in the night.

"What the heck is that?! Is that land?!" Matuka yelled, which made the rest of the crew reveal themselves.

"It's beautiful," Kotoyami said softly, as she walked closer to join Matuka and Jubilaree.

"No freaking way!" Dayhoon said as he looked from the ship at the distant island.

"Interesting, it's the same glow," Tahma said as he walked closer to starboard side.

"This just keeps getting weirder and weirder," Umbati said as he walked over to Matuka and Jubilaree.

"Yeah," Jubilaree said as he covered his once glowing red eye with his gray bandanna.

"Is that how you found Kotoyami?" Yanielle asked as she walked up to Jubilaree.

"I don't know what you are talking about, last I checked, the Captain found Kotoyami," Jubilaree said before he walked closer to starboard side.

"Whatever," Yanielle said as she turned to Matuka.

"Is that really an island Tahma?" Matuka asked as he looked to the young genius.

"Well Captain, there's only one way to find out," Tahma said as he turned to look at Matuka.

The crew became quiet before they all turned to look at Matuka, to know what they were going to do next.

"To your places!" Matuka said before he ran to the helm deck.

"Places?" Umbati asked with a look of

confusion over his face.

"Hurry!" Yanielle said before Tahma and her ran to the sides of Matuka.

That's when Kotoyami ran towards the bowsprit and Jubilaree jumped to the crow's nest.

"Come up here! To guard this front deck!" Kotoyami yelled from the tip of the bowsprit.

"Yes ma'am!" Dayhoon said with a smile before Umbati and him ran to stand on the front deck of the ship behind her.

"You guys ready?!" Matuka asked as he reached for the warm and inviting helm.

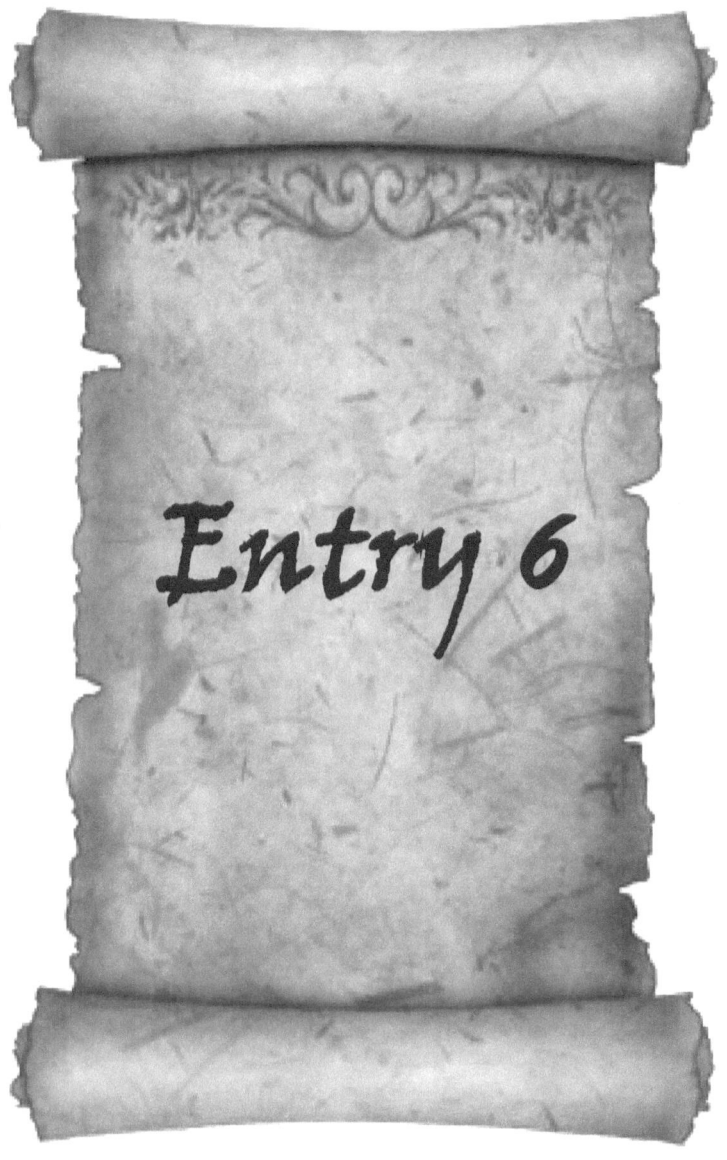

Entry 6

HIDDEN

The night was beautifully doused with stars and the ocean was soothing to the ears of the young children. They silently stood in their places and stared off into the distance at the luminescent island; that shined like the northern lights. The moment Matuka grabbed the helm, all their clothes and hair began to float. Tears of blood fell from his eyes, while warmth from his soul transferred from his body, through his hands, to the ship's helm.

Fog quickly seeped from the boat's exterior until the ship was completely shrouded in a blanket of invisibility again. Matuka was immediately met with a vision and was able to see the island at an aerial view from where he was standing. He instinctively knew it was theirs and only theirs to claim. Then suddenly, the ship took off like a bullet towards the glowing island with superior speed.

"So cool!" Umbati yelled as he tried to look to his left towards Dayhoon.

"I knew you two would like it here," Kotoyami said as she looked over her right shoulder at the brothers.

"Yeah!" Dayhoon screamed as he enjoyed the rush and looked forward to Kotoyami.

The closer they got to the island the brighter it grew, which alerted a nearby ship.

"Captain! Do you see that?!" a guild member asked their Captain.

"Let me see," the Captain said as he took the spyglass to have a look.

His crew began to whisper and asked each other where it came from.

"I see! Well men! We have ourselves an entire freaking treasure island it appears! Ready the sails!" the Captain said before he tossed back the spyglass.

The guild of thieves slowly made their way to the island, while Matuka and his guild already closed the gap. Suddenly, an invisible wave exploded and went out in all directions from the island. Although the winds were great, it passed through Matuka's and the guild of thieves' ship without doing harm to anyone. The wave cloaked the entire island and was no longer visible, only to the ones within the force field.

"I don't like the looks of this Captain," one of the guild members said as he looked at his Captain.

"Onward!" the Captain yelled as he looked towards the west side of the island.

At this time, Matuka and the guild drifted down a large river that led into a hidden cove on the east side of the island.

"Iraja are you okay? Can you fit?" Matuka quickly asked as the ship stopped and their bodies were released to move again.

"Yes Master, I am fine. There is more than enough room for me down here," Iraja said to everyone telepathically.

This place is freaking insane!" Dayhoon said as he looked around at the beautiful, and different illuminated colors coming from within the elements of the island.

"Interesting, this place seems to be alive but on a different level. It's like the rooms on the ship," Tahma said as he looked at the glowing green vegetation and then towards the different colors screaming from the trees.

"Yeah, no kidding," Yanielle said as she looked to her left past Matuka towards Tahma.

As the crew got closer to the shore, Iraja lifted one of his enormous tentacles out of the water and made it hover over the glowing beach sand, so the guild could have passage to shore.

"Interesting," Tahma quickly said as he fixed his glasses.

"No way," Dayhoon said with a shocked facial expression as he gazed at Iraja's large, grayish-brown, and dark-purple spotted tentacle.

"Iraja, you're the best dude!" Umbati said with a large child-like grin and with his eyes closed.

Jubilaree smirked with his eye closed and arms crossed before he jumped from the crow's nest, down to the main deck.

"Thank you Iraja," Kotoyami said as she bowed to his tentacle while she stood on the bowsprit.

"Yes, thank you Iraja, you read my mind," Matuka said with a smile and with his eyes closed as he held the back of his head with his right hand.

"Yes, thank you Iraja, you the man, I mean the..." Yanielle said with a nervous smile before she was interrupted by Iraja.

"All aboard, young Masters and Mistresses, there are foreigners closing in on the island. You must hurry to shore to touch it first!" Iraja sternly said to all the young lads and lasses telepathically.

The guild looked confused for a second as they tried to wrap their minds around what Iraja had told them.

"Okay Iraja, we trust you. Alright team! Let's go!" Matuka said before he left Yanielle and Tahma to run down the helm deck.

"Interesting," Tahma quickly said as he fixed his specs.

Matuka then ran past Jubilaree, across the main deck past Dayhoon and Umbati, towards the front deck above his quarters, to the tentacle that was awaiting them all.

"You coming?" Matuka asked with an eager smile and warm presence as he looked towards his left at Kotoyami on the bowsprit.

Kotoyami then tucked the hair that was in front of her face behind her left ear and took off running on Iraja's tentacle, towards the glowing beach sand.

"Hey! Wait for me!" Matuka said before he pushed his hat down onto his head and took off running after Kotoyami.

"Well bro, let's get a move on," Dayhoon said as he looked down to his right at his little brother.

"Sure thing bro," Umbati said with a smile while he looked up to his left at Dayhoon.

The two brothers took off, one after another, like bullets onto Iraja's arm.

"You two coming or not?!" Jubilaree shouted as he turned around; looked to the helm deck at Yanielle and Tahma before he leaped onto Iraja.

"Interesting, maybe we should get a move on, huh Yanielle?" Tahma asked while he looked to his right at Yanielle.

"Yeah, I'm just a little nervous," Yanielle softly mumbled while she twiddled her thumbs.

"You must hurry young Master and Mistress," Iraja said gently to Tahma and Yanielle telepathically.

Tahma then grabbed Yanielle's hand and fixed his glasses as he glared into her soul.

"I won't let you slip off, okay?" Tahma asked with a smile as he looked to Yanielle.

"Yeah," Yanielle replied with a smile and with her eyes closed.

Tahma and Yanielle then ran down the helm deck, across the main deck, to the front deck and jumped onto Iraja's tentacle. One by one, the crew hurried across Iraja's arm while the other ship was closing in on the west side of the island.

"Ahhh!" Matuka yelled as he shot past Kotoyami, jumped and landed onto the glowing beach sand; headfirst.

"Pitiful," Jubilaree said as he walked up

behind Kotoyami.

Kotoyami jumped off Iraja onto the shore, knelt and then picked up a glowing seashell.

"Hey! No fair!" Dayhoon yelled as Umbati and he caught up to the others.

"Yeah, I almost fell thanks to you!" Umbati said as he looked up to Jubilaree with his fist balled.

"Training never ends, boys," Jubilaree said with a smile as he stepped off Iraja onto the shore.

"Why I oughta…" Dayhoon said before he was swept off his feet by Tahma and Yanielle.

"Hey!" Umbati yelled after he was caught off guard by the collision.

Tahma, Yanielle, Dayhoon and Umbati all flew off Iraja's wet surface, then fell onto the shore in a bundle. Immediately after, a huge shock wave went out in all directions from around the crew, Iraja, the ship and the island once again.

"Success young Masters and Mistresses!" Iraja said telepathically with joy to the entire guild.

"Alright!" Matuka jumped up and yelled as he fixed his hat.

"Can someone explain?" Umbati said as he tried to stand from the pile.

"Yeah, start with these enemies," Dayhoon quickly replied as he stood up.

"Of course, young Master. Well, I could sense the other ship in the water from the vibrations as well as the other sea creatures who communicate with me on a regular basis. The intruders are drawing near to the west shore as we speak. Once they land, I cannot help you physically. There are no animals here either that could aid you as well. However, this is your home away from the ship, so you'll feel strangely comfortable and safe. Like you've already been here," Iraja said to the entire crew telepathically.

"Interesting, like how you communicated with the shark, tell me, was that telepathy or vibrations?" Tahma asked Iraja aloud in front of the rest of the guild.

"Both actually young Master," Iraja replied telepathically to them all.

"Interesting," Tahma said as he looked back to the ocean.

"What are you cooking up over there?" Jubilaree asked with his arms crossed as he opened his right eye and looked to Tahma.

Meanwhile, the guild of thieves had just felt the wave and wind from the invisible energy.

"Uh, Captain, did you feel that? And did the island's light dim?" a guild member asked as he looked for a glimmer of hope from their overconfident leader.

"I, Okokobi, Captain, leader of the deadliest guild of swashbuckling, good for nothings, best treasure hunting, conniving bastards I love and hate, will claim us all victory and riches beyond your wildest imaginations! The moment we step foot on that damn island! So, all speed ahead!" Captain Okokobi yelled as he looked at the magnificent island that was drawing nearer to him.

Back on the island, the crew had left Iraja with the ship and headed off into the unknown of the glowing barren jungle. The island was breathtaking, the lights shined through the dirt, grass, trees, fruits, herbs, flowers, and bushes, just like the objects back in the rooms.

"Interesting," Tahma said softly as he looked around at the trees.

"What's that?" Matuka asked as he turned around in the front of the line to look at the young genius.

"From afar, the island was extremely visible with the arrays of colors. However, now that we are here, they're illuminated like the things from the ship. You know, just enough for us to see. It seems like the moment we stepped foot into this thicket, the island calmed down and produced less light..." Tahma said before he was interrupted by Jubilaree.

"As though it was just to draw us here," Jubilaree said as he stood in line behind Matuka with his eye closed and arms crossed.

"Here? To this spot in the jungle?" Umbati asked as he looked up to the back of Tahma's head.

"No, what Tahma means is that we were drawn here to the island and the moment we stepped foot on the shore, the lights began to dim. I noticed it as well," Kotoyami said as she looked at Jubilaree's back; before she turned around.

"So now what?" Yanielle asked with her left hand on her hip while she faced Kotoyami.

"Onward?" Dayhoon asked sarcastically from the end of the line with both his palms up.

"Exactly!" Matuka said before he turned around and began to march through the thick, glowing bushes.

One by one, the crew pressed through until they reached a small open patch of land with a small creek. The creek was absolutely stunning with its glow, and it was accompanied by a huge, illuminated Banyan tree.

"Water!" Umbati yelled as he started to run towards the creek.

"Wait!" Tahma yelled to Umbati before he could get any closer.

The rest of the crew realized that Umbati was standing in the midst of some very strange-looking plants. The plants looked somewhat like mushrooms but were yellow with white spots, the top of the plants were green and round, unlike a mushroom. Suddenly, the mushroom-looking plants began to open from the top and glowed even brighter.

"Brother!" Dayhoon yelled as he tried to run to Umbati's rescue.

"Big bro!" Umbati yelled before he was caught in an explosion of pollen.

Immediately, Umbati dropped to the ground as the plants wilted and died simultaneously. By the time Dayhoon reached Umbati, he was still unconscious and laying in the dead patch of strange plants.

"Umbati! Lil bro! Wake up! You guys help! Yanielle help!" Dayhoon yelled as he looked back to the crew that was closing in quickly.

"I'm coming!" Yanielle screamed before she reached the brothers.

Yanielle quickly pulled out her silver, healing tool and placed it over Umbati.

"That's strange," Yanielle said as she looked down to her right hand and the retractor.

"What's going on? Why isn't it glowing?" Dayhoon asked with fear and frustration as he looked to his right towards Yanielle.

"He'll be fine," Kotoyami said as she walked up behind Yanielle.

"You sure Kotoyami?" Matuka asked as he knelt between Yanielle and Dayhoon.

"What do you mean he'll be alright?!" Dayhoon yelled with tears in his eyes.

Suddenly, Jubilaree walked up behind Dayhoon and slapped him on the back of the head.

"Hey! You wanna die?!" Dayhoon yelled as he looked over his right shoulder to Jubilaree.

"Umbati is fine; you don't see the snot bubble coming from his nose?" Jubilaree asked with his eye closed and arms crossed beneath his dark-blue cape.

"He's sleeping?" Yanielle asked with a confused look on her face.

"Interesting," Tahma said as he knelt from afar to look at the strange dead plants.

Tahma's quietness caused the rest of the guild to grow uneasy; however, they patiently awaited the analysis from the young genius.

"Interesting," Tahma said as he stood to his feet with one of the dead plants in his hand.

"What is it?! Will Umbati be okay?" Dayhoon asked while a tear rolled down his cheek.

"Calm down damn it!" Jubilaree said before he hit Dayhoon across the head again.

"Why I oughta!" Dayhoon said as he stood up to face Jubilaree.

"Come on guys, chill out," Matuka said as he stood up with a nervous smile before he tried to break up Dayhoon and Jubilaree.

"This appears to be some sort of sleep-inducing plant," Tahma said as he looked to the rest of the crew.

"Huh? Are you sure?!" Dayhoon asked after he rushed over to Tahma.

"Yes, indeed. This powder-like substance is a form of pollen. A form of which I never saw or at least recall seeing," Tahma said as he walked past Dayhoon and looked over Umbati's body.

"Tahma, how can we be sure that Umbati will be okay?" Matuka asked with a serious face as he stood and faced him.

"I guess we have to trust the island, that it wouldn't do anything to hurt us," Tahma said as he fixed his glasses and looked up at the night's sky.

The rest of the crew looked up as well before they all became captivated by the stars in the sky that night.

"Well, someone build a fire, we camp here tonight," Matuka said as he walked away from the group and looked around the small open patch of land.

"That's pretty bold, even for you, there are enemies here now. Are you sure Captain?" Kotoyami asked as she turned around to face

Matuka.

"Yeah, seems kind of reckless," Jubilaree humbly whispered as he opened his eye.

"This is our island, right? So, we have nothing to be afraid of. I'm sure if we were in any danger, the island would have rejected the enemies by now. Besides, if we are lucky, we might get some answers about the war. Maybe get some clues and information on our memories," Matuka said after he turned around to face his uncertain crew.

"Interesting," Tahma said as he fixed his specs with his left hand.

"We don't even know how many of them it is! We could be outnumbered, we're already just kids," Dayhoon said as he looked to the young Captain.

"Yeah, he has a point, we're a man down," Yanielle said as she stood up over Umbati.

"Just kids?! Who else was the ship given to?! Who else can communicate with sea creatures?! We have skills, perks and more on our side than they could ever have! We will rest! Now is not the time to be afraid you guys, it's only time to be brave!" Matuka said with a serious tone and look in his eyes.

"Fine," Jubilaree said as he began to walk off into the thicket.

"Where are you going?" Matuka quickly

asked as he looked to his left towards Jubilaree.

"This firewood won't collect itself," Jubilaree said as he threw his left hand over his head to signal, he'll be back later.

"I'll go with you," Tahma quickly said as he rushed after Jubilaree.

"I'd rather you not," Jubilaree replied as he looked over his right shoulder towards Tahma.

"Aw come on, this is the only way I can get some quick research done," Tahma said as he looked to Jubilaree with a child-like hope.

"Whatever," Jubilaree said before he walked further into the glowing forest.

Meanwhile, on the west side of the island, the guild of thieves had made it to the shoreline in their rowboat.

"Men, tonight we become kings!" Captain Okokobi yelled as he looked on at the island. The Captain and his crew all exited the rowboat and walked onto the beach.

"Look Captain! There is light shining throughout the environment!" Kuraba, the right hand of the Captain said as he looked up to him.

The rest of the crew gathered around the Captain to have a closer look at the sand and seashells.

"How strange," one of the thieves whispered.

"Yeah, I don't have a good feeling about

this Captain," one of the crew members said as he looked at the Captain.

"Silence! Especially from you Chumbry!" Captain Okokobi yelled to the older, overweight buffoon.

"Yeah shut up!" the rest of the crew yelled in unison at Chumbry.

"Okay," Chumbry said softly and sadly as he dropped his head in shame.

"Now! Grab your sacks! Fill it as much as you want! Tonight, we become rich!" the overzealous Captain yelled as he marched forward to leave the beach.

"Hey Captain! I think half of us should stay behind," Kuraba shouted before the Captain could get too far.

"What was that?!" Captain Okokobi yelled as he turned around to look at his crew.

"Well, Captain, I think half of them should stay behind and watch the ship. We have no idea what and who is on this island. Plus, some of the crew have been whispering. They're scared and are unsure if this place is worth their lives," Kuraba said as he fully walked up on Captain Okokobi.

"Fine! You stay behind with the rest of the picaroons; I'll take the willing with me," Captain Okokobi said as he looked past Kuraba at his crew that was closer to the seashore.

"Sir, I'm more than willing to go, but do

you really want to trust one of these idiots with the ship? I mean, I wouldn't be surprised if they hightailed it out of here and left us for dead; if we took too long to return," Kuraba whispered to the Captain as the rest of the crew looked on at the two of them.

"You're right, you have a point. Keep my ship safe and right here at all cost! Do you understand me?!" Captain Okokobi yelled to Kuraba.

"Indeed Captain," Kuraba said before he bowed to him and turned around to the crew.

Meanwhile, Matuka and his crew had set a fire and were resting their boots from the long night.

"You really are resourceful, huh Tahma?" Yanielle asked with a smile as she looked to her right past Jubilaree at Tahma.

The crew sat in the same circle-like formation when they were in the saloon.

"Yes, very useful," Kotoyami said as she took a sip from a cup Tahma made.

"Yeah Tahma, you're the best," Matuka said with a smile as he also took a sip of water from the cup that was made for him.

"I guess you're alright for a weirdo," Jubilaree said with a smirk as he sipped out of his cup with his eye closed.

"Interesting," Tahma said with a smile as he took a sip of the ice-cold and fresh, glowing water.

"No doubt about it bro!" Dayhoon said as he took a sip from the glowing green, bamboo cup that Tahma fashioned.

After Dayhoon took a sip, he leaned over to his left and opened Umbati's mouth. Umbati was still unconscious when Dayhoon slowly poured the glowing, aqua-blue water in his younger brother's mouth, so he didn't expect what came next. Without warning, Umbati jumped to his feet and startled the entire guild.

"What the?!" Jubilaree said as he spit out a mouthful of water.

"Interesting," Tahma said as he looked down to his cup of water while the lights reflected on his glasses.

"Tahma?" Matuka asked as he looked to his right towards Tahma.

"Let me at em! Let me at em!" Umbati said as he swung his fists around with his eyes closed.

"Little bro calm down! It's me, Dayhoon!" the older brother yelled to the youngest as he grabbed his arms.

"Dayhoon?" Umbati asked softly as he began to come to his senses.

"There you go, have a seat," Dayhoon said as he guided Umbati down to the ground.

After Umbati opened his eyes, he let out a deep sigh and looked to his left at Tahma.

"What happened?" Umbati asked as he took a sip from a cup that was lying next to him.

"You ran into a sleep-bomb field genius!" Dayhoon said as he grabbed Umbati with his left hand and put him in a choke hold.

"Huh?" Umbati asked as he looked up to his big brother.

"Interesting term, but you ran into a pollinated, sleep inducing, mushroom field," Tahma said as he looked to his right towards Umbati and Dayhoon.

"Yanielle," Kotoyami said as she looked to her left past Matuka.

"Yes?" Yanielle answered as she looked to Kotoyami.

"Do you think that the plant is safe for digestion?" Kotoyami asked as she took a sip of water.

"Interesting," Tahma said as he looked at the dead patch of plants.

"I mean, there is no real way to know without trying, but from the looks of it, it doesn't appear harmful," Yanielle said before she took a sip of water and looked at the plants.

"What do you mean? What don't look harmful? Look at what it did to my little brother!" Dayhoon said as he released Umbati from the choke hold.

"Yeah!" Umbati said as he stood up.

"Tahma," Kotoyami said as she looked to her left across the fire at Tahma.

"Yes?" Tahma replied as he looked towards Kotoyami.

"Do you think you three could weaponize the pollen?" Kotoyami asked before she took another sip from her cup.

"Interesting, I mean, I suppose," Tahma said as he looked across the fire at Kotoyami.

"What's bothering you?" Jubilaree asked as he looked to his left towards Matuka.

Matuka had his head up, arms leaned back for support and was staring at the night's sky.

"Huh? Oh nothing, just soaking all of this in; wondering what's next to come," Matuka replied to Jubilaree before he looked back up to the stars in the sky.

The crew grew silent and joined Matuka in thought by staring at the stars as well. The night was calm, the wind throughout the island carried delicious scents to the noses of who all were there, and the island kept its sacred glow kindled for its guest. Meanwhile, on the west side of the island, less than half of the guild of thieves were still exploring the mysterious land.

"Alright men, if you get lost, then you're lost! This place is too unfamiliar and possibly dangerous, so if you want a ride back home, you better stay close!" the Captain yelled as he swung a machete with his right hand through the illuminated thicket of tall grass and bushes.

"Yes sir!" the small reconnaissance team said in unison as they followed behind the Captain into the unknown.

One by one, the brave and armed team of thieves pushed through the island until they came upon a clearing on the island.

"Captain, a few members are fatigued, and this seems like a decent place to relax," Sivilo, the guild's alchemist and philosopher said as he walked to the right side of his Captain.

"Rest your boots gents! We continue shortly! And keep your eyes open! We are still on unknown land!" the Captain shouted with a grin after he turned around to look at his tired crew.

"Yes sir!" the band of thieves said as they all sat down.

"Thank you, Captain," Sivilo said as he bowed his head before he and the Captain sat down next to each other.

Captain Okokobi and Sivilo sat facing the guild while everyone sat looking around at the beautiful scenery of the hidden island. A few moments passed and one of the thieves stood up from noticing something out of the corner of his left eye.

"What are you doing?" Chumbry asked

Saiyu, the curious guild member who was walking towards a mushroom field like the one Umbati stumbled upon earlier.

Captain Okokobi and Sivilo looked towards Saiyu as he slowly made his way closer to the glowing plant.

"Hey stop! I wouldn't move another step if I was you!" Sivilo shouted as he stood up in concern.

"Sit Sivilo," Captain Okokobi said softly with his eyes closed, arms crossed and legs as well.

"Captain," Sivilo said softly as he looked down at the composed leader then back up to Saiyu.

After Sivilo sat down next to his Captain, Captain Okokobi opened his eyes, lifted his head, and turned to his right to look at Sivilo.

"If he wants to learn the hard way, then let him," Captain Okokobi said with a serious face before they both turned to look at Saiyu.

The closer he got to the plant field, the more they appeared to open and glow.

"I'm going to be rich," Saiyu mumbled with a greedy smile as he inched further and further.

Suddenly, just like before, the mushroom-like plants exploded with a huge pollinated cloud, which caused Saiyu to fall unconscious.

"And just like that, we have our first test subject. Boys go retrieve that idiot and try not to make the same mistake!" Captain Okokobi yelled with a slight grin as he closed his eyes and dropped his head.

A couple of the crew members ran over and each grabbed a foot to pull Saiyu back. After they pulled him over to the rest of the crew, they all noticed that Saiyu was unconscious instead of dead.

"What should we do with him, Captain?" one of the crew members asked.

"Take him back immediately and await our return," Captain Okokobi said.

Without hesitation, the same two members grabbed Saiyu, and made their way back to the ship through the thick jungle.

"Captain, may I go have a closer look? Only for research and data purposes of course," Sivilo asked with a nervous smile and chuckle as he kept his eyes closed.

"Knock yourself out," Captain Okokobi said as he looked up to Sivilo.

"Thank you, sir," Sivilo quickly replied as he immediately stood to his feet.

"Sivilo," Captain Okokobi said with a serious tone.

"Yes Captain?" Sivilo asked as he turned back around to face him.

"I need some form of intelligent conversation and the rest of these guys are on the downswing from that. So, don't literally knock yourself out," Captain Okokobi said with another slight grin as he continued to keep his eyes closed and head down.

"I'll do my best sir," Sivilo said with a smile before he turned around to walk away.

The rest of the crew watched Sivilo inch over to where Saiyu had fallen into the consequences of greed. The first thing Sivilo noticed was that the strange mushroom-like plants further away did not explode but instead crystallized from the other plants' explosion.

"Intriguing, I bet now I could touch them without the risk of becoming a victim to its somniferous pollen," Sivilo said as he looked at some of the more distant plants.

After Sivilo kneeled to have a closer look, he picked up a few dead plants and pulled out a sack for storing items. The sack was pearl white and made from a silk-like material. It had golden tassels that held its secrets captive and away from strange eyes.

"Wow, that's a nice bag there Sivilo, where did you get it?" Chumbry innocently asked as he pointed to the open sack in the focused alchemist hand.

"Fool! This is no mere bag or satchel your mommy makes. This is an enchanted object!" Sivilo snapped back at Chumbry.

"What is an enchanted object?" Chumbry hesitantly asked.

"It's an object that can do mystical things because it has been imbued with the power of magic," Sivilo said with an annoyed tone.

"When did you get that?" Chumbry asked as he looked on at Sivilo.

"Oh, come on Chumbry! How dumb are you really?! You were there in the dungeon of Dujumblen just as well as the rest of us! We all picked something from the dungeon we wanted after defeating those damn monsters! How could you forget such a thing? You picked that worthless piece of gold trinket there around your neck. You better get ready because the next place we're headed is Habanarah to defeat that dungeon's bastard of a king and all his demon monsters to obtain more magical items!" Sivilo yelled, which made Captain Okokobi crack a slight grin.

Chumbry bowed his head and walked away from Sivilo, while the rest of the crew was either watching or relaxing in the field. Sivilo continued to get a closer look at the crystallized plants, while Chumbry unnoticeably snuck out of sight into the thicket of the island; headed towards the east side where Matuka's guild was.

"I bet these could be weaponized, I better take as many as possible," Sivilo softly said as he hurried and grabbed as much as possible.

"Sivilo," Captain Okokobi said sternly as he kept his eyes closed, head down, with his arms and legs crossed.

"Yes Captain?" Sivilo quickly asked as he stood up and turned to face the Captain.

"What do you have for me?" Captain Okokobi asked before he looked up to his right towards Sivilo in the distance.

"Bastard! Always taking everything! I'll destroy him and all these losers once I gain the magic I need! I'll rule this entire planet's water supply! I'll be the world's strongest sorcerer!" Sivilo shouted within his mind as he smiled with his eyes closed at Captain Okokobi.

Sivilo then hurried over to the Captain and the rest of the guild to show them what he discovered. Meanwhile, Chumbry was already more than halfway near the children and coming up on an unnoticeable ditch.

"Such a beautiful island, I don't think we or anyone should take from you. Is that smoke I smell?" Chumbry asked as he looked up over his head at a glowing vine; wrapped around an illuminated mango tree branch.

Suddenly, a glowing, reddish-yellow mango began to fall from one of the other branches.

"I got you!" Chumbry yelled before he fell very hard and loud into the ditch from trying to dive for the fruit.

"Did you hear that?" Jubilaree asked Kotoyami as they both looked in the same direction towards the west side of the island.

Unknowingly, Chumbry wasn't too far from them and was all alone in the ditch that kept him prisoner.

"I'm lucky I have this mango here or else I'd be in real big trouble," Chumbry said as he dusted off the mango and prepared to taste its glow.

The moment Chumbry bit into the glowing mango, tears of joy fell from his eyes and he began to slightly dance.

"Amazing, this is the best mango ever!" Chumbry said with a stuffed face and tears in his eyes.

After Chumbry finished the mango, all that was left was the glowing seed that rested in his left palm.

"I wonder how long it will take for the Captain and the crew to find me," Chumbry softly said as he pushed the glowing seed into the dimly glowing dirt next to him with his left hand.

Several moments ended up passing and Chumbry heard something moving next to him, so he looked down to his left.

"Peace to this island, I wish you were big enough for me to climb right out of here,"

Chumbry said as he watched the mango seed, he planted grow into a radiant sapling.

Chumbry then fell asleep next to the sapling as the night grew darker and as the island blossomed with sweet smells. Back at the thieves' camp, Sivilo has just explained to the Captain and the remaining expedition team what the plant could be used for.

"Splendid intel Sivilo! Crew, raise your mugs! This one is for a new weapon discovered by Sivilo and under my great rule! Tonight, we have become kings and rulers!" Captain Okokobi shouted with joy as did the rest of his crew.

"Awe, thanks Captain, you guys," Sivilo said as hate grew more in his heart towards everyone.

"Hey where is that dummy Chumbry?" one of the thieves questioned with a drunken smile as he leaned on one of the other guild members.

"Where is that fool of a man?" Sivilo asked slowly as he looked from the crew to the Captain.

"I was wondering why it was so quiet around here," Captain Okokobi said with his eyes closed and arms crossed as he sat.

"He headed that way, towards the east of the jungle," another one of the guild members said as he pointed into the glowing thicket of trees and bushes Chumbry passed through.

"And no one thought to stop the moron?!" Sivilo shouted at the crew.

"Calm down Sivilo," Captain Okokobi said gently with his eyes still closed.

"Captain?" Sivilo questioned with a look of confusion over his face.

"It's okay! Chumbry has been our good luck charm thus far. Remember it was he that found that dungeon by falling into that well after trying to get water from it. Also, it was that idiot who found out the last dungeon king's weakness by a mere accident. So, he should be fine for now and if not, good riddance! But, for the sake of discovery, we will go recover this lost, dumb sheep and bring him back to the fold," Captain Okokobi said after he opened his eyes to look at Sivilo.

The guild of thieves raised their mugs and took a final, large sip of rum and began to ready themselves to find Chumbry.

"Relax, he couldn't have gotten too far," Captain Okokobi said as he looked to Sivilo.

"Yes sir, Captain, it's just…this island is alive, and I've noticed things. Even on the way here, to this part of the island, I saw things that didn't even fit into my realm of work," Sivilo nervously said as he bowed his head in respect.

"Well let's get a move on. Ready up, you rascals!! Onward!!" Captain Okokobi shouted with a grin as he pushed through the glowing thicket of trees and bushes.

One by one, they followed the brave Captain into the unknown with greed in their eyes and hunger is their souls.

"Remember! Keep your eyes open and grab what you can carry!" Captain Okokobi yelled as he looked over his right shoulder at his guild members.

"Yes sir!" the guild said in unison.

The small group of thieves inched on; step after step, through the illuminated landscape, astonished at is magnificent display.

"I never smelled anything so good before," one of the guild members whispered to another.

"Yeah, it's intoxicating," the other thief replied softly as they followed behind Sivilo and Captain Okokobi.

"Make sure you grab as many as possible men! The seeds to these plants will be worth a fortune!" Captain Okokobi said as he looked over his right shoulder towards his guild members.

The guild of treasure hunting thieves took no time in carrying out their Captain's order by making sure their sacks were full.

"Do you smell smoke?" Sivilo asked Captain Okokobi before he fell in the same pit with Chumbry.

"Sivilo! Can you hear me?!" Captain Okokobi screamed into the dark ditch.

Moments passed and Sivilo awoke to see Chumbry asleep on the ground of the ditch.

"Sivilo! Can you hear me?!" Captain Okokobi yelled once more from the surface, as the rest of the guild gathered around to have a closer look.

"Yes Captain, I'm fine!" Sivilo shouted as he looked up.

"Alright I'm sending some help down!" Captain Okokobi replied as he stood to his feet.

"You won't believe who's down here!" Sivilo quickly replied with an annoyed tone after he turned to his left and looked to the ground.

"Well now we know why you fell in there," one of the superstitious guild members said.

"Well I be damned," Captain Okokobi replied with a grin.

"Chumbry wake up! It's time to go, you dumb bastard! It's your fault I'm in this hole!" Sivilo shouted at the heavily snoring Chumbry.

After a few more harsh words, the sleeping imbecile began to move.

"Huh? Sivilo?" Chumbry questioned as he awoke and stood up.

"You cause more trouble than good Chumbry! We went looking for you and I fell in here face-first!" Sivilo shouted before turning his back to Chumbry.

Suddenly, the mango sapling that Chumbry planted earlier began to grow very rapidly.

"What the?!" Sivilo quickly shouted after he turned around and witnessed the glowing mango sapling transform into a tree.

Back above, outside the ditch, the Captain and guild of thieves could see something coming their way that was producing light.

"What?!" Captain Okokobi questioned before he quickly leaned back to avoid being hit in the face by the oncoming, glowing tree.

The Captain and the guild members back above ground were speechless to what they saw.

"Thank you, lady mango tree," Chumbry said softly with a smile as he watched the mango tree extend further out the mouth of the ditch.

"Remarkable, I've never seen such a thing! The speed at which this tree has grown is thought to be impossible! I could rule the world by its food source if I could research this fully," Sivilo thought to himself with a sinister and shocked facial expression.

"What's taking you all day?! Climb up!" Captain Okokobi yelled from above inside the illuminated hole.

The moment Chumbry tried to climb the

radiant mango tree, Sivilo pushed him out of the way, which caused him to fall to the ground.

"Out of my way!" Sivilo shouted before he climbed up the mango tree.

"Sorry sir," Chumbry said with an innocent smile as he held the back of his head with his left hand.

"*How dare that village idiot try to go before me?!*" Sivilo thought to himself as he climbed the tree.

Chumbry then dusted off his pants with a smile and followed Sivilo out of the ditch. When Sivilo and Chumbry made it to the top of the ditch, the Captain and crew lightly cheered for their return.

"Welcome back," Captain Okokobi said as he reached for Sivilo's hand to pull him up.

"Good to be back sir," Sivilo said as he was pulled upward and out the ditch.

When Chumbry reached the top of the pit, he could see the glowing, green grass peeking over inside. As Chumbry admired the scenery and mango tree, he shortly noticed that he was receiving angry looks from everyone outside of the ditch.

"Some good luck charm. Such filth!" Sivilo mumbled before he kicked dirt in Chumbry's face and turned his back to him.

"Alright men pull him up! We got some exploring to do!" Captain Okokobi said as he began to march forward.

"Sir!" Sivilo shouted as he looked to his right at Captain Okokobi.

"What is it?" Captain Okokobi asked with a glare in his eyes and a serious face as he looked back to his left at Sivilo.

"Sir, I smell smoke! That means either lightning struck something or there is someone else out here with us. Although the weather has been weird lately, I think we can all agree that it hasn't been any storms since we've been here," Sivilo said nervously as everyone started to look around themselves.

"Good point, maybe we should tread softly until we are sure the coast is clear," Captain Okokobi said as he looked on at Sivilo.

"*I do think it will be wise, you buffoon of a Captain! If it wasn't for me and my brains, we'd all be dead by now! Fool doesn't even think! No wonder he has a soft spot for that dummy Chumbry and thinks he's some type of good luck charm. These dummies belong together!*" Sivilo thought to himself as he faced the east of the island.

"Hurry and get that idiot out of that hole," Captain Okokobi said as he turned back around to face the east of the island as well.

"Onward Captain?" Sivilo asked Captain Okokobi with a smile and with his eyes closed.

"Onward it is!" Captain Okokobi yelled

before immediately getting hushed by Sivilo.

"Not that loud sir," Sivilo said softly with a smile and his eyes closed.

"Oops! Sorry, onward you animals," Captain Okokobi whispered as he looked over his right shoulder at the small crew he had left.

After Chumbry got out of the ditch, the rest of the crew followed Captain Okokobi and Sivilo. One by one, the anxious crew pushed through the glowing island until they were able to see the smoke from the children's fire, that was rising above the trees into the night's sky.

"Halt men," Captain Okokobi said softly as he threw up his right hand to signal stop.

Captain Okokobi and his guild of thieves were finally near the source of the smoke and little did they know that it was the start of their end. The guild of thieves could see at the root of the smoke in an open clearing was a fire accompanied by seven young children that were sound asleep.

"Well I'll be damned, Sivilo pass me your spyglass," Captain Okokobi said softly as he stood from a crouched position with a shocked facial expression.

"Sure thing sir," Sivilo said before he looked for his spyglass.

"*I have a funny feeling about these children,*" Captain Okokobi thought to himself before he received the spyglass.

Captain Okokobi looked through the spyglass and immediately felt uneasy as he zoomed in on their faces.

"Well, what do you see sir?" Sivilo asked as he looked from the lads back to his Captain.

"It's seven of them, five lads and two lasses. These children, it's strange, they're dressed in very old clothing. So old it may even be worth something. They look familiar as well; very familiar. Where have I seen them? Who do they remind me of? This one is wearing a Captain's hat. Wait a sec! Is that what I think it is? It's impossible!" Captain Okokobi said as he snatched the spyglass from his eyes and fell to his knees.

"What is it sir?" Sivilo whispered with a look of concern as he looked back to his Captain.

"Have a look for yourself, look at the one who has a Captain's hat," Captain Okokobi said as he passed the spyglass to his left.

"Strange, they are dressed in old attire and they do look very familiar," Sivilo said as he looked over Matuka's guild.

Once Sivilo scanned all the other children, he then looked to Matuka.

"What the hell?! No way! That's the legendary necklace of Déjà Vú! The Witch of the Triangle! The necklace that grants its master the power to control the seas and oceans!" Sivilo slightly yelled as he removed the spyglass from his eye.

"Exactly," Captain Okokobi said as he looked to Sivilo, then back to Matuka and his guild.

"Just how in the hell did he come to possess it?! It was told through the generations that it was forever lost. No, it's impossible!" Sivilo lightly shouted after he looked at Matuka and the necklace.

Captain Okokobi started to softly chuckle because he felt as though he found the find of the century.

"Why are we whispering? They're just children. I mean, if we wanted, we could just take them out," a guild member said as he prepared his bow to aim at the children.

"What do you think you're doing?! I didn't give you any orders," Captain Okokobi lightly snapped at the guild member as he looked back over his right shoulder.

Suddenly, a large glowing vine wrapped around the guild member's mouth and entire body.

"What the?!" everyone asked in unison as they watched their guild member lift off the ground.

"Oh boy, this isn't going to end well," Chumbry whispered as he dropped his head.

In a blink of an eye, the vine had taken him up and threw him all the way back towards their ship at the coast. As he went soaring, they could hear his loud cry quickly fade away. The cry inadvertently awoke Jubilaree and Kotoyami but Sivilo quickly noticed.

"What the?" Jubilaree asked as he tried to come to his senses.

"They're here," Kotoyami said as she sat up and looked towards the trees.

Without hesitation, Sivilo threw a couple of the crystallized mushrooms-like plants towards the group of lads and lasses. Jubilaree and Kotoyami tried to stand after the plants exploded; however, it caused them both to fall unconscious again. The rest of the children didn't even know what was going on, and the explosion of pollen kept them asleep through what was next to come. Back at the guild of thieves' ship, the members were still awaiting the return of their Captain and other guild members.

"Ahh!!!" the guild member that was flung out of the island to the ship yelled before he hit the main deck.

"What the hell?! Is he dead?!" Kuraba yelled after he watched the thief fall from the night's sky and hit the deck.

"No sir! It does appear he managed to survive that fall, however..." a guild member said as he stood and leaned over their fallen guildmate.

"Impossible!! How?" Kuraba asked aloud as he walked over to get a closer look.

The rest of the members of the guild encamped around the fallen member and awaited his recovery. The thieves all waited patiently to gain insight on what conspired before his dramatic and mysterious entrance, until Kuraba became very anxious.

"Jutah! Wake up! What happened?! Are you okay?! Where is the Captain and others? Are they dead?!" Kuraba asked as he knelt over him.

Suddenly, Jutah sat up from being unconscious and began to cry.

"What happened?" Saiyu asked as he also knelt over Jutah.

"This island is cursed!! Cursed I tell you!!" Jutah yelled and cried.

"And the Captain and others?" Kuraba asked again as he stood up over Jutah and Saiyu.

Meanwhile, the small guild of thieves were all in disbelief from the moments passed.

"What the hell is going on?!" a guild member asked as he looked to Captain Okokobi and Sivilo.

"Sivilo," Captain Okokobi said softly as he turned to look at him.

"Sir?" Sivilo quickly and softly replied.

"Just what are we dealing with here?" Captain Okokobi asked as he looked back to the children.

"I have a theory but if I'm right, we have a serious problem," Sivilo said as he looked through his spyglass at the children with a sweat bead dripping down his face.

The night was calm as though nothing had occurred, and the island's glow danced without cease. The stars were bright, and the night was perfectly dark. The temperature was ideal as a light breeze flowed throughout the island, which carried the different scents to the ocean and the heavens.

"It's no way I'm gonna let this clown or any of those dimwits get their hands on this find! I have to come up with a plan!" Sivilo thought to himself as he looked to his left at Captain Okokobi.

As the gears in the conniving man's brain began to turn, his heart grew even colder. After Sivilo was able to form a plan, he was ready to carry it out.

"Captain?" Sivilo asked with his eyes closed and with a smile.

"What is it?" Captain Okokobi quickly replied as he anxiously awaited a reply from his trusted ally.

"Command Minoka to throw his machete at one of the children with the intent to kill and

Benoby to fire an arrow at one of them as well," Sivilo whispered before he lowered his spyglass and turned around.

Captain Okokobi trusted Sivilo so much that he did not hesitate to give the order.

"Minoka! Benoby!" Captain Okokobi quickly said with a stern voice.

"Sir!" the two quickly replied in unison as they hurried forward to the right of Captain Okokobi.

"I want you two to kill those children. Throw your machete as hard as you can and aim without hesitance. I will not accept failure. Have I made myself clear?" Captain Okokobi said as he turned to face them both.

"Sure thing boss," the two replied in unison with a devious smile before they turned around and readied their weapons.

"I hope you're right about this," Captain Okokobi said softly as he looked to Sivilo then back to the children.

"*Well I hope I'm not right about this,*" Silvio thought to himself as he looked back to the children.

"Ready sir!" the two men said in unison with a grin and hate in their eyes.

Once the men launched their weapons, several glowing tree branches rapidly extended into the open field and stopped their weapons from harming the children.

"What the?!" Minoka and Benoby said in unison as they stared at the branches.

Immediately after, just like before, the vines quickly wrapped around both the attackers' bodies and threw them out of sight. This made Captain Okokobi, Sivilo and Chumbry the only ones left from their guild on the island.

"Just as I thought," Sivilo said as he immediately turned around to face the children.

Meanwhile, back at the ship, everyone was still on the main deck discussing their next plan of action.

"Ahh!!!" Minoka and Benoby screamed as they fell from the sky before they hit the main deck.

"Not again! What the hell is happening in there?!" Kuraba asked as he watched Minoka and Benoby try to sit up from the deck.

As the guild gathered around them, Saiyu and Jutah went forth to help them up.

"This place is cursed land!" Benoby yelled before he started to whimper and cry.

"Where is the Captain?!" Kuraba asked as he ran and slid on his knees in front of Benoby and Minoka.

"They're fine for now, but... I don't know for how long," Minoka whimpered as well.

The other members grew more concerned about the outcome as time slipped away.

"Captain," Kuraba said with a look of fear as he looked back to the island.

After Minoka and Benoby got to their feet, everyone except two members went down below deck.

"Do you think we should send men in there for the Captain and others? Or should I just go myself?" Hedesah, the guild's cook said with a serious look as he began to walk over to Kuraba.

Hedesah slowly walked with a freakishly large sword, held across his back with his left arm as though it was light as a feather. Kuraba was standing against the bulwarks on starboard side, staring off into the distant and radiant island as he felt Hedesah walk up.

"Although I am worried for the sake of the Captain and the others, I cannot disobey his orders. From what we've heard and seen tonight; from the moment we sat foot on this island is, we're not supposed to be here. This place is rejecting our men left and right. I figure either the Captain will have the same entrance, or they'll figure out a way to come back unscathed," Kuraba said as he turned to look over his right shoulder at Hedesah.

"Whatever you say boss," Hedesah said as he shrugged his shoulders and threw up his right palm.

The two of them stood together and

watched the mysterious island's light show dance with the wind. Meanwhile, back within the illuminated island, Captain Okokobi and Sivilo were discussing their next move.

"What do you suggest we do?" Captain Okokobi asked as he looked through Sivilo's spyglass at the unconscious children.

Sivilo thought long and hard before he attempted to answer Captain Okokobi.

"It's killing me, I swear I saw their faces before," Captain Okokobi said again after a while as he looked through the spyglass.

"Okay, I think we should send Chumbry over to collect the necklace and bring it back to us," Sivilo said as he looked to the Captain and then to Chumbry.

Captain Okokobi then removed the spyglass from his right eye and turned to look at them both. Chumbry was sitting on the lightly glowing ground behind the two of them with his legs crossed, eyes closed and with a smile on his face.

"I see, well I guess it can't be helped," Captain Okokobi said as he handed back the spyglass to Sivilo.

"He'll be fine, if I'm correct that is," Sivilo said as he looked to his right at Chumbry with disgust.

"Okay, Chumbry, get over here, you big goof," Captain Okokobi said with somewhat of a friendly tone as he looked at him.

Chumbry then stood and walked up to Captain Okokobi and Sivilo with the same smile.

"Yes Captain?" Chumbry replied quickly.

"I need you to do your ole Captain here a favor, what do you say?" Captain Okokobi asked with a sneaky smile.

"Anything for you sir!" Chumbry quickly replied with a child-like joy.

"Sivilo?" Captain Okokobi questioned as he gestured for Sivilo to explain further.

"Right! Chumbry, we need you to sneak over and remove the necklace off the young lad with the Captain's hat on his head. Once you do that, we want you to quietly come back over here to us," Sivilo said with a serious look in his eyes.

"He stole your hat Captain?" Chumbry sincerely asked as he turned to look in his face.

Captain Okokobi started to laugh and that didn't make Sivilo so happy.

"No, you idiot! Are you blind?! The Captain is wearing his hat! Focus! You're only to bring back the necklace off the neck of the lad with the tri-cone hat on his head," Sivilo sternly said as he grabbed Chumbry by the shoulders and turned him to face the children.

"Are we stealing it?" Chumbry asked

with a sad look in his eyes.

"Of course not ole pal, we just want to have a closer look at it and don't want to wake them, is all," Captain Okokobi quickly said to put him at ease.

"Okay then, no problem sir," Chumbry said before he yawned and stretched.

"That a boy Chumbry, make me proud," Captain Okokobi said with a smile as he slapped Chumbry's back with his left hand.

Chumbry then slowly pushed through the glowing bushes and entered the open field where the children were sound asleep.

"That a boy Chumbry, you can do it," Captain Okokobi lightly shouted as he watched him walk slowly over to the unconscious lads and lasses.

"*Morons,*" Sivilo thought to himself as he sucked his teeth and watched Chumbry slowly walk forward.

By the time Chumbry got up on the kids, he was extremely nervous and already sweating.

"They all seem so peaceful," Chumbry said softly as he stood over the young leader.

Chumbry's back was turned to Captain Okokobi and Sivilo so they could not see what was to come next. As Chumbry knelt over Matuka, both of their necklaces began to lift, glow, and gravitate towards one another.

"Wow," Chumbry said as he looked down at both of their necklaces.

The moment Chumbry began to reach for Matuka's necklace, a huge rain cloud appeared in the sky over the island and it started to violently rain.

"What's going on?! Where did that cloud come from?" Sivilo lightly shouted as he looked up to the sky.

"Something is not right," Captain Okokobi said as he looked at the storm forming over them.

Back on the ship, Kuraba and Hedesah were quickly surprised at the weird weather they could see forming over the island.

"Where did that come from?!" Kuraba quickly yelled as he leaned over the bulwarks with both his hands.

"It's only over a certain part of the island," Hedesah said as he looked inward to the east side of the island.

Meanwhile, back on the island, Chumbry's hand grew closer to Matuka's floating necklace.

"Get a move on Chumbry! We don't have all day!" Sivilo shouted through the loud sound of the raindrops hitting the ground.

Suddenly, a huge ball of lightning began to form in the sky over Chumbry and the children.

"This is not going to end well," Captain Okokobi said as he looked to his left at Sivilo.

"Chumbry! The moment you grab the necklace! Throw it to me and I'll catch it with this!" Sivilo shouted as he held his enchanted bag open over the glowing bushes.

"Okay," Chumbry said after he turned around and saw Sivilo holding open his sack.

The moment Chumbry grabbed Matuka's necklace, the ball of lightning sent down seven large bolts.

"Get out of there you idiot!" Captain Okokobi yelled to Chumbry as he watched death descend on the island.

Suddenly, the lightning paused over him in mid-air and seemed to hesitate on striking.

"What the hell?!" Captain Okokobi yelled as he looked at the lightning that floated above Chumbry's head.

"Wow," Chumbry said as he looked up at the large, sword-like bolts of lightning.

"Chumbry! Throw the necklace! Hurry!!" Sivilo quickly shouted over the rain with his enchanted sack open and ready.

After Chumbry removed Matuka's necklace, the lightning bolts began to thicken in size. Meanwhile, back at the thieves' ship, Kuraba and Hedesah were still watching the weather phenomenon.

"That doesn't look good at all," Hedesah

said as he looked from the storm to Kuraba.

"Oh Captain," Kuraba said with fear in his eyes as he stared at the lightning.

Back on the island, things were about to get much worse for the old imbecile. The very moment Chumbry threw the necklace, one of the bolts followed the necklace as it flew towards Sivilo. The moment Sivilo caught it with his open bag, the bolt of lightning was sucked into his bag as well. Once that happened, the rest of the bolts struck Chumbry simultaneously. Without hope and a possible chance of survival, Chumbry immediately dropped to the wet ground.

"Chumbry!" Captain Okokobi yelled as the storm completely disappeared.

"I can't believe it, we got it!" Sivilo said with a sinister smile before he let out an evil laugh.

Captain Okokobi, dropped to his knees out of disbelief and began to cry.

"What's wrong sir? This is a win for us!" Sivilo asked with a smile and eyes wide open like a lunatic.

Captain Okokobi then dropped his head as a tear rolled down his left cheek.

"I never lost a man before, not one crew member has ever died at my hand! Oh Chumbry!" Captain Okokobi said as he stood and looked back into the open field at Chumbry.

"The moron served his purpose! I guess he was our good luck charm after all," Sivilo jokingly said before he threw his head back and laughed.

The sound of Sivilo's laughter caused Captain Okokobi to become enraged beyond measure.

"Say another word and you'll surely join him in the afterlife," Captain Okokobi said with a serious tone and glare in his eyes before he snatched the enchanted bag from Sivilo's hand.

"But Capt..." Sivilo started to say as he watched Captain Okokobi put his right balled fist over his heart, take his hat off and face Chumbry.

"Goodbye you dumb fool, maybe now you can rest. You've seemed pretty restless lately and unhappy. May you find happiness in the spirit realm. You will not be forgotten, thank you for your sacrifice and all the laughs you provided all of us," Captain Okokobi said before he turned around and wiped the tears from his eyes.

"Good job Chumbry," Sivilo said with a sincere smile as he looked out into the field at him.

"Come on, let's go. It's a wonder they didn't awake from all the commotion and some-thing tells me that we don't want to be here when they do," Captain Okokobi said as he pushed through the glowing thicket and bushes.

Without hesitation, Sivilo followed him into the dense vegetation. The sun was due to rise in a few hours and the walk back to the ship was a quiet one.

"It always feels much shorter of a trip when you head back instead of going somewhere for the first time. Why is that Captain?" Sivilo asked to strike a conversation with Captain Okokobi.

However, Captain Okokobi did not immediately reply because he was still thinking about Chumbry.

"I don't know Sivilo, maybe because you are already anticipating the trip, so therefore you think more when headed somewhere. Like remembering the directions and landmarks. While on other hand, when you head back, you don't think about the journey as much because you already know your surroundings from seeing it before. Now quit the useless chatter, I don't want to hear another word," Captain Okokobi said as he continued to walk in front of Sivilo.

"*How dare he?! He even took my enchanted bag,*" Sivilo thought to himself as he stared angrily at the back of Captain Okokobi's head.

Minutes passed and they were now coming up on the hole that Chumbry and Sivilo both fell into.

"Look familiar?" Captain Okokobi asked before Sivilo unsheathed his long sword and stabbed it in his back.

"What?!" Captain Okokobi screamed as he looked down to his chest.

The long sword was sticking out of Captain Okokobi's chest and Sivilo wore a satisfied grin on his face.

"I thought you said I couldn't speak?! Then you ask me a question?!" Sivilo shouted with a smile and a demonic glare in his eyes.

A cold breeze swept throughout the island and around them as Captain Okokobi's knees began to tremble.

"Bastard! How could you?!" Captain Okokobi asked after he coughed up blood.

Sivilo laughed and then snatched his enchanted bag out of Captain Okokobi's left hand from behind.

"Well this was a long time coming anyway. But I thought about it long and hard on this cold and quiet walk you took me on. While you were busy sulking and being depressed over a complete moron, I was plotting. I quickly realized I had what I wanted within reach and it was only us out here. There was no one to witness and stop me from taking action. Pretty clever thinking from me to get rid of all the witnesses huh? Oh yes, I've been planning this since Jutah went flying," Sivilo said before he let out yet another sinister laugh.

"Curse you! You won't get away with this," Captain Okokobi softly said before he coughed up more blood and grabbed the end of the sword that was sticking out of his chest.

"Oh yes I will! You and that dummy deserve each other, now you can be with him. Don't forget to tell him hello for me!" Sivilo said with an evil smile on his face as he stood behind him.

After Captain Okokobi took his last breath, Sivilo removed the fallen Captain's tricone hat and kicked him off his sword with his right foot into the ditch.

"Whew, I'm starving," Sivilo said as he wiped his bloody sword and put it up.

The evil alchemist then walked over to the glowing mango tree that was protruding out of the ditch and picked off an illuminated mango.

"This shall do just fine I might say," Sivilo jokingly said as he looked at the peculiar fruit.

After Sivilo took a bite from the mango, he continued onward to his destination like nothing happened at all. Meanwhile, back in the open field, the seven lost souls started to awake.

"What happened? My head is killing me," Matuka said as he slowly lifted his head

The Entries of the Black Sails

off the wet ground.

"What happened to the fire? I'm freezing!" Yanielle said as she sat up and began to shiver.

"Did it rain? Why am I wet?" Umbati softly asked before he let out a deep yawn.

"Yeah, this is not how I remember going to sleep," Dayhoon said with a raised left eyebrow after he slowly sat up.

"Wait, I remember something," Jubilaree said as he too lifted off the ground.

"Yeah, wait! It's coming back. Wait a second! Hey! The enemies, they were here!" Kotoyami shouted after she sat up and fully came to her senses.

"Interesting," Tahma said as he too sat up from his slumber.

"Uh guys, who's that behind Matuka?" Dayhoon asked as he pointed to the lifeless body on the ground.

Everyone jumped to their feet and turned to face the man lying on the ground. Matuka shrieked and immediately grabbed for his necklace, only to realize it was gone.

"I think he's dead," Umbati said as he walked past Kotoyami and stood to the right of Matuka.

"Where's my necklace?!" Matuka shouted before he dropped to his knees.

At that moment, Sivilo was walking

392

through the open field that his crew first came across.

"I'm almost there and I gotta make sure my story has no leaks. While the others brain capacity is in question, Kuraba's and Hedesah's are not. Those two are very wise as serpents, they'll be useful to me while I'm the Captain," Sivilo thought to himself as he walked into the glowing bushes after he crossed the open field.

Back at Matuka's camp, the children were all gathered around their mysterious guest. The lifeless body was an older heavyset man. His face was chubby, his cheeks were rosy, his glasses were big, and he was quite hairy. On his head was a small burgundy cap and beneath it was a yellow bandanna that exposed his hair. He was short with gray, short, curly hair and he smelled very familiar.

His skin was a light-tan color but he was wet and dirty so you couldn't really tell unless you were close enough. His pants were baggy, burnt, and cream colored. He was wearing a green vest that was burnt and did not have a shirt on beneath it, which exposed his big belly. The man also wore a strange gold necklace. His shoes were brown and had a few holes in them.

"Interesting," Tahma said as he stood from his crouched position after looking around the lifeless body.

"What's that?" Matuka quickly asked Tahma as he stood up and faced him.

"It's strange, he's not dead at all, he's only unconscious," Tahma quickly replied as he began to look around Chumbry's body at the ground.

"How is that possible?" Yanielle asked as she looked back to the lifeless body.

"Yeah, you just said earlier he was struck by lightning," Umbati quickly chimed in.

"So was Koto and she's still alive," Jubilaree said with his eye closed and arms crossed.

"Yeah but Kotoyami is not human," Dayhoon quickly replied with a smile as he looked to Kotoyami.

"Oh, I'm human alright, females can just take more pain than the average male," Kotoyami said with a smirk before she walked over to Dayhoon, and lightly punched him in the left arm.

"Ouch!" Dayhoon quickly said as he rubbed his arm.

"See?" Kotoyami asked with a light chuckle.

"My necklace is missing and he's the only one that can give us a clue to what happened here, and what happened to it. He's coming back with us!" Matuka said with anger in his eyes as he stared at the lifeless body before he turned and walked away.

"Wait, what?!" Yanielle asked before she removed her right hand from her right hip and began to walk over to Matuka.

Everyone came and stood in front of Matuka to get a better understanding from what he said.

"From the look of it, the same thing happened to him that happened to Kotoyami when she tried to remove my necklace. Well, from what Jubilaree told me the other day at least," Matuka said as he quickly looked to Jubilaree.

"Yeah, you must be right, but it doesn't make sense," Jubilaree said before opening his eye and unfolding his arms.

"What's that? You think so?" Matuka questioned as he sat down and crossed his legs in front of everyone.

"What Jubilaree means is that this was strategically thought out," Dayhoon replied before he took a seat next to Matuka.

"Correct. Whoever they were, they knew that getting our Captain's necklace wouldn't be an easy job. They threw those bombs to keep us unconscious when they saw Jubilaree and I awake. Also, judging by it only being one person here denotes anyone else was hit with the lightning. Which means they must've had a run in with misfortunes beforehand. Maybe the island did protect us somehow and they witnessed it," Kotoyami said as she walked over to

Jubilaree.

"Which beckons this question, why leave your guildmate? If somehow you managed to do the impossible and succeed, why not take your guy back with you? I mean he's alive, did they even check? They would have had to in order to get the necklace, right? Or is it a trap? Is he a spy?" Jubilaree questioned as he looked up to the trees that surrounded the open patch of land.

"Interesting," Tahma said as he fixed his glasses and sat down next to Matuka.

"Point taken Jubilaree. Either they were in a rush and didn't check his pulse or they are just completely evil," Matuka said as he crossed his arms and held his chin with his right hand.

That's when Jubilaree and Kotoyami looked to each other, took off without warning and ran towards the trees. In a split second they jumped to the trees' tallest branches and looked all around the island for a clue or sign of life.

"I'll never get tired of seeing that," Umbati said as the rest of the guild looked at the pair.

"See anything?" Kotoyami asked as she scanned the north and the east side of the island.

"Yeah," Jubilaree stoically replied as he looked to his right at her.

"What?! Where?!" Kotoyami quickly

asked after she looked to her right at him.

"There, a ship by the west shore," Jubilaree said softly as he pointed towards the west side of the island.

After Kotoyami turned to face the west side of the island she followed his index finger as a reference.

"*The ship looks weird, different from any ship I've seen before*," Jubilaree thought to himself.

"How can you see that far?! Oh, let me guess. Your eye? With such a great quirk you shouldn't be so ashamed to show it, you know?" Kotoyami said with a smile as she turned to her left and looked at Jubilaree.

"Focus woman, they haven't left. They still may be trying to make their way back to their ship," Jubilaree said before he opened his eye and crossed his arms again.

"It is quite beautiful up here isn't Jubilaree?" Kotoyami asked as the wind blew hair in front of her face and as her cheeks began to blush.

Jubilaree began to blush and nearly slipped off the branch from being caught off guard from seeing too much beauty at once.

"You see anything?!" Matuka yelled after he stood up and walked closer to the glowing trees.

"Time to go," Jubilaree stuttered before

he jumped down to the ground in front of Matuka.

"Whatever you say," Kotoyami said with a smirk before she jumped down as well.

"What did you see?" Matuka asked with a serious glare in his eyes as the wind blew his locks in front of his face.

As Jubilaree and Kotoyami walked in front of Matuka, the rest of the guild gathered behind him.

"I saw a ship by the west shore. From the looks of it, it could possibly be more than fifteen men on the vessel," Jubilaree said with his eye closed, head bowed, and arms crossed.

"We believe that they are headed to the ship now and could be departing shortly," Kotoyami immediately chimed in before she dropped her head.

At that very moment, Sivilo ran out the thicket onto the glowing beach sand and screamed as loud as he could, to alert the others of his return. He soon noticed that there was a rowboat already waiting near the shore to escort him and the others back to the main ship.

"Sir! Where is the Captain and Chumbry?" one of the thieves asked with a look of concern in his eyes as he looked down and noticed Captain Okokobi's hat.

"Get me back above at once, I'll tell you all together. It's what they would have wanted,"

Sivilo said with a fake, sad tone of voice as he dropped his head.

Ukata grew sad as Sivilo helped him push the rowboat away from the shoreline.

"Captain, Chumbry," Ukata said softly as a tear fell from his face into the dark ocean.

By the time Sivilo and Ukata boarded the ship, the rest of the members were all above deck awaiting his report.

"Where's the Captain?!" Kuraba yelled as he ran over to Sivilo and grabbed him by the neck of his shirt.

Sivilo pulled away and began to fake cry so good; that everyone believed he was being genuinely serious. That's when Jutah, Minoka and Benoby came forward to comfort Sivilo.

"Brothers! You're alive! I thought you all were dead!" Sivilo shouted with fake tears of joy before he ran and hugged them.

"We're fine now, just tell us what happened. We told them everything before you came. So now all you have to do is fill us in on what happened afterwards," Jutah said as he let go of Sivilo.

"It all happened so fast!" Sivilo shouted as tears ran down his cheeks and before he fell to his knees in front of everyone.

"Take your time and breathe Sivilo," Hedesah said as he walked closer with his sword held across his back.

"After this cursed land did harm to you guys, we were watching the seven entities we thought were children sleep. We then tried to figure out how we could still recover the lost and legendary necklace of Déjà Vu without alerting them. So, we sent Chumbry over, being he was the Captain's good luck charm. That's when those seven demons awoke! They called down lightning from the heavens and struck with supreme precision, nearly killing me as well by accident from the aftermath! If it wasn't for the Captain telling me to stay behind in the bushes, I would be dead as well," Sivilo said before he stopped to wipe the fake tears from his face.

"Sivilo, while the storm was taking place, we saw the seven lightning bolts freeze in mid-air. What happened?" Hedesah asked with his eyes closed and head bowed.

Everyone then looked back to Sivilo and awaited his response. The ship grew quiet and the only things that could be heard were the waves beating against the ship and the wind dancing around their ears.

"The demons paused in action after Captain Okokobi ran out and tried to reason with them for Chumbry's life. Then, without any remorse and a second to spare, they let their evil ways rain down onto them both. Afterwards, the demons disappeared, and I ran over to the Captain and Chumbry. I quickly noticed that Chumbry was dead and that the Captain was soon to follow. I grabbed him by the hand and with his last words he said..." Sivilo said before he paused and wiped a tear from his eye.

The crew patiently waited for Sivilo to gather himself to gain more knowledge of Captain Okokobi's final words.

"Sivilo, forgive me and tell my beloved crew I asked for their forgiveness as well. Tell them I was proud to be their Captain and I'll see them in hell. To you, I leave my ship and guild, so take care of my men," Sivilo said before he let out a loud, fake cry.

The rest of the crew also grew more in pain from the loss of Captain Okokobi.

"And then he took his final breath," Sivilo said softly.

Suddenly, all the members dropped to their knees and saluted their new Captain with tears in their eyes. Shortly after, the heavy-hearted men began to softly cry and hum their guild's song. Moments passed and the rest of the crew was still feeling very fatigued from the bad news when Kuraba approached Sivilo.

"Well, where to now Captain?" Kuraba asked as he wiped his tears and looked to Sivilo.

"Should we go after those bastard demons who killed Captain Okokobi and Chumbry?" Hedesah asked with a serious face.

"No, we couldn't possibly know where they went. And personally, I don't want to lose anyone else I care about to this God forsaken island! No, we will press onward! To the dungeon of Habanarah!" Captain Sivilo shouted before all the men cheered with their fist and weapons in the air.

Meanwhile, Matuka and his crew were discussing their next move.

"We need to hurry and cut them off before they get too far away," Kotoyami said as she looked to Matuka.

The young Captain became silent and everyone could see he was in a deep thought. Several minutes passed and the crew couldn't take the silence anymore.

"I hate when he gets like this," Yanielle softly said to the others as she watched Matuka walk around in a circle.

"Jubilaree, check one last time to see if they are still there," Matuka said after he took in consideration what Kotoyami suggested.

"Sure thing Captain," Jubilaree said before he ran over and leaped back up to the top of the trees.

"Well?!" Dayhoon yelled as they all awaited an answer from the young warrior.

Jubilaree then jumped down, crossed his arms, closed his eye, and walked over to the rest of the guild.

"They're gone, even too far for me to see at this point," Jubilaree said before he walked past everyone to where Chumbry was.

"Interesting, their ship is quite fast then, I presume," Tahma said as he walked over to where Jubilaree was standing.

"Indeed," Jubilaree said as he stood and looked over Chumbry.

"That's insane!" Umbati said as he looked up to Dayhoon.

"Don't worry little bro, no one can out sail our ship," Dayhoon said before he leaned over and put his hand on Umbati's thick afro.

"Well guys, let's get a move on then," Matuka said as he led the rest of the group over to Chumbry.

"So, what? We're supposed to carry this heap of lard?!" Yanielle asked with an attitude before she walked in front of Matuka to face him.

"That necklace is very important to me Yanielle. I must get it back. Dayhoon, Jubilaree!" Matuka said before he walked past Yanielle.

"Sir," the two lads responded in unison.

"Each of you grab one of his legs, we're leaving," Matuka said with a serious facial expression as he looked at them both.

"Yes sir," Jubilaree and Dayhoon quickly replied in unison before they carried out his orders.

Matuka and his guild then left the open patch of field to reclaim what had been stolen. Meanwhile, on the guild of thieves' ship, one of the guildmates looked back towards the island once they went through the force field, and he could no longer see the island.

"What the hell?! Where is the island?! Ukata asked as he pointed to where the island would be.

"Strange," Hedesah said before he closed his eye with his sword held across his back and shoulders.

"See men? Just in time!" Captain Sivilo said as he too looked back towards the missing island.

Back on the island, Matuka's guild began to make their journey back to the cove where their ship was safely awaiting their return, and the beauty of the island seemed to increase.

"Is it me or is this place shining brighter?" Yanielle asked as she walked past a glowing pineapple bush that seemed to glow brighter by the second.

"Interesting, it's almost like the island knows that they're no longer here and can now be free to shine as it pleases," Tahma said as he looked at the glowing apple tree he walked past.

"How are you guys doing back there?" Matuka asked as he looked over his right shoulder towards Jubilaree and Dayhoon.

"Fine," Jubilaree said as he continued to drag the unconscious thief.

"This guy is heavy! How long until we're there?" Dayhoon asked as sweat dropped down his forehand to his nose.

"Not far, we'll be there shortly," Matuka reassured him as they continued to press through the uninhabited island.

"You're awfully quiet Yami," Yanielle said as she looked to her left at Kotoyami.

"Am I? Sorry, I was just thinking," Kotoyami softly replied as she continued to walk with her eyes locked on the back of Matuka's hat.

"Interesting, what about?" Tahma quickly asked as he sped up to walk next to the left of Kotoyami.

"I was just wondering why they wanted his necklace, like how did they even know it was special to begin with?" Kotoyami said before she looked at Tahma.

"Yeah, that's a good question," Yanielle said as she became captive to a deep thought.

"Maybe they know what it really is and how to use it?" Umbati questioned as he threw both of his palms up.

"Whatever it was, it got this guy here in

his predicament and pissed the wrong guy off," Dayhoon said as he held onto Chumbry's left leg.

"Yeah, whoever knocked me out with that plant is going to suffer a pain far worse than death," Jubilaree said with his eye closed as he held onto Chumbry's right leg.

"That's a promise," Matuka quickly stated as he kept his head forward as he continued through the glowing island.

By the time the kids made it to the cove and to the water's edge, they were exhausted.

"Welcome back young Masters and young Mistresses, I see you have company," Iraja said telepathically to everyone as they stopped to take a well-deserved breather.

"Iraja, can you sense the enemy's ship in the water?" Matuka asked aloud as he walked closer to the shore.

"I cannot Master, but they will not be hard to find with the help of the other sea creatures," Iraja quickly replied telepathically to everyone.

"Okay, sounds good. Can you give us a lift up? We need to lock this guy away before he awakes," Matuka said aloud as he pointed to the lifeless thief.

Without hesitation, Iraja quickly lifted two of his large, grayish-brown tentacles out of the water and placed one of them on the glowing beach sand. When everyone sat down on Iraja's tentacle that touched the shore, the other tentacle gently picked up the unconscious intruder.

"This sure beats walking and running!" Umbati shouted with excitement as the wind flowed through his thick, golden afro.

"I will second that," Yanielle said as she threw her head back and closed her eyes as the breeze flowed through her hair as well.

"Are you okay Captain?" Tahma asked Matuka after he noticed how quiet the young Captain was.

"I'll be better once I have my necklace back," Matuka said with a serious tone before he looked to his right at Tahma.

"Interesting, I understand. Hopefully, we get the answers we seek, soon," Tahma said as they drew closer to the ship.

"Agreed," Matuka quickly replied before they finally made it to the ship.

"Here you are, young Masters and Mistresses," Iraja telepathically said as he gently placed them all on the warm, black deck of their ship.

"Thank you, Iraja," Matuka said as he fully stood up on the deck.

"Yeah, thanks," everyone else said in unison aloud.

"My pleasure," Iraja said before he

pulled his tentacles back beneath the water and went silent.

"Now! To put this thief where he belongs!" Matuka shouted as he turned around to his crew.

"Yeah," everyone said in unison as they looked to Chumbry.

"Dayhoon, Jubilaree, you know what to do. Let's go," Matuka said as he walked towards the bow of the ship.

After Jubilaree and Dayhoon took a leg of their own, everyone followed Matuka off the main deck. One by one, they marched through the door and down the black stairs, until they all were in front of the glowing jail cell.

"Alright, Yanielle," Matuka said before he looked back at her.

"Yes Captain?" Yanielle asked as she walked to the right of him.

"Open the cell, I'm going to help the guys put him in the bed," Matuka said.

"Sure thing Captain!" Yanielle quickly responded.

"I knew I could count on you," Matuka said with a smile which caused Yanielle to blush.

"Kotoyami," Matuka said after he turned his head to the left to look at her.

"Yes Captain?" Kotoyami quickly questioned as she turned to face him.

"I need you to be my guard just in case he wakes up in the process. You know what to do," Matuka said with a serious look in his eyes.

"Kill him?" Kotoyami asked as she began to crack her knuckles.

"No, just knock him out," Matuka replied with a nervous smile as he closed his eyes and laughed.

"Gosh! She's brutal!" Umbati said with a smile as he looked to Kotoyami.

"Yeah, you don't want to piss her off," Dayhoon said as he looked down to his left at Umbati.

"Not even a little bit," Jubilaree said with a smirk as he kept his eye closed.

"We're going to need you too for this one Tahma," Matuka said with a smile after he turned around and placed his left hand on Tahma's right shoulder.

"Interesting, no problem boss, my pleasure. I'm here to serve," Tahma said after he fixed his glasses with his left hand.

"Alright fellas, let's do this!" Matuka said as each of the boys grabbed hold of the heavy and unconscious thief.

"Crap!" Dayhoon yelled.

"What does he eat?!" Umbati yelled as he nearly slipped from trying to help carry the sleeping beast.

"This is insane!" Jubilaree yelled as he pushed past his physical limits.

"Almost there boys!" Matuka yelled as sweat dropped from his face onto the floor.

"Hurry! My grip is slipping!" Tahma yelled as his glasses began to fog up.

The boys struggled to lift the unconscious man into the cell for a few minutes but were eventually able to get him into the bed and safely lock the cell.

Entry 7

AWAKENING

It was a couple of hours before day-break. Everyone was tired except Matuka, and the sleeping guest had yet to awake.

"Ugh! How much longer are we gonna allow him to get the sleep we deserve?" Jubila-ree asked with an attitude before he sucked his teeth as he stood in his usual pose.

"Yeah! I'm getting tired!" Umbati com-plained as he looked up to his left at Matuka.

"Not any longer. Hey!! Wake up!!!!" Matuka yelled after they all started complaining at once.

Suddenly, the once sleeping beast began to slowly move and accidentally rolled off the small bed onto the floor.

"Huh, what happened?" Chumbry asked himself as he struggled to open his eyes, sit up and find his glasses.

Chumbry's back was facing the children and he still didn't realize he was on their ship, until he put on his glasses.

"Hey you!! Wake up! Turn around! And face me!!" Matuka yelled as he hit the silver bars of the cell with his right balled fist.

Everyone was silent as they watched the old heavyset man try to come to his senses to face them.

"Where am I? Oh, it's you!" Chumbry said with a child-like grin as he completely turned around to face the guild.

"Oh, it's you? Why I oughta!" Dayhoon said as he raised his right hand as if he was going to slap him somehow through the bars.

Chumbry soon noticed that none of them were happy at the same time he realized he was in a jail cell.

"Am I in trouble?" Chumbry asked like a child afraid of a father's chastisement.

"You damn skippy you are!" Umbati yelled as he ran and grabbed the vibrant, silver bars of the cell.

"What have you or your men done with my necklace?!!" Matuka yelled once more before he completely walked up to the cell.

"You two should stand back Captain, he may try to grab you guys," Jubilaree said with his arms crossed as he opened his eye.

"That's why I'm here," Kotoyami said as she cracked her knuckles and stared at Chumbry with a red gleam in her eyes.

Chumbry took a big gulp as a small river of sweat poured down his face, neck, hairy chest and necklace.

"I was just taking orders," Chumbry said before he dropped to his knees and began to cry like a young child.

"Huh?" Matuka asked softly with a look of confusion as he leaned his head to the right.

"Interesting," Tahma said as he fixed his glasses and walked forward to have a closer look at the thief.

"What's with this guy?" Yanielle asked as she looked on at the crying, old man.

"Hey! What guild are you from?" Jubilaree shouted over the thief's loud crying.

"My guild?" Chumbry quickly asked with fear.

"Yes!" Jubilaree yelled as Chumbry wiped his tears.

"I'm from, uh, from uh, from uh, from…" the poor fool said as he scratched his head and tried to remember.

"I think that lightning fried his brain dude," Umbati jokingly said as he looked over his right shoulder at his older brother.

"Don't fall for his tricks! He's probably trying to play us because he thinks we're young and naive!" Dayhoon said as he balled his left fist and leaned forward with his left foot.

"I see," Matuka said after he looked to his right at Dayhoon and back forward.

"You're wrong, all of you. We have some type of luck man," Jubilaree said after he turned around, closed his eye and walked a couple feet away.

"Interesting, quite perceptive there Jubilaree," Tahma said as he looked from the prisoner to Jubilaree.

The rest of the guild immediately turned around to face Jubilaree to hear what he meant.

"Explain Jubilaree," Matuka said as he closed the gap between the two of them.

"We got the village idiot on our hands! The runt of the litter, can't you tell? He obviously has a birth defect. He don't even have theirs or any other insignia on his body to prove allegiance. He couldn't even save his life if it depended on it," Jubilaree said before he slapped his own forehead with his right palm and turned around to face them all.

Matuka and the rest of the guild quickly

turned around to see if they could see what Jubilaree had claimed he discovered.

"I should be ashamed," Kotoyami said before she turned around.

"Yeah," Jubilaree said with his head down and eye closed.

Kotoyami then walked past everyone and sat on the stairs to face them. Jubilaree shortly followed her, while Matuka and the rest remained.

"So, what's next with this guy then, Matuka?" Yanielle asked as she looked to her right at the young Captain.

"Yeah, what's next Matuka? I'm tired," Umbati whined after he turned around, leaned up against Matuka's right leg, and stared with his puppy dog eyes.

Matuka then looked up from Umbati and back to the crying imbecile.

"Hey you!! What's your name?!" Matuka shouted to the thief to stop him from crying.

"Who me?" the thief asked as he wiped his tears and snot from his face before he pointed to himself.

"Gross and that's coming from me," Umbati said as he turned his head to the left and closed his eyes to avoid seeing the rest.

"Ew, disgusting," Yanielle said as she covered her mouth with her right hand before she made a gagging sound and motion.

"What are we supposed to do with this guy?" Dayhoon asked with a raised left brow as he turned to face Matuka.

"Watch and see. Yes you! What is your name?!" the annoyed young Captain shouted to his prisoner.

"Well, my name is Chumbry. What is your name?" the child-like fool asked with a smile.

"My name is not important! What is important is you tell me where my necklace is!" Matuka said as he pointed to Chumbry.

"This should be good," Jubilaree said before he opened his eye and looked to his left at Kotoyami.

"Well, you see, Captain Okokobi told me to come get your necklace. He said he only wanted to have a closer look without waking you," Chumbry said with his head down as he twiddled his thumbs before he sniffed and wiped his tears.

"Captain Okokobi," Matuka softly said as he crossed his arms, grabbed his chin, and closed his eyes.

"Never heard of em," Umbati jokingly said as he held his palms up in the air with his eyes closed.

"I think I'll take a seat to that," Dayhoon said as he looked down at his younger brother.

"Yeah, it's okay guys. You all can take a

seat or something. You can relax now, I got this," Matuka said as he looked at each of them with a smirk.

"Interesting, will do, Captain. If you need me, I'll be on the stairs," Tahma said as he fixed his specs with his right hand.

"Sure thing Tahma," Matuka said with another smirk as Tahma, Dayhoon and Umbati walked away.

"You sure you got this Matuka? I mean, I believe in you, it's just…" Yanielle said before she hesitated to continue.

"Thank you Yanielle for caring for my mental state. I know you feel like you have to act as some type of grounding rod for me. However, it's okay. We're clearly not dealing with someone who was born normal, so you don't have to worry. I will be nice," Matuka said with his eyes closed and with an open smile as he grabbed the back of his head.

"Good to hear it Captain," Yanielle said before she started to blush.

Yanielle then walked away to join the others on the stairs so the young Captain could continue. After the crew sat down on the stairs, Matuka resumed his interrogation.

"So, he told you to get my necklace. What happened next Chumbry?" Matuka asked his frightened prisoner as he sat down in front of the cell.

"Well, after that. All I can remember is throwing your necklace to Sivilo. He caught it in his very special bag," Chumbry said with a smile as he fully sat on the floor in front of Matuka.

"Special bag?" Matuka asked with a look of confusion as he stared into the holding cell.

"Yes, Sivilo said it was a magical bag," Chumbry said with a child-like grin as he placed each of his hands on a knee and leaned forward.

"Interesting," Tahma said before he fixed his glasses as he watched from the black, alligator-skinned steps.

"Who is Sivilo? And how many men came to the island with you Chumbry?" Matuka asked as he intensely looked on at him through the gaps of the silver bars.

"Sivilo was one of the three men Captain Okokobi really trusted. He is very smart, unlike me," Chumbry said with a smile as he closed his eyes.

"Don't say that Chumbry, you are smart. You're going to help me get back my necklace. But first I need you to show me how smart you are by telling me how many men were with you," Matuka said with a smile as he grabbed hold of one of the bars with his right hand.

"Okay! I'll do my best!" Chumbry said with a huge smile before he stood up.

Chumbry then began to pace around his cell as he softly called out names and counted them on his fingers.

"*That a boy Chumbry!*" Matuka thought to himself as he watched him.

As the crew sat on the stairs, they talked amongst themselves as they watched the boy-like man try to reveal a secret to them.

"You think he'll be any help guys?" Yanielle asked softly as she looked on at Matuka and Chumbry.

"I hope so," Jubilaree said softly before he opened his eye and looked down to his left at Yanielle.

"Even if he's not, couldn't Iraja and the sea creatures just find them?" Umbati asked as he looked around at everyone on the stairs.

"Interesting, it would save us time," Tahma said as he fixed his glasses and looked to his left at Umbati.

"Smart thinking little bro," Dayhoon said as he looked down to his right at Umbati before he wrapped his right arm around his neck.

"That's all good and said, however, we are all tired. What good would it do to find them in the state we are in now?" Kotoyami asked as she looked down at the back of Dayhoon's head.

"Interesting, I see where you are coming from Kotoyami," Tahma said as he turned around and looked up, over his left shoulder.

"Yeah, I suppose you're right," Jubilaree said before he closed his eye and let out a sigh.

"This sucks, why us?" Yanielle asked as she buried her face in her palms.

"Yeah," the rest of them said in unison as they continued to watch Matuka and Chumbry.

A couple more minutes passed and Chumbry finally had a breakthrough.

"I got it!" Chumbry shouted with joy before he sat back down in front of the young and patient Captain.

"Great! Let's hear it," Matuka said with a smirk as he leaned forward.

"Finally," Umbati said as he rolled his eyes before he stretched and yawned.

"There were about eleven of us that came to the island. While about twenty stayed behind on the ship," Chumbry said before he fell to his back from the exhaustion of thinking.

"Well, you were close Jubilaree," Koto-yami said as she looked to her right at him.

"Yeah," Jubilaree said stoically as he kept his normal pose.

"So, Chumbry. Why did they want my necklace?" Matuka asked the child-like man as he watched him catch a breather.

Chumbry slowly sat up and looked at Matuka before he scratched his head again.

"Oh, not again!" Dayhoon said with an

attitude as he rolled his eyes and before he shook his head.

"Sivilo told Captain Okokobi that your necklace was very special, like the treasures we hunt," Chumbry said with a smile as he looked at Matuka.

"Interesting," Tahma said as he fixed his glasses as he sat up straighter.

"Yeah, very," Kotoyami said as she moved the hair that hung in front of her face to behind her left ear.

"So, you and your guildmates are treasure hunters?" Matuka asked with a raised right eyebrow as he hunched over.

"Yes sir! And Captain Okokobi always tells me I'm his good luck charm," Chumbry said with a smile before he chuckled.

"Is that so?" Matuka asked Chumbry as a plan began to form in his mind.

"Yes sir," Chumbry quickly replied.

"Chumbry," Matuka said as he leaned forward and stared into his prisoner's eyes.

"Yes sir?" Chumbry asked as he leaned forward as well and gazed into the young Captain's eyes.

"I only have one final question," Matuka said sternly and with a serious look before he stood on his feet.

Everyone, including Chumbry, stared and patiently awaited his final question.

"Where is your guild headed?" Matuka asked as he looked down at Chumbry.

The thief then scratched his head and began to think as hard as he could to remember.

"You can do it," Yanielle whispered as she looked on from the stairs.

A couple of minutes passed and Chumbry finally remembered their next destination.

"Habanarah! We were headed to the island of Habanarah!" Chumbry said after he stood up from the floor.

"Never heard of it," Umbati said with a smile as he threw his palms in the air and looked to Dayhoon.

"Do you know what direction it's in?" Matuka asked as he crossed his arms.

"No, but Captain Okokobi always encourages me to read if I can't find the answer to something. So, maybe you should read," Chumbry replied with an innocent smile.

"Thank you Chumbry for your help. Get some rest," Matuka said before he turned around to walk over to the others.

"Am I going home?" Chumbry asked as he looked to Matuka.

"Where is home?" Matuka asked with a raised brow.

"Eseville," Chumbry said after he paused and scratched his head.

"Eseville? Never heard of it," Umbati

jokingly said as he threw his palms up.

"I will do my best to get you home," Matuka said before he turned around and walked to the others.

Chumbry then wiped his tears, smiled, and laid back down on the bed. By the time Matuka stood in front of the others, they could already tell there was a lot on his mind.

"So, what's the verdict?" Dayhoon asked as he looked at Matuka.

"There was so many other questions you could have asked him," Kotoyami said before she stretched and yawned.

"Like what?" Matuka quickly asked as he walked closer to them.

"For starters, you could have asked what year it was or where is the nearest civilization," Jubilaree replied as he uncrossed his arms and opened his eye.

"Interesting, I didn't think of that. Perhaps it's not too late," Tahma said before he looked past Matuka to Chumbry.

"What's the use? We don't remember anything or anyone," Yanielle said before she dropped her head.

"Well if we did find land, maybe we could ask someone something. It may jog our memories," Dayhoon said as he stood up and looked around at everyone on the stairs.

"I thought of that Dayhoon, however, my

necklace is the top priority. Like Chumbry said, his Captain said my necklace was special. If I can't remember anything about it and they know something, I have to find them to ask," Matuka said with a serious look in his eyes as he looked on at everyone.

"So, what's next?" Kotoyami asked as she stood up as well.

Everyone else that was sitting, stood to their feet and awaited their Captain's response.

"Well, for now we rest. I know we're all pretty tired and I got some reading to do," Matuka said with a smile.

"Thank God!" Umbati said as he hunched over and wiped his forehead from sweat.

"Interesting," Tahma said as he fixed his glasses with his right hand.

"Reading?" Jubilaree quickly asked as he crossed his arms.

"Yeah, Chumbry gave some good advice. I still have my father's journal. Maybe there are some clues in there I could find that will tell me more about the necklace," Matuka said as he looked at all of them.

"Okay, well I'm out! You coming girl?" Yanielle asked Kotoyami before she began to walk away.

"Most definitely," Kotoyami said before she let out a sigh.

"Alright! It's settled! Everyone get some rest, our mission starts after we awake," Matuka said with a smile and with his eyes closed.

The crew said their goodbyes and went down their hallways, into their rooms. Matuka then walked up the stairs and out onto the main deck. The once dark sky had begun to lighten as the sun promised its return. Matuka slowly walked across his main deck with his arms behind his back, as he tried to process everything that took place. It had been a long night and the young Captain needed a good rest. By the time Matuka reached the door to his quarters, he was drained and ready to collapse.

"Almost there," Matuka said before he let out a sigh and his door opened on its own.

The moment Matuka's door opened he was met with the smell and feeling of comfort that he most surely missed. He soon remembered how dark the room was after he stepped in and closed the door behind him.

"It's so dark," the young Captain said as he took a step forward.

As Matuka walked down the steps, his once dark room began to glow.

"This never gets old," Matuka said as he looked up at the ceiling.

Matuka then looked to the right at his bed before he slowly made his way over to it.

"What a night," Matuka and the others

all simultaneously said as they each landed on their beds.

Suddenly, Matuka heard something fall near the west wall of his room.

"What was that?" Matuka said as he laid on his back and looked to the west wall.

Matuka then sat up to see if he could see anything on the floor.

"That's weird," Matuka said before he stood up and slowly walked over to the long table on the west wall.

When Matuka reached the table, he immediately noticed the journal he was planning to read had somehow fallen off the table onto the floor.

"How did that happen?" Matuka questioned himself aloud as he stared at the dark-green journal.

Matuka then picked up the journal and walked over to his desk in the middle of his cabin.

"Maybe it was the wind and me closing the door," Matuka said as he looked down at the journal.

The young Captain then pulled out his chair and sat down at his desk.

"Okay, let's see what we have here. Hopefully, father wrote something about my necklace," Matuka said as he looked down at the journal before he opened it.

The moment Matuka opened the journal, his head began to pound, and he got extremely dizzy.

"What the heck?" Matuka questioned as he took off his hat and held his head from the pain.

Matuka then took a second to breathe and to fan himself with his hat. Once the dizzy sensation subsided and Matuka was able to shake the pain, he began to read.

"Today has been a long and exhausting day. I, King Matuka...Wait, what?!! King Matuka?! Isn't this father's journal?!" Matuka yelled as he looked down at the journal.

The young lad was confused and couldn't believe what he just read so he started over.

"Today has been a long and exhausting day. I, King Matuka, met with the other kings and queens today to come to an agreement. King Jubilaree, Queen Yanielle, Queen Koto-yami, King Dayhoon, King Umbati and King Tahma all had something to say," Matuka read before he and all of his crew simultaneously fell unconscious.

Matuka and the others were transported to an astral plane where they could all see one another but they could not speak or move. They were all terrified of what was to come and didn't understand how they got there. When they all started to think it was a dream, they then heard a familiar voice ringing in their ears.

"Welcome young Masters and young Mistresses to your hidden memories," Iraja said as a mist began to grow in front of them.

They were in the same circle formation as they were when they sat in the saloon, so they could all see each other perfectly.

"This is the story and past of seven kings and queens from long ago that has been nearly forgotten until now," Iraja said to them all telepathically.

Suddenly, within the mist, a clear image of a continent began to form.

"Once upon a time, in the distant past, on the continent of Eseville, there were seven great countries, and they were filled with countless different guilds. The seven great countries were ruled by seven kings and queens. With time, the once flourishing continent took a turn for the worst. This is their story.

There once lived a king in the north who ruled over his people with grace. His country's name was Schivala. This king was the king of justice and might. He was a man of few words, but whenever he did speak, he had the hearts and ears of his listeners. He spoke with love and taught peace with patience. His people were heroic like he was. They all achieved great feats and would proudly die for him. From the young to the old, he reached each of them on a personal level. This king was you, Master Matuka," Iraja said before tears of blood fell from Matuka's eyes.

The image of Matuka faded and another image began to surface.

"There also lived a king in the west. His country's name was Mezera. He was a manly man. A serious and loyal man. He was the king of assassins and strategists. No one could ever match his foresight. His people were nearly unstoppable and unstoppable to many. He never took life for granted and taught that mentality to his people. His people loved him and his open-minded way of thinking. This king was you, Master Jubilaree," Iraja said aloud before blood crept from both of Jubilaree's eyes.

The image of Jubilaree faded and another image began to surface from the mist.

"Now, there once lived a queen in the northeast. Her country's name was Mikoto. This queen's country was known to be the leader in spiritual enlightenment. She was the queen that had the best culinary specialists on the continent. Her food filled all her citizens' bellies with ease. She was beyond tough and ruled with an iron rod. However, her people loved her dearly. This queen was you, Mistress Kotoyami," Iraja said before blood flowed from Kotoyami's eyes and dripped down her cheeks.

The image of Kotoyami faded and another image began to surface out of the mist.

"Now, there once was a queen in the northwest. Her country's name was Yahanna. She had no competition in the field of medicine and communication. She was like a queen of heaven, one who could heal the nations in a blink of an eye. Her people were skilled naturalists and builders. Her people loved her with no bounds and would sacrifice themselves in order to save her life. This queen was you, Mistress Yanielle," Iraja said before blood flowed from Yanielle's eyes and trickled down her cheeks.

The image of Yanielle faded and another image began to surface.

"There once was a king in the southwest. His country's name was Tilosta. He was the king of sorcery and advanced technology. All his people were either skilled magicians or skilled engineers. He gave his people hope and provided them with a perfect environment for imagination. He was a kind genius although he had no competition in intelligence. His people loved and cherished him for his humbleness. This king was you, Master Tahma," Iraja said before blood crept from behind Tahma's glasses.

The image of Tahma faded and another image began to surface from the rising mist.

"There also was a king in the southeast. His country's name was Wulara. He was known as the king of weapon crafting and animal taming. His country's citizens used wild and ferocious beasts to travel. This was a great fear tactic for a lot of enemies. He was strong and very brave. He ruled his people with sureness and love. His country held the best hunters and held some of the greatest fighters. Although he was lethal, he disliked confrontation above all. His people loved and adored him for it. This king was you, Master Dayhoon," Iraja said before blood fell from Dayhoon's eyes.

The image of Dayhoon faded and another image began to surface from the mist.

"And last but not least, there also was a king in those days that ruled in the east. His country's name was Vinyarra. He was the king of agriculture and art. He was also the younger brother of the King of Wulara. Whenever they got together with their guilds for battle against someone, they were a force to be reckoned with. This king loved weapons as a youth but as he matured, he became a kind and gentle man. In his younger days, he was known as the relentless one amongst his peers. He was extremely brave and determined. He was known around the continent for creating the best wine and rum, in his older teen years. His people were geniuses when it came to the musical arts, painting, as well as sculptures and entertaining. His people were also the best at farming and irrigation. His citizens loved him without cease. This king was you, Master Umbati," Iraja said before blood crept from Umbati's eyes and ran down his cheeks.

The image of Umbati faded and another image began to surface from the rising mist. The crew couldn't believe what they heard and what they saw, but they had no choice, because they began to remember it all. As another image began to surface, Iraja began to speak.

"You all lived in peace and worked together perfectly until the Great Famine. The overindulgence from all the countries except King Matuka's caused jealousy, fear and hate to sweep the unexpecting countries. Since Schivala, King Matuka's country was thriving; citizens from all the other countries went to seek refuge. This ignited a flame within the other kings and queens. Somehow, King Matuka's country was excelling enough to draw foreigners in the midst of a famine, and they couldn't understand it.

This enraged King Tahma so much he started sending scouts to Schivala to see why the country was still prospering and full of life. Upon doing so, King Tahma discovered that all King Matuka's luck and good fortune came from a magical artifact that King Matuka had in his possession. One of King Tahma's scouts gathered information and told him that he heard King Matuka was found on the beach as an infant. That he was found in a rowboat that was broken in half, and that he had a strange necklace around his neck.

It didn't take long for King Tahma to realize it was the legendary, long lost necklace of Déjà Vu, The Witch of the Triangle. The same necklace, that over the centuries, the sailors would gather to whisper about. The stories always started with one man who experienced a terrible sea wreck at the hand of The Witch of the Triangle. It is told that she only let the pure of heart survive, and so far, it has only been one each from all the ships she's taken down.

The one lucky survivor, the pure of heart sailor, was allowed to keep their life. It is said that she even assisted the men with the aid of sea creatures to swim them back to land. Throughout the centuries, one man would come forth and tell the unbelievable tale of Déjà Vu, The Witch of the Triangle. A tale of a ghostly woman that controlled the water as lightning danced with her. The witch that's accompanied by tornadoes, whirlpools, and hideous sea monsters. The supernatural woman that stands on the water, screaming for the return of her necklace.

After each incident, one brave sailor

would come back trying to remember how she briefly described her necklace. Each giving a small description of the item until its depiction became a picture that needed deciphering. After King Tahma had a chance to see King Matuka's necklace in person, he was able to confirm it was indeed the same necklace of legend. This old ghost tale was known to be over four hundred years old. And that she got the name Déjà Vu from people hearing and seeing the same claim resurface throughout time. The necklace from legend that could grant the wielder all power to the water supply on the planet. King Tahma quickly became highly interested in Matuka after he learned more of the legend.

King Tahma also heard that after King Matuka was found on a seat of a broken row-boat on the beach with the legendary necklace of Déjà Vu, he was taken to a small village. And it was the same land where he grew up, expanded the territory, and became king over," Iraja said as the image faded and another image began to surface out of the mist.

The entire crew was paralyzed and had no choice but to watch as their haunted, hidden past unfolded before their very eyes. As another image began to make itself known and clear, Iraja began to speak again.

"After King Tahma got wind of all that interesting news, he began plotting and planning on how he could possibly find a way to benefit from the necklace as well. He then started to sow more jealousy within the other rulers by letting them know what he had discovered about King Matuka. All the other kings and queens eventually began to despise King Matuka.

King Tahma, with the other kings and queens, eventually decided to request a meeting with King Matuka. This gathering was about the future plans of the continent in regard to the Great Famine. They named it the Hyungetta Council in hopes to solidify an alliance. However, each of the rulers wanted King Matuka's necklace to advance their own specific agenda.

King Jubilaree and his assassins were unstoppable on land, but they wanted to be assured that on water they would also be unstoppable. Eventually, he would have destroyed the world from his ambition and lust for power. Queen Kotoyami wanted to be able to cook, eat and provide the rarest and highest end of seafood known to man. In doing so, the number of sea life would have dwindled and eventually gone extinct. Queen Yanielle wanted to create a crack in the ocean floor in order to get a purer form of water for her healing practices. Her actions would have set loose an ancient demon from the abyss that would have sunk all the continents.

King Tahma wanted to achieve a new form of energy to advance life on earth by merging magic and science. By doing so, the people would have annihilated themselves and destroyed the world in the process. King Dayhoon wanted to extract precious metals from the earth and sea floor in order to build new weapons and gear for his guilds. This would have disrupted the balance of the ecosystem and destroyed the earth in the process. And lastly, King Umbati wanted the necklace to be able to control the food growth of the entire continent by controlling the water supply and charge as much as he saw fit. If he was successful, he would have destroyed the world with a flood, like back in the ancient days.

After King Matuka met with the other kings and queens, he soon saw past their blind, selfish desires. He could see what their plans really meant for the entire continent and even possibly the entire world. King Matuka let it be known that he didn't want to give up his necklace and insisted on another way. In doing so, the other kings and queens left the meeting upset. They threatened to wage war if an agreement couldn't be made because they felt he was being a hypocrite. King Matuka ended up ignoring the other rulers and their demands which caused the Great War," Iraja said to them all as blood profusely fell from all their eyes.

The image then faded, and another image began to surface from the mist. Within the mist, once everyone could see the adult version of Matuka slowly dying on his ship, Iraja began to speak.

"With King Matuka's last breaths drawing near, he cried out to his maker. He cried and wished that things could have been different. He desired for the other kings, queens, and himself to have a chance to do things over. He wanted to give his life saving lives instead of taking them. He wanted to save as many lives that were lost that day. He was truly sorry for being selfish and not giving more thought to the needs of his neighboring rulers. He wished that he could have had the opportunity to save as many lives as he just helped destroy.

King Matuka's emotions were so strong, that his pain and remorse vibrated his entire ship. However, King Matuka was severely injured from his gunshot wound and died after the battles stopped. After everyone was deceased, an electrical wave of energy exploded from King Matuka's body. The wave of energy quickly traveled to each of the other kings and queens in an instant. That's when his necklace lifted off his chest and the legendary power activated.

The seven rulers' bodies vanished along with all the casualties and the destruction.

Much time passed while the rulers were incubating but after they were done, they were transported back to the same location, many years later. Soon after, a new ship was created and appeared in the water near King Matuka's ship. I was abruptly awakened from my sleep and I was instantly drawn to the ship. The moment I latched onto the bottom; I received all knowledge of the rulers' pasts. The vessel was brand new but rang with echoes from another time it seemed. The vessel was designed with a piece of each of them in mind.

It was a majestic and supernatural vessel for the leader of the Hyungetta Council, King Matuka. It was handcrafted from a miracle and no one could move it but him. It also had enough books and secrets to keep Queen Yanielle from ever being bored. Inside, held a one of a kind training facility to keep King Jubilaree and Queen Kotoyami busy. It had enough weapons for King Dayhoon and King Umbati to get lost in. It even had enough mysteries for King Tahma to try to solve and never run out. I was bound to all of them forever, once I saw their past, present and future," Iraja said as the images of the mist slowly faded away.

All the children continued to cry tears of blood as an image of Iraja began to appear from the mist.

"After I received the knowledge of them

all, I found King Matuka's ship about to sink, so I held it up with my tentacles and the rest is history. The reborn kings and queens eventually all met as children but had no recollection of their past. They didn't know that after the war, one-hundred and fifty-years later, that all their countries would be corrupt. That their countries had chaos amongst their guilds and that they all were abusing the citizens. They didn't know that all the guilds within their countries had gone rogue. They didn't know that other continents with guilds that possessed powerful magical users and artifacts, heard of their demise.

The reborn kings and queens didn't know that one of those foreign guilds took their land for themselves. They had no clue what was to come because of amnesia and the time they loss," Iraja said before his image faded from the mist.

Once the mist faded away and the children could all see one another, Iraja began to speak again.

"Once again, young Masters and young Mistresses, these are your hidden memories from long ago. Yes, there is a lot you must make up for. There is a lot you must remember still. There is a lot you must learn from a one-hundred and fifty-year gap. There are new possible enemies at every turn and on each adventure. You must retrieve your necklace from the wrong hands. Restore the balance and take rule again as the true rulers you are all destined to be. Now awake, my young Kings and Queens! Your memories have returned to you!!!" Iraja shouted before everyone awakened from the vision, they all shared.

As Matuka woke up, he soon noticed he had an excruciating headache. At that very moment, down below deck, all the crew members ran out of their rooms into their hallways. Yanielle and Kotoyami paused to look at each other before they bolted down the hallway towards the stairs. The boys also stopped to look at each other before they bolted down the hallway toward the stairs.

One by one, they came around the corner until they all were by the stairs. The children paused in their tracks and stared at one another without saying a word. Suddenly, Tahma ran up the stairs and out onto the main deck. The others quickly followed until they all reached Matuka's door to his quarters.

When they all reached the door, Matuka stepped out of his room and saw them all standing there with bloody tears in their eyes. The sun had just begun to peak over the horizon and the silence was unbearable. The children all then ran into a huddle, grabbed hold to each other, and started to cry their hearts out. Bloody tears fell from all their eyes as their long lost, hidden memories rang in their minds.

"I'm so sorry!" Matuka cried as he held onto his crew.

Everyone else started crying more once they heard Matuka apologize because it made them feel even more guilty. That's when they all fell to their knees in the huddle as they held onto one another.

"I'm sorry Matuka! I'm sorry everyone! It's all my fault!" Tahma screamed and cried as he held everyone.

"No, it's my fault!" everyone else shouted simultaneously.

"I shouldn't have ignored you all!! It's my fault!" Matuka cried as blood continued to pour out his eyes.

"No, it's my fault!" everyone else said in unison.

The crew sat there crying for several minutes before Iraja started to speak.

"Young Masters and young Mistresses, although you all played the dominant role in the chaos, you all have been given a second chance," Iraja said before he caught all their attention.

The children slowed in their crying and all looked to the ocean.

"Like I said before young Masters and young Mistresses, yes, there is a lot you must make up for. Yes, there is a lot you must remember. Yes, there is a lot you must learn from a one-hundred and fifty-year gap. Yes, there are new possible enemies at every turn and on each adventure. But you have each other now. You have seen the error of your ways and now that you have, you can figure out how to avoid repeating the same mistakes. You must retrieve that necklace before any more damage is done. And yes, you must restore balance and take rule again as the true rulers you are all destined to be. Now stand my Kings and Queens, you are royalty!" Iraja shouted with pride as an army of sea creatures came to the surface of the water and started to splash.

"He's right," Matuka said as he slowly stood up above his crew and wiped his face.

Everyone then looked up to him as he fixed his hat and stood over them. One by one, they all started to rise to their feet after they wiped their bloody tears from their faces.

"Iraja is right guys; we have been given a very special opportunity; a super rare blessing. A second chance at life; fate has called us all into her chambers. It's up to us to be our brother's keeper. We have destroyed so much and took so many lives. We are forever in debt of the people and the ocean.

We will never run from any fight because we have the strength to overcome any opposition. We will be the strongest guild amongst the waters and known to man. And once we regain our power, we will reclaim our continent!

The waters of the rain, the rivers, lakes, ponds, swamps, bayous, canals, puddles, the oceans, and seas will be our footstool. The animals will hear our cries and aid us always and forever. For we are their friends, protectors, and their family. The fog will be our shield everywhere we go and this vessel has no limits. This is our ship, we are now and forever more, the Hyungetta, the crew with the black sails," Matuka said as he held out his hand in the huddle.

After everyone placed their hand in the huddle, the once still ship began to vibrate.

"What's next Captain?" Umbati said with a smile as he looked up to Matuka.

"Yeah, I have so many questions," Kotoyami said as she looked at the young Captain.

"Yeah me too," Yanielle quickly replied.

"Get in line I have some myself," Jubilaree said with a smile as he looked to Matuka as well.

"Interesting, I have a few of my own," Tahma said as he fixed his glasses with his right hand.

"Hey, no fair, I have questions!" Umbati whined as he waved his arms around in the air.

"Don't worry little bro, we got time,"

Dayhoon said with a gentle smile as he looked down to his younger brother.

Matuka smiled as he looked down to Umbati and then turned around to face the helm.

"Next, we go get my necklace," Matuka said with a smirk as he looked on at the helm.

***

Meanwhile, Sivilo was enjoying being the new Captain over everyone.

"Hurry up and fetch me a bottle from the saloon Hedesah before I get upset!" Captain Sivilo threatened before he threw an empty bottle of wine down to the deck and wobbled away.

"Jerk!" Hedesah said softly as he left the main deck to go grab a bottle from below.

Without warning, a mysterious fog came out of nowhere and surrounded the guild of thieves' vessel.

"Where in the hell did all this fog come from?!" Sivilo asked as they all tried to make sense of it.

Suddenly, the crew began to see glowing red eyes shining through the thick fog and began to hear sinister laughing.

"What's that?!" Saiyu screamed as he pointed into the fog at a pair of the gleaming red eyes.

"Could it be the demons that killed Captain Okokobi and Chumbry?!" Jutah asked with fear in his eyes.

"*Impossible! I made that all up!*" Sivilo thought to himself as he looked around at the different pair of glowing red eyes.

"It's seven of them!" Minoka yelled before falling backwards to the deck.

"*Seven?*" Captain Sivilo thought to himself as he grew more terrified by the second.

"It's them! The demons from the island," Minoka said as he pointed into the fog after he saw a quick glimpse of Umbati.

The children continued to laugh which caused some of the men to get angry and some to become horrified. Without warning, the thieves' ship came to an immediate standstill, which caused the ship to jerk and everyone on it to tumble over on their face.

"Run! It's the demons!" Benoby said before he caused the rest of the crew to panic, scream and scramble for their lives.

"How could this be?!" Captain Sivilo asked before he became enraged from fear.

As Iraja held the enemy's ship from escaping, the fog dissipated, and the guild of thieves could see Matuka and his guild. The guild of thieves could not believe their eyes because they were scared to death by mere children.

"Are those children?! That's what we

were so afraid of?" one of the thieves asked before he laughed hysterically.

Once all the crew knew they were only facing children, they relaxed and began to laugh.

"These can't be the demons Captain Sivilo was talking about," another one of the guild members said as he too started to laugh.

"No! You're wrong! That's them!" Benoby yelled.

"Yeah! Tell them Captain!" Minoka yelled as he looked at Captain Sivilo.

Sivilo stood speechless until Matuka stepped forward with Chumbry, who was told to be dead.

"Is that Chumbry?!" Hedesah asked as he dropped the unopened wine bottle to the deck which caused it to shatter.

"It is Chumbry!" Kuraba said as he looked on at their thought to be dead guildmate.

"What's the meaning of this?! How is Chumbry alive?!" Hedesah asked Captain Sivilo as the rest of the guild of thieves walked closer to see if it really was Chumbry.

"This must be a trick! I saw him die with my own two eyes!" Captain Sivilo quickly and nervously replied as he looked around at his crew and then back at Chumbry.

"Then how can you explain this?" Kuraba asked Captain Sivilo as he pointed to

Chumbry.

"Enough!" Matuka yelled as he looked on at the baffled men.

"Who does he think he's talking to like that? They're just children! We can take them men!" Captain Sivilo shouted as he looked over his right shoulder towards his men.

"Chumbry, who was it that you gave my necklace to?" Matuka softly asked Chumbry with a smile.

"There, Sivilo was the one and he put it in that bag," Chumbry said with a smile as he looked and pointed to the silky-white bag that hung from the thief's waist.

"You have something of mine! My necklace!! And I want it back!" Matuka yelled as he looked on at Captain Sivilo.

"A trade for a trade!" Umbati yelled as he walked across the bulwarks and put a knife to Chumbry's throat.

Captain Sivilo then started to laugh so hysterically that he caused tears to form in his eyes.

"Huh? What's so funny?!" Matuka asked out of frustration.

"Do you think I'd really give up anything for that stupid idiot?! Keep dreaming!" Captain Sivilo said before he continued to laugh.

"What are you saying Sivilo?" Kuraba asked Captain Sivilo with a look of confusion and anger on his face.

"Yeah, didn't you say that you didn't want to lose any more men, after the demons killed Captain Okokobi and Chumbry?" Hedesah asked as he too looked at Captain Sivilo with anger.

"Yeah, they don't look like the normal demons we killed in the past either!" one of the guild members chimed in as they surrounded Captain Sivilo.

"Maybe you should let Chumbry tell you all what happened!" Matuka shouted as he looked on at the confused guild of thieves.

"Chumbry, tell us what happened," Hedesah said as he stepped forward to the bulwarks.

Chumbry then looked back to Matuka to make sure it was okay to speak.

"It's okay Chumbry, go ahead and explain your side of the story," Matuka said softly with a gentle smile.

The guild of thieves all stood around and listened to what Chumbry had to say. After each passing second, the guild of thieves grew uneasy and more suspicious of Captain Sivilo's story.

"Wait, so only you got struck by the lightning?" Kuraba asked Chumbry before he looked to Captain Sivilo.

"Yes sir!" Chumbry said with a serious

look in his eyes.

"Come on! You're gonna believe this moron?! He's already the village idiot and he got struck by lightning! How credible is he?!" Captain Sivilo yelled as he turned to face his crew.

"How credible are you right now?! You said they were demons and they look pretty human to all of us!" Minoka quickly replied with an attitude.

That's when Hedesah looked down and noticed what looked like fresh blood on Sivilo's sword's scabbard. By the time Chumbry was finished talking, everyone began to suspect Sivilo of killing Captain Okokobi.

"How dare you? You bastard! You'll pay!!" Kuraba yelled as tears fell from his eyes.

"You killed him!! You don't deserve to be called Captain you piece of filth!!" Hedesah yelled after he raised his enormous sword in the air.

The guild of thieves began to cry and grow in anger as they mourned the loss of Captain Okokobi all over again.

"This is madness!!" Captain Sivilo shouted as he looked around at his guildmates.

The guild of thieves had Captain Sivilo completely surrounded and began to close in on him.

"Stay back!!" Captain Sivilo screamed

before he pulled out a gun from behind his back.

Captain Sivilo then backed up until he was no longer surrounded.

"Give me back my necklace!!" Matuka yelled from his ship at Captain Sivilo with a balled fist.

"Who's gonna make me?! You can't stop me! Who would even try?!" Captain Sivilo shouted before he started to laugh like a maniac.

"I will!!!" Matuka yelled as loud as he could.

"We will!!!" Matuka's guild yelled in unison.

"See, you can't kill us all Sivilo!" Jutah said as he began to walk forward.

"You're right! All I need to do is kill one! These magic bullets feed on blood! Good luck!" Captain Sivilo said after he turned around to face Matuka.

Without warning or hesitation, Captain Sivilo pulled the trigger and shot Matuka in the chest.

"Noooo!" Matuka's crew yelled in unison as their Captain hit the black deck.

Suddenly, Iraja telepathically let out an eardrum bursting scream. Immediately, everyone on both ships dropped to their knees from the pain and tried to cover their ears. That's when Matuka's ship started to vibrate and all the sea creatures came to the surface of the water.

"Look! In the water!! Its monsters!!" one of the guild members screamed before all the thieves looked as well.

Shortly after, what followed next was a very loud bang because Iraja used his tentacles to rip through the enemy's ship. One tentacle burst through the hull and projected some of the men in the air, while another destroyed the poop deck. All the men screamed for their lives while they ran about the sinking ship. That's when another tentacle ripped through the sick bay and exposed all the men to the justice-hungry killer whales.

As another tentacle destroyed their beloved sun deck, another one threw a man into the tiller head-first. Some of the men tried to climb the masts but were yanked down into the water by an enormous squid and eaten. Iraja then wrapped his gigantic tentacles around the three masts on the vessel and crushed them. That's when he ripped the ship in half and more men fell out to be eaten alive. Iraja then threw both halves of the ship into the air. The mizzen fell in the water over the men who were trying to escape the angry sea monsters, as the rest of the men were falling from the sky.

Before Sivilo could hit the water, Iraja

took his silky-white bag, grabbed his head, grabbed each of his arms and each of his legs, then pulled his body apart. Silvio's body parts were completely eaten before they hit the water. The feeding frenzy continued, and all forms of sea life took a part in the act because of Captain Sivilo's fatal choice. The crew gathered around Matuka's lifeless body and cried as they listened to the screams of the thieves. All the while, Chumbry was afraid and crying next to the bulwarks.

"Yanielle, hurry up and heal him!" Jubilaree yelled as he looked at her.

Everyone was crying and leaning over Matuka as Yanielle reached for her healing tool in her pant leg pocket.

"Hurry Yanielle!" Umbati cried as he leaned over Matuka.

When Yanielle pulled out her healing tool, she soon realized it wasn't working.

"What's going on?! Why won't it work?!" Yanielle screamed from frustration and fear as she looked at the silver retractor in her hand.

"What's the matter? Is it broken?" Kotoyami asked as tears continued to fall from her face.

"We gotta hurry before it's too late!" Dayhoon yelled as tears fell down his face as well.

"Oh Matuka," Tahma cried as he laid his head on Matuka's legs.

"This can't be happening! This can't be! You stay with me! You hear?! You little bastard!" Jubilaree screamed as tears fell from both his eyes.

"Why didn't the force-field around the ship work?!" Yanielle screamed from fear and frustration.

Minutes passed after all the thieves were completely eaten alive, and all the sea creatures were still at the surface of the water; awaiting a miracle. The crew was all lying across Matuka when out of nowhere, the ship began to vibrate and Matuka began to lift off the ground. The crew then stood up to get a better look at what was happening. The more he rose the more everyone began to step away from him.

"Whoa," Umbati said after he wiped his tears.

"Interesting," Tahma said as he began to wipe his tears.

That's when all Matuka's dried blood throughout the ship began to glow red.

"What the hell?!" Jubilaree asked as he looked around at the deck.

"Are you guys seeing this?" Dayhoon asked as he looked around the main deck.

"Yeah, what's happening?" Kotoyami asked as she wiped her face and paused.

Everyone watched without blinking as Matuka floated in mid-air in the upright position. Suddenly, a black cloud appeared above the ship in the sky. The sudden weather changes caused Chumbry to look up and notice Matuka floating in mid-air.

"Whooa," Chumbry said as he wiped his tears and stood to his feet to look at the young Captain.

Suddenly, all Matuka's dried blood that was across the entire ship came to life and began to travel to where he was floating.

"Guys, are you seeing this?!" Yanielle asked as she looked down by her feet.

"Interesting!" Tahma yelled as he fixed his glasses and looked back and forth at Matuka's blood.

Shortly after, all the blood formed a huge puddle under Matuka, and Yanielle's silver retractor started to glow green.

"Yes!" Yanielle shouted with joy as tears leaped from her face.

"Alright!" Dayhoon and Umbati yelled in unison.

"That a boy Captain," Jubilaree said with a smile as a lonely tear ran down his cheeks.

"Come on Captain you can do it! Come back to us!" Kotoyami lightly shouted as she attentively watched Matuka's blood glow brighter and brighter.

When Yanielle walked over to Matuka and the light from her retractor shined over him, his blood began to glow brighter. Without warning, the blood shot up off the deck and entered his body through the bullet wound.

"Interesting," Tahma said as he fixed his glasses with his right hand.

A minute passed and all Matuka's blood entered his body before Yanielle's healing tool stopped glowing.

"What happened? He didn't wake up!" Jubilaree said as he looked at Yanielle.

"I don't know! That usually does the trick!" Yanielle cried before she dropped back to her knees.

That's when Iraja passed the enchanted bag that contained Matuka's necklace to Yanielle.

"You must return his necklace," Iraja said telepathically to them all.

"Interesting," Tahma said as he looked at Iraja's wet tentacle.

"Huh? Okay, right!" Yanielle said before she leaped to her feet.

The moment Yanielle opened the bag, a lightning bolt shot out of the bag into the sky, which nearly hit her in the face.

"What the?!" Yanielle screamed as she looked up to follow the lightning bolt with her eyes.

That's when everyone else jumped back and looked to the sky with her.

"Was that dude carrying around lightning?!" Umbati asked aloud to everyone.

"Young Mistress you must hurry," Iraja said to Yanielle telepathically.

Yanielle then dug in the bag for Matuka's necklace to return it to him. After quickly finding his necklace, Yanielle tied the bag around her wrist and walked over to him. After she watched him float for a second, she took off his hat and slowly slipped his necklace over his head. Suddenly, in a blink of an eye, lightning and fire rained down from heaven. The continual stream of fire and lightning from the cloud merged as one as they descended rapidly. Once the combined elements hit Matuka's head, a wave of energy caused everyone to fly backwards onto the deck.

"Ow!!" Umbati yelled as he sat up from the deck.

"What the hell?!" Jubilaree asked.

"Ow!!" Tahma cried as he rubbed the back of his head.

"That actually hurt," Kotoyami said with an attitude.

"I'm going to need to use this myself at this rate," Yanielle said as she looked down at her retractor.

"That's definitely gonna leave a mark,"

Dayhoon jokingly said as he rubbed his head.

The crew watched in awe, for they had never seen anything like it before. The merged elements surrounded the young Captain as thunder clapped throughout the sky. Their mouths dropped as they watched the combined elements surround and then enter his body.

Suddenly, the stream of merged elements stopped flowing from the heavens as though it ran out. That's when Matuka opened his eyes and all they could see was a white light shining through them. He immediately raised his right palm in front of him and screamed with a beastly echo. That's when a surge of electricity leaped from his body as the fire from within engulfed him outwardly.

"Interesting," Tahma said before he fixed his glasses with his right hand and looked at the others.

Just as quickly as the phenomenon started, was as quickly as it ended. The storm cloud disappeared, and the sun came forth from the shadows. Immediately after, Matuka dropped to the black deck of his ship. It took no time for everyone to run and crowd around him again.

"Matuka! Matuka!" everyone yelled as they patiently waited for a response.

Without warning, Matuka quickly sat up from the deck and looked around at everyone.

"Matuka!" everyone yelled and cried as

they all wrapped their arms around him.

"Are you guys okay? What happened?" Matuka tried to ask while he was nearly choked as everyone hugged and squeezed him tightly.

"I think you died you big dummy!" Yanielle cried as she held onto him.

"Wait, what?" Matuka asked as he tried to make sense of what she said.

"You don't remember?!" Kotoyami cried as she held onto him.

"I remember getting shot but not dying," Matuka said with a look of confusion on his face.

"Interesting," Tahma said before he cried with joy as he held on as well.

"That bastard shot you in the chest and killed you, moron!" Jubilaree said as tears fell from both of his eyes.

"We thought you were a goner," Umbati cried.

"Yeah man! Don't scare us like that!" Dayhoon cried as he held on with everyone.

"But don't worry, we got our revenge!" Jubilaree said with a serious look on his face before he looked to the water.

"Welcome back young Master," Iraja said to Matuka telepathically as everyone stood around him.

"Good to be back friend," Matuka replied aloud with a smile.

"I must say, fine work you did out there, Iraja," Umbati said with a grin as he threw up his right thumb to signal a good job.

That's when Jubilaree, Yanielle, Koto-yami, Dayhoon, Umbati and Tahma agreed in unison.

"Thank you young Masters and young Mistresses, my pleasure," Iraja telepathically said to them all.

"Hey, where is Chumbry?" Matuka asked as he looked around.

Matuka and the crew then noticed Chumbry was still by the bulwarks, so they all walked over to where he was.

"Welcome back sir!" Chumbry said before he picked up Matuka and hugged him.

"Glad to see you again too Chumbry," Matuka said with a smile as he hugged the child-like man back.

After Chumbry put Matuka back down on the deck, Matuka stepped back away from him, and the crew gathered closer around them.

"So, what's next Captain?" Jubilaree asked Matuka with a smirk before Yanielle gave him his tri-cone hat back.

The young Captain slowly put on his hat before he saw the smiles on his crews' faces. That's when Matuka looked to the helm, then back to everyone and smiled. The day was still young, and the weather was beautiful. The rubble from the guild of thieves vanished beneath the water's surface and the ocean never looked better.

As Chumbry held onto the back of a swimming dolphin, he looked back over his right shoulder. Chumbry smiled as he watched the ship engulf itself in fog. He was grateful for his life, so he cried as Matuka and his guild sailed away. He remembered that Matuka told him to warn the people of Eseville of their return and that they'd be back very soon to reclaim what's rightfully theirs. He told Chumbry to tell them that when they see the fog that appears out of thin-air, with the form of a ghostly ship within the midst, to know it is the return of the Hyungetta… the crew with the black sails.

The Hyungetta

Glossary

Terms

Astrolabe – a two-dimensional model of the celestial sphere that once was the most used, multipurpose astronomical instrument.

Basin – a wide, round open container, especially one used for holding liquid.

Bilge – the bottom part on a ship.

Boom – a long pole attached to the bottom of a boat's sail that is used for changing the direction of the sail.

Bow – the front part of a ship.

Bowsprit – a long pole that stick out the front of a ship.

Bulwarks – side of the ship above deck or railings along the ship.

Cabin – a private room on a ship for a passenger or one of the people working on the ship.

Coat of arms – the distinctive heraldic bearings or shield of a person, family, corporation, or country.

Crow's nest – a place near the top of a ship's mast where a sailor stands to look out over the sea.

Cue – a signal that encourages someone to take action.

Dap/Dapped – a hand greeting amongst friends.

Deck – the outside top part of a ship that you can walk on or one of the levels on a ship.

Forecastle – the front part of a ship.

Galley – kitchen on a ship.

Guild – an association of people for mutual aid or the pursuit of a common goal.

Guildmate – a member of the same guild.

Gunsight – a device on a gun that enables it to be aimed accurately.

Head – toilet on a ship.

Helm – a wheel or handle used for making a boat go in the direction you want.

Hull – the body of a ship.

Jib – a small triangular sail near the front of a boat.

Lanyards – a short rope used on ships for fastening things such as the sails.

Lever – a handle or bad that is attached to a piece of machinery and which you push or pull in order to operate the machinery.

Main sail – the largest sail on the ship.

Mast – a tall pole that the sails hang from on a ship.

Mast head – the top of the mast on a ship.

Mizzen – the sail behind the main sail.

Octopi – Plural of octopus.

Picaroon – a rogue or scoundrel.

Pectoral – relating to the breast or chest.

Poop deck – the higher part at the back of an old sailing ship usually above the captain's cabin.

Port side – the side of a ship that is on your left when facing forward which is the left side.

Porthole – a small window in the side of a ship.

Quiver – an archer's portable case for holding arrows.

Retractor – a surgical instrument used for holding open the edges of a wound.

Rigging – the ropes and chains used for supporting a ship's sails and masts.

Rudder – a flat piece of wood or other material at the back of the ship that is moved to change direction of travel.

Sail – a large piece of strong cloth fixed to a tall pole on a boat, used for catching wind to move the across water.

Saloon – a big room on a ship where passengers can sit together and talk or play games etc.

Seats of ease – toilets on a ship.

Scallywag – a disreputable person, a good-for-nothing.

Scabbard – a sheath for a blade or a sword or a dagger.

Scuppers – openings along the edges of the deck that allow water on deck to drain back to the sea rather than collecting in the bilge.

Sick bay – a room where sick people go to rest and get medical treatment on a ship.

Squiffy – somewhat intoxicated; tipsy.

Starboard side– the side of a ship that is on your right when facing forward which is the left side.

Stern – the back part of a ship.

Stowage – place for storing things in a ship.

Stowaway – a person who hides aboard a vessel in order to obtain free transportation or elude pursuers.

Sun deck – an open area on a ship where you can enjoy the sun.

Swashbuckling – the characteristic behavior of a swashbuckler; loud boasting or bullying.

Three sheets to the wind – to be completely drunk.

Tiller – a long handle at the back of a boat that is used for controlling the direction that the boat moves in.

Tri-cone – a brimless triangular hat pointed at the front, back and top.

Touché – an acknowledgment during a discussion of a good or clever point made at one's expense by another person.

Water-line – the highest point where water touches the side of a boat.

Virago – a domineering, violent, or bad-tempered woman.

Acknowledgments

I would like to thank my Heavenly Father, first and foremost. Thank you, for the gifts, talents, and abilities that you gave me. Thank you, for blessing me, keeping me, and loving me unconditionally. Thank you, for the vision for this book and those to come, and thank you, for the strength and endurance to complete this project.

Thank you, to my father, Rafael P. DeFreitas, Sr. for always encouraging me to make something of myself and live the way God intended for me to live. Thank you, for the words of wisdom in the moments of my life when I felt like giving up, especially after the manuscript for this book was deleted.

Thank you, to my mother, Dr. Olivia J. Mack, for your continued unfailing love and belief in me. Thank you, for your support with this project, for reading and editing. Thank you, for praying for all the gifts I have and for praying for me, in general.

Thank you, to my wife, Tanya DeFreitas, for suggesting that I write a story about young black pirates. If it wasn't for your suggestion this book may have not ever come forth. Thank you, for the motivation, support, prayers, your help with formatting, editing, and publishing this story.

Last, but not least, thank you, to ICU Computer Services, a Christian based company in Riverside, California. Bob Plourde, you were a God-send and answered prayer. Thank you, very much, for recovering my file that was maliciously deleted.

About the Author

Born and raised in Palm Beach County, Florida, Rafael is an artist, author, story developer, and musician. He is a U.S. Marine Veteran, who has been writing since he was in the fourth grade. His work includes comics, cartoons, novels, poetry, and music.

Rafael is the Founder of Love Wins Publishing (www.lovewinspub.com), a consulting company that offers bundled packages and writing services for writers and authors. He manages the company with his wife and they both serve as Publishing Consultants. He is the Co-Founder of the Youth Author's Club (Y.A.C.), an organization that helps youth ages 5 - 17 years old to become published authors, where his youngest children serve as leaders.

Rafael is the lead author and anthologist for Brutal Courage, Men's Edition, a compilation of stories by men overcoming traumatic experiences. He is passionate about God, marriage, family, helping Veterans, and helping the homeless. He is a husband, father, entrepreneur, and inventor. In his spare time, Rafael enjoys cooking, traveling, making music, writing, and creating.

Contact the Author

Follow Rafael on Facebook:

www.facebook.com/authorrafaeldefreitasjr

Check out other books by Rafael:

www.amazon.com/author/rafaeldefreitas

For guest appearance and speaking engagement requests, send requests to contact:

admin@lovewinspublishing.com

Interested in publishing your own book, visit:

www.lovewinspub.com

Book Club Discussion Starters

What was your favorite part of the book?

What was your least favorite part of the book?

Which character in this book would you most likely like to meet?

Did you race to the end, or was it more of a slow burn?

Which scene has stuck with you the most?

Who is your favorite character and why?

Who is your least favorite character and why?

Which character do you connect most to?

What did you think of the writing? Are there any standout sentences?

Did you reread any passages? If so, which ones?

Did reading the book impact your mood? If yes, how so?

What surprised you most about the book?

How did your opinion of the book change as you read it?

If you could ask the author anything, what would it be?

How does the book's title work in relation to the book's contents?

If you could give the book a new title, what would it be?

Is this book overrated or underrated?

Did this book remind you of any other books?

How did this book impact you?

Do you think you'll remember this book in a few months or years?

Would you like to see this book on the big screen, as a movie or television series?

If you were making a movie of this book, who would you cast?

Share a favorite quote from this book. Why did this stand out to you?

What other books by this author have you read, or would you want to read another book by this author?

Would you ever consider re-reading this book? Why or why not?

Who do you most want to read this book?

Are there lingering questions from the book you're still thinking about?

Did the book strike you as original?

What do think about the book's length? If it's too long, what would you cut? If it's too short, what would you add?

****

Thank you, for diving into my imagination. Please share your feedback, good, bad, or indifferent, on Amazon. – *Rafael P. DeFreitas, Jr.*

"Nothing is ever truly forgotten, just hidden."
– Rafael P. DeFreitas, Jr.

Stay tuned...

www.ingramcontent.com/pod-product-compliance
Lightning Source LLC
Chambersburg PA
CBHW021946010726
47494CB00018B/1440